I0739531

Artifacts of Conspiracy

ALSO BY DONY JAY

THE WARRIOR SPY

Artifacts of Conspiracy

OF

A WARRIOR SPY THRILLER

Dony Jay

Merry Hill Publishing

Merry Hill Publishing

Artifacts of Conspiracy

Cover design by Damonza

For more information visit the author's website at **DonyJayBooks.com**

ISBN 978-0-9969270-3-1 (hardcover)
ISBN 978-0-9969270-4-8 (softcover)
ISBN 978-0-9969270-5-5 (mobi)
ISBN 978-0-9969270-6-2 (epub)

For all those who are still missing in action.
May you come home soon.
Never give up. Never lose hope.

And for God and country.

Truth will ultimately prevail where
there is pains to bring it to light.
– George Washington

If you are going through hell, keep going.
– Winston Churchill

ARTIFACTS OF CONSPIRACY

1

Leesburg, Virginia

THEY were after him. A pack of starved wolves desperate for the taste of flesh. One of them lunged for him, but Rainey managed to dodge from the man's outstretched hands at the last second. He was on his own now; there would be no one coming to rescue him.

Their panting was loud and incessant; their footfalls grew closer and closer with each passing second. With malice in their eyes, bad intentions in their hearts, they would finish him this time for good. He was just too great a threat.

A large, razorback of a man stormed into view while another man, every bit his equal in size, emerged on the opposite side. They converged on him with frenzied zeal. Instinctively, Rainey drove his foot into the ground and spun, still at full speed. One of the snorting beasts threw out an arm—a sharp elbow that struck him in the ribs. Rainey growled as his fury began to redline.

No one is going to stop me.

Suddenly, there came a firm tug on his shirt. Rainey shot a glance over his shoulder and saw another snarling man in his early twenties, fit as a fiddle, with spittle spewing from his clenched teeth. Rainey churned his legs even harder, leaned to the left then blasted back across the open space on his right. The man now used both hands, leaned backward and pulled with all his might. But Rainey was too strong, his resolve unlike any his adversaries had likely ever seen. He would never relent, never give in. They would have to kill him. The fabric of his shirt stretched taut against him. The sinews of his arms, chest and abdomen rippled with each of his powerful movements. Rainey ripped free of the man's grasp as his T-shirt gave way. It hung open now, exposing the entire left side of his lean, sun-tanned frame. Long strands of the torn red and blue fabric—a tattered American flag on a war-weary battlefield—waved behind him.

Send it, Ray.

In a fraction of a second, everything slowed down. He focused on his target, calculated the proper angle, knew exactly where to aim. He took two more lightning-fast strides then just as another man was about to crash into him, he pulled the trigger. The ball took off like a rocket, then began to curve, rotating counter-clockwise about its axis, which was on a 30-degree tilt. The spinning orb managed to clear the diving goalkeeper's gloves, then like a missile homing in on a specific set of geo-cords, dipped sharply. The ball slammed into the side netting just beneath the crossbar—upper 90— and snapped around the white, nylon mesh with authority.

Reagan Rainey, eyes wide with triumph, let out a primal scream of exhilaration then sprinted in a wide, looping arc.

"Goooaaal!!!" Tito Salazar raced across the fifty-yard line with arms raised, his fists pumping the air.

As Rainey neared the sideline, his teammates enveloped him. They all went to the ground in a heap, each of them whooping and hollering with childlike excitement.

When the boisterous celebration finally drew to a close, the men got back to their feet and headed for their end of the field. Ten seconds after the kick-off, the referee blew the final whistle. It was bedlam en route to the benches. A few players from the opposing side walked over and congratulated him on the game and his four goals but the majority eyed him with scorn.

"Man, oh man, Ray! Their back line is still looking for their jock straps. That spin move was sick! And that shot… I haven't seen a shot like that since… I can't remember when. Unbelievable!" said Tito.

Rainey smiled. "You know, I didn't even think about what I was doing. It just happened. Muscle memory, I guess. Funny how stuff like that just comes back to you." Rainey slipped a water bottle from a backpack, squirted his face and head before drinking greedily for several long seconds.

"You know, if you'd like, I could arrange a tryout with the club."

He and Tito had competed against each other for most of their lives. Top-level club stuff when they were youngsters, then four straight years of high school ball. During Rainey's final two years at Annapolis High, they had squared off against each other in back-to-back state final games, which they split. They met yet again when Rainey was at Duke and Tito at Clemson. Theirs had been a storied rivalry, which—as rivalries sometimes do—developed into a keen friendship built on mutual respect and admiration. The rivalry ended unceremoniously in the fall of 2004, when Rainey abruptly left school and joined the Army. It was shortly after his college roommate's brother—a highly decorated Special Forces soldier—had been killed fighting the forces of evil on a craggy mountain ridge in Afghanistan. Rainey often traced the trajectory of his life back to that singular point. It was a definable moment in time, where his life shot off in an unexpected direction. He often wondered about what might have been. What if he had stayed in school? What if he hadn't left everything and everyone to run off and fight a war thousands of miles from home? Would he be practicing law now and not the art of killing? Would he be a husband, a father?

In contrast, Tito did complete his degree requirements and used up all four years of his soccer eligibility, which paid off in the form of a decent pro contract with D.C. United. He played for five years until a terrible knee injury ended his career for good. Now, he was heavily involved in recruiting and training talented, young prospects for the D.C.

United Academy while he also coached the Gonzaga College High School boys' team.

Tito spit a mouthful of water into the grass. "You're definitely in shape, and, *my gosh*, you still got the moves. Might not start right away, but I think you could easily make the squad. I've got a lot of pull with the front office, you know. They could use a big bruising forward like you, especially one with your speed."

Rainey chuckled. "Thanks, my friend. It's a gracious offer, maybe a little too gracious, but my competitive playing days are over. Nevertheless, I still love the game. There is nothing like walking across a freshly cut pitch with cleats on." Rainey dragged his boot back and forth in the plush grass. "I'll tell ya, man, I miss it big time. Thanks again for asking me to come out today."

"Hey, my pleasure. After the way you played… That spin move… I still can't believe your touch on the ball… And you say you haven't been practicing. Ha. I don't believe you. But that shot… I mean, that thing was a rocket! The guys are going to beg me to have you back next week. You just helped us beat our toughest rival. They've kicked our behinds mercilessly over the past three years. I don't think we've scored more than one goal against them in that whole entire time. And you score four against them in one game." Tito laughed. "I love it."

Rainey was about to respond when he noticed a black sedan drift into the parking lot and ease to a stop. He took another swig of water as he watched a man in a dark-colored suit step from the rear of the car and squint through a persistent, ochre-colored dust cloud as thick as wax paper. When the dust finally cleared, the man drew a hand against his forehead and shielded his eyes from the glare of the mid-afternoon sun. He was twenty years older than most of the men on the pitch and less imposing in stature, yet still looked rather fit for his age. His thinning gray hair was shorn close to a scalp free of blemishes and was carefully swept to the side, giving him the appearance of an accountant or a loan officer, the kind who takes pride in exercising due diligence in all aspects of life. What the man really did for a living was largely a secret and a closely guarded one at that. The man was a spymaster after all, and his boss, which was why Rainey knew upon seeing him that his plans for the day were about to change. There was no equivocation in his musing. He was about to embark on something dangerous or important or both.

"You want to go out and get something to drink with us? We're all going to… Oh wait. That's right, you don't drink. Well you can still come." Tito pushed his socks down, popped out his shin guards and slipped off his cleats.

"Afraid I'm gonna be busy, T." Rainey's eyes were still locked on the man in the parking lot.

"All right, but if you change your mind, call or shoot me a text."

"Will do. Thanks."

Rainey removed his cleats and slid into a pair of running shoes he had had since his freshman year at Duke. He didn't bother with tying the laces. He threw his backpack over his shoulder and plodded off toward the parking lot. He circled around to the driver-side door of a 1989 Ford Bronco that was black as crude oil with a sand-colored topper and matching trim. The previous owner had been his late father and for that very reason he labored to keep it looking as cherry as the day his dad had driven it off the Koons Ford lot.

Rainey's lips came together as he rubbed a speck of road grease from the Eddie Bauer emblem on the fender. He opened the door and tossed his bag across to the front-passenger seat then stripped off his torn, wet T-shirt, rolled it into a ball and lobbed it into the waste bin that stood a few paces off to his left. With a towel he had retrieved from the back seat, he began wiping the sweat from his face, arms and chest.

"So *this* is how you relax?"

"Sure. Why not?" said Rainey.

"I gave you a week off to rest and take it easy, not run around like a madman and maybe blow out a knee." Job Jackson wiped the beads of sweat now gathered on his forehead with a handkerchief.

"Okay, mom."

Job cast a disapproving frown then gazed out over the soccer complex. "So you survived then? The Academy, I mean."

"No offense, Job, but that was a picnic compared to the Q Course."

"Maybe I should have had them push you a little harder."

Six months ago, Rainey had signed on to work for the CIA, specifically the Agency's Directorate Twelve, having previously served there while on temporary duty assignment care of JSOC and the Army's Special Operations Command. Before that he had worn the Green Beret and been a special operator in an assault troop within the Army Compartmented Element, what is popularly referred to as Delta Force. Since joining the Directorate, however, the Agency had gone through a bit of an overhaul. A housecleaning some might say. There had been a recent reorganizing of the various directorates and subdivisions within the Agency. Directorate Twelve had been re-designated Directorate X. For all intents and purposes though, Directorate X—aside from the name change—remained the same.

"Tell you the truth, the Academy isn't designed to weed people out. That part is done in pre-phase. In recruitment. After all, the DX is invitation only. We fully expect candidates to graduate."

Using his fingertips, Rainey massaged the area of his ribcage where he had taken the elbow. "So what brings you out here? I mean, I'm guessing you didn't bring your cleats."

Job wiped his forehead again. In the second it took him to do so, he grew serious. His expression dark, he flatly said, "Get in and I'll tell you."

2

RAINEY twisted at the waist as he examined the four cherry-red claw marks that streaked across his back in the reflection of the car window. Just above them was a thin pink scar where a sniper's bullet had once grazed him—a souvenir of his first deployment with 3rd Special Forces Group. Six inches higher was the remnant of another wound he had incurred on behalf of his country. During the operation in Montreal last year, he had been hit in the shoulder by a piece of shrapnel. Rainey often joked about the way the jagged scar resembled a three-pronged lightning bolt.

He shook his head. "Man, that guy had some nails."

"Who?"

"The guy who ripped my shirt." Rainey dabbed his face with the towel as they both eased into the air-conditioned sedan. "So what's up?"

Job held up his index finger. He leaned forward and asked his driver/bodyguard to go for a walk. When they were alone, he began. "The director came to see me this morning."

"What about?"

"Before I tell you, I want to make it absolutely clear that I am taking this very seriously. Do you understand?"

Rainey's eyes narrowed as he nodded. "I understand."

Job pulled out a cell phone from his inner breast pocket. He swiped the screen several times with the tip of his finger then hesitated. He drew in a controlled breath as his eyes rolled up to the headrest in front of him. Finally, he turned toward Rainey and handed him the phone.

Rainey accepted it with his left hand, brought it in front of his chest. The glow of the screen against his face and nude torso stirred a haunting effect within the vehicle's dim interior. Rainey was motionless as he stared into the screen. It was a photo of a piece of paper. A typed letter. After a moment, he worked his fingertips across the screen, causing the image to enlarge. He glanced back at Job then began to read.

You can call me Moses. I am Russian. I am a spy. For some time now I have worked outside my country's borders. In the interest of my own security I cannot reveal my current location or even my past areas of operation. I hope you understand and can appreciate this necessary precaution.

I wish to meet. I have specific information that I am willing to share. My reasons for wanting to share this information are my own and shall remain so until such time that I deem otherwise. This information is just that, information. It's not conjecture or opinion. It is factual. It is true.

What is this information? Let me just say that it involves a man named, Benjamin Rainey. Mr. Rainey was a CIA officer, who was killed in a plane crash in the mountains of southern Venezuela in September, 1996. At least, this is the official account of his death. But I attest to you that Mr. Rainey did not die in any plane crash. In fact, and I have verifiable proof, Benjamin Rainey is not dead. He is alive. You should also know that I have information about Mr. Rainey's current status and location.

I will share this information in a personal meeting only. I do, however, have a few stipulations thereto. I will only disclose what I know to one man. Ben Rainey has a son, his name is Reagan. Last I knew he was in your army's 3rd Special

Forces Group. He would be 31 now. As of a few days ago. It is with him that I wish to meet. And him alone.

Secondly, the date, time and location of the meeting shall be of my choosing. I'm afraid these stipulations are non-negotiable.

If you are receptive to a meeting under these terms, post the following comment exactly as it appears on the blog site RobertSchumannFans.blogspot.com: "RobeRt Schumann was a master of his cRaft."

You have five days to consider my offer and respond. If I do not see a response by the end of the five days, my offer will expire and the information that I possess will be forgotten forever. This is a one-time offer. I will be watching.

Moses

◆ ◆ ◆

After Rainey had finished reading the letter for the second time, he lowered the phone into his lap. His mind was upside down. He felt weightless. No, he felt…nothing. His mind was too rocked, too disoriented to perceive feeling. Confusion consumed him like a tidal wave.

Dad. Alive? But how? Can't be. Could it? No. Not possible.

The letter loosed a river of memories. So many memories. He consciously swallowed the thick knot in his throat. It felt like a baseball going down.

Breathe, Ray. Breathe.

He looked at the phone again with unfocused eyes. The service at Arlington played in his mind. His mother was seated there in a white chair in perfect green grass. Her black dress flapped in the gentle breeze. Her face was solemn, her eyes red and lifeless. Like she could physically cry no more tears. She was broken. Her hands clutched at the folded American flag in her lap. She clung to it as if her life depended on it. His younger sister, Maddie, pressed up against her, her cute little face all streaked with tears that sparkled like diamonds in the sun. Now, it was as if he were floating above the ceremony and looking down upon himself. Little Reagan Rainey sat there in his Sunday best, his hair combed over with the military precision he had inherited from his late grandfather. His bottom lip quivered as he fought the urge to cry. His hands were folded tightly in his lap. Rainey remembered, even now, sitting there silently praying—shouting—to God, *"Please, God! I want my daddy back. I want my daddy! Please, God! Please! It's not fair. I need him! Daddy, I need you!"*

He felt a hand on his arm. Just like that day. It gently squeezed him at the wrist. It was Job offering comfort. The man had since become like a father to him. And just like that awful September morning in Arlington, Ray turned his head and quickly wiped a tear from his cheek. *Be tough. Don't let them see you cry.*

Job spoke softly. "You okay?"

He cleared his throat. "Yeah."

"Like I said, Ray, I am taking this very seriously. Remember, he was my best friend."

He swallowed again with a sniffle. Then his warrior face returned. "Is there any shred of truth to this?"

Job put the phone away. "Honestly, I don't know. I mean… I can't see how, but I *will* get to the bottom of it."

"Why does this guy want to meet with me?"

"I don't know that either. I've already had Spencer and his people go over the letter with a fine-tooth comb. They didn't find anything. No DNA, no prints, no nothing. Best they can tell is the brand of typewriter with which it was written, the ink, the paper, what have you. They say it is all commonplace in Europe. Whoever wrote the letter knew what he was doing, knew we would check for all that."

"How did it surface?" He dabbed his face with the towel again.

"A case officer in Lisbon found the letter in his car as he was headed into work. It had been slipped through his cracked window sometime overnight. We are still trying to assess how he was identified as an Agency officer."

"When did he find it?"

"Yesterday, oh five thirty, Zulu. It was brought to Langley by courier. Arrived on my desk this morning."

Rainey looked at the clock on the dash, did the time conversion in his head.

Job nodded. "We have a few days yet."

"For what? It's a no-brainer, Job. Post the comment. I'm ready now."

"Moses has given us some time, doubtless so we can do a little digging of our own. You know, see if this is just a tickle or if there is any merit to it."

Rainey's forehead scrunched up. "So now what? What do we do in the meantime?"

"The director is meeting with POTUS, as we speak. They're going to discuss the letter and its ramifications, but I'll tell you… The director has already given me the authority to see what we can uncover internally. His only qualifier is that we do so quietly. Get packed. The next couple of days are going to be busy."

"Do Mom and Maddie know?"

Job shook his head. "No. I thought that I would let that up to you. My recommendation? See what turns up here initially. If we find anything probative then we'll have a talk, but—"

"I want them to know. They have a *right* to know. If it turns out to be nothing, then so be it. But if I were them, I would want to know. They're adults, Job. They can handle this."

Job grimaced. "I just don't want to get their hopes up, kid. Stir up an emotional cauldron. This smells of a hoax. Could even be some kind of trap. You torqued off some very dangerous people last year. I think it best to proceed with caution."

"I'm not saying we run off half-cocked. I'm just saying that I think Mom and Maddie should be told about this. They deserve to know."

Job scratched his chin, obviously torn about what to do. Finally, he said, "Okay. But the sooner, the better. Go home, get cleaned up. Pack your suitcase. I'll meet you at your mother's place at twenty hundred."

"I'll be there."

3

Washington, D.C.

KEN Thompson followed the president into the Oval Office. He had been here countless times, yet each time he walked into the room, its significance to world events, to history, struck him anew. Today was no different. This was the inner sanctum of the most powerful man on the planet. Thompson had seen three administrations come and go throughout his run as director of the Central Intelligence Agency. Each one seemed to take pride in putting its own unique touch on the office and the White House as a whole. Some of the alterations were subtle, some less so. As a matter of principle, he was generally averse to change, especially when it had anything to do with America's traditions and historical institutions. Thus, he was glad to see the painting of George Washington still in its rightful place over the fireplace. But he still could not stomach the bust of Woodrow Wilson on the credenza. In his mind, it had no business being there. Mostly because President Winslow's predecessor had had a bust of Ronald Reagan in that very spot. Two men could not have been more different.

To a man, President Grantley Winslow was not fit for the presidency, but Thompson kept these feelings to himself, even amongst those within his charge. Though he personally abhorred Winslow's politics, his blatant lack of integrity and respect for anything relating to America's founding doctrines, Thompson was a patriot, a man of honor. And he conducted himself as such.

President Winslow circled around the Resolute Desk, stripped off his suit coat and draped it over the back of his chair. Once seated, he interlaced his fingers behind his head, leaned back and put his feet up on the desk, something Thompson found grossly disrespectful to the office.

Vera Lysniak entered. She was the president's senior advisor and closest friend. In many respects, she was closer to the president than the man's own wife. Some even intimated that she was the real president, the *shadow* president.

Vera slid her tiny frame around the heavy door and nudged it shut with her hip. In her clutches were a leather-bound brief, some file folders and several stacks of paper, which were separated with black binder clips. The giant bundle seemed almost bigger than her. She held her Sectera Edge smartphone and her iPhone, in her left hand, the screens pinched together.

Director of National Intelligence Hank McManus and National Security Advisor Valetta Ivory were quick on her heels. McManus jabbed out his hand and stopped the door from closing. He held it open for Ivory then clicked it shut after they were both inside.

"Where's Karen?" snapped the president. Karen Griggs was the secretary of state—someone who Thompson also felt was severely unqualified to serve as the nation's top diplomat.

Vera fell into one of the sofas in front of the president, almost losing a stack of files in the process. "She just texted me, Grant. She's feeling under the weather, apologizes for not being here." Vera was the only one in the room who could get away with calling the president by his first name.

"She couldn't send one of her deputies?"

Vera glared at him. A teacher admonishing a student who had spoken out of turn.

The president conceded. "All right. Okay." When they were all settled, he said, "So what's this all about, Ken?"

"Mr. President, sir." Thompson explained how the Agency had received the Lisbon letter. He also related the details contained therein. As he did so, he looked around the room, noting the facial expressions and body language of each person present. The president, of course, was his normal aloof self, as was often the case in matters of national security. His feigned interest was obvious. Thompson noticed several times during his soliloquy how the president's eyes darted to and from a document on the desk in front of him: a detailed breakdown of the latest poll results according to demographics and other categories held in high esteem by his reelection campaign. Meanwhile, Vera eyed him as she always did, with naked contempt. In contrast to the president, Vera Lysniak was a careful listener. She missed nothing. Her soft coffee bean eyes belied an arsonist's insatiable thirst for fire. She was a ruthless political warlord who relished pillaging and plundering her foes. No holds barred. As beautiful as she was vigilant, she was the president's perfect vanguard.

McManus on the other hand had the look of restrained consternation about his face. Like he was sitting on a thumb tack, but was too embarrassed to admit it. He fidgeted in his seat, crossed his legs then just as suddenly uncrossed them.

The only one in the room who seemed genuinely interested in what he had to say and did not have the appearance of holding some secret, private agenda was Valetta Ivory. Thompson liked her. She was extremely bright and always professional. He watched her jot down some notes then lift her head back up in eager anticipation of the last bits of his monologue.

"I don't understand. Who is Ben Rainey? CIA?" said the president.

"Yessir. Used to work for the Agency, he—"

"Used to?" blurted Vera.

Vera Lysniak was a witch. Many of the power players in D.C. were afraid of her. But he'd seen her type before. Just another self-absorbed ideologue drunk with the power of her position. There was no question, Vera wielded an awesome amount of power. Truth be told, she had the president wrapped around her little finger. And she made sure everyone knew it, too. For someone so small in stature, she sure liked to throw her weight around. A female Napoleon, some called her, but always behind her back. The woman had a true passion for intimidation and routinely exercised it to get whatever it was that she wanted.

Thompson continued as if she weren't even there. "Sir, Ben Rainey was a case officer with the Agency. Came aboard in eighty-one. Had some pretty tough assignments. Worked all over. Russia, France, Germany. You name it. He was killed in ninety-six when his plane went down in the mountains along the border between Venezuela and Brazil."

"So what's the significance of the letter then? If he's dead, then why would this—what was his name, *Moses?*—say otherwise."

Thompson nodded. "Well, Mr. President, sir, that's the peculiar thing. My people are digging into the archives, looking at the operations in which he was engaged back then. There is a chance that this letter is just some type of provocation. At any rate, we're doing our due diligence to prove its merit one way or the other."

"What's your gut feeling, Ken? Could there be any truth to this?"

"Well, Mr. President. I don't know enough to be able to intelligently speculate. We're looking into it."

"He just wants your gut feeling! That's all he's asking for. Yeesh!"

Thompson regarded Vera with little affect, but inside he wanted to snatch her up and toss her face-first out into the Rose Garden. He loathed her.

Valetta Ivory adjusted her reading glasses. "Do we know if any agents or current operations are in jeopardy?"

"Again, we're looking into it," said Thompson.

Vera put her elbow on the armrest of the sofa. She sat on the end nearest the president and directly across from Ivory. It was rumored that the two women hated each other. Valetta Ivory was smart and for the most part apolitical. A straight shooter. Based on everything he had seen and heard about the woman, Thompson knew she hated the politics of the job and gave it her all to simply advise the president on how best to keep Americans safe. Like him, she was a patriot first. For all the cronies the president brought into his administration, Valetta Ivory was the exception and one of the few people that he truly admired.

Vera huffed. "*Rainey*... Is this the same guy that went off the reservation last year? Left a trail of bodies all over the place. He's lucky he's not in jail. This is about him?"

Are you kidding me?

Thompson glowered at her. "Ben Rainey is Reagan Rainey's father. Try to keep up, Vera." He couldn't help himself. "And by the way, *Reagan* Rainey saved the lives of most of the people in D.C. That includes everyone in this room. He—"

"But he had no authority to go running off, engaging in his own covert operations. There was never any finding that authorized that! He could have..."

Easy, Ken. Easy. She's not worth it.

When she finished her rant, he simply turned to the president and ignored her. "Sir, again, we don't know anything about the validity of the letter or what to make of the mention of either Rainey. But one thing is certain: the author knew that Alan Beckett—our Lisbon case officer—was CIA. *And* he knew about Ben Rainey, how he died. That's never been publicized."

"What are you saying, Ken? Give it to me in a nutshell."

"Well, could be that this is more fallout from what happened last year. Or..."

"Yes?"

Thompson drew in a long breath then let it out slowly through pursed lips. "Or we have a whole new problem on our hands."

"But why would someone go to the trouble of telling us that he's not dead? What do they have to gain? And what proof could they have?"

"I haven't the foggiest, sir."

"What does this mean in terms of the election?" said Vera.

Ivory folded her arms. "The election, Vera, seriously? That should be the least of our concerns. If Ben Rainey *was* involved in some highly classified operations, regardless of whether he is alive or not, someone knows things. Worst case, human sources and collection methods could be in peril. We don't need any more of our people turning up dead like last year. Furthermore, our intelligence capability might be compromised." Ivory shook her head, whispered under her breath as she examined her notepad.

The president carried on as if this were a regular occurrence, a feud he enjoyed watching from the sidelines. "You've been quiet so far, Hank. You have any input?"

McManus frowned. "I think this is a waste of time, sir, to be perfectly honest. I worked with Ben back in the nineties. Very closely, in fact. His plane went down. Simple as that. I was part of the team that was on the ground right after it happened. He's dead. I saw his body. Case closed."

"So why the letter then?" said the president.

McManus shrugged. "No idea, sir."

"All right, well, let's do this: Ken, if your people find anything, let me know. But I don't want a lot of Agency resources spent on this. We could just end up chasing ghosts here. This sounds to me like a hoax. Probably a counterintelligence operation of some kind."

Thompson almost rolled his eyes. The president came across at times, especially with respect to matters of intelligence, like he had seen one too many episodes of *24*. Yet ironically he never seemed all that interested when it came to his daily briefings. "Yes, sir."

◆ ◆ ◆

As they filed out, McManus looked down at Vera. When their eyes finally met, he mouthed the words, "Can we talk?"

She nodded, bit off the cap of her pen. She kept it clenched between her teeth as she scribbled something onto one of the papers in her arms.

McManus tilted his head ever so slightly as he read the chicken scratch. He nodded back, then spirited out of the room.

There was much to do.

4

AMIDST the shadows, she heard the soft clang of metal on metal as someone worked the latch of the wrought iron gate down by the street and slipped inside. The figure hesitated, looked both ways then proceeded up the flagstone steps that curled around the perfectly manicured lawn.

From the rear landing of her sprawling D.C. mansion, Vera Lysniak watched him against a background of boxwoods, Leyland cypress, cherry laurel and silver maple. Save for the occasional scuffing of his soles, McManus climbed the stairs quietly, taking a few deliberate breaths on every fourth step or so. She grinned to herself, content with the fact that the director of National Intelligence would be exhausted by the time he reached her.

Vera sipped a glass of pinot noir, staring at the man like a tiger patiently tracking its unknowing prey. She swallowed the smooth liquid, took another sip then swirled the remnant in the bottom of the glass, which she cradled in her palm like a crystal ball. A gentle breeze played at the scalloped collar of her sleeveless blouse, tickled her bare feet. For a moment she forgot all about Hank McManus and his struggle up the stairs. The breeze came again. It was divine. Soothing. She was suddenly a teenager again, lying on the beach with her friends on the southern coast of her native Iran. It was right before the fall of the shah, after which the religious police cracked down hard on such activity. Women were no longer permitted to swim with men, let alone wear bikinis. But further north, near Isfahan, where she had spent the bulk of her childhood, that didn't much matter, because there were no beaches. Nevertheless, Vera reveled in her Persian heritage and her Muslim faith, but not outwardly so. Not ever. She wasn't nearly as pious as the fundamentalists in Tehran and Damascus, Beirut and Baghdad—she did cherish her indulgences, after all. But America—the entire world for that matter—would be a far better place if Islam were the supreme law of the land.

Someday…

McManus wheezed as he reached the summit. "Why…did…you have…me…come in…the back?" he panted.

Vera smiled.

"You *are* a witch. You know that, right?"

"Oh, come now, Hank. I couldn't have you traipsing in the front door for all the neighbors to see. You of all people should know that affairs such as these are to be handled with utmost discretion."

Vera's house sat on an exclusive piece of real estate situated in an area of D.C. known as Embassy Row, where, as the name suggests there are a considerable number of foreign embassies. And where there are embassies, there are spies.

"Affairs such as these, huh…"

"Clearly this is about the letter. Am I right?"

McManus muttered several curse words between breaths which only made Vera's smile grow bigger. Leaning against the railing, the DNI wiped his forehead with the back of his hand. It was still a sweltering 93 degrees though the sun had already sunk well below the treetops.

Vera slipped on her shoes and stood. She walked up to the older man, stared at him for a handful of seconds as he huffed and puffed. His hair was wet at the edges, his skin clammy. "Let's get you inside before you keel over."

McManus fell in behind the diminutive woman. "You wouldn't happen to have a glass of lemonade or iced tea would you?"

Her back to him, Vera grinned. She called out and a uniformed woman with hard facial features and wide hips appeared. Vera instructed her to bring them both a glass of lemonade. The woman offered a mirthless "yes, mum" and briskly disappeared.

"So what is it that's troubling you?"

The DNI adjusted his glasses, which were now fogged up due to the coolness of the air conditioned room. He removed them from his face and wiped the lenses with an embroidered handkerchief he had tugged from his pants pocket. As he did so, he wound around the opulent, great room, past a shiny black Bechstein with a hand-painted design on the case. He stopped, pushed his glasses back on. "Nice piano."

"It was my grandfather's. Would you believe that a certain German chancellor once owned it?"

"You don't mean—"

"Hitler, yes. After the war, it wound up in the hands of the French. The French foreign minister *assumed* ownership. I forget his name. Anyway, my grandfather was the ambassador to France back then. The piano was eventually given to him as a gift. I don't think it's ever been played since it's been on American soil."

McManus whistled as he plopped down in a leather sofa next to an elegant end table. He was still studying the intricate artwork on the case of the grand piano. Finally, he took a deep breath and let it out as the servant woman appeared with a silver tray that contained a pitcher of lemonade and two full glasses.

Vera watched him drink greedily then said, "So?"

"This really is a nice place you have here."

"Hank, you've been here before. Quit stalling. I'm a busy woman. Can we just get to it?"

"It's about the letter."

"What about it?" Her eyes narrowed. "It's true, isn't it? Tell me it isn't true."

"I… I don't know. I—"

"Freakin' spit it out, Hank! Stop stammering."

"I don't know! But… The part about Ben Rainey dying in a plane crash… Well, let's just say he *didn't* die in a plane crash."

Vera crossed her arms.

"Okay, okay. First of all, just so we're clear, I came to you because you and I understand each other. And I'm confident that you will know how to handle this." He sighed. "And also because this has the potential to cause some major damage to the president."

"How much damage?

"The kind that can destroy any hope for reelection and much more. This is the type of thing that those right-wing radio whack-jobs will harp on for years to come."

Vera eased into a flowered print wing chair in front of a stone fireplace that lay dark and dormant. "Tell me everything."

He nodded as he looked at the floor. "All right. Here goes."

When the DNI had finished, she stood, walked over to him and offered him her hand. "Thank you for bringing this to my attention, Hank. This is why you are DNI." She led him to the door, her demeanor calm yet severe. "Don't you worry about anything. Let me handle this. Okay?"

He stopped short of the threshold, turned and looked down into the small woman's dark, flagrant eyes.

"It'll be fine, Hank. Trust me, I know just what to do."

5

Annapolis, Maryland

DUSK had come. The last remnant of daylight pressed upward against a ragged line of ominous blue-gray clouds that made the horizon resemble the edge of a torn page.

Rainey rolled to a stop behind his sister's brand new Mustang GT. Flecks in the navy blue metallic paint shone like glitter in his headlights. He dragged his hand over his jaw, as if there were still a full beard there. After so many years in Special Forces and Delta, the smoothness of his face was unfamiliar.

On his way to the front door, he heard voices hearken from off in the distance. He squinted into the darkness. Two silhouettes were moving toward him from the far end of the boat dock that jutted out from the wooded point beyond his childhood home. Behind them in heavy shadow, a boat with its deck lights switched on, glided across the calm, glassy water of Aberdeen Creek—more a small harbor than an actual creek. The steady gurgle of its outboard motor echoed in the sticky August air, offering a modicum of tranquility to his jumbled thoughts.

"Ray!" Maddie—his twenty-seven year-old kid sister—and her fiancé emerged into the soft glow of the lamppost standing over by the front door. They were holding hands and grinning like they had not seen each other in months.

Rainey batted a mosquito from his eyes. "Hey, sis."

Maddie hugged him. "What's up, big brother?"

You'll find out soon enough. "Hi, Wes." The two men shook hands. Wes had a slight smudge of lipstick on his chin just below his bottom lip. *Oh, brother.* "How's business?"

Maddie ran her own martial arts studio in D.C. Wes had come aboard as a business partner after quitting his job at the *Washington Post* late last year. He was also now endeavoring to write a book that focused on corruption in the federal government.

"Good. Couldn't be better actually." Maddie and Wes exchanged quick glances.

Something's up, he thought, before deciding to let it go. There was too much on his mind right now. "Good. How's the book coming?"

"Painfully slow, I'm afraid. But I'll get there. Research takes time. Good news is that I'm getting a ton of ideas for future projects in the meantime."

"Sounds promising."

Maddie playfully punched him on the shoulder. "You'll never guess who I ran into the other day outside Kramerbooks. Kayla." When Rainey didn't reply, she said, "Did you hear me? *Kayla.* As in your old college girlfriend Kayla."

"I heard ya."

"You're not still bummed about her, are you? I mean how long has it been? Ten years? At some point you have to let go of the guilt, Ray. You have to forgive yourself."

"Yeah, well…"

"C'mon, Ray. It's not like you cheated on her with some other chick. You went to fight for your country. You're a war hero for crying out loud. I'm sure she understands that." Maddie punched his arm again, this time harder.

He ignored the sisterly gesture. His eyes drifted to the water again, the treetops and the last vestige of sunlight beyond. "I abandoned her."

"You were a kid back then. You've matured now. You're a man. Don't you think it's time to move on?" Maddie turned to Wes, who seemed desperate for the full story but was too polite to say so. "Back in oh four, the fall of Ray's sophomore year at Duke, his roommate's brother was killed in combat in Afghanistan. He was Special Forces, right, Ray? As you can tell, he doesn't like to talk about it. Anyway, when the news broke, Ray decided to drop out of school to join the Army so he could avenge his death."

"That's not why I enlisted, Maddie."

"No? Then why did you?"

Rainey shook his head.

"Like I was saying… Ray and Kayla were a pretty hot item up to that point. I mean, there was talk of marriage and all that stuff. Right, Ray?" She didn't give him time to respond. "Ever since then, Ray's been plagued by guilt. Can't let it go. I don't know if he's embarrassed or what, but it's been a sore subject with him ever since."

Rainey bristled.

"See," said Maddie. "Can't let it go."

He frowned then finally relented. "How's she doing?"

"I didn't get to talk to her for very long, but I take it she's doing well. I will say this, Ray. She looks gooooood. And I didn't see any wedding ring on her finger either." Maddie grinned conspiratorially. "She told me to tell you she said hi. I know it's none of my business, Ray, but I got the sense that she's still carrying a torch for you. Gave me her number…"

Rainey sighed as he stuffed his hands into his pants pockets. He wanted desperately to believe her, but his mind was elsewhere now. Back to the matter at hand. His father. The letter from Moses played in his thoughts again. Mentally, he was on a forced march through quicksand and was carrying an eighty-pound rucksack. "Job call you?"

"Yeah. Just said to meet him here. Said you guys have something important to discuss."

"We do."

6

SARAH Rainey was seated next to Job and his wife on a sectional in the spacious living room. She and Iris were like sisters. With Ben gone and Job frequently pulled away on Agency business, they could usually be found together shopping, making crafts, planning day trips or just enjoying each other's company the way best friends do. The fact that they lived next door to each other compounded their time together. More than anyone, Iris understood her, because she, too, was the wife of a CIA man, which was certainly not an easy thing to be.

Sarah met the trio as they entered, gave them each a big, warm hug and a kiss on the cheek. Wes got the same treatment. He was very much considered a part of the family already. "Reagan, have you lost weight? Iris, doesn't he look like he's lost weight?"

"Maybe a few pounds."

Rainey glanced down at his body, rubbed his stomach.

"But your arms look bigger," said Iris. "You've been working out." Sarah gave one of his biceps a squeeze. "She's right. Make a muscle."

"Ah, Mom."

"We're just teasing you." Sarah looked at Maddie. "You tell him yet?"

"No, not yet." Maddie smiled, her big, honey-colored eyes gleaming with pure joy. She looked at Wes then faced him. "I'd like you to give me away. At the wedding, I mean."

Wes put his arm around her. "We both would, Ray. It would be an honor."

The mention of the wedding seemed to catch him off guard. He started to choke up, but masked it well. "The honor will be all mine. I'd be happy to, Maddie, but…"

"*But?*"

"Please. Can everyone just sit down?"

◆ ◆ ◆

The silence was deafening. Job had just broken the news about the letter sans the part about the blog and the proposed meeting with him. Rainey watched his mother. It was as if she had been smacked across the face. All at once her eyes began to melt. She let out a gasp and began sobbing.

"What does this mean? He's alive?! How?! Where?! Where is he, Job?!" Maddie pleaded through her own tears.

The muscles in Job's jaw flexed as though he were trying to will himself to get control of his emotions. "We don't know. We don't know anything yet. But we're doing everything we can to find out if there is any shred of truth to this. I need for you to understand that this could be a hoax, some kind of cruel joke. Or—"

"Or he could be alive." Sarah stood up slowly. She walked to the rear window overlooking the water, steadying herself as she went. She brought her trembling hands up, covered her mouth. Her head sunk and she began to weep with her whole body. She fell to her knees and rocked forward onto the floor. Iris quickly ran over and consoled her, followed by Maddie. After a moment, she collected herself enough to say, "I just want to know the truth. Not some Agency doublespeak. I want to know the *real* truth. Please, Job!"

Rainey went to her, knelt and wrapped his arms around her. "I'm sorry, Mom. I wanted you to know. Both of you." He cupped the back of Maddie's head in his hand. "I'm sorry. I'm sorry to cause you more pain."

Sarah leaned into his chest, her face puffy and red and streaked with tears. "No, Reagan. It's not your fault. You did what you thought was best."

They stayed like this for several minutes each of them dealing with the news and their emotions in their own way. Mom, Maddie and Wes were aware of what he did for a living now, not with great specificity, but they each knew he worked in some capacity for the CIA. They knew he did things about which he could never speak. Important things. Dangerous things.

Maddie and Wes had both signed non-disclosure agreements after their part in the episode that played out on American soil back in January. But this was different.

This was family.

"Mom, we're going to get to the bottom of this. Do you hear me?"

She looked up at him, with pleading in her eyes. "If it's true, *if* he's alive… Find him, Ray. Please. Bring him home to me."

"I will, Mom. I will."

7

RAINEY and Job stepped outside into the calmness of the summer air. Rainey had never been good at sharing his emotions, always seemed awkward and uncomfortable when he tried. The atmosphere inside the house didn't help things either. It was downright suffocating in there.

He took in a chest-full of oxygen, exhaled as he raked his fingers through his close-cropped, brown hair. A pair of crickets chirped away, their shrieking a sort of mournful duet. As the men walked along the sidewalk toward the driveway, the crickets stopped. Then, after a few seconds, one of them resumed its rhythmic, monophonic performance in solo.

Rainey swung around at the sudden sound of a woman screaming.

"Easy, Ray. Just some shrill laughter. From over there."

Far across the harbor, someone was throwing a grand party. Lively piano music spilled from a set of French doors that had been left open, along with a throng of unintelligible voices.

Carnaval, Op. 9.

Schumann. How ironic.

There was an occasional outburst of laughter from a particular woman who evidently had a good set of lungs. He could not decide whether the cricket or the howling woman was more annoying. The big house from which she continued to bellow her boisterous jocularity was alive with lights and activity. Several groupings of silhouettes milled about the terrace. His eyes traced the grassy knoll to the water's edge. He had to squint to see them, but in the glow of the house, was a couple—lovers by the looks of it. They seemed lost in each other's embrace. Their heads came together, stayed that way. The woman with the good lungs burst out again.

The contrast with the mood over here could not have been any more stark. A sense of jealously crept into his thoughts. Would he ever get to experience that again? Happiness. Contentment. Evenings full of serenity and serenades. A godly woman to love and embrace.

It was stupid, he told himself, especially considering the news about his father, but right now in this very minute he would give anything for someone, someone like Kayla, to hold and to hold him. If only for a little while.

She told me to tell you she said hi…

"I'm sorry about all that," said Job.

Rainey cleared his throat. "It had to be done. They needed to know. They're upset, but, as you well know, our family's faith is strong. Mom and Maddie have each other. More importantly they have God. He will be their refuge, their comfort."

"And what about you? Are *you* okay?"

His eyes shifted to the black sedan in the driveway. Job's bodyguard stood beside it, a Marine dutifully awaiting his orders. The man would stand there all night if he was told to do so. "I'm okay. You?"

Job nodded. "Have to be. There's work to do." Job patted Rainey on the arm. "You *are* packed, right?"

"I'm all set. Gear's in the truck."

"Good. Throw it in the trunk and get in. I have some news."

◆ ◆ ◆

The sedan zoomed along I-97 toward Baltimore-Washington International Airport. He and Job were seated comfortably in the back seat. The light from passing motorists flashed across their faces as they gently rocked with the vehicle's movements.

"I thought it best to wait until after…you know, after we told your mother and Maddie."

Rainey accepted a file folder from Job, clicked on a small interior cabin light. He flipped through its contents as Job continued.

"Not sure anyone's ever told you, Ray, but your father was a field man. An operations officer. He was stationed in some pretty busy places. From the few records I've been able to locate, we know his last assignment was rather complex, but very significant.

"Officially, your dad was posted to Berlin Station, but he was seldom there. Best I can tell he was last working on some kind of operation out of a clandestine office in Estonia. But the records are…"

"Yeah?"

"Gone."

"Whaddya mean, *gone?*"

"I mean everything pertaining to your father's last assignment is gone. There's nothing left."

"There has to be. It's computerized. There's at least gotta be an audit trail."

"We were an agency in transition back then, Ray. Some things had yet to be digitized. The databases and digital records that did exist, some people had trouble utilizing. It was all new. It wasn't like today where everyone has a solid baseline of computer knowledge. Sometimes records weren't indexed properly. Staff were still working to familiarize themselves with the coming digital world. We may well have the records, but even if we do, they're not searchable. At least not in a way that can be accomplished with any degree of speed. It could take an eternity.

"This I know: any records, paper docs especially, pertaining to whatever your dad was working on from ninety-five to ninety-six were either misfiled, improperly classified and indexed, or purposely removed."

Rainey hung his head. "Are you telling me what I think you're telling me?"

"Let's not jump to conclusions. There may be a valid explanation. It's definitely unusual, I'll say that, but mistakes have been made. Not often, but—"

"But there could also be a more sinister explanation."

"I'm not going to lie to you, Ray. It's crossed my mind." Job kneaded his hands. "Yes. It's possible."

Rainey gazed through the dark, tinted window. A mosquito that had been buzzing inside the cabin, landed on the glass. He thrust out a hammer fist and decimated it, leaving a wet, burgundy smear on the window. He wiped his hand on his pant leg. "Who was he working with?"

"I'm already ahead of you, Ray. The director and I are meeting with the DNI in the morning. He ran the operation in Estonia. If anyone can shed some light on this thing, it will be him. We're going to get answers. One way or the other. I promise you."

The sedan shot across the tarmac to a waiting jet; its airstair was already down. The lights from the airport shimmered against its white fuselage, making it appear a pastel orange, the royal blue striping a deep purple. Soft yellow light burned from within the open door of the plane.

"You'll be briefed on the way. I'll be in touch. And Ray, be careful."

He nodded as they shook hands. "Will do."

Rainey grabbed his gear from the back of the sedan and stood there, watching it buzz away across the tarmac. He hoisted the bag over his shoulder and boarded the plane. As soon as he rounded the corner into the cabin space, a familiar voice boomed.

"Hiya, kid."

"Pappy. What are *you* doing here?"

The slight grin on the face of Saul Baker faded. "Sit down, Ray. We have a lot of ground to cover."

He dropped his duffel bag on one of the supple leather seats and plopped down in the one next to it. "By the way, where are we headed?"

Saul stretched out his legs, placed his interlaced fingers in his lap. "To see an old friend. Now fasten your seatbelt."

8

THE Bombardier Challenger 350's powerful engines droned in the background like a hairdryer set to low. It was a new edition to the Directorate's fleet of clandestine aircraft. Registered to a Greenbriar Foundation affiliate—another Directorate X front company—based in Miami, the jet was luxurious and spacious. But Rainey didn't care about any of that right now. Rather, his focus was solely on Saul.

Saul "Pappy" Baker had worked at the Central Intelligence Agency for over thirty years. His daring exploits were still talked about in the corridors of Langley and Washington, D.C. After his retirement and late wife's passing, he had sold his historic Virginia horse farm to Rainey for almost nothing. Saul had no longer been able to physically keep up with the amount of work required to maintain it and Rainey had been searching for a decent place of his own with a lot of land. One of their agreed-upon stipulations was that Saul could live there for as long as he wanted. Since then Saul had become like a grandfather to him.

"So who's this friend?" said Rainey.

"Ernie Wells. He's retired Agency, too. Left a little after me. Still keeps his finger on the pulse of what's going on in the world. Ernie worked in the Directorate of Administration back in the seventies, eighties and nineties. At least that's what it was called back there. Now I believe they call it the Directorate of Support. Ernie's a good guy. He's quiet. Doesn't say much unless he's got something to say. And he's smart. Probably one of the smartest men I've ever known. He's got a photographic memory, which I guess comes in handy if your purpose in life is records management."

"How does he factor into discovering the truth about my dad?"

"Ernie was the go-to guy when it came to Agency archives back in my day. And he's a good friend. If anyone will know about the operation, it will be Ernie. The man is a veritable encyclopedia on you name it. Hopefully, he'll at least be able to steer us in the right direction, maybe tell us who the players are or were. Bottom line is that we're looking to substantiate whether this Moses character has any credibility. If we can't come up with anything, then we'll know that Moses is full of it. Thus we'll be able to conclude that he is a provocateur."

"The missing records seem to portend that he's legit though. Wouldn't you say?"

"Yeah. That's a very good point. But that's not enough in my book to prove what Moses is saying is true or even possible. Coming out of the woodwork to tell us after all these years that Ben is alive, is a very big deal. Unprecedented to my knowledge. And very hard to swallow. It's going to take a lot to convince me that Moses is not angling for something here."

"Angling for what though?"

"I don't know, kid. I don't know."

After several moments of staring at the fingermarks on the powered-off flat-screen affixed to the wall in front of him, Rainey said, "You used to work with my dad, right?"

Saul straightened the stack of files in front of him. "Yes. He came to the Agency in eighty-one. I had just been sent to Moscow as the new station chief after stints in Sudan and East Germany. His first posting was in my house. He may have been new to the mission back then, but your dad was good right out of the gate. Very bright. A lot like you, I might add.

"Ben excelled at recruiting agents. He was a natural. Your dad could recruit a fruit basket. Some people just have a knack for it. He could also shake a tail better than anyone. He was one of the best officers I had working in Moscow Station. None had the success he had. The KGB's surveillance was suffocating. Most of the time my people just ended up loading drops for agents who'd been recruited elsewhere, that type of thing. But he was one of the few who seemed to thrive in that atmosphere. Eventually, I requested he be cycled out to another station where he would have more elbow room. He was posted to Paris and West Berlin. While he did far better than his peers in Moscow, he was still inhibited. There was always much more freedom to run operations from outside Russia.

"Anyway, I was still station chief in Moscow when the Wall came down. The Soviets were wobbled like a prize fighter who'd been clocked good but was still somehow able to stay on his feet. When the curtain finally did fall in ninety-one, everything changed. After all those years of matching wits against the Soviets, it was finally over. Langley was thrilled, we all were, don't get me wrong. But to be perfectly honest, Ray, the Agency was a little disoriented. When the Cold War officially drew to a close, I was brought back home and re-tasked to fight the new and growing threat: Islamic fundamentalism. Iraq. Iran. Hezbollah. Al-Qaeda. They put me in charge of the Near East Division. That's when I began to work more closely with Job. He'd just come over from South Asia Division."

Rainey kicked off his shoes, wiggled his toes. "What was my dad working on when you left Moscow?"

"When I left, he was still wrangling spies, developing networks and running cases. I know he had some pretty good agents. Loyal ones, too. Like I said, your dad was a natural. The plan back then was that he would keep the bulk of his agents in place until after the dust settled. While SE Division kind of fell apart, or at least was in search of a new identity, Langley wanted to keep track of the players. There were suddenly a lot of KGB and GRU officers and others out of a job. They all had to go somewhere. A large number went to work for banks or other private enterprises doing security or consulting work. Some tested the global markets, sold their training and expertise to the highest bidder. Yet many were rolled into new positions, given new titles within the new Russian government agencies. The FSB, the SVR.

"As far as I know, Ben continued recruiting spies, developing his agent networks, culling key intel from the rapidly shifting sands of former Soviet-bloc countries. Last time I saw him was March of ninety-four." Saul closed his eyes. "He was a good man, your dad. A rock. He used to tape scraps of paper to the walls of the communications room. Do you know what was on those scraps of paper?"

Rainey shook his head.

"Bible verses. He used to write out *Bible* verses, a different one every month, and hang them on the walls where staff would see them. I remember one specifically: Psalm one eighteen, six. *The LORD is on my side; I will not fear. What can man do to me?*"

"Any idea what he was doing in ninety-six? At the time of his... When his plane crashed."

"I've heard different things over the years. I've heard that he was working out of Berlin Station under State Department cover to help vet the wave of defectors and others seeking asylum in Europe and the U.S. One person told me he was chasing around some old KGB targets in Tajikistan. Another former colleague said she had heard he was involved in something sensitive in the Baltics. Estonia or Latvia, one of those countries.

"Honestly, I don't know what he was working on. But Job has culled enough information to say with a relatively high degree of confidence that he was working out of Estonia. As good as Ben was, I have to believe he was still running agents."

"What else do you know?"

"That's pretty much it, Ray. The only other thing I know for sure is that whatever it was he was working on, he answered to Hank McManus."

"The DNI."

Saul's face soured. "The one and only."

"You don't seem to care for the man."

"That's because I don't."

"Why not?"

"Because he's a politician. Was then. Is now. Remember how I said some officers are just naturally good at recruiting agents and some aren't? Well, Hank McManus falls into the latter category. He was horrible at it. Truth be told, the man couldn't recruit a walk-in. And frankly I've never trusted him.

"See, McManus was brought in as my replacement to run Moscow Station. You know me, I'm a humble guy, Ray, but McManus was like a third-string quarterback who came in when the game was already well in hand. Had a strong entitlement mentality. And *boy* was he arrogant. In his mind, he could do no wrong. Somehow he moved up through the ranks. He sure knew how to play the game with those on the seventh floor. After his stint in Moscow, he went on to become division chief. SE had become Central Eurasia Division by that point. From there, he climbed the ladder to deputy director of administration. Like I said, he's a politician. Smart, but smarmy. Somewhere along the way, he ran an operation with your dad. After Moscow."

"Funny how the records are now missing, huh? Specifically records pertaining to that operation."

Saul chewed on his bottom lip. "Yeah. Funny."

"Is that why Job and the director are going to see him in the morning?"

"That's exactly why. They're gonna poke the beehive."

9

Vienna, Virginia

HE entered through a rear door, addressed the alarm system at the keypad panel just inside then made his way through the large kitchen, down a short hallway and into a study that smelled faintly of cigar smoke. A few steps into the room, he stopped, gazed around and took it all in. The house was quiet and dimly lit. He pulled out a small penlight and clicked it on. The safe was behind the desk in the den. He already knew the combination.

Rolling the leather desk chair out of the way, he approached a large bookcase behind the desk. He touched several of the books on the second shelf, which were not books at all, but rather a finely crafted outer door. He opened it and began spinning the dial of the safe within.

Click.

The door of the safe was thick and heavy, the handle cold even through the fabric of his glove. He probed the dark box with his penlight then stuck the light in his mouth while he extracted a stack of dusty files. After several minutes rifling through them, he found it. He smiled then suddenly had the urge to sneeze. Quickly, he pinched his nose until the feeling subsided then placed the rest of the files back inside the safe, closed the door and spun the dial back to where it had been.

The man bent the yellow-gold envelope in half and stuffed it inside his shirt. He pulled the desk chair back in its proper place then made his way upstairs. The carpet muted his careful footfalls until he was in the master bathroom. It was spacious, smelled of lilac or… *No. Lavender. Yes, it's definitely lavender.*

Gently, he opened the medicine cabinet and examined each prescription bottle with his eyes until he located the right one. He picked it up, screwed off the cap. Emptying its contents onto the vanity, he reached into his pocket and pulled out a Ziploc baggie that contained tiny pills that visually were identical to the pills on the counter. He counted them twice to be sure the amounts were equal then exchanged his pills with the ones that had been in the prescription bottle, closed the lid and set it back inside the medicine cabinet. With a cupped hand, he carefully herded the pills on the counter into the baggie, sealed it and shoved it back into his pocket.

He glimpsed himself in the mirror of the medicine cabinet door, trying to think of any trace of evidence he might have left behind that could betray his careful tradecraft though he knew there was none.

His tasks complete, he made his way back downstairs where he reset the alarm and exited the same door he had used to enter. Once over the fence, he retrieved his night-vision goggles and set off into the woods that surrounded the property on three sides. He easily made it back to the rendezvous point. Crouching down, he waited just inside the dark, shadowy tree line along Lawyers Road.

It wasn't long till the headlights of a dark SUV swept around the bend. The vehicle drifted past and suddenly stopped. He bolted from the woods and hopped into the front seat, dropping his NVGs on the floorboard between his feet. The driver said nothing, just handed him a cell phone.

Zarek Tarło brushed a few gnats out of his hair as he waited for the call to connect. When it finally did, he brought the phone closer to his mouth.

"It's done."

10

Potomac, Maryland

S HE had seen some dazzling estates in her lifetime, but this one was truly sublime. Stedman Carter knew how to live the good life, how to spend money. He knew how to make it, too. The lavish estate must have easily cost the billionaire well over two hundred million dollars to build. The main house had over 80 rooms and was bigger than some five-star hotels. It had everything you could ever want or need and a doting staff to make sure you got it. Outside, there were fountains and statues and gardens scattered about. Most of the grounds now, though, lay dormant and in dark shadow, but for the areas that clung to the gigantic mansion—the terraces, the flagstone walkways, the enormous forecourt and the Olympic-size swimming pool. Some of the guests sauntered about these areas, which were lit by iron lampposts, recessed fixtures, spotlights and bulbs that were strung to artful perfection. But for a moat and a princess up in the tower, it was the quintessential storybook setting. A castle fit for a king.

This is heaven.

Vera stood next to a Greek pillar in the grand reception hall, the place where Stedman Carter could often be found wining and dining his guests with the purpose of separating them from their money or to celebrate the latest multi-gazillion dollar business deal. In tonight's case, he was raising money for the final leg of the president's reelection campaign.

Her left arm tucked beneath her right, Vera sipped at her champagne while musing about recent events. Her sultry Persian eyes swept over the eclectic gathering of American aristocrats. The eighty-five year-old media baron with the potbelly and a curvy blonde on either arm, each of whom could be his granddaughter. The senator from Nevada, the Party's eloquent, soft-spoken hatchet man. The effeminate man by the bar, CEO of one of America's biggest clothing retailers, acclaimed social justice warrior and media darling, all; he was one of the campaign's fiercest and most cunning weapons and had an army of like-minded souls he routinely rallied via his considerable social media following. Then there was the hedge fund manager with shark teeth and the revolving door of debutante wives. The president of a famous Ivy League school that had the heralded tradition of inviting the world's most egregious human rights offenders to lecture her student body—and America at large—on the ills of Western society, the plight of the Palestinian or the need for a more robust and expansive Progressive agenda especially with respect to Christian and Jewish hegemony.

Soon Vera became fixated on the tall man in the center of the room. He stood amidst the throngs of people, the men in black tie, the women in gaudy dresses with thousand-dollar handbags. His hair was neatly combed, his face tanned and well-groomed. The suit was probably Italian. Its lines complemented his lean, sturdy form. At sixty-two, Stedman Carter was still a gorgeous man. She had often fantasized about him, what he must be like under his suit. In it, he certainly exuded godlike power.

With envy, she watched him smile at a young bosomy thing in front of him who was eyeing him the way a dog eyes a steak. He shook the hands of several people then stepped a few paces away from them and pulled out a cell phone. She was well outside of earshot to hear his words, but she could read his lips, those wonderful kissable lips: *Yes? I see. Thank you.* After pocketing the phone, he lifted his chin and began searching the room with his eyes. When they landed on her own, a charge of electricity pulsed through her body. Stedman Carter raised his glass as if to make a toast from afar, a hint of satisfaction in his visage.

She responded with a slight nod, offering a discreet grin over the bubbles in her glass.

Excellent.

Slithering from her perch, she milled through the crowded room, past senators and congressmen, lobbyists and news media puppets, CEOs and moneychangers. She brushed by a pair of A-list Hollywood celebrities who as best she could tell were engaged in a rather serious discussion with the under secretary of education. She was almost to the arched doorway that issued into the next room, when the IRS's deputy commissioner for services and enforcement touched her on the elbow.

"Vera, can I get a word?"

"Not now, John."

She left the obsequious man in her wake and entered Stedman Carter's private gallery, where he kept a collection of some of the world's most valuable works of art, just for the sake of showcasing them to his guests. Rumor had it, though, that somewhere on the premises Carter had another room—a secret room—and it was chock full of paintings, jewels and other priceless artifacts that had been acquired through less than legitimate means.

Vera ambled past several well-coifed guests, nursing drinks and gawking at a Cézanne landscape called, *Vignoble en Hiver.* She continued across the room and placed her small hand on a pocket door that led into Stedman Carter's massive library. It was heavy but she was able to slide it open without much effort. She stepped inside and was about to close it, when a man's voice called out in a loud whisper from halfway across the gallery.

"Vera. *Vera!*"

She looked up at the man lumbering toward her then scanned the room to see who might be watching. Her mouth stretched into a polite smile in the spirit of pretense. "Yes, Hank."

"I need to talk to you."

She stepped back and permitted him entry then slid the door closed. As soon as they were alone, she chastised him. "Don't whisper, Hank! It's poor form. What's more, it looks like we're up to something sinister."

"Yes. I'm sorry."

"What is it? You look a bit frazzled. Is anything the matter?"

"It's about tomorrow. Thompson is bringing someone with him. Job Jackson. I'm a little concerned," said McManus. "Job's got something of a reputation for—"

"Hank," she said while placing her hand on his arm. "Relax. I've given this a great deal of thought. I want you to tell them everything. Be honest."

"What about… I thought we had agreed that—"

"We did," she said with an earnest nod of the head. "But I've had time to digest. After further deliberation, I think it would be unwise to be anything other than completely forthcoming. Whatever the consequences, we'll endure. The president's popularity has never been higher. And we've got a few things up our sleeves for our opponent. Don't worry. Everything's going to be fine. I plan on having a chat with Director Thompson myself tomorrow afternoon. The Agency doesn't need dragged through the mud yet again. He'll get the picture. If he chooses to pursue this, I'll see to it that there are hearings held regarding last year's activities. Very *public* hearings. He'll be finished. He and everyone involved. Maybe even criminally charged. What they did was engage in covert activities on foreign soil without a presidential finding or any semblance of authority to do so. Rest easy, Hank. Thompson doesn't want to pick a fight with me."

"Well… Okay. That makes me feel a lot better."

She smiled, showing a perfect set of teeth. "Good. Now go relax and enjoy the party. Tell you what. How about you stop by my office tomorrow sometime around eleven or so and you can tell me how the meeting went?"

"Sounds like a plan. Thanks, Vera."

"Thank you, Hank. I'm happy you came to me in the first place." Her smile faded as soon as he turned his back to her and shuffled out of the room. She raised her glass, nodded her head as if to acknowledge an unseen audience then gulped the last of her champagne.

Thank you, Hank.

11

Kingston-Upon-Hull, UK

RAINEY rocked in the front-passenger seat of the rented Skoda, as Saul plowed through one of the puddles that spotted the road. He wiped the gentle spray from his left hand, which had been hanging out his open window. The quick summer downpour had ceased only minutes after they had landed. Steam now rose from the pavement as sunlight shimmered against the wet veneer of the street. Saul downshifted and accelerated around a double-decker bus that had been frustrating their egress from the city.

When traffic finally cleared, the office buildings and neighborhoods had fallen away, Saul opened her up. After a mile into the lush farmland, he said. "Kinda reminds you of home a little. Wouldn't you say?"

"Little flatter, but yeah."

The English countryside was pastoral, peaceful, a quilted patchwork of green, tan and more green. He tried to comprehend a sky full of German bombers. He recalled the pictures he had seen in history books about World War II, of wrecked British cities, population centers that had been mercilessly hammered by the German Luftwaffe.

"A lot of history here, Ray."

"No doubt. A resilient people, the Brits. You'd have to be to endure the type of bombings they've suffered. Not just endure, but thrive."

Saul smiled. "They are. If we had more time, I'd show you some of my old haunts. Here and down in London."

Rainey said nothing as he took in the beautiful landscape. They passed an old man on an old red Massey Ferguson pulling an old tiller. A small boy, who could be the man's grandson, sat in his lap, holding the steering wheel as the farmer drove across the field. The little boy turned his attention to the passing vehicle, waved at them. Rainey waved back.

As they swept around the next curve, Saul slowed, put on his blinker and waited for an oncoming car. After it passed, he turned onto a private lane. They continued through a small metal gate, which was nothing more than a break in the fence that had skirted the road for the last half mile. The lane shot forward in a line that disappeared at the horizon. On either side were endless fields of green grass, undefiled and rolling like an ocean tide in the steady breeze. As they crested the slight grade, a mammoth red-brick building came into view. Its spires and turrets with crenellated parapets seemed to grow up out of the earth as they moved closer. Ivy climbed several stories high on the left side of the hulking structure.

Saul drove them through a formal looking entranceway with a brushed bronze plaque that read, *The Institute for the Preservation of Knowledge and Learning.*

"Wow, it's huge. What is this place? Some kind of old castle?"

"Close. The former Beverley Manor. It was originally built by the French back in the fifteen hundreds. Changed hands a few times over the years. In the mid-seventeen hundreds, Lord Milton Beverley acquired it. I forget the whole story. Anyway, some of his heirs still live here. In the mansion over on the western edge of the property. The main house—I know, it looks more like a college campus—was hit hard by the Germans in forty-one. Half of it burned to the ground. It's since been fully restored and expanded several times over, as I understand. British Intelligence used it briefly during the war as a listening post and a place to bring captured German spies for interrogation. Later it was used as a training academy for MI6 and MI5 recruits. Like I said," he chuckled. "A lot of history here.

"Now—as the sign says—it's the Institute for the Preservation of Knowledge and Learning and it's owned by the Greenbriar Foundation, but that's a well-kept secret. Even most of the employees here aren't aware of that little nugget." Saul smiled, his thick hands hugging the wheel like a race car driver. The Greenbriar Foundation was the public entity—in reality, one great big CIA front—that housed Directorate X personnel and functions. It had many associations, affiliates, partner institutions and businesses, NGOs and other types of organizations within its purview. Each one contributed invariably to the DX's covert existence and its stellar operational capability.

A man inside the gatehouse checked their credentials and happily sent them through a black iron gate beneath a red-brick archway. They parked on a cobblestone lot. Rainey got out and stretched. It had been a long trip. He felt sluggish from all the sitting. The faint scent of the sea was in the air. That and the fact that it was a balmy 90 degrees harkened back to a week he and some Unit buddies spent in Duck, North Carolina a few years ago while on leave. They had stayed in a house owned by a former Unit commander. What a blast. It was always great spending quality downtime with his brother warriors, when they didn't have to think about planning and conducting dangerous operations or the stresses of war. Jumping into the swimming pool from the rooftop, throwing football on the beach and meeting pretty local girls tended to quell the anxieties of the job if only for a short time.

He had been away from his Unit mates only six months now and he missed them terribly. Missed their humor, missed the camaraderie. But he was committed now to the Directorate. And he was a man who honored his commitments. In the end, he knew he would see them again. Doubtless sooner than later.

His mom and Maddie had just begun to creep into his thoughts as he glanced back toward the gatehouse. The man inside was talking on the phone. When he noticed Rainey observing him, he smiled and signaled with an outstretched forefinger that they were to continue toward the massive front door. In a matter of seconds, it swung open and another man stepped into the bright sunlight. His face was intelligent and ruddy, his hair white and thinned with age, but neatly combed. He wore thick spectacles and a tweed blazer that gave him the appearance of a lifelong academic.

"Gentlemen, welcome. I've been expecting you," he said, offering each man an affable though delicate handshake.

"Reagan Rainey, I'd like you to meet Dr. Ernie Wells."

"Ah, yes, Mr. Rainey. Pleasure to meet you. I knew your father. He was a great man, your dad. It's remarkable, the way you resemble him."

"Thanks," said Rainey.

"That's why we're here, Ernie. We need to talk to you about Ben," said Saul.

"Of course. Please come inside. I'll have Winnie bring us some sandwiches." Wells led them inside a spacious foyer decorated with meticulous precision and care. "So, Mr. Rainey, this is your first time at the Institute, yes?"

"Yeah, first time."

"How 'bout I give you the tour first?" said Wells.

"I wish we had time for that, Ernie."

Wells regarded his old friend with a crestfallen frown. "Well maybe later then. You really must see the place."

12

AFTER being issued visitor badges, they walked through the lobby beneath a large purple banner on which was embroidered in gold script, "The fear of the LORD is the beginning of wisdom, and the knowledge of the Holy One is understanding." He read it again then looked down at a bustling cluster of high school-age kids who were beginning to filter out of a small gift shop. Their leader assembled them in congregation like a conductor commanding the movements of a marching band during the halftime performance of a college bowl game.

"Think of the Institute as a giant library—a very *special* library. A library with a dedicated purpose: to preserve Western foundational ideals and foster critical thought. Does that mean we only maintain pro-Western resources? Heavens, no. What would critical thought be without the study of opposing viewpoints, yes?" He ushered them past an ornate wooden stairway. "We are open to the public, by appointment only, mind you. Each day you can find student groups here, intellectuals doing intense research, or just history lovers enjoying a guided tour of the property. Sometimes government leaders hold meetings or conferences here. There is a small retreat complex further east on the property.

You'd be surprised to learn who has stayed here. Heads of state, ambassadors and ministers. Once a year we host a rather large bible conference. Pastors and clergy can gather and have fellowship. We hold book fairs and benefit parties. All with the sole purpose of preserving those ideals on which America, and the West as a whole, has been built. The bedrock principles that have fostered true prosperity. We hold arguably the most extensive and best-preserved collection of writings and resources pertaining to the American Revolution in existence. Ironic that it's right here in England, wouldn't you say?"

Rainey marveled at a mosaic of stained glass windows that rose up along the wall on the left side of the main stairs. The vibrant palette of colors was unlike anything he had ever seen.

"You should be here at sunrise. The way the sunlight hits those windows. It's positively magnificent!"

"Neat," said Rainey.

"In a few months, we are going to be unveiling plans—keep this to yourselves, please—of a brand new facility in Virginia. Probably going to be three times as big as this place. I can't wait! We'll be introducing something else truly remarkable in another year or so." Wells was like a kid on a Christmas Eve. "You wanna know what it is?" Without giving them a chance to respond, he whispered, "The Institute is going to start a college. Yes, indeed. Stay tuned. It's going to start a revolution in post-secondary education."

When they reached a bank of elevators, Wells smiled at the men, adjusted his glasses. "One of the modern amendments. One for which I'm very grateful. I'm too old to go running up and down stairs anymore."

Rainey stepped inside. "So what exactly do you do here, Dr. Wells?"

Wells smiled with glee. "I'm special assistant to the curator. I do some consulting on collections, but my primary remit is managing the Institute's huge repository. It's quite extensive. Dare I say, the amount of resources here on this property alone rivals that of the Library of Congress."

"Wow."

"My job is to keep track of it all, streamline retrievals, along with various other related tasks. I have a small staff of very capable people. There is always something to do here. We are very busy. But I must say, I love my job."

◆ ◆ ◆

The man pressed his face into the phone. "Yes. They're here now. Two of them. They just went inside."

"Okay. Keep an eye on them. We'll be there in a twenty minutes. Let me know if anything changes."

"All right, but hurry." The man disconnected the call and pocketed the phone. He reached under the counter and gripped a Walther PPQ M2. With his eyes still on the front door, he slipped the pistol into his waistband and made sure his shirttail covered it.

Please hurry.

◆ ◆ ◆

Wells' office was on the fourth floor. It was furnished with antiques and trinkets that assuredly held historical and personal significance. Rainey recognized the signature on a framed document inside a glass display case. He drew closer and inspected it.

Wells stepped up beside him, leaned over and tilted his head back, making use of his bifocals. "Ah, yes. A letter from Washington to the head of his spy network."

"Tallmadge. The Culper Ring."

"You know your history, Mr. Rainey." Wells smiled, shuffled past him. "Here, gentlemen. We can talk in here." Wells opened a wooden door at the back of his office that issued into a small conference room. Inside, it was insanely quiet and smelled of old wood and dust. A hand-carved clock on the credenza indicated it was just past noon. In the center of the room was a small, but beautiful, polished walnut table with brass-handled drawers. A tall wing back chair with blue and burgundy and gold upholstery was positioned in the corner. "It's really good to see you, Saul. How many years has it been now?"

"Too many." Saul took a seat next to Rainey, folded his hands on the polished walnut table.

"I thought you had retired."

"Me, too. I'm doing a little consulting of my own now, I guess you could say." A middle-aged woman knocked on the closed door. When Wells advised she could enter, she slipped in and delivered a silver platter of triangle sandwiches and tea then quickly receded to wherever it was she had come from.

"Ernie, something's come up. I didn't want to say over the phone, but... It involves Ben Rainey. There's a chance he may still be alive."

Wells' face went white. His forehead wrinkled in confusion as he sat up in his chair. "Well, that's great. But I don't understand, I thought he...," His eyes flitted to Rainey.

Rainey nodded. "It's okay, Dr. Wells. You can say it."

"I thought he *died* in a plane crash." Wells' eyes widened as he said the word "died."

"So did we. But some information has come to light to suggest otherwise. Nothing's confirmed, mind you, but we're looking into the possibility. Basically we are trying to substantiate its validity."

"Okaaay. How can I help?"

"Ernie, we need you tell us what you know about the operation Ben was working on prior to his death. All I know to this point is that he was working out of Estonia. What was he working on? Who were the players? That type of thing. Think back to ninety-five/ninety-six. Hank McManus was running it."

"Hank. Yeah. But I don't understand. Why come to me about this? Why not go to Hank?"

"Suffice it to say, we're not the only ones looking into this." Saul sipped some tea then set his porcelain cup on the saucer in his left hand. He maintained his grip on the cup handle with his index finger and thumb. "Ernie, the files are missing. Those that were digitized have been wiped. Everything. It's all gone."

"That's impossible. How?"

Saul sighed. "That's what we need you to help us figure out."

Wells sloughed back in his chair. "Holy cow!" He removed his glasses and massaged the bridge of his nose. After several seconds, he pulled out a handkerchief and began furiously cleaning his lenses. "I just don't see how that's possible. We had checks in place to prevent that type of thing from happening. How could all those records be gone?"

"Who else had access? What I mean is, who had the means to destroy the records, including the digital files?" asked Rainey.

Wells pushed his glasses back in place. "There was any number of people, myself included. But the notion that someone could do that and do it successfully—without getting caught—is ludicrous. It…" He placed his hand over his mouth as if he had been struck with a sudden revelation. "It must have been… Son of a… It must have been Hank. He asked me to pull some reports once. It was right after he'd taken over the DA. I thought it had something to do with an audit, you know, something to do with an ongoing internal review. He said Security needed them. I just assumed… I didn't suspect anything untoward. I had no reason to. Plus, it wasn't my place to ask questions. I just pulled the files he'd requested and gave them to him."

Rainey stood up, walked to a window that overlooked the sprawling grounds. The North Sea was off in the distance. The sunlight made the water that lay on the horizon appear pale blue, almost white. "That doesn't explain the digital files."

"He's right," said Saul.

Ernie looked at Saul, then the table, shaking his head. "I can't explain that. Frankly, I can't fathom it. Like I said, there were checks in place."

"But someone could get around those checks if they really wanted to? Someone who knew how the system worked?"

Wells pursed his lips. "I take your point. I suppose anything's possible."

Saul assessed the sandwiches on the tray, selected one. "Tell us about the operation."

"I will tell you what I remember. It was a long time ago." Wells reached for his tea cup, lifted it to his mouth. "It was called Triumph. Operation Triumph. Hank's part of the op was run out of Tallinn."

"Estonia," said Rainey.

Wells nodded. "Hank was in charge, just like you said. Overall, the operation had two objectives. The first was to track down stockpiles of surplus Soviet armaments. When the USSR disintegrated, there were so many weapons and materiel that suddenly hit the black market. I'm talking heavy equipment, too. Ships, submarines even. It was crazy. As a seller, all you needed was a buyer with enough money and a broker to find him and facilitate the transaction.

"The second objective was to locate and monitor certain people who had either gone missing or slipped into other roles. Scientists, GRU and KGB officers and other key members of the Red Army. A number of rather significant people seemed to have just vanished into thin air. Sometimes the two operational objectives converged."

"Who was involved in the op?" asked Saul.

"Most of CE Division's North Group, but those involved were split up into specific locations with their own areas of responsibility. With respect to the cables and reports I pulled, the only names I recall seeing were those associated with Hank McManus and Benjamin Rainey. Not their names, of course, but…well you know, their operational pseudonyms."

"Hank told you what to look for? He told you their op names?"

Wells nodded.

"What about support staff?"

"Well, yes, Ben did have a communicator. Crystal Hartley-Breeland, if memory serves."

"Anyone else?"

"I'm afraid not. They kept things very compartmentalized. It was a highly sensitive operation. Remember, this was not long after Ames was arrested." Aldrich Ames had been a CIA case officer who specialized in recruiting agents from the Russian intelligence services. He was arrested by the FBI in February of 1994 for spying for the KGB.

"Targets or agents? You recall any of them?" asked Saul.

"I'm sorry. No."

Rainey polished off a sandwich, wiped his mouth with a napkin then mused aloud. "If my dad operated out of Tallinn then how is it he ended up on a plane over South America?"

"I can't answer that. What I mean is, I don't know. All I know is what I saw in the reports and cables."

"Which is what?" asked Saul.

"That he was flying along the border area between Venezuela and Brazil when his plane crashed. I seem to remember one of the reports indicating that the plane had experienced *mechanical failure* mid-flight. McManus flew to the scene and documented it, took photos, you know." Wells set his cup down, massaged his hands. "Locals were on scene, too. State had to smooth it over a little in order to have the bodies shipped back in a timely manner."

Rainey was stone-faced until his jaw muscles involuntarily flexed.

"You don't know what Ben was really doing there?"

"No."

"What was the cover story?" said Saul.

"That he was part of a group of missionaries, transporting Bibles to a local tribe, something along those lines."

"There should have been a report from the local station, too, am I right?"

"Should have been, but they were kept out of the loop. Their reports essentially summarized what the operational cover story ended up being. They were none the wiser."

"I see."

"Any idea who else was on the plane?" said Rainey.

"No. I'm sorry. I wish I could tell you more."

13

THEY stepped back out into the early afternoon sun. Rainey squinted as he flicked out his shades and put them on. "Whaddya think?" Saul looked as if he'd bitten into a lemon. "What's wrong, Pappy? Do you not feel well?"

"Honestly, I feel a little sick to my stomach. He's holding something back. There is something he's not telling us."

"What? And why?"

"I don't know. Ernie's always been a good friend. Something's just not right. I've always hated that line: 'I *wish* I could tell you more.' It's a red flag, one you learn to pick up on when you work in the field for as long as I have. There are others, too. Some are even more subtle. Regardless, you learn to detect them. Better still when you know the person, the way they act in a normal conversation. You get to know their mannerisms, their vernacular. It's why parents can almost always tell when their kids are lying. I'll grant you the fact that kids aren't all that sophisticated at deception, but the principle is still valid.

"Back when I was in the Agency, debriefing agents in the field, if I heard one of them say that phrase—*I wish I could tell you more*—it almost invariably meant they were being deceptive. Count on it. Ernie's basically telling us that he knows more but can't or *won't* tell us what it is."

"Well, let's go back in there and make him talk."

Saul shook his head. "No. Ernie's smart, probably smarter than you and me, combined. He would be prepared for that. If we were to press him, he would probably have a rather convincing story to tell that is backstopped in concrete. We just have to think of a way to convince him it's in his best interest to cooperate and tell us *everything*."

"While you think, I'm gonna check in with Job. His meeting with the DNI should be over by now."

Saul looked at his watch. "Good idea."

Rainey pulled out his cell phone. It was a special piece of hardware that all DX field operatives were issued. The phone looked and operated much like a typical smartphone, but this one had a few special features including state-of-the-art encryption. And when inserted into a high tech sleeve, it quickly became a sat phone.

"Greenbriar Foundation. How can I help you?"

"Nine. Nine. Alpha. San Diego."

"Stand by."

There was a series of clicks then the DX duty officer came on the line. "Code please?"

"Valley Forge. Four. Three. Six. True."

"Authentication confirmed. Go ahead, sir."

"Put me through to the chief, please."

"Yessir. Connecting you now."

In a matter of seconds, Job answered. "Go four-three-six."

"Hey, Chief. How'd the meeting go?"

"It didn't."

"Whaddya mean? I thought you were meeting with the DNI this morning?"

"Yes, well, he never made it into the office. He was found dead this morning. At his home. Sometime around six-thirty or so."

Rainey's eyes widened. "Are you serious?" He cupped his hand over the phone, which was still pressed against his ear and said to Saul, "DNI's dead. Found this morning."

"Not good," said Saul shaking his head.

"Any details?"

"Nothing solid," said Job, "but preliminarily they're thinking it was his heart. He'd had some heart problems in the past and was on medication. When things settle down a bit, I'm going to see if I can speak with his wife. It's awfully coincidental, him dying. And you know me. I don't believe in coincidences."

"Right."

"How about you guys? How'd you make out with the doc?"

"Decent, but Pappy thinks he's holding something back." Rainey rattled off the information Wells had given them.

"Triumph, huh? Okay. I'll look into it. I'll also check with State and the Bureau, see what they have. At least you've given us something to work with."

"You want us to head back?"

"No, sit tight for now. Let me see what I can find out. Head over to the flat in Grimsby. I'll call you later."

"Roger that." Rainey snapped the phone back into the rugged plastic holder on his waist. "Do you believe this, Pappy?"

"No. And you know what? I've changed my mind. We need to go back in and confront Ernie. Wild as it sounds, if the DNI was taken out, Ernie could be in danger now, too."

They trudged back into the Institute, stopped at the big visitor's desk in the lobby. Saul leaned in front of a pear-shaped lady who was bellied up to the chest-high counter. "Excuse me. We need to see Dr. Wells right away. It's urgent."

The man behind the desk frowned at the breach in etiquette. With a forced smile, he said, "I will be with you just as soon I help this kind lady."

"Did you not hear him?" boomed Rainey. "It's urgent!"

The woman turned at the waist, cocked her head at an unnatural angle and made a noise that sounded like she had been punched in the stomach.

The glare from Rainey must have frightened the man because he picked up the phone without further delay. As they waited, Rainey looked over at the woman. "I'm sorry. But it's an emergency."

The man placed the phone back in the receiver like it were made of fragile porcelain. "I'm sorry, gents, but Mr. Wells has retired for the day."

"What?" said Saul. "That's impossible. We were just up in his office."

"Yes, well. He's gone now. That was his assistant."

"Where to? I mean, did Winnie say where he's going? It's a rather urgent matter we need to discuss."

"She doesn't know. He left without telling her."

"Well, do you have his cell phone number?" blurted Rainey.

"No. I'm sorry. We don't do that. If you'd like to come back tomorrow, that will be fine. You can see him them."

Rainey's face flashed with anger. "I'm going up." He began to push away from the desk, when Saul grabbed his arm.

"No, no. That's fine. We'll come back tomorrow. Thank you. Very sorry to bother you."

They exited and made their way across the lot toward the Skoda. Rainey dragged his hand through his hair. "Why do you think he left so abruptly?" When Saul didn't respond, he said, "You think he's still up there?"

"Beats me. But good luck trying to find him in there. That place is full of secret passageways, tunnels, hidden rooms. Sometime you really must take a tour. It's pretty impressive. But it's all good, Ray. We have his home address in the car." Saul smiled as if he had been down this road before. "C'mon. We'll find him."

Rainey slid his sunglasses on. *That's odd. The gatehouse is empty.*

He caught movement coming toward them in his periphery. A man—the man from the gatehouse—stepped out from between two cars.

He was holding a gun in his right hand and was just starting to bring it up to fire. Rainey lunged at him. With his left hand, he grabbed the top of the gun, shoved it in a safe direction and punched him hard in the jaw with his right then in rapid succession punched him again. Rainey switched hands, wrapping his right hand over the slide now, careful to keep his palm away from the muzzle. The man became rigid and pulled his arm back, which caused the pistol to fire a single round. Rainey delivered a lightning-fast knee strike to the man's outer thigh then another and another. The guy winced and hinged over at the waist.

BRAAAP!!!

A burst of gunfire clamored from behind him. Rainey flinched, but still kept hold of the man and the pistol. With his left foot, he swept the man's right leg, forcing him to the ground then looped his left elbow over the man's extended right arm. Rainey pivoted to his right and pointed the man's gun toward the car that was racing into the lot. A man armed with a submachine gun was leaning out from the front passenger-side window.

BRAAAP!!! BRAAAAAAAP!!!

Bullets slammed into the cars beside him. Glass shattered. Sparks flew.

"Get down!" yelled Saul.

The man began to squirm within his grasp. Rainey elbowed him hard in the face then looked back up at the fast-approaching car. Both of them still locked onto the pistol, Rainey squeezed the man's hand inside the trigger well but the gun did not respond. It was jammed. He quickly ripped the pistol from the man's grasp, cleared the stoppage and aimed at the car. Several rounds found the windshield. Bullets spotted the hood and grille. The vehicle swerved then slid sideways, careening right for them. At the last second, Rainey released the man and leapt onto the hood of the vehicle next to him. The speeding sedan slammed into the gatekeeper full-on before smashing into the vehicles behind him, each one striking the next in a domino effect.

Rainey jumped from the hood of the car, rolled to a crouched position with the gun up and ready. "Pappy! You okay?!"

Saul grunted. "I'm good."

"Stay down!" Rainey popped up. A man with a submachine gun was alighting from the back seat of the car through the broken-out rear windshield. Rainey fired three rounds, striking him in the head and neck. The man fell forward onto the trunk with a thud and hung there, dead. Rainey ducked back down, quickly scrambled behind another car. This time when he popped up, he caught the front passenger still focused on where he had just been. He fired two more rounds then dropped back down.

The man yelled in agony then screamed, "GO! GO! GO!"

The vehicle's engine whined loudly. Its tires chirped against the cobblestones as the driver managed to untangle the vehicle from the ones he had crashed into and sped off. As the car slalomed through the lot, the dead man on the trunk was thrown clear. He rolled like a rag doll over the surface of the lot until he struck the gatehouse with a loud crack.

Rainey glanced back at Saul. "Pappy, throw me the keys!"

Saul hurriedly fished the keys from his pants pocket, threw them to him.

Rainey jumped into the Skoda, turned the ignition and revved the engine. "Get in!"

Saul dodged over to the vehicle. He clawed opened the front passenger door and scrambled inside.

"Put your seatbelt on. Tight!" Rainey sped out of the lot, blew past the gatehouse and whipped down the lane in pursuit of the other car. The vehicle's tires screeched as he slid sideways out onto Hull Road. "You okay?! You hurt?!"

"I'm okay. I'm okay. Just drive!" Saul was breathing heavily. "He set us up, Ray. He set us up."

14

RAINEY'S head was tilted downward. His eyes were dark with intensity, with rage. He shifted gears and stomped the accelerator.

"How are you with a pistol?"

Saul looked at him as if he'd just been asked the stupidest question in the world.

"Here." Rainey pulled the gatekeeper's gun from the seat beneath his leg and handed it to Saul. "Back left tire."

"Gotcha. One thing, Ray. They still have more firepower than we do. Even *if* we stop them, we're going to be outgunned."

"Then we'll have to improvise. Back left tire. Got it?"

"Got it."

Rainey pressed the pedal to the floor as Saul put down his window, propped his wrists on the door and prepared to aim.

"Ready?"

"Ready."

Rainey pushed the car faster. They were ten yards away from the back of the Renault and closing.

The Renault's driver looked back while his front passenger climbed into the back seat and leaned out the driver-side rear window. The man poked the muzzle through the open window and let loose with several bursts of gunfire. Rainey darted back to the left, moving out of the guy's field of fire. The man edged further out the window, hooking his right arm inside as he did so. He was all but sitting on the door ledge. He fired again. Bullets stitched up Rainey's side of the car. It sounded like he was back in his blacksmith shop pounding on metal, save for the engine noise and the screeching tires. Rounds tore into the car. His side mirror exploded.

Rainey whipped the car further to the left. The passenger-side tires of the Skoda fell into the shoulder kicking up dust and gravel. Stones pinged against the undercarriage. The man fired again. He felt a sudden, sharp pain in his foot, like he had just been stomped on by someone wearing soccer cleats.

"Give me the gun!"

Saul handed it back to him without protest.

He gripped the gun in his right hand, propped it on the door and accelerated. He didn't need to use the gun sights. He would aim the gun with the car. He steered to the left ever so slightly and fired a round. Then another. The first went a little high. But the second was dead on. Center mass.

The man twisted and all but fell out of the fast-moving vehicle.

HOOOOOONK!

Wide-eyed, Rainey yanked the steering wheel hard to the left just as a big, oncoming semi decimated the guy's torso. A pink mist sprayed the windshield. The pulped figure disappeared behind them, rolling across the pavement like tumbleweed.

Rainey flicked on the windshield wipers, which drew wide greasy smears across the glass.

"There's an intersection up ahead, Ray!" Saul braced himself. "We're never gonna make the turn."

"Neither is he."

Both vehicles skidded across the road, through the T intersection and shot into a field of golden barley. They were jostled violently but Rainey kept his foot pressed to the floor.

The Renault shot out the other side. The vehicle leapt from the shoulder and landed hard on Beverley Road. Sparks flew as its undercarriage scraped the asphalt. Rainey followed suit.

"There's a town up the road a bit, Ray. End it, or it's gonna get messy."

Both vehicles swept around the bend onto Lambwath Lane leaving black yaw marks across the road. Rainey stomped the gas again. He aimed the vehicle for the right rear corner of the other car and made his move. The vehicles collided with a jolt. As the other driver tried to compensate for the unexpected movement of his vehicle, Rainey accelerated and steered to his left. The Renault spun out of control. It skidded sideways off the pavement, dropped into the shoulder and rolled. Once. Twice. Three times. It finally came to rest upside down in the adjacent wheat field. One of the back tires was still spinning.

Rainey brought the Skoda to a controlled stop on the side of the road and hurried into the field toward the wrecked car. Gun pointed, he approached the driver's door. He peered inside quickly and prepared to shoot.

The cabin was empty.

He heard a grunt followed by a few short moans. Fifty feet away lay the driver. He had been thrown from the vehicle. His limbs were twisted and in places they should not be. His face was a bloody mess; a puffy hunk of brain matter was showing through his cracked skull.

Rainey secured the gun in his waistband. He walked over and knelt beside him. "That's why you always wear your seatbelt."

The man made a gurgling sound, exhaled a breath of air and went completely still.

Rainey shook his head, winced as he rifled through the man's pockets. No wallet. No ID. *Gee, go figure.*

He was about to stand up when the sunlight flashed against something off to his right. He reached over, picked it up. "How 'bout that "

The phone was perfectly intact, not a scratch on it. He hit the power button. The screen came alive then self-adjusted to the brightness of the day. *Great. Locked.*

Saul tramped through the wheat stalks to him. "I jotted down the tag number, Ray, but it's probably either stolen or rented under a fake name. Guaranteed, it's a dead end."

Rainey pocketed the phone. "Okay. We'd better get going. Cops are going to be all over this place."

Saul followed him back to the Skoda. "Now what?"

Rainey handed him his phone as he sped away. "Call Job. Let him know what happened. Ask him where I can dump a phone. Tell him it's urgent."

"We gotta get rid of this car, too."

"I know, but it's gonna have to wait until we get closer to town."

After being patched through to Job, Saul turned to Rainey with the phone against his cheek. "Got his voice mail."

"Leave a message. Tell him to call us back ASAP."

After Saul disconnected the call, he gave the phone back to Rainey.

"You said you had Ernie's address, right?"

Saul opened the glove box, pulled out a file folder. "Yeah, it's right here. Four Jarratt Street in Hull."

15

THEY had made good time to the city center though it was a perfectly sunny Saturday afternoon and there was a considerable amount of activity on the streets. They had already dumped the Skoda in the Asda lot in Bilton and grabbed a taxi after hoofing it for several blocks.

Saul had the taxi driver continue past Wells' front door, turn onto Charles Street and drop them off on the Johns Street side of the Kingston Theatre Hotel.

"Whaddya think?" said Rainey.

"I'm not sure. C'mon, let's cut through the park. If his place is being watched, I would expect to find someone posted there."

Rainey followed along, his hand ready to draw the pistol that was beneath his untucked shirt. He had precisely three rounds left. Not ideal, but it was certainly better than nothing.

He considered the conversation he and Saul had had en route to their present location. It was only a matter of time before the police showed up at Wells' front door. When investigators began questioning people at the Institute they would quickly learn that he and Saul—the apparent targets of the shooting—had met with Wells, a man who had now curiously gone missing. Rainey and Saul were traveling under alias and had signed in with such at the Institute; there was no way the police could identify them from that information. So it would be only logical for the authorities to seek out Wells at his home. But even if the police were to do just that, they were not likely to set up surveillance on the place—at least not this quickly, which meant that if Wells' place was being watched, it could only be for nefarious purposes and by nefarious characters.

They stopped walking midway through the small tree-filled Kingston Square.

"What is it?" said Rainey.

"Look at those two cars over there."

Rainey knelt to tie his shoe. As he did so, he glanced over at the sidewalk to the left of the pillared Hull New Theatre. Two hatchback coupes were parked there. Each was occupied with two men. It was as if they were waiting for something…or someone. When he stood up, Saul nodded toward a man seated on a park bench at the southeast corner of the plaza.

"There. That man. He's reading the newspaper, but he's not *reading*. He's flipped back and forth between the same two pages too many times to be reading, and… See how he keeps looking to his right, toward Ernie's house. He's a static post."

Rainey studied the man. His lips were moving. "So you—"

Suddenly, the two cars to their left started moving.

"Crap! Ernie must have just arrived," said Saul.

But Rainey had already taken off at a sprint. He blew past the man on the bench, racing after the two cars that were now headed down Jarratt Street. Ernie Wells was on the sidewalk ahead of him. A taxi was just pulling away from the curb. Engines revved. Tires squealed. Wells' head snapped toward the sudden commotion, his eyes saucers.

The two cars crossed over to the curb beside Wells and screeched to a halt. Rainey was just reaching the back of the second car when both front-passenger doors whipped open. A man with a submachine gun jumped out right in of him. The guy was oblivious to the human missile that was now locked onto him. Rainey didn't even slow down. He hit him square in the middle of the back with his right shoulder. The man's neck and back snapped backward at an unnatural angle and he crashed to the pavement with Rainey riding him all the way to the ground.

Rainey drew his pistol and fired at the other man alighting from the first car directly in front of him. The bullet struck the man at the base of the skull. He fell lifeless against the fender of the car. Rainey swung quickly to the right and fired two rounds into the stunned driver of the second car. The man grimaced then slumped over the wheel, causing the car's horn to blare without ceasing.

Rainey dropped the empty pistol and quickly picked up the submachine gun from the unconscious man on the ground next to him.

The driver of the first vehicle flung his door open now and turned toward Rainey, let loose with several bursts of gunfire. Rainey dove behind the engine block of the second vehicle. Bullets cut into the hood, making long oval gashes in the thin metal and throwing off a brilliant shower of sparks.

Rainey rolled onto his right side. He aimed the SMG at the other man's ankles and fired into them not caring if some of his rounds bounced off the surface of the road.

The man howled as he fell.

Rainey leapt onto the hood of the second car and then onto the roof of the first. The driver lay on the sidewalk, still clinging to his gun. He seemed surprised when Rainey appeared above him, tried to swing his muzzle upward. But Rainey drilled him in the chest and head before he could fire.

Rainey hopped down to the sidewalk, took a quick peak inside both vehicles.

Wells had dove onto the steps leading into his flat when the violence first erupted, which is where he still lay. His entire body was shaking like a wet dog.

Rainey scanned the street for more threats. There were none. As he picked up the empty Walther—it carried his fingerprints and DNA, he looked back toward the park, expecting to find Saul. Instead, he saw no one, not even the man with the newspaper.

Tires squealed. The sound of an angry engine echoed down the street.

Crap!

Rainey lifted Wells off the ground by his shirt and stuffed him into the first car along the street. He gunned the engine, popped the clutch and whipped around the corner onto Worship Street. Rainey screamed down the short road and took a hard left onto the A165 using the hand brake to facilitate a long skid. The vehicle's momentum threw Wells against his left shoulder. He shoved the old man back into his seat, straightened the vehicle and stood on the accelerator. The engine growled in response.

"Put your seatbelt on! Do it now! This might get a little wild."

The quivering man did as he was told.

Rainey pumped the brakes for some slowed traffic and noticed two dark-colored sedans in the rearview mirror.

"Hold on." Rainey downshifted and swerved around the back end of a Nissan Cabstar, crossed over the center median and sped into on-coming traffic. The two sedans followed. He slalomed back and forth through cars and trucks. Horns blared, people shouted.

He hammered the gas in the empty stretches, blowing lights and intersections with abandon. When the road became Spring Bank, he downshifted again and shot between two cars crossing in front of him. Two guys walking in the crosswalk with briefcases, jumped out of the way. One of the cases hit the front end of the car and exploded on impact. A cloud of papers burst into the air. The men bellowed profanity at the top of their lungs, shook their fists in anger.

The road quickly became long and straight and Rainey used every inch of its width to dodge back and forth through traffic. It soon doglegged to the left and Rainey could no longer see the sedans behind him. He gave the car more gas and raced down Spring Bank West, skidded left onto Walton Street then made a quick right onto Lowther. Here, he slowed his speed dramatically. He followed Lowther around to Albert Avenue, where he turned left and wound his way to Hessle Road.

He wiped the sweat from his forehead and looked over at Wells.

The man responded with a fretful gaze. "Are you going to kill me?"

"No. If I wanted you dead, I would have let those goons back there finish you off."

Wells closed his eyes. "Thank you."

"Don't mention it." Rainey gripped the steering wheel tightly, a sublimation of what he really wanted to do to the man for lying, for setting them up.

"Where are we going?"

"Just be quiet."

They soon pulled into the park-and-ride lot at Priory Park along the River Humber. Rainey backed into a spot along the tree line and shut off the ignition. There was silence for a few seconds except for the ticking of the engine and some birds screeching from somewhere beyond the trees. The stench of burnt brake pads radiated throughout the cabin space. Adrenaline was still coursing through him.

"Wait here. If I come back and you're gone, I'll find you and I *will* kill you."

"I'm not going anywhere," pleaded Wells.

Rainey soon returned with a Toyota minivan. He hit a button on the dash and the sliding door on the right side of the vehicle opened. From the driver's seat, he waved for Wells to get in.

When the door clicked shut, Rainey put the van in drive and drove away.

16

Arlington, Virginia

THE polished marble sign outside the tall, smoky glass and concrete behemoth at the corner of 17th Street N and N. Fort Myer Drive, read *Carter Tower*. Office space here was among the most prestigious and sought after in all of northern Virginia. And while the twenty-story building paled in comparison to Stedman Carter's skyscrapers in New York, Los Angeles, London and Dubai and about five dozen other cities around the globe, Carter Tower was his favorite because of its proximity to Washington D.C., the epicenter of global power.

Stedman Carter felt alive here. This was a place where his Congressional henchman could be summoned at a moment's notice, where loose-lipped Pentagon officials or Cabinet-level cronies could be wined and dined, and where, over a hearty breakfast of eggs and toast and tea, he could receive what was comparable to the President's Daily Brief from one or more of his numerous intelligence community informers.

Carter rolled out of his limousine in the exclusive section of the parking garage below, his personal bodyguard in tow. Out of habit more so than anything, he adjusted his tie knot in the gleaming brass doors of his private elevator. He uttered nary a word in the time it took to ride to the top floor, yet the look on his face spoke volumes.

His hard-soled, leather brogues clipped at a fierce pace down the shimmering, recently waxed hallway floor. As he entered his luxurious office suite, an aide appeared and wordlessly handed him a stack of messages, which he received in likewise fashion. He continued through a set of heavy wooden doors with long, antique bronze handles. His route took him past an empty executive lounge and a dormant conference room, which contained a table of reclaimed wood that was bigger than some hotel swimming pools.

He finally pushed into his private office. It was bigger than what could be described as spacious, yet the rich wood accents somehow made it feel cozy. On the one side was a stainless steel wet bar, the other an assortment of wood and glass shelves that held vases and plates, trinkets and tomes. Each shelf was awash in the soft glow of a small recessed light that tastefully showcased some of the billionaire's most prized possessions. There were illuminated manuscripts from the 15th century he had acquired in Italy; a solid gold clock he had picked up in Riyadh—a gift from a Saudi prince; a three-hundred-year-old African walking stick that had once belonged to a king of some renown; and a magnificently chiseled kilij with matching scabbard that dated back to the Timurid Empire. All of this was but a mere glimpse of his staggering wealth.

Carter paraded across the quiet carpet, staring daggers at the man seated in the leather sofa on his left. For as much as he loved it here, he was never in the office on a Saturday afternoon. By now, he should have had two rounds of golf in and be chatting over a late lunch with a pair of senators on the Senate Select Committee on Intelligence. The fact that he had to be here because of such utter incompetence irritated him like nothing else.

He removed his suit coat and hung it on a sleek metal coat rack in the corner of the room next to a bulletproof, floor-to-ceiling window. His hands still on the jacket, he closed his eyes and tried to calm himself. He took in a slow, deep breath and let it out over the course of several seconds. Important decisions were always best made when the emotion of the situation was set aside. He hadn't become a billionaire several times over by flying off the handle at every little bump in the road. Ruthless, yes. Calculating? Of course. But he was never irrational. Never out of control. And yet this was not a little bump in the road. This was a fiasco.

"I don't understand. They had a simple job to do. Tell me how they failed," said Carter.

Zarek Tarło stood up, walked over to a chair in front of Carter's massive mahogany desk and sat down. "The gatekeeper acted prematurely. Seems one of the Agency men disarmed him and went on the offensive. I admit, the men from London made a pretty big mess of things. But they paid for it with their lives."

"What about at the old man's flat? How on *earth* did your people fail there?"

Tarło's eyes skirted past his boss and allowed him to escape out the window for a few seconds. "My source at MI5 says it was the same guy—the guy from the Institute. Somehow he managed to intervene, snatched Wells right out from under us. I've never made excuses, sir, and I'm not going to start now. They failed and they will be dealt with severely. But…"

"But?!" Carter turned toward the window, his hands on his trim hips. A passenger jet silently descended into Reagan National. It looked like a toy airplane from this distance. For a few fleeting moments, he thought back to a recent trip he had taken to his island in the Caribbean. His week with Zaina, the goddess. But even devilish thoughts of her now could not temper his rage.

"Sir, I've studied the surveillance footage from the Institute and from the street outside Wells' flat. I recognize the younger of the two men. His name is Reagan Rainey. They call him *Bronco*. I rubbed elbows with him in Iraq and later did some joint training with his unit at Fort Bragg before I left GROM."

"Are you saying that Ben Rainey's *kid* is responsible?"

"Yes."

"Bragg. He's Delta?"

"Was, sir. He's no longer in the Unit."

"So who does he work for now?"

"From what I've been able to gather, no one knows where he went or for whom he works. A man like that doesn't just disappear. I can assure you he's not flipping burgers in some backwater town in Arkansas."

Carter's eyes narrowed. He pursed his lips as he mused. "You think he's working for the CIA?"

Tarło nodded. "I do. And he's going to be a tough out, sir. Reagan Rainey is…"

"Yes?"

"He's one of the best I've seen, sir. If you want him dead, we will need to go in heavy with some skilled operators. Or be very, very lucky."

"It was supposed to be a nice surgical little operation. Kill Wells, kill anyone he might have told about Triumph. Hank said the Agency was sending two people. He didn't say anything about them sending a Delta, Ben Rainey's kid or not."

"I know sir… Obviously, the shooters Alvin hired in London weren't up to the task. I will deal with him, personally."

Carter sat down in his high-backed leather chair, rotated it toward the window, which was treated to defeat any high-tech listening devices. He crossed his legs, tented his hands under his lower lip and studied a bass boat wandering down the Potomac. His success was due largely to the fact that he could plan three, four, five steps ahead of his adversaries.

After several minutes of deliberation, Carter swung his chair around, a steely resolve now in his shark-skin eyes. He had made his decision.

"Okay, listen. Go to London. Tidy up. Contact me when you're done. And Zarek… No more surprises. I'm not paying you to make mistakes."

"Yes, sir."

17

Vienna, Virginia

JOB sparred with a wasp on the front porch as his colleague cupped his hands to his face and peered through a front window; they were waiting for McManus' widow to answer the door. Keller soon returned to his side, reached out with a finger and jabbed the doorbell again. The sun had been beating on the porch all day, generating enough heat on the stone landing to fry an egg.

"She said she'd be home," said Curt Keller, the CIA's head of security.

"Relax. Her husband just died."

After another two minutes, the door cracked open and a woman in her sixties eyed them warily, squinting into the glare of the sun behind them. "Yes?" It was obvious she'd been crying.

"Ma'am, I'm Curt Keller…from the Agency. I called earlier. This is Jim Bell. He's my assistant."

Job wasn't keen on using an alias especially right now, but maintaining cover was vital due to Directorate X's clandestine nature.

"Forgive me, gentlemen. It's been a rough day. Please come in."

They followed her into an airy living room with books and picture frames. She carried the cordless phone with her along with a box of tissues.

"Please, won't you sit down?"

"Thank you." After they were seated, Job said, "We're very sorry for your loss, Mrs. McManus. We both worked closely with your husband."

"He had many friends." She sniffled and dabbed her nose. "I'm sorry. I must look absolutely dreadful."

"Not at all," said Job. "You're fine. Curt, do you mind getting Mrs. McManus a glass of water?"

"Uh, sure." Keller got up and walked to the kitchen.

"Thank you. And please, call me Lana."

"Okay, *Lana.*" Job offered an empathetic grin. "I don't want to take up much of your time, so I'll be quick."

"It's okay. I've just been making phone calls. Kids are coming in later today to help me with the arrangements."

Job leaned forward. "Lana, how much do you know about Hank's work at the CIA? Did he ever talk about it?"

"The CIA… Well, that was a long time ago. And he didn't really like to talk about work at home. Even when he did, he never discussed details."

"That's understandable," said Job. "Perhaps I should be a bit more specific. Did Hank ever speak about his time in Russia? Or for that matter any of his postings overseas?"

She sniffled again, wiped the corner of her eyes. "I'm not sure I understand, Mr. Bell. Why are you asking me such questions, especially at a time like this?"

"Yes, I know. Our timing is not ideal, but I assure you that the reason why we're here is important." Job bit his lower lip as if debating whether to disclose some secret bit of information. He leaned closer and in a voice just above a whisper said, "We're looking into something. I'm afraid that's all I can say right now. Perhaps I'll be able to speak more openly in the near future." Job tilted his head and using his eyes probed the house behind Mrs. McManus while she blew her nose and drew another tissue from the box on the cushion beside her.

"What do you mean you're *looking into something?*"

"Suffice it to say, Mrs. McManus…er, Lana…it could be related to Hank's passing."

Her forehead wrinkled with confusion. "Hank died of a heart attack. Wha—are you saying that there may have been foul play involved?"

"No. That's definitely *not* what I'm saying." Job let the words sink in, hoping she might perceive what he was intimating, but certainly *not saying.*

"Then what on earth are you talking about?" Suddenly, her eyes shot open, the blood drained from her face. "Wait. Wait, wait, wait."

"What is it, Lana?"

"Oh my… I had forgotten."

"Forgotten what?"

Keller walked in with a glass of water. When neither of them looked up, he said, "Is everything okay in here?"

Job made a face that translated to words said: "Don't speak. I'm on to something here."

"Go on, Lana," he said gently.

"A number of years ago, I think it was sometime after he was promoted to director of administration, Hank mentioned that if anything ever happened to him, to—" She got up.

"To what, Lana?"

She walked out of the living room, past the kitchen and into the study. Job looked at Keller then followed after her.

"Hank told me that if anything ever happened to him unexpectedly to go to the safe and find the envelope."

"An envelope containing what?" said Job.

"I don't know exactly. It was a long time ago. I didn't even think about it until just now." She wrung her hands, looked at the ceiling. "Oh, that's right. It was a letter, some photos, I believe. Oh, and a little, you know, um…computer disc. Two of them, if I recall correctly. Hank had placed the letter, photos and computer discs in an envelope with a set of instructions for me to follow then sealed it. Told me never to open it unless he…" She trailed off with a sniffle.

Job and Keller exchanged glances.

"I don't know if this is what he meant, but…well, he's gone now. I don't see how it can hurt." She shuffled past a painting on the wall—some big, colorful attempt at Expressionism. In the center of the piece was a blob that could have been a beetle or a dog or a gingerbread man. Next to the painting, directly behind her late husband's desk, was a hand-carved bookshelf. She nudged his chair out of the way and pulled on one of the books on the second shelf. As she did so, a part of the bookshelf swung away from the wall, revealing a rather large safe. She began to work the dial of a combination lock. Her hands were shaking. "I'm sorry. I can't seem to remember… No! Wait." She worked the dial again and after a third try, she grinned. "There." She tugged the safe door open and stared up into the void. "Do you mind? Without a footstool, I'm not quite tall enough to see all the way inside."

Keller, easily a head taller than the woman, stepped forward, reached in and grabbed the contents of the safe with both of his meaty hands. He set the stack of files and folders on the desk and shifted out of the widow's way.

"Thank you." She quickly swept through the items a few at a time. "No. No. No, that's not it. It's a gold-colored manila envelope with the words "*Artifacts of Triumph*" written on it in red pen."
Job watched the woman's hands sift through the files. When she'd reached the bottom of the pile, she went through it again.

"I don't believe this! It's gone."

18

Greenville, South Carolina

TRAFFIC on South Rutherford Street was moving along nicely for a Saturday evening. Madison Rainey read aloud the sign of a quaint red-brick church on their right, "Triune Mercy Center." The arched red doorway and stained glass windows reminded her of the Pilgrims and Plymouth Rock for some reason. "Certainly are a lot of churches in Greenville."

"I'd say. Ours is up here on the right just a little further." Evelina Krantz breezed through the green light, one hand on the steering wheel. "Remember, Maddie, be yourself. I hear you're a natural. If you're anything like your brother, you were born for this. Speaking of your brother, what does he think of you working for the DX?"

Maddie grinned. "Well, Evie, I mean *Miss Smith*, he doesn't know yet."

"I see. What do you think he'll say or do when he finds out?"

"He's gonna flip. But you know what? I'm a big girl. I can take care of myself. The people at the Academy have taught me well."

The Benjamin Tallmadge Special Services Training Academy— named after the head of George Washington's famous Culper Spy Ring—was a top-secret CIA-run school where new recruits destined for special-service programs within the American intelligence community were sent for high-level instruction. For the last six grueling months, Maddie had sat under the intense and careful tutelage of some of the best artisans of espionage and special operations that America had in her arsenal. While almost all CIA new hires were sent to Virginia's Camp Peary, aka the Farm, to receive their *year-long* training, Directorate X, in conjunction with a few other top-secret American intelligence programs, had its own facility and its own hiring standards. Situated on the banks of Albemarle Sound near a small town in North Carolina called Merry Hill, the Academy enjoyed a great deal of privacy as well as strategic proximity to such places as the Harvey Point Defense Training Activity, the Dam Neck Annex at NAS Oceana, and the John F. Kennedy Special Warfare Center and School at Fort Bragg, among others. Training at the Academy wasn't just limited to the thousand-acre plot of land, either. Trainees were sent all about the United States and even to several undisclosed points overseas. But even after a trainee had graduated from his or her initial six-month course to become a full-fledge operations officer, the training continued. There were always new techniques, new technologies to master. And there was no greater teacher than real-world experience.

"I have no doubt, but what about Wes? He's okay with his fiancée running off to play warrior spy?"

"Well, he thinks I've become an analyst or something. You know, Agency protocol... Nevertheless, he does have reservations, but he is very supportive of my interests and pursuits. Always has been. It's one of the reasons I love him so much. That and the fact that his cooking is to die for." She giggled. "Like I said on the plane, I can always go back to teaching martial arts. But I realized something profound about myself after what happened back in January. I realized that I have a great need to do something that will make a difference. I want to be in the center of the action. God's given me these talents for a reason. When I finally found out what Ray's been doing, what *you've* been doing, I knew right then that it's what I needed to do as well. Yes, I know I might be some wide-eyed, idealistic newbie, but... I feel I was born to do this."

"Well, I for one am thrilled to have another gifted, warrior chick in the mix. We can do things and go places that the boys simply cannot. Which makes us that much more effective."

"Here, here," said Maddie. "Thanks again for convincing Job to let me in on this. It means a lot."

Evelina smiled. "We all have to start somewhere. Besides, you have a vested interest in what is going on in this case. That is, you deserve to know the truth on a personal level. If it were my father we were talking about, an army of commandos wouldn't be able to keep me away. Not saying I know how you feel, but—"

"I know what you mean. Thanks, Evie."

They pulled into the church lot and parked in front of a small one-story, red-brick house that had been converted into offices for the pastoral staff.

Evelina removed her sunglasses, hung them on the steering wheel. "Well this is it."

Maddie unbuckled her seatbelt and nodded. "Let's do this."

The pastor greeted them warmly and ushered them out of the dreadful humidity and into the cool air-conditioned office.

"Miss Smith, I presume?"

Evelina offered a professional smile, shook his hand. "Yes. We talked on the phone. Pastor Daly, this is my associate, Miss Green."

"Nice to meet you both. Please have a seat. Can I offer you something to drink? Coffee? Tea, perhaps?"

"No, thank you."

"So you ladies are researching the plane crash? Interesting."

Evelina collected her straight blonde hair in her hand and deposited over her shoulder as she sat down. "That's right. We're very interested in stories such as this one. When I first heard about it, I knew I had to learn more. We would especially like to learn more about the people involved." She crossed her legs and folded her hands in her lap.

"Yes, of course."

"Thanks again for seeing us on such short notice." said Evelina.

"Sure. Well, I was coming into the office anyway to go over my sermon notes for tomorrow. How can I help?"

"As I mentioned on the phone, we're interested in the plane crash in ninety-six. September, right?" When the pastor affirmed, she continued. "We've gone through all the newspaper clippings we could find, mind you, but we wanted to get a little better picture of what happened before, during and after. You know, touch on some more detail for our readers."

"So you're writing a book or doing a story for a newspaper? I'm sorry, I'm a little confused on *why* you're looking into the crash."

Evelina nodded. "Oh, by all means. Yes, well, if we can come up with enough material a book is a possibility. Speaking for myself, I would love to see a book published about these fine men." She turned to Maddie who smiled in agreement. "But we don't want to get ahead of ourselves. We're starting out with our focus being on a documentary on missionaries who have died in the field. Not just died in the field, but were killed as a result of their ministry."

Maddie's eyes fell on a shelf full of Bibles of various versions and pastor reference books. A shock of guilt charged through her. The idea of not being completely honest with a man of God made her shift uncomfortably in her seat. She unconsciously smoothed a wrinkle in her slacks. *Great. First assignment and I'm lying to a pastor. Well, Wes is always looking for book material. Maybe a book will come out of this after all.*

"Wow. A book would be great!"

"So as I understand it, the missionary team had been delivering Bibles to a native tribe in southern Venezuela?"

"Bibles and supplies, yes. They were flying to a tiny village just north of Venezuela's southern border. We've had a mission presence in the region now for decades, still do. We've partnered with a Christian aid organization as well as several other churches in the U.S. to serve the Ye'kuana people. We provide medicine, educational and other types of supplies while also teaching them about the Gospel of Jesus Christ. It's been a largely successful endeavor." He paused and looked up at a photo on the bookshelf across the room. Inside a beach-store wooden frame, was a picture of a group of four men standing by a large sign that read, "Welcome to Sullivan's Island." Over their shoulders, far in the background, were the rocky bulkhead and sand-colored ramparts of Fort Sumter. They were all wearing shorts and T-shirts and wide smiles. Pastor Daly stood up and retrieved the photo from the shelf. He stared into it for a moment then carried it back to his chair and sat down.

"That was the year we stayed on Station Twelve. Place was right near Fort Moultrie. Gary's right here, standing next to me," he said, pointing at the picture. "I obviously had a lot more hair back then. We were on our yearly fishing trip to Sullivan's Island. Come to think of it, that was the last trip before he died. Man, we had a blast together. I miss those trips though I don't think we ever really caught much. Except for this one time." He chuckled, tilting his head upward and toward the window. "It was a few years earlier. We had just come in from the jetties to fish the harbor a little before lunch. Davis—that's him on the other side of Gary—wound up and cast his line. You've never seen such a beautiful cast. Thing was way out there. But, see, when Davis drew back his rod, he hooked Gary's hat—Gary was standing behind him on the opposite side of the boat with his back to him." Pastor Daly laughed. "Snatched the hat right off his head and deposited it out there in the surf. You should have seen the look on Gary's face. Talk about priceless."

Maddie and Evelina exchanged glances as the pastor took a breath and continued on.

"So Gary spins around franticly trying to solve the mystery of his disappearing hat. It's got all these hand-tied flies on it, you know, it's his lucky fishing hat, right? Anyway, he finally sees it. It's out there bobbing up and down on the surface of the water forty yards off the port side. He looks at Davis, looks at the rest of us who are by this time laughing our heads off. But Gary doesn't say a word. He just secures his rod, steps up on the edge of the boat and dives in. He swims over to his lucky hat then returns to the boat, climbs in and goes right back to fishing. Guy's drenched to the bone, but he doesn't even seem to care. But that's not even the funniest part. See, when Davis goes to pull in his line, something big—and by big I mean *humongous!*—latches on. He ends up pulling out the biggest red I've ever seen.

"So we buzz up Shem Creek to a place called RB's and are having lunch and you know, just carrying on and having a good time. Soon a guy from another fishing group hears us and comes over. Davis gets to telling him about his record catch. Guy's eyes go wide when he hears how big this sucker was. He waves over his buddies and Davis tells the tale of his monster catch again. When Davis is finally finished, one of the guys in the other group leans in and says, 'So what are you guys using for bait?' Davis turns to Gary and says, completely deadpan, 'I don't know. Whatever he has on his hat there.' Well, we all just lost it. I think Dr. Pepper shot out my nose. I laughed so hard I nearly peed my pants.

"Man, we shared a lot of laughs on those trips. Had some really good times of serious fellowship, too."

"Gary Robertson. He was the pilot?"

"Yes."

"So what happened?"

Pastor Daly's mood grew dim. "The mission team had left the airfield at Puerto Ayacucho and was flying at capacity for about an hour and forty minutes, when something terrible happened. I'm told it was something mechanical in nature—catastrophic, in any case. The plane disappeared over a treacherous area of the rain forest. Mountains, fog, and weather all hampered the search effort. Four and half days had gone by until rescuers were finally able to get to the crash site. There were no survivors, obviously."

Evelina jotted down some notes. "I understand the Venezuelan military assisted in the recovery."

"That's right. Search party workers were flown to the area where they had to rappel down into a large ravine. Couldn't have happened in a more remote area."

"Who all participated in the recovery? What I mean is: do you know who specifically was at the site?"

The pastor shook his head. "Some locals, some members of the Venezuelan military, a number of others associated with the mission team and of course a handful of people from the State Department."

Before her Academy training, Maddie would not have had a clue. But now she knew better. *State Department. You mean CIA,* she thought to herself.

"I don't know exactly how many or precisely who was actually at the scene, but there weren't many. Based on the photos I've seen, the only ones who seemed to be there were those necessary to extract the bodies, what was left of them. Wasn't much room for anyone else. It was so dense, conditions so severe, that the plane was just left there. There was no way to get it out."

Evelina tapped her pen on her knee. "You mentioned photos."

"Yeah. One of the mission team members had snapped a few photos of the crash site. It wasn't… I'm sorry." The pastor closed his eyes and swallowed. "It wasn't pretty."

"I can imagine."

Maddie felt a bubble of emotion. "Excuse me. Do you have a restroom I could use?"

"Sure. It's around the corner, second door on your left."

Evelina uncrossed her legs and leaned forward with a face that said, 'I'm sorry for the interruption.'

Maddie slipped into the bathroom and closed the door. She turned the faucet on and stood in front of the mirror, hands gripping the porcelain vanity. Finally, she looked up and stared into her own eyes. *God, give me the strength to deal with this. I know You won't give me more than I can bear.* She splashed some water on her face and patted it dry. She took a deep breath. *Be strong, Maddie. You can do this.*

As she opened the bathroom door, she heard Evelina ask, "Any chance we might be able to take a look at the photos?"

"Well, I wish I could accommodate you there, but when Hurricane Hanna came through in oh eight, we had severe flooding. See that mark on the wall over there? That's how high the water was in this building. Needless to say, all of our files were destroyed, including any photos."

"Darn." Evelina flipped a few pages back in her notepad. "How long was it until the remains of the five individuals arrived stateside?"

"*Four.* There were four," said the pastor.

"Really? I have it in my notes that *five* bodies were recovered from the plane. Yeah, here it is… State Department records—which I obtained via a FOIA request—indicate that five bodies were flown to Puerto Ayacucho and then on to Caracas before being brought back to the States."

"That's gotta be a mistake."

Evelina paged through her notes. "Now, all the articles that I've been able to find only show four names, which as you can imagine is a big part of why I'm here. So the question is: who was the fifth person?"

The pastor looked like he was trying to do graduate-level calculus in his head. "It's gotta be some kind of mistake. I mean…"

"I don't think so, the—"

"Miss, it has to be. I know how many people we had down there. And I know how many people came back…in boxes. There were four." The pastor rubbed his nose beneath his eyeglasses. "I'm sorry for snapping. I still get emotional when I think about them."

"There's no need to apologize, sir. Listen, we've taken up too much of your time already. Is there anyone else with whom we should speak that might be able to assist us in nailing down the details? We obviously want to be accurate with our facts."

"I'll tell you who you should talk to: Vic Humphreys. He was down there when it happened. He's the one who *took* the photos."

"Awesome. Do you have his phone number on hand?"

"Won't do you any good. He's there now. In Venezuela, I mean. If you'd had been here last week, you would have caught him. He and his wife were here on furlough. But they just went back down for another two-year stint. They check in every other week or so depending on the weather."

"Very well. Here is my card in case they should be in touch. If it's not too much trouble, could you give me a buzz if and when you hear from them? I would love to interview them both."

"No problem. Sorry I couldn't be more helpful."

"Ah, but you've been a *big* help to us. Thank you, sir."

19

"YOU okay?" said Evelina. "What happened in there?"

Maddie cracked her window, allowing the suffocating heat inside the car to escape. "I'm sorry. I was just thinking about my dad and the crash site. And what the pastor said about it not being pretty…"

"I understand, Maddie, but it's not going to get any easier. If you're not going to be able to handle—"

"*No.* I'm okay. I… It's just hard, you know. My father was my hero growing up. Even though it feels like I only knew him for such a short time, he was my hero. And Ray… He idolized him. I can't imagine what he's going through. But to picture my father all twisted and mangled, it… It just took me by surprise, is all." She took a deep breath. "I'm good. Won't happen again."

Evelina pulled out into traffic. "All right. If you say so."

They drove to the Westin Poinsett on South Main Street and once they were settled in, they contacted Job about what they had learned. The cell phone lay between them on the table, speakerphone switched on.

"Okay. Listen to me," said Job. "I want you to head down there. Speak to the missionary, see if he'll take you to the crash site. If that plane is still there, I want photos. I want documentation. I want to know—if at all possible—what brought it down. Was it engine failure or a Stinger missile? Understand?"

Evelina and Maddie exchanged glances. "We understand," said Evelina.

"Miss Green, are you okay?"

"I'm good. Why would you ask me that?" hissed Maddie. Her brown hair was still wet from having just taken a shower. A few stray locks hung down along her face. She pulled a hairbrush from her over-night bag and began dragging it through her hair, little flecks of water dotting the table in front of her with each swipe. She was angry with herself mostly. Her first assignment and she already had Job doubting her. *You'll see.*

"Just checking. I went against my better judgment on this one when I let Miss Smith talk me into bringing you in. Don't let me down."

Seriously? Maddie snarled, crossed her arms.

"She's fine, Chief," said Evelina. "She's a rock. Glad to have her on board." She winked at Maddie.

"Very well. I'll email your itineraries in a few hours. Your travel docs will be ready in the morning. Be safe, ladies."

"Yes, sir."

20

Grimsby, UK

RAINEY cradled a chipped enamel mug with both hands. He brought it to his lips, breathed in the coffee's strong, intoxicating essence, then took a sip, all the while staring at Saul's old friend and former CIA archives man, Dr. Ernie Wells. He took another sip then set the cup down on the turquoise Formica table, which looked as if it could have been perfectly at home in any American diner in the 1950s. The chairs, too. There were four of them. Their chrome legs and vinyl upholstery would be considered *retro* back home. But they could be sitting in a log cabin for all he cared. His mind was focused entirely on Wells and why he had not been honest with them in the first place.

"Could you loosen this please? My hands are starting to go numb."

Rainey considered the duct tape he had wrapped around Wells' wrists and affixed to the chair, which incidentally was the reason the old man had not budged out of his seat since they had arrived at the safe house. He stood up, removed a butcher knife from the wood block beside the refrigerator and approached Wells. "You gonna be good?"

Wells tilted his head upward with obvious pleading in his cloudy blue eyes. "Of course. I'm not going anywhere. After all, you saved my life."

Rainey gripped the tape in his left hand and sliced through the make-shift manacles in one quick motion. He walked to the coffee-maker, filled another mug then set it on the table in front of Wells. He sat back down without a word and studied the man now massaging his wrists. Rainey wanted him to have no illusions. He had better tell the truth this time, the whole truth and nothing but the truth. Or there would be trouble. The old man's eyes were focused on the shiny blade of the butcher knife as Rainey dug its sharp tip into the surface of the table and began twisting it back and forth, carving a small divot in the table's veneer. *Good, I've got your attention.*

There was a soft thud outside—a car door. Rainey went to the window and, with the tip of the blade, pulled back the canvas-like curtain a centimeter from the wall, peaked out. A figure was moving along the shadowy sidewalk. A car's headlights swept over the face of Saul Baker as he shuffled up to the front door. He raised his arm to knock, but Rainey swung the door open before he could do so. Saul entered quickly, a cigarette clenched between his lips. Rainey took a moment to scan the street then closed the door.

"Oh, good you went back and got our stuff."

"Can't have us running about without a change of underwear. Didn't they teach you anything at the Academy?" Like Rainey, Saul had a dry sense of humor, which he wielded often. He dropped their two overnight bags on the sofa and walked into the kitchen. As he passed Wells, he rendered a portentous glance then ground the cigarette butt into the empty sink.

"I didn't know you smoke," said Rainey.

"You sound like my late wife." Saul smiled. "I don't. At least, not any more. Used to smoke like a chimney back in my operational days. I know it's a filthy habit, but it does give you a plausible reason for standing around outside when doing mobile surveillance or waiting for an agent to show up in the park." Saul rolled up his sleeves, washed his hands then dried them with a towel that hung on the oven door. He poured himself a cup of coffee and leaned against the counter. "Whatcha got there?" He jerked his head toward the knife in Rainey's hand.

"A lie detector."

Wells' eyes widened as they flashed from Rainey to Saul then back to Rainey.

With steely assurance in his voice, Saul said, "You can put that away. That won't be necessary."

Rainey looked down on Wells, held his gaze for several seconds then threw the knife into the wall where it stuck like a dart.

The safe flat in Lisburn Grove was modest, but clean. Located in a fairly secluded neighborhood near the Scartho Road Cemetery it was perfect for hiding out from police, hostile intelligence services or the smell of fish drifting in from the processing plants up on the docks along the River Humber.

Saul finished his coffee then paced over toward the sofa, signaling Rainey to follow him. They walked across the living room, to a spot far enough away from Wells to be out of earshot but where they could still keep their eyes on him.

"What happened to you back in Hull?" whispered Rainey. "I thought they might have grabbed you."

"I slipped into the park, watched everything unfold from within the trees. I knew I couldn't keep up with you when you took off, so I decided to hang back and observe. When the bullets starting flying, I decided to focus on the man with the newspaper."

"And?"

"He tried to disappear in the confusion."

"You followed him?"

Saul grinned like a fox.

"Where to?"

"He went a couple streets over and got into a Mercedes panel van. I flagged down a cab and managed to trail him for a few blocks, but…"

"Then what?"

"I lost him in the city."

"Tell me you got the tag."

"Of course, I got the tag."

"Good deal. Job's on his way. He has to make a pit stop in London first, but then he's headed here. TOG guy should soon be here to SSE the phone we recovered."

Saul looked at Wells as he nodded.

"You ready for round two?"

"Darn right."

21

I don't understand, Ernie. Why would you do that? Why on earth would you destroy Agency records? Especially for someone like Hank McManus?" said a bewildered Saul Baker.

Rainey watched Wells lower his head and bury his face in his hands. The old man began to sob. Their tack had been different this time around. They had been firm, direct and relentless. Wells was not someone who was accustomed to the rigors of interrogation. After all, he was an academic, not a field operative. He had caved in a matter of minutes.

"I did it for Michael."

"*Michael.* Who's Michael?" said Rainey.

Saul uncrossed his arms and softened his tone. "His son. Talk to me, Ernie. What happened?"

Wells sat up, wiping his face with his liver-spotted hands. Behind his spectacles, his eyes were puffy and red. Rainey dropped a box of tissues on the table in front of him and then stepped back against the counter. This was now a conversation between old chums.

"I'm sorry. I'm sorry for not being forthcoming before, but I was scared. It's the only blemish on my otherwise untarnished career. I've been wracked with guilt for so many years. I knew it would catch up to me one of these days. I was just hoping…" He blew his nose then reached for another tissue.

"How does Michael play into this?"

Wells' lips quivered. A fresh tear escaped the corner of his eye, streaked his cheek and dripped to the floor. "When Hank first came to the DA, he seemed really squared away, eager to make it more efficient and organized. He also seemed to take a personal interest in us…and our families. I thought he genuinely cared. We all did. I told him about Michael and how one of the doctors had suggested an experimental drug, but that it was very expensive. Far more than our insurance would cover. He said that there might be a way for him to come up with the money for the medication, but that it would require me to do something for him in return.

"I told him that I would do whatever it took to keep my son alive. He said that all I had to do was pull some files and see that they never saw the light of day again. He also wanted me to destroy a block of dig-ital archives and the back-up tapes. He was very specific."

"The Triumph files," said Saul.

Wells nodded. "I meticulously went through them and made sure they were all gone. He wanted there to be no trace whatsoever of anything re-lated to the Tallinn office. There could also be no suspicion of what I was doing. He was adamant. He gave me a little money here and there, said that the rest would be forthcoming when the records were all gone."

"So what happened?"

"Michael's condition worsened. I begged Hank for the money he'd promised me, so Michael could finally get the drug the doctors thought would stabilize his condition, maybe even cure him."

"Lemme guess. He reneged."

"I pleaded with him. I even threatened to go to Security, but he just laughed. He said that to do that I would have to admit to what I had done. I would be arrested and sent to jail. Then Michael would have no one. I was a single parent raising a very sick child. What could I do? I kept quiet. Michael… He needed me."

Saul reached out, embraced the arm of his old friend.

"He was so thin, so frail. He… He died a few months later. He… I'm sorry," he sobbed.

Rainey looked at the floor. He tried putting himself in Wells' position. What would he have done? Tough stuff. Ernie Wells had been desperate. And desperate men do desperate things. On some level, he couldn't fault the man for doing what he did.

"Ernie. Ernie, look at me. This is *Ben Rainey's* son. Think of your situation, but in reverse. A son is trying to save his father's life."

"I don't understand."

"We have reason to believe that Ben *could* be out there. Alive. If that's the case, then we both will stop at nothing to find him. Please, Ernie. Help us. Do it for Michael. Honor his memory by helping to make things right."

Wells removed his glasses, blew his nose again. When he'd finally gathered himself, he said, "For Michael. Whatever happens to me, so be it."

Rainey filled the empty coffee cup with water from the tap and set it on the table.

Wells looked up at him. "I'm sorry. I truly am. I didn't know…"

Rainey's jaw muscles flexed. "You aren't responsible for what happened to him, Dr. Wells. Just help us find out what did. Help us learn the truth."

"What else do you remember about Operation Triumph?" said Saul.

"Actually, not much more than what I've already told you. It was a long time ago. Except…"

"Yes?" prompted Saul.

"I remember that the Tallinn office seemed to have a particular interest in someone they referred to as Keynote. If I recall correctly, he was a former KGB officer and was believed to be behind a lot of the black market sales coming out of the former Soviet states, specifically the Baltics."

"Keynote?"

Wells finished off the water in one gulp. "A code name. Yes. I don't know the man's real name. There was someone else, too. It started with an E. It'll come to me. Anyway, I remember the two names appearing together in many of the files. Kind of like a tandem."

"Any idea what they were into?"

"Nothing specific, just that they were involved in the sale of Soviet weapons and/or military hardware." Wells moved his empty cup back and forth between his hands. He stared past Saul into the living room then turned his eyes to the ceiling. "Oh, it's on the tip of my tongue. Let me think."

After several minutes of watching Wells draw invisible circles on the table with his cup, Rainey opened a cabinet and tore into a box of Power Bars. He was starving. He tossed some on the table for Saul and Wells.

"Echo!" said Wells. "The other guy's name was Echo. Echo and Keynote. Although I should qualify that. What I mean is that I don't know whether Echo was male or female. But someone apparently had an affinity for music terminology," said Wells with a self-satisfied smile and a mouthful of Power Bar. "Somehow those two were linked. Echo and Keynote, yes, siree."

"One more question," said Saul. "Why did you set us up at the Institute?"

"What are you talking about?"

"The men at the Institute."

Wells cocked his head. "What men?"

Saul squinted. "Ernie, three men tried to kill us. Four, if you include the man on the gate."

"This happened today?"

"Yes. Right after we met with you. Are you saying you didn't know anything about that?"

Wells receded into his chair. He swallowed his food and stared into the bottom of the empty cup. "No. I didn't tell anyone you were coming. Honest."

"Then someone else did."

22

WHILE they waited for Job and the Technical Operations Group member to arrive, Saul cooked them a proper meal. He had unearthed some fettuccine pasta in a cabinet and a bag of frozen vegetables in the fridge. It wasn't the best meal Rainey had ever eaten on an operation, but it certainly wasn't the worst.

As they were finishing and Rainey was putting on another pot of coffee, the TOG officer arrived. He looked to be in his mid-twenties and had a spindly frame but for a doughy stomach that protruded from his spine in such a way that made it seem he was hiding a football beneath his shirt. His face was intelligent though ruddy. His features including his walk across the carpeted front room were birdlike. The thick, twill pants he wore left little to the imagination while conversely his blue Oxford shirt was too big at the collar. With thin, pincer-like fingers, he adjusted his dark-framed spectacles and greeted each of them with an awkward nod.

They cleared a spot on the kitchen table for him and he quickly set to work. The Stork, as Rainey had immediately dubbed him, if only in his private thoughts, opened a briefcase, pulled out a laptop and another electronic device that was about the size of a handheld GPS unit along with several neatly bundled cables. Rainey watched the man connect the phone he had recovered by the wrecked car to the smaller device and then the device to the laptop. The Stork pressed a few buttons on the device then clicked open a program on the laptop. After a few moments, he lowered his head, spied Rainey over his eyeglasses and offered a confident grin.

"You're in?"

"I'm in."

"You tech guys always amaze me." Rainey stepped behind him, looked down at the screen from over the man's shoulder. "May I?"

"Absolutely," said the Stork. He slid back the chair, stood and headed toward the coffee pot.

Rainey sat down and began clicking through the contents of the phone, which were now displayed on the computer screen in logical categories. *Call History. Messaging. Email. Media.* He examined the call history first. "Here. This was about when we arrived at the Institute. It's a call received."

"Looks like a Hull area code," said Saul. "Probably whoever it was that tipped them off to our arrival."

Rainey looked at Wells.

"It wasn't me. I swear."

"Relax. I believe you, Dr. Wells. But who could it have been? Had to be someone on the premises."

"What's the number?" asked Wells.

Rainey rattled it off and watched the old Agency man search his memory banks.

"That's not an Institute extension."

"Probably a cell," said Rainey.

"What about the gatekeeper?" offered Saul.

"Could be." Rainey scrolled back in the history. "But this number here," he said, pointing to the screen. "This is the one I'm more interested in."

Saul craned his neck so his head was closer to the computer. "That what I think it is?"

Rainey nodded. "Zero. Two. Zero."

"Area code for London."

"Someone in London knew we were coming to see Wells."

"How would they have known?"

"I don't know, but that's our target." Rainey sifted through the rest of the contents of the phone. "I don't see anything else here that's going to help us."

After the Stork had gone, Rainey kicked off his hikers and stretched his legs under the table. As he did so, something small fell out of the gummy toe of his right shoe. He leaned over and picked it up. It was a bullet. The copper jacket was peeled back giving it the appearance of a small metal flower. *That's what hit me in the foot during the car chase in Hull.* He had seen bullets do some pretty crazy things over the years, but this was ridiculous.

He leaned back in the chair, twisting the projectile back and forth between his fingertips.

"What is it, Ray?"

"Nine mil."

"No, I mean what are you thinking? I've seen that look before."

Rainey stared at the ceiling for a minute or so then got up and paced around the room. "I'm just trying to make sense of everything that's happened. You know, put it all into context. What started all of this was the letter from Moses, remember? So what, if anything, did Moses say that might be helpful to us for the purposes of developing the situation?" He pushed his hands into his pockets as he leaned against the wall beside Saul. He stared across the room with a pair of intense, resolute eyes. "He said he was *Russian* and that he was a *spy*."

"Moses could be a woman. Have you considered that?"

"Yeah. That's definitely a possibility. But for the sake of discussion, let's assume he's a man."

"All right."

"If we take what he wrote as true on its face, then he can't be affiliated with Triumph. Unless… Perhaps Moses was a one of Dad's agents?"

Saul scratched his five o'clock shadow. "Yeah. Or he could be some smart Russian spy hunter who's trying to flush *out* an agent or two."

"Anything's possible, but I'm not sensing that from the letter."

"Yeah, you're right," said Saul, rubbing his chin.

"If you listen to his tone, it's personal in nature. He wants to meet with me, specifically. And he knows that I was in Third Group." Rainey pulled the knife from the wall, studied the blade. "What would he have to gain by meeting with *me*?"

"Yeah. I don't get that part at all."

Rainey tossed the knife in the sink and crossed his arms, which caused his shirtsleeves to stretch at the biceps. "Then the question becomes: who would have an interest in preventing the truth about my father from coming out? I mean, first they target us and then they target Wells. Seems whoever is behind the attacks is determined to keep Triumph a secret. At least whatever part my dad and McManus had going. Could be McManus was working for that person."

"Or the Russians. Or some other foreign service." Saul crossed his arms, too. "Well, hopefully when Job arrives, he'll have some answers for us."

Rainey plopped down onto the sofa. He looked over at Wells on the recliner. He had fallen asleep over an hour ago; his snoring was now beginning to sound like a steam locomotive setting off from station. Rainey closed his eyes. If he allowed himself to do so, he too could be asleep in a matter of minutes. He cracked his eyelids, tilted his left wrist and examined his Casio G-Shock GWG1000 Mudmaster.

04:16.

What on earth is keeping Job?

23

THE first thing he noticed was the sound of birds in joyful sing-song. He opened his eyes slowly. A wide band of sunlight that had forged through the window blinds on the opposite side of the room and lay across his face, forced him to squint. A firm, steady breeze with the rhythm of an ocean tide washed against the house, rattling the brass doorknocker on the front door. The leaves on the poplar, ash and elm trees outside swished to and fro. Their volume fluctuated from soft to loud, as if a conductor were out there directing them in some grand symphony of nature.

Mezzo Piano. Crescendo. Crescendo. Fortissimo!

The sound of the wind in the trees brought back memories. He was fifteen years old, a high school freshman. He had just come home from a tough soccer match—homecoming, in fact—during which he'd scored the winning goal in the last two minutes of play. It had been his very first goal in his very first start for the varsity team. The stands were packed with fans. His mom and Iris were there, of course; they were there for every game. Job made the ones he could, which weren't many. Rainey really wished his dad could have been there that day. Especially for that game and for that goal.

It had been sometime later that night when he awoke on his mother's bed and found her there seated beside him, stroking his forehead and choking back tears. At first, he had no idea why she was crying, but then quickly realized she must have seen him talking to his dad before drifting off, if only in the framed portrait on the pillow next to him. Ray had chronicled each thrilling quarter of the game, related what it felt like to score the winning goal and how much he missed him. His mother's whispered words still echoed in his head, even now. *"He's watching from heaven, Ray."*

Miss you, Dad. Miss you every single day.

Rainey sat up and stretched the stiffness from his neck and shoulders. He arched his back and twisted from side to side. Wells was still asleep on the recliner in the corner. A large, colorful Afghan lay draped over him. Rainey looked down. Saul had covered him with a blanket, most of which had fallen to the floor.

As he wiped his eyes, he detected the invigorating scent of freshly brewed coffee and…bacon and eggs. A garble of hushed voices came from the kitchen. He stood up and peeked around the corner. Saul and Job were sitting at the table each with a cup of coffee in front of them. Saul looked as fresh as a daisy; Job like he had been up the entire night.

"There he is. Mr. Sleepy Head," said Saul with a grandfatherly twinkle in his eyes.

"Morning, Pappy." He looked at Job. "When did you get in?"

"About thirty minutes ago. I've been busy."

Saul pushed back from the table. "Have a seat, kid. I'll fix you some breakfast."

Rainey yawned and squinted into his watch. "What time is it?"

"Eight fifteen," said Job.

Saul brought over a plate of scrambled eggs, some strips of crispy bacon and two pieces of toast. "Here ya go. Breakfast of champions, dinner of spies. You can thank Job for bringing the grub." Saul also slid a cup of piping hot coffee in front of him and handed him a fork.

Rainey bowed his head, said a quick prayer then sunk his fork into the eggs and took a bite.

Saul smiled as if he were reading his mind. "Yeah, I'm up half the night as it is. Figured I'd pull guard duty and let you sleep. Ernie's not going anywhere now anyhow. He's with us. You know, I don't condone what he did, but I feel for him. He was in a tough spot. His son was his life."

"You didn't sleep at all?"

"I'll have plenty of time to sleep when I'm dead. Besides, you do enough for me back home on the farm and all."

"Thanks, Pappy. And Job, thanks for this." He held up a forkful of eggs.

"Sure thing, bud." Job sipped his coffee. "So, you ready to hear what I've found out?"

Rainey bit into a strip of bacon. "Hit me."

Job slid a file across the table. "Operation Triumph. It was a CE Division-wide op, with the lion's share of the work tasked to North Group. There were a total of twelve covert offices spread out at strategic locations within the former Soviet republics. Each of them had different responsibilities and thus different targets. We don't know what the office in Tallinn was concerned with because those records are missing, but we do know that McManus was the ranking officer there. Meaning he ran the office. Ben was the field man. Ran an agent network is my best guess. And Crystal Hartley-Breeland was the comms officer, just like Wells said."

Rainey flipped open the file as he scooped up another mouthful of eggs.

"Now, Breeland had a number of key assignments during her career…from the Baltics to the Middle East. In two thousand four, she took a desk job at Langley then resigned in oh seven to go live on the West Coast with her husband, a retired Foreign Service officer. She's had a full career and was as solid as they come."

"Anyone talk to her?"

"No."

"Why not?"

"Because she's dead. Killed in a car crash in the summer of oh eight."

"Dang it!" spat Rainey, a piece of toast in one hand and his fork in the other.

"I know."

"So where does that leave us?"

"Well, checks with State and the feebies turned up nothing, so I'm afraid we're back to square one."

"I'll tell you what I think, Job. It's time to post the message to Moses," said Rainey.

Job frowned. "I don't know, Ray. I'm still thinking about that."

"What's to think about? Obviously this Moses knows something. I think Pappy and I have effectively determined that something very bad happened to my dad. Don't pull back on me now."

"It's not about pulling back, bud. It's about your safety. Moses said he wants you to come alone."

"Then I go alone. I'm not afraid of any man."

"I get that. But just because you're not afraid doesn't mean I want to risk losing you. Remember, it could still be a trap. You pissed off a lot of people last year. Could be that one of them wants to lure you out into the open, so they can finish what they started. Moses clearly stated he was Russian. Based on what you did last year, I'd say it's a safe bet that the Russians are behind this. We already know Levka Borovsky wants you dead.

"Plus, there's one more thing I need to discuss with you before I would even consider an actual meeting, but we can talk about that later."

Rainey stood up, wiped his mouth then dropped his empty plate and fork in the sink with a clang, which caused Wells to stir in the other room. "We're talking about my dad, Job. If he's out there…" He gripped the faucet handle tightly as if he were about to rip it from the sink, closed his eyes and sighed through clenched teeth.

Job and Saul exchanged thoughtful glances. Finally, Saul nodded.

"Okay. I'll post the message, but no promises until we see how Moses responds."

"Understood," said Rainey, a spark of jubilation in his voice. He sat back down. Now it was their turn. He and Saul briefed Job on what they had learned. When they had finished, Job left to touch base with the Agency's London station chief and a high-ranking counterpart within MI5. He returned a few hours later with a smile.

"Okay, the phone number," he said. "No name or credit card attached, probably a burner. Not sure if it's still in play. If it is, whoever's using it has been smart for the most part. Last activity was in London yesterday after your little skirmish outside Wells' place. GCHQ is on it though. Hopefully, it'll pop back up and we'll be able to nail down a location. I can tell you it doesn't have much of a history. Which means the guy probably changes phones like he changes underwear."

"And the tag?" said Rainey, referring to the license plate on the vehicle Saul had seen leaving the area of Wells' flat after it collected the man with the newspaper. "Whaddya come up with?"

"Dead end, right?" said Saul.

"Yes and no. It's registered to a name and address that don't exist, but that doesn't mean your grabbing that tag was fruitless."

"I don't follow," said Saul.

"As you both well know, the UK is littered with surveillance cameras and—"

"LPRs," blurted Rainey.

"Exactly."

"LPRs? What's an LPR?" said Saul.

"License plate reader. Essentially, cameras that can *read* plates. They snap a photo of the tag and the vehicle and capture the exact date and time. That information then gets stored digitally in a searchable database. We may not know who is rocking that tag, but we *do* know where that tag has been for the last six months. If we wanted to go back further, we could, but I thought a six-month window was sufficient. For the past six months, we have every LPR capture of that tag and therefore the vehicle on which it was displayed in the entire UK. So… Mercedes panel van, right?"

"Right."

"I'm told that the highest frequency of LPR captures is in London, in an industrial area called Park Royal. MI5 is going to focus their search there. If the van pops up on an LPR somewhere else in the meantime, great. In either case, we have people ready to launch.

"Boy, you guys these days are spoiled with all your hi-tech gadgets."

Rainey smiled. "Makes it nice, that's for sure. Human eyes and ears still reign supreme though in my book. The key is balance. And synergy."

Job suddenly looked grim.

"What?" said Rainey.

"Brits are pretty torqued about the bodies you've left behind. It's all over the news, by the way."

He shrugged. "So let 'em be torqued. We were defending ourselves and Wells."

"I know. But they don't like cleaning up other peoples' messes. I've managed to smooth things over for the time being. Just try not to kill anyone in the UK for the foreseeable future." It was more a jest than a direct order. "The London station chief is another story, but he's just gonna have to deal with the director on this one. The DX has been given wide latitude, here. At least to this point, we have.

"By the way, MI5 has identified the men you killed. They're local thugs. We're not talking world-class talent here, but they were professionals nonetheless. Maybe that phone number you gave me will lead us to whoever hired them."

"So the next course of action?" said Rainey.

"We post the message to the blog and see how Moses responds."

24

Washington, D.C.

A limousine pulled to the curb in front of her. Behind a pair of Tom Ford Mirandas, Vera Lysniak examined her sleek figure in the reflection of the dark, tinted windows. She smiled. Wow. She looked good. Real good. The man inside had to be noticing.

She didn't wait for the driver to scurry around the car and open the door for her. She hated when men did that. She could open the door for herself, thank you very much. She slid into the supple leather seat and pulled the door closed. Crossing her legs in such a way that any man was sure to notice, she pushed her sunglasses to the top of her head, batted a strand of hair over her shoulder and turned toward the man seated on the far side of the limo. Stedman Carter was on the phone. He was always on the phone.

The car began to move. After two blocks, Carter dropped his phone on the seat between them and said, "Women!"

"Trouble on the home front, Stedman?" said Vera.

"My wife wants to go to Paris this week." He shook his head with a huff. "I told her to go. I could use the peace and quiet. I swear!"

Vera smiled.

Perfect.

"You know not all women are like her," she said.

"Don't kid yourself, Vera. Now, what do have for me?"

Her smile faded into a pout, which she managed to hide well. "There is a meeting tomorrow morning. Apparently there are some whisperings about McManus' death being looked at now as a homicide. The president wants to know if there is anything with which he should be concerned in the investigation."

"No, not anymore. We recovered the files he had squirreled away. Trust me, Vera, I've got as much to lose as he does. The only way anyone is going to find out now about the president and me is if one of us talks."

"Or if Ben Rainey does. I still don't get why your friend would keep him alive after all this time."

"You and me both. He told me that he would take care of the problem. I just assumed that meant putting a bullet in his head, not a bag over it and running him off somewhere to play sick, twisted games."

"Why don't you just reach out to him, tell him what's at stake," said Vera.

"Because I can't. He's in hiding. No one knows where he is. Even yours truly. I just… I just wish I knew who this Moses character is and what he knows. But, first things first. My sources in British Intelligence tell me Ernie Wells and his two saviors are still in England. And that someone by the name of Jim Bell has come into the picture. He's asking a lot of questions. What do you know about him?"

"Jim Bell? Never heard of him."

"Well, find out what you can, will you? The only thing my people have been able to unearth is that he is somehow affiliated with the Agency."

"My pleasure."

Carter nodded.

"How much has he learned?" said Vera.

"Enough to put him and British security officials on the trail of the men we hired. But it's being dealt with."

She held his gaze. *Gosh, he's gorgeous.*

"Even if Wells tells them everything he knows about Triumph, I think we're still covered. Don't get me wrong, I'd still like to see him dead, him and the other two, but McManus and his little stash of files were priority one. He could have ruined me, *and* the president, as well as some of our closest friends. Still makes me mad just thinking about it. How on earth could Hank have thought he was going to get away with trying to double our arrangement? The *idiot*."

"How *did* you get by his security detail by the way?"

"You shouldn't ask such questions, Vera. It's poor form. But, I'll tell you anyway. Tarło and I have many well-placed sources. One of them is on the DNI's security detail. You see, I've kept a close eye on Hank ever since our initial arrangement back when he was station chief in Moscow. He's a politician at heart. Always looking out for himself. I have paid him well over the years to keep me informed. That's why I strongly recommended to you that he be appointed DNI.

"Anyway, our source on Hank's detail is how we found out about the Triumph files in the first place, got the alarm code and the safe combination, knew when and how we could burgle the house without detection. The specific meds he takes… I mean *took*. And how we might best eliminate the problem." Carter smiled. "Having a guy like Tarło and his people working for you is like having your own private little CIA. Well, I've already said too much. I expect that information to be kept between us. Understood?"

"Of course."

"I tell you all of this because I think you and I understand each other. We know how the real world operates. I want to thank you for the tip about the Moses letter, Vera, and for coming to me about Hank's sloppy play for more money. He should have never told you about those files. But I'm glad he did. He really was an idiot."

"Oh, you're quite welcome. I think very highly of you, Stedman." She slid closer to him.

"Only two things concern me now. Like I said, this Moses person, whoever he is, he's an X-factor. A big one. I don't know a thing about him or what cards he might be holding. That troubles me a great deal."

"And the second thing?"

"The plane. It's still down there. In the jungle, I mean. This Moses person might just stir things up enough for someone to begin a rather thorough investigation. If any free-thinking investigators were to ever go down there and nose around… Well, they just might find something that could raise some serious questions."

"So, send a team down there to deal with the situation. I hear C-4 does wonders. It's one of the most desolate places in the rainforest, love. No one's ever going to know. Say, if C-4 explodes in the forest and no one is around to hear it, does it really make a sound?" She frowned at her failed attempt to lighten his dark mood.

Carter continued picking at the stitching in the seat. "Explosives leave behind residue, Vera. That's what I'm worried about them finding as it is."

"You're not understanding me, Stedman. I'm no expert, of course, but it occurs to me that if you use enough C-4 and pack it appropriately in the downed plane, you might be able to break the plane apart into pieces. Then you let nature do the rest. The rains there are relentless and severe this time of year. They wash away everything. Even your troubles, love. Give your hypothetical investigators nothing to investigate."

"I don't know. Wouldn't that be just as suspicious as the blast hole in the side of the plane?"

"Ask a homicide detective what he would rather investigate: a crime scene with a body that holds clues and yields potential evidence or one in which there is no body whatsoever?"

"I take your point."

She watched him look off into space. "Well, you'll think of something. You always do."

"Yes."

"But for heaven's sake, Stedman, don't worry. I'll keep you abreast of what's going on with the Agency's inquiry into Moses and any developments concerning Ben Rainey. Haven't I always been a good girl?" She tilted her head toward him with an eyebrow raised. Her rose-colored lips curled into a smile. *Go for it, Vera!* She placed her hand on his leg.

"Good? I'd say you're a very *bad* girl. And that's why I love you, Vera. You're as ruthless and conniving as I am." He leaned into her, kissed her on the mouth.

She cupped her hand around his head and pressed against him with all the passion she could muster. As they kissed, an intense heat flashed inside her.

He's mine.

25

London, UK

IT had been years since he had actually killed someone with his bare hands, but that didn't mean he had grown rusty. In many ways, Zarek Tarło had grown even more lethal at his craft. Maybe it was because now he trained harder than ever before. As a result, his appearance was nearly identical to how it was back when he was in the prime of his operational career. He had a full head of hair, which had once been jet black, but now appeared frosted with charcoal dust. With an intrepid manner and sinewy frame, at forty-nine he could still attract the ladies. His arms were powerful and tanned from days spent on the shooting ranges in Texas and Montana and from the frequent jaunts to the Caribbean aboard Stedman Carter's carrier-size yacht. His cardio was the thing of which he was most proud. The specially tailored CrossFit training had turned him into a model of fitness such that even most of the younger men in his private little army couldn't keep up with him.

After the failure by the hired men in Hull, Tarło felt compelled to take matters into his own hands. Literally. It was pure irony that one of his best teams of highly trained special operators had been tied up on an unrelated operation just across the North Sea in Amsterdam or else they would have been the ones tasked to kill Wells and the two CIA men sent to debrief him. In order to make do, Tarło had hastily hired on some local talent through a man he had on his payroll in London. Rory Alvin worked in the Marine Policing Unit with the Metropolitan Police and was a key figure in RWS'—that is, Stedman Carter's—arms trafficking operation in the UK, especially with respect to waterborne shipments in London. But whatever role—significant or otherwise— Alvin may have once played in Carter's criminal enterprise, he had since squandered it away with the hiring of a bunch of overzealous shooters who failed to complete their simple mission in Hull.

Tarło looked down at his rough hands. The red lines crisscrossing his palms and the pads of his fingers from the ligature he had just used had not yet fully faded. When his anger had diminished and the blood was once again flowing in his fingers, he searched the flat for anything that might connect to him. Thankfully, he found nothing.

At least that part Alvin did right.

◆ ◆ ◆

A fog was settling in as Job Jackson scurried into the MI5 safe flat at Number 55 in Tufton Street. It was a well-appointed space, rich with the hallmarks of a Churchill legacy and easily within spitting distance of Thames House. Job glided up the stairs to the second floor, past rooms full of books and wing back chairs, dark wood and fireplaces. He found the Security Service man sitting at a small conference room table within an opaque miasma of cigar smoke. Gavin Cheffers was a short man, thick around the middle with jowly cheeks and sharp, slate-colored eyes. He wore a tweed jacket over a white dress shirt, a tie the color of wet sand and brown corduroy slacks that were starting to show some wear at the knees. His pate was nearly bald, but for the U-shaped blend of gray and silver that he had carefully combed behind his ears.

Cheffers exhaled a column of brown smoke that drifted in a slow spiral toward the antique ceiling fan above him, which was switched on but barely moving. He could have been Churchill himself at the ripe age of fifty-five, thought Job, as he took a seat beside him.

Job extended his hand. "Thanks for the heads up, Gavs."

Cheffers' hand shot out. The man had a vice-like grip. "My pleasure, mate. I figured you might like to see the play-by-play while you're still on my side of the pond."

"Where is he?" said Job.

Cheffers angled an open laptop toward him, stabbed at the screen with a fat, cigar-stained finger. "Here. In a flat at the corner of Golders Green and Armitage."

"Is this a live feed?"

"Aye. Coming from a drone that's about sixty meters overhead."

"How'd they find him?"

Cheffers' eyes narrowed as he turned his head away from Job and puffed out another cloud of thick smoke. "Camera picked up your Benz in West Acton. We tracked it from there to an industrial block in Abbeydale Road over in Park Royal. We feigned a traffic stop then mugged the driver, who as it turned out was armed with an Uzi. Van was packed to the gills with all manner of stolen goods, mostly the drugstore variety." Cheffers picked a piece of tobacco from the tip of his tongue. "The lads went at him pretty hard. Didn't take long for him to see the light. In exchange for consideration at sentencing, he agreed to tell us who hired him and his mates to kill your friend, Wells."

Job looked at the screen intently. Police vehicles were swiftly moving in, blocking off the streets around the intersection. Flashing blue LEDs bled into the fog, which seemed to soak up their color like a sponge.

"Name's Rory Alvin," Cheffers lowered his forehead, "and he wears a badge. Works for the Yard's marine unit. He oversees a lot that goes on with respect to maritime security in London."

"Is that it? Just a name?"

Cheffers shook his head. "Gave us the email account through which Alvin and he communicated. IP resolved to the store right across the street from Alvin's flat. Alvin also provided the guns for the hit. The van driver's Uzi was among them. We were able to raise the serial number, which had been filed nearly to the bone. Turns out the gun had been seized from a storage shed during a drug pinch down in Putney two years ago. Alvin was one of the men in charge of that investigation. He's a dirty one for sure. Well, his time has come, all right." Cheffers' eyes moved about the screen. "Looks like they're about to hit it." He turned the volume knob on a handheld radio that stood on the table next to the laptop. "Now we have a bit of audio."

Job inched forward as he heard the on-scene commander and his people going back and forth over the air.

"Here we go," said Cheffers.

♦ ♦ ♦

It was just past 4:00 P.M. Tarło took one more pass around the apartment. He had found an unused burner phone by the ceiling atop a kitchen cabinet, but nothing else that could even remotely link to him or Stedman Carter. Rory Alvin may have hired subpar hitters, but at least he wasn't sloppy in his tradecraft.

Tarło strolled back over to the slack-jawed man on the floor. It was a shame really. Over the years, Alvin had been quite a useful source of intel about British security protocols and police activity especially around the ports. Have to find someone else now. He frowned, considering the work that would be involved in such an endeavor then kicked Alvin in the stomach. The dead man absorbed the blow with little movement.

A horn sounded outside followed by a man's angry shout. Even from inside the flat, two stories above the street, Tarło immediately suspected something was amiss. He went to the window overlooking the intersection of Golders Green and Armitage and assessed the attitude of the street with careful, hawk-like eyes. Traffic had completely died. There were no vehicles buzzing past, no pedestrians either. At this time of day?

Something's wrong.

He titled his head and gazed all the way down Armitage. A police sedan was parked across both lanes of travel with its blue overheads pulsating against a gauzy blanket of fog. Suspicion confirmed. They had come for Alvin.

Tarło withdrew from the window and receded into the flat. He stood in the middle of the living room next to the dead man as his eyes darted about. He kicked him again just for the heck of it.

Think, man. Think!

I've got it.

He jogged into the kitchen, cranked open the gas for all four burners on the stove then did the same thing to the valve for the fireplace in the living room. He grinned as he sniffed the gas rushing into the room.

Tarło cracked the door and peaked into the hall. It was empty. For now.

He stepped into the hall, locking the door behind him. He walked to the next flat over, pulled his suppressed 9mm and held it behind his thigh so it wouldn't be seen. He knocked softly with the knuckle of his index finger. When no one answered, he knocked again, this time with a bit more volume.

A pudgy woman with a smudge of flour on her cheek opened the door and at the sight of him offered a friendly smile. Tarło smiled, too then pushed his way inside. He quickly raised the pistol and fired one suppressed round into the center of the woman's forehead and watched her fall backward onto the sofa like she had tripped or was simply too tired to stand. She bounced into a seated position then listed to the side like the Leaning Tower of Pisa, her eyes halfway closed. A rivulet of blood oozed from the dime-size hole in her head, ran to the corner of her eyebrow and spilled onto her shoulder.

Tarło jogged to a window that faced Armitage and unlatched the lock, made sure the window wasn't painted shut, but was careful not to open it. If there were people watching the building, which there surely were, they would be alert for anyone opening a door or window right now. He then returned to the door, drew up against it and spied the hallway through the peephole.

Then he waited.

Twelve minutes later, the first man appeared in the hallway. He was clad in a black tactical vest, helmet and gloves. In his left hand, he carried a ballistic shield with a tiny window through which he peered. In his right hand was a pistol bearing a weapon-mounted light, which was wrapped around the side of the shield and pointed downrange. The man cleared the stairs and headed for Rory Alvin's flat. A train of men attired in similar fashion followed close behind him. Each of them carried a carbine and other gear necessary to their industry.

Tarło studied them and their movements. *Not bad.* They were careful yet negotiated the hall with appropriate speed. No noise generated by shuffling feet or battle rattle. The team of men paused as one of its members stepped forward with a door ram.

Time to go.

The former GROM commando made for the window he had staged for his escape. For some reason, he started counting down in his head. *Three, two, one...*

He threw open the window and dropped to the gable below, then ran across the landing toward Golders Way—a one-lane alleyway to the rear of the building. He leapt for an adjoining rooftop. As he sailed through the air, a terrific explosion ripped apart the second-floor, corner flat. Brick, glass and other projectiles shot out in all directions. The ground shook for blocks. Car alarms blared.

◆ ◆ ◆

Job and Gavin Cheffers were silent. Radio traffic had died as the men inside the apartment building moved toward the target. Cheffers rolled the cigar back and forth between his lips with his fingertips.

The streets were deserted. All was quiet.

The calm before the storm.

Job pictured it in his head: a team of men moving down the hall. A few paces before the door to the flat, one of them would pop out and ram the door, another would toss in a stun grenade. Then it was game on. The tactical team would take the flat with an overwhelming show of force until Rory Alvin was in handcuffs and the rest of the flat was deemed safe for the investigators to move in and turn the place upside down for evidence.

Job waved away the smoke that lingered in front of his face and studied the screen. Suddenly, a figure emerged from a window on the north side of the building and ran across the rooftop. What followed was a brilliant flash of light that momentarily blinded the camera. As the lens adjusted itself, clouds of smoke began to billow from all sides of the flat, growing blacker and more intense with each passing second.

Wide-eyed, Job gripped the edge of the table and leaned closer to the screen.

The ash-end of Cheffers' cigar drooped toward the floor as his mouth fell open. "Ah, bloody hell."

◆ ◆ ◆

Tarło raced to the edge of the rooftop, gripped a light standard and rappelled down to the street. He took off in a sprint until he found a bicycle leaning against someone's trash bin. Brushing a piece of broken glass from his hair, he turned the bike in the direction he was heading and pedaled quickly away. He passed a man with a handheld radio, who was running in the opposite direction.

Tarło shot across Golders Green Crescent and into a small, walled-off parking lot. He skidded to a stop at the far end of the lot and alighted from the bicycle. Glancing back toward the bobby with the radio, he picked up the Gary Fisher carbon-fiber hardtail and flung it over the five-foot wall, then scrambled over after it. When his feet hit the pavement, he snatched up the bike and mounted it again. He pedaled hard onto Finchley then leaned into a right turn, ramped the sidewalk onto Rotherwick where he narrowly avoided a woman and her yapping little terrier. When he reached Corringham, he slowed his pace to blend in with his surroundings. Soon he crossed into Hamstead Heath and was cruising along a bike path, thankful he still trained the way he did.

Like his boss, his main concern now, as he rode casually past families and joggers and others gleefully oblivious to world events, was this Moses person. He—assuming it was a man—was an unknown variable. Maybe Moses was bluffing about knowing what had happened to Ben Rainey, but if he wasn't and truly was intent on exposing dark secrets to the CIA, he was a very serious threat to a lot of very wealthy, very powerful people, not least of whom was Stedman Carter.

Boss is going to want answers. He's going to want a plan.

And I think I just came up with one.

26

Southern Venezuela
39 Miles North of the Brazilian Border

THE chartered helicopter emerged from a small cloud and circled the northern rim of Cerro Sarisariñama—one of the flat-topped mountains, known as tepuis—in Jaua Sarisariñama National Park. The heavily forested terrain below was dotted with rocks. It was the rainy season, the pilot had said, though the sun right now was shimmering brightly in the bluest sky Maddie had ever seen. Puddles the size of large ponds filled every depression and reflected the intense sunlight. It looked like a thousand fires were raging across the vast panorama. Down over the steep edge of the tepui, was a carpet of vibrant green foliage, with rivers and streams slithering back and forth through the flora like snakes, large and small. Despite its idyllic beauty and serenity, the landscape surely held secrets within its hidden recesses. Secrets about her father.

She tilted her head toward the window. Her large, honey-colored eyes focused on a huge circular void off to her right. It was as if someone had taken a giant scoop right out of the jungle forest.

"Sima Mayor," said the pilot. "Es a seenkhole. A beeg one."

The man's voice seemed distant through the headset though he sat mere feet away. His head craned right, left and back again while he scanned the terrain for a proper spot to put down. He repositioned his lip mic and turned toward those seated behind him in the passenger cabin. His eyes locked onto her and at the same time, he let loose with a wide smile that made his thick mustache flatten out and his aviator sunglasses rise on his full cheeks.

The bearded man seated next to her nudged her with his elbow. "I think he likes you."

Maddie rolled her eyes.

"Set us down over there," said Evelina in perfect Spanish with a finger extended toward a flat, dry area below.

Maddie and Evelina had left Greenville, South Carolina on separate commercial flights eventually meeting up with their male counterparts in Miami, where they collected their travel documents from a DX courier. There, they were issued cover identities, which were fairly close to their real ones. This made it easier for them to memorize on such short notice. The courier had advised that their gear would arrive ahead of them at their destination. A few particular items had to be sent under diplomatic pouch.

It was not lost on Maddie that she was part of something very special now. The Central Intelligence Agency. Directorate X. Hard to imagine, looking back, just how she had wound up here. She considered the fact that Job had acquired entry visas for them essentially overnight. That was even more difficult to fathom. She studied the landscape as she mused. Could the DX have someone under thumb in the Venezuelan Embassy back home?

They had arrived as a foursome in Caracas on a private jet registered to a studio production company based in Hollywood, California. The company was legitimate even if its resources were sometimes utilized to the contrary. Shrouded in secrecy was the fact that the CIA had long ago become a shadowy partner through its Directorate X—known publicly as the Greenbriar Foundation—in order to provide cover from time to time for its officers and operations. In this case, Maddie and her colleagues were here to scout out locations for an up-coming documentary on the tepuis of southern Venezuela that focused on the effects climate change had had on erosion and other aspects of the delicate ecosystems of the region. Though not the real reason for their visit, the reality was, in essence, a different kind of documentary.

The pilot kept the rotor blades spinning as they unloaded their gear. He then lifted off and disappeared, leaving them in the middle of one of the most isolated places on earth. Unless they transmitted an emergency signal via satellite back to DX headquarters, they were on their own for the next five days.

"So, you're Bronco's…uh Ray's…sister," said one of the bearded men with a smile. "I can see the resemblance. You both have that same fire in your eyes."

"Yes, but I'm much better looking," quipped Maddie.

"No argument there. Now that we can make proper introductions… People call me Mouse. This is Tonka."

Hefting a sizeable rucksack onto his shoulders, the big Native American turned at the mention of his call sign and nodded. "Hi, Maddie."

"You know my name."

Mouse nodded. "We've heard a lot about you. What I want to know is do you have any good dirt on Bronco. Stuff we can use, I mean, to really bust his balls. He's always razzing us. I want some good stuff on him for a change."

"Oh, there's plenty, believe me."

"Well, it's a long hike to the crash site. I'm all ears."

"That why they call you Mouse?" said Maddie.

"Oooh!" Tonka laughed. "Yep. You're Bronco's sister all right."

"C'mon you guys. Get sprayed up." Evelina slid a can of bug repellent back into her pack, slung it onto her back and tugged the straps tight. "We've got two miles to cover before we lose daylight and that includes our descent."

Tonka turned to Mouse. "Hope you're wearing your whitey tighties, bro. Chiggers in the crouch make for miserable hiking."

"Dude, there are ladies present." Mouse looked at Evelina and Maddie. "Relax, you two. There's no going commando on this trip."

Maddie adjusted her ponytail. *Were these operator guys always this jokey?* Then she stopped and considered for a moment just how much they were like her brother. Like him, they were quick with the dry wit and had an easy, unflappable disposition. They each exuded a disarming, but confident charm and were keenly alert to their surroundings though not obviously so. They were also very intelligent even if they kept it hidden behind school-boy antics. But the thing that struck her most of all—Ray and all of them had this, herself included—was the glimmer in their eyes of a raging fire within, that once unleashed was nearly impossible to quell.

As they picked their way across the top of the tepui, several downpours came and went, each one retarding their progress. After finally reaching their waypoint at the base of the mountain, they searched for a proper place to bed down for the night.

"It's a little cramped, but this one will work," Mouse called out. He stood at the mouth of a small, flat cave that was wider than it was high. One by one they stepped toward him and examined his find. "It's up high enough. Don't you think?"

"What do you mean?" said Maddie.

Tonka wiped the sweat from his forehead with a small towel then stowed it back in his pack. "He means if the rain falls overnight like it did earlier then the water is going to rise very fast down here. Flash floods appear out of nowhere. Rainy season, remember?"

"It's the *Rainey* season all right. We Raineys are always in season," she replied.

"You know, this is a little scary. You even have Bronco's bad jokes," said Mouse. "And I gotta say… That was really bad."

Evelina guzzled some water from her canteen then wiped her wet brow with the back of her hand. The mixture of rain and sweat had transformed her normally yellow-blonde locks into a dark gold color. "All right, let's camp here for the night."

Tonka bent over, clicked on his flashlight and angled it back and forth.

Maddie patted him on the shoulder. "Don't worry big guy, you can stay close to me if you get scared."

"Seriously, she's just like Bronc," said Mouse with a grin. "I love it."

Tonka was still shaking his head. "Here you have to look out for scorpions. They're poisonous. Make sure you get your netting wrapped around you good. Oh and watch out for the tarantulas, too. They're not harmful, but if they bite you, you'll know it."

After constructing rudimentary bedding that would keep them off the ground and away from the relentless chiggers, Tonka proclaimed the cave safe for overnight accommodation.

Mouse was the first one in. He had his mosquito netting out and was working it into a cocoon.

When Maddie had finally reached an acceptable level of comfort and closed her tired eyes, a torrential rain erupted from the obsidian darkness. Electric strands of lightning suddenly flashed before them, revealing a sky full of sea foam-colored clouds. Water tumbled down over the slope toward them. It had the sound of an avalanche. All at once, a waterfall appeared over the mouth of the cave.

"That's what I was talking about," said Tonka.

There was a long pause.

"Hey, will sleeping behind a waterfall turn us into leprechauns?"

"Go to sleep, Maddie," said Tonka.

27

WHEN she awoke, she found Mouse's face mere inches from her own. He was so close, in fact, that she couldn't quite focus on him. Mouse opened his eyes and stared back without emotion. As he rolled away from her onto his back, she continued to watch him. Even through the netting, his brilliant blue eyes were hard to miss. A stripe of sunshine found his face through the gentle jostling of jungle flora in the morning breeze. His features were rugged, his jaw well set and sturdy. He had a lean, muscular frame that in many ways resembled Ray's though Mouse was a few inches shorter. Along the upper fringe of his beard on the right side of his face, were tiny flecks of scar tissue as if he'd once been thrust through a windshield or bits of shrapnel had ripped at his skin.

Mouse closed his eyes and let out a sleepy sigh. "It's not polite to stare."

"Sorry."

Mouse grinned through a yawn. "You remind me so much of your brother." He scratched his ankle with the heel of his other foot. "I know you're a gifted fighter and all, but, man, you even kick hard in your sleep. Nailed me a couple times right in the shin."

"Did I? I'm sorry…"

"*Mouse.* If we're gonna be working together, you're gonna have to grow accustomed to our call signs."

"All right… Mouse."

"That's better. That reminds me. We have to come up with a good one for you. Gimme some time. I'll come up with something."

She was silent for a few seconds. "So you guys were in Delta with Ray?"

"Mmm hmm. But just so you know, we don't say that word. We prefer to call it the Unit." He yawned again. "Followed him over here…to the dark side," he chuckled. "To the DX. He's the best, you know. There's no one better. Never seen someone as driven as he is. Of all the operators I've rubbed elbows with, Bronco dwarfs them all. Mostly because of his will to win. Guy is unstoppable. I mean, we're all very good at what we do, but… Bronco's the best."

Maddie wiggled within her mosquito netting, eventually creating enough room for herself to rise up on her left elbow. She lifted her head and gazed beyond Mouse, through the mouth of the cave and into a wall of jungle. The water on the rain-soaked leaves glistened in the sunlight like diamonds. A pair of chestnut-mandibled toucans shrieked from high up on the branch of a nearby barrigona tree. They seemed to be engaged in some form of duet…or duel. Their shrill screeches sometimes bled together into a haunting echo. However, these were not the only sounds that pierced the morning air. On the contrary, the jungle was alive with activity. It was as if the animal kingdom were singing in joyous refrain, celebrating the slight reprieve from the constant rain.

"To be in the DX, Maddie, you have to be among the most capable people on the planet. I get the sense that you're not quite sure you belong here yet. Let me be perfectly clear when I say that you do. You wouldn't be here if Job and the people back home didn't think you were able to do the things we do. And don't let the fact that you didn't serve in the military bother you. There are many things you'll learn as you go. Some things take years, it's true. But you're here for a reason. You made it through the DX Academy with flying colors from what I've heard. That's saying something. That means you've mastered some very special skills. I don't know how they kept you and Bronco from running into each other during your training, but…

"Bottom line, Maddie, you're here because people believe in you. The *right* people believe in you. And that includes me, Tonka and Evie. So be easy. And let's take care of our business. I know this op is a tough one for it to be your first… It's personal. I get it. But don't dare let emotion affect the way you operate. Ever. There's no time for it when the bullets start to fly. That's what debriefs are for. And what keeps the shrinks on the payroll.

"In those times when doubt raises its ugly mug, remember this two to the chest and one to the head. Put it down and move on. It's normal for it to come knocking sometimes, but give it no quarter in your mind."

Maddie nodded. "Thanks, Mouse."

"You bet. Now let's get something to eat. See how you like breakfast taco MREs." Mouse chuckled. "Just kidding."

Due to the limited amount of space in the cave, they had slept shoulder to shoulder. It had been awkward at first, her being a woman engaged to marry Wes, yet sleeping up against another man—a handsome man, at that. But Mouse was a true professional. He'd been the perfect gentlemen throughout the entire night, even going out of his way to make her feel more comfortable about the situation. As comfortable as anyone could be sleeping inside a jungle cave, that is.

In fact, so far they had all made her feel like a legitimate part of the team and not like some rookie who didn't have a clue. She was one of them. She was going to love working with these guys.

Maddie shed her netting and tied on her boots. Mouse did the same. "I'm starving," she said.

"Me, too."

"Freeze. Don't move." The voice was Tonka's though she couldn't see him.

Maddie's eyes flicked to Mouse. Like her, he was a statue. Then she saw it. The triangle-shaped head. Hooded eyes. The bright green snake was nearly three feet in length and was probing the lip of the cave. Like most snakes it looked angry, evil. Its tongue flitted in and out as it analyzed the air. The ghostly creature slithered closer to her left hand as she clutched a jumble of mosquito netting. It hesitated, poked its head into the air and looked at her. The tongue nearly touched her thumb. As it continued into their space, it dragged its length over her wrist. It felt like sandpaper against her skin.

Her nose began to itch. *Ignore it!*

"I'm serious, you guys. Don't move a muscle. That's an eyelash pit viper. One of the most venomous snakes out here. Stay calm. Just breathe."

She could see Tonka now in her periphery. He was off to her right just outside the cave. He was frozen, too.

There was a crunching sound on her left, but she dared not turn her head to see what had caused it. Slowly, something came into view beside her that made her want to burst out of the cave. It was long and tan and drifted across her field of view.

Another snake!

Wait. Not a snake. A stick.

Evelina hedged around the left side of the cave and inched the stick closer.

Then closer still.

The snake stopped and inspected the air again, raising its head a few inches into the air.

Maddie swallowed hard. Her eyes followed the snake as it lowered its head and moved closer to her torso. It would soon be in the area beneath her, in the triangle formed by her chest and arm as she remained propped on her elbow.

The stick drew closer.

"Trust me, Maddie. Just don't move," said Evie. "You, too, Mouse."

Evelina negotiated the stick into the cave a little further, placing it behind the snake with a sniper's patience and stealth. The tip of the stick was just above the viper's head. The snake rose up again without warning and brushed against the edge of the stick. Reflexively it recoiled and angled away, then moved around the obstruction and curved closer to her, licking the air as it went.

Thwap!

Maddie started as Evelina pinned the snake to the ground with the stick. Its mouth sprung open widely as if it were screaming. Evie held the stick firmly behind its head. She hunched over and lowered herself to her knees all the while exerting more pressure downward. She crawled forward into the cave. Soon she was right over it. With her right hand, Evelina reached down and grabbed the yellow-green snake where the stick had it pinned to the ground. She adjusted her grip then picked up the snake and shuffled backward out of the cave.

Evelina stood and held out the snake as if admiring it in some way. She turned the head toward her and studied its face. "That would have been bad," she said as she tilted the snake's head toward them. The snake writhed for a few seconds then just hung there in Evelina's fist.

Maddie crawled out of the cave and took a good look at it. "Kind of pretty."

"Kind of deadly," said Tonka. "Get rid of it."

Evelina plodded away from their small campsite and released the snake carefully onto the floor of the jungle. After she had returned, she grabbed her pack and summed up the episode by saying, "Well that was fun."

28

AS they hiked to their next waypoint they all shared bits and pieces about themselves. Maddie learned that Evelina was single and had five older brothers. Mouse and Tonka were both married. Tonka had two boys waiting back home; he talked about them constantly. Mouse had three girls—all of them had hair of gold like their mother. He and his wife were still holding out hope that the next one would be a boy.

"So what's it like being away from your families for so long and so often?"

Tonka grimaced. "It's hard, *very* hard. But, you know, someone has to do what we do. Someone has to go do the dirty work that most of the public doesn't want to even think about."

"But when we come home, it's like a honeymoon all over again," said Mouse with a bright smile. "Right, brother?"

Tonka blushed. "I guess."

It was like this until nearly dusk. The combination of the terrain, the humidity and the heat made for a tortuous trek. Not only did they have to forge through the native jungle foliage, but they had to deal with chowder-like mud and regular driving torrents of rain.

Darkness came quickly in the jungle, like someone all at once draped a blanket over their life-size diorama. Thankfully, they found the small Ye'kuana village before nightfall.

The villagers greeted them with less surprise than what they had anticipated. The foursome was led to a grouping of thatch-roofed huts that formed an elongated circle within a small clearing a few hundred yards from a river, which the continuous rain had turned into a monster that audibly raged.

Now, Maddie and the rest of the team were huddled around a table in the missionaries' domicile, their wraith-like faces illuminated by flickering candlelight.

Vic Humphreys was a cheerful, middle-aged man with gray hair and the wide shoulders of an NFL linebacker. "Man, this is the busiest I've ever seen it here."

"What do you mean?" said Evelina.

"Another group just came through. I thought y'all were them at first, returning because y'all had forgotten something or had decided the journey was too difficult." He chuckled.

"How long ago did they leave?" said Evelina.

"They came through a few hours ago. Five of them. Said they were Venezuelan Army and were hunting narco-traffickers rumored to be in the area. They were just passing through. We gave them some food for their journey."

"What is it, Mr. Humphreys?" said Maddie. She had a sense that there was something bothering him.

"Well, they were *dressed* like Venezuelan Army soldiers, but from the equipment they were carrying I find it very hard to believe that they have anything to do with the Venezuelan government, military or otherwise."

"What do you mean?"

"Well for one, of all the military officials I've seen in Venezuela, I've never seen one of them with a Kimber on his hip. Good gun, yes. But it's an American gun. Second, their web gear looked brand new. And third, their gear didn't match their story. They had ropes and climbing gear like you all. And from the size of their packs and the amount of rations they had with them, I'd guess they only intended to be in the jungle for another day or two. No more. That's why I offered them some food. They all looked fit, but it seemed to me anyway that the jungle was beginning to take its toll on them as it often does with people who are not accustomed to its unrelenting recalcitrance. This is not a place to be ill-prepared or ill-equipped. You can die out here real fast."

"You've got a sharp eye, Mr. Humphreys," said Maddie.

"Served in the Navy in my younger years. Spent most of my time on the *USS New Jersey*. That there was back when America had *real* leadership. My opinion: the world, not just America, desperately needs another Ronnie Reagan—someone with a backbone who stands for and advocates traditional American values. The culture these days… Ugh. It's sad and at the same time scary where the world is headed."

"Totally agree," said Maddie. "But God is still in control."

"Ain't no doubt about it."

Evelina brought up the plane crash in 1996 and advised why they were there, but made no mention of Triumph or the CIA.

"Y'all suspect foul play?" said Humphreys with incredulity.

"*Suspect*, yes. We're inclined to believe that the plane was brought down on purpose. But we have no proof to substantiate our suspicions. We're hoping to find it at the crash site."

"Who are ya then? CIA? FBI?"

"I really can't say, sir. But the work we're doing is important."

Humphreys face grew serious. "How can I help?"

"I'd like to show you some photographs," said Evelina. "See if maybe you recognize anyone from being at the crash site back then."

"It was a long time ago, but I'll do my best."

Evelina laid a stack of photos on the table and kept quiet as Humphreys went through each one. They were all official government headshots. The photos included several legitimate State Department officials who had worked in Venezuela back in the nineties and even some Agency people who did as well. There was also a dated photo of Hank McManus. There were no names attached to any of the photographs.

Several times Humphreys paused, went back a few photos before continuing on. When he was finished, he pushed the photos to the side save for one he kept on the table in front of him. He tapped it with his thick index finger. "This one right here. He was definitely there. I can't say with one hundred-percent certainty that *none* of the others were there—it was a long time ago—but I'm fairly confident none of them were. But this guy—," he tapped the photo of Hank McManus again. "*He* was *there*."

Evelina made a show of examining the photo then passed it to Maddie who in turn passed it to Mouse and so on.

"Told us he was from the State Department. Was kinda rude, too, considering the circumstances. I mean my friend and colleague had just died. That's why I remember him." He drew in a breath. "There were some other guys with him, too, but they didn't say a whole lot."

Evelina nodded as she accepted the photo from Tonka and placed it with the others back in her rucksack. "I understand you took some photos yourself back then. At the crash site."

"That's right. Mr. Mean Jeans ordered me not to, but I managed to snap a few anyhow. I didn't see what the big fuss was about."

"Mean Jeans?"

Humphreys smiled. "Guy wore mom jeans. Tight, brand new. Behaved like he was unfamiliar with, or at least didn't like, the outdoors. A real dandy, he was."

"Any chance we might be able to take a look at your photos at some point?" said Evelina.

"Sure. But I'm not due back in the States for quite some time. Although… I could have my son retrieve the pictures from my house. I keep them in a footlocker. Y'all are welcome to 'em as long as you promise to get 'em back to me when y'all are finished with 'em."

Evelina nodded. "That would be fantastic! Thank you. Now, getting back to the men that were here in the village. Do you know in which direction they were headed?"

Humphreys jerked his head. "Northwest. Toward the crash site, actually."

The team members glanced at each other.

"If you'd like, I could take y'all over there first thing in the morning. I'm sure I can get one of the locals to go along. I gotta tell ya, the villagers are pretty doggone intrigued with y'all. They're fascinated with yer blonde hair and her yellow eyes," he nodded toward Maddie. "I'm sure ya hear this a lot, miss, but your eyes look like honey. They're very unique. And you, too, there fella. Villagers ain't never seen anyone with eyes the color of the heavens. Y'all are kinda like celebrities here."

"Hear that, bro." Maddie elbowed Mouse in the ribs. "We're celebrities."

Mouse grinned. "Aw shucks."

◆ ◆ ◆

When they were finally alone, Evelina said, "Does anyone think it's suspicious that these five mystery guys dressed in military fatigues are headed toward the crash site, now of all times?"

They all nodded in agreement.

Maddie dragged her finger over the woven fronds of a hat that one of the villagers had given to her. "They could've been sent to destroy the crash site, you know, whitewash the entire scene from history just like they did with the Triumph records. In light of recent events in the UK, it makes logical sense for the person or persons responsible to try to wipe out any evidence anyone might find at the site. Think about it. As the investigation back home intensifies, someone will surely be sent down here to snoop around. If the wreckage is destroyed, then—"

"Then how do you prove anything? No records. No physical evidence. I'm tracking," said Mouse.

"Right." Maddie looked over at Tonka, who was working on his second plate of wild boar steak that the villagers had prepared for them. "Enjoying it, big man?"

Tonka held up a cashew then made a show of popping it into his mouth. "Need fuel. We burned a lot of calories in the past two days. I suspect tomorrow will be no different." He gobbled up a handful of acai berries and smiled with glee. "Good stuff."

Mouse picked a few cashews out the hand-carved wooden bowl on the table. He chomped them down as he spoke. "You think we should check in with Lynn Street, Evie?"

"No. I think that would be a mistake. If someone else *is* down here and headed to the crash site, they might have people monitoring the airwaves for comms traffic. No need to send up an electronic flare. Let's keep quiet for now. Our objectives were clear: make contact with the missionary and get to the crash site. We're halfway home."

"Yeah, you're right."

Maddie stole some berries off Tonka's plate. "You think those guys know we're here?"

Evelina took some berries, too. "Hard to say. We know they're ahead of us and we know where they're likely headed. Still, we need to be very careful. I'd like to take Humphreys up on his offer of a guided tour, but that would expose him and his friend to far too much danger. The entire village could suffer.

"With the jungle as thick as it is, it shouldn't be hard for a couple of D-boys to track a group of five men. Am I right?"

Mouse shook his head as he pushed a wad of chewing tobacco into his bottom lip.

"In any case, we have to get to the crash site before it's compromised. Everyone, prep your kit now. I want to be ready to clear out at first light."

◆ ◆ ◆

Maddie unzipped her rucksack and pulled out an HK MP7A1 submachine gun. She dropped the magazine, worked the action several times then eyed the empty chamber. She was back in the Academy now disassembling, reassembling various weapon systems. Pistols. SMGs. Sniper rifles. She'd been taught about countless firearms to include those she might find in foreign lands while on assignment. Her hands moved without much thought. She slid the optical sight onto the Picatinny rail then adjusted the sling to fit her frame. They each had their own hardware with exactly seven magazines of ammunition. The items had been shipped over in diplomatic pouch. *"Just in case,"* the courier had said.

The candlelight flashed and flickered as rain pounded the roof of the hut. Her desire to be with Wes was strong; she missed him terribly. The Academy had tested her mentally, physically and emotionally. Not only had it taxed every fiber of her being, but it had also kept her away from Wes for six long months. Was she doing the right thing by joining the DX? Tonka's words came back to her. *"Someone has to do what we do."*

Maddie set the gun down on a low wooden stand beside her wood and thatch cot. Next to it was a box of Bibles. Some were in English and some were in a language she didn't recognize. She picked up one of the English-language Bibles and opened it. The first verse that appeared caused a tear to squeeze from the corner of her eye.

"Cause me to hear Your lovingkindness in the morning, For in You do I trust; Cause me to know the way in which I should walk, For I lift up my soul to You."

She read the psalm again then a third time, committing it to memory. She did. She did trust in the Lord, the Sustainer of all things.

She lowered herself to her knees, leaned across the cot and folded her hands. She had done this many times as a little girl alone in her bedroom. With eyes closed and head bowed, she prayed the psalm she had just memorized back to God. She asked him to be with Wes, to help him know that she was thinking of him. She asked God to make His presence felt in Ray's heart, too. He loved their dad beyond what he could ever express in words. This operation had to be weighing on him greatly.

Give him strength, Lord. Give those of us here strength and endurance as well. Keep everyone safe from harm and grant us wisdom. And may it be all to Your glory. In Jesus' name. Amen.

In that very moment, all doubt, all reservations she had about joining the DX, about her abilities, about her path in life faded from her mind.

This was where she was supposed to be.

29

Málaga, Spain

THE reply to their blog post had come in less than an hour. If Moses had had any thoughts concerning their delay in responding to his initial proposal, he had made no mention of them.

On Job's orders Rainey had left Saul and Wells in Grimsby and took a taxi to Humberside Airport where he boarded a DX jet en route to Málaga, Spain. The three-hour flight had given him time to review his new identity documents, which Job had rushed over from a DX field office near London Station. But more so, he used the time to further digest Moses' response on the blog. He saw the words in his head as they had appeared on the laptop computer screen.

Indeed. He was. Ever hear Schumann's Spanische Liebeslieder, *Op. 138? Not among his best works, but the way in which it was performed last night in Madrid was simply divine. I've got tickets to see Maurizio Pollini next week in Seville. He's slated to play a number of Schumann's sonatas. I'm really hoping for the opportunity for us to meet after the show. One thing is for sure, when you heaR the masteR played by a pianist like Pollini, it will make you think you've died and gone to heaven. So looking forward to seeing him play.*

The message was clear and yet cleverly tucked within the post. *I'm really hoping for the opportunity for us to meet.* Then the two capitalized letter Rs.

Moses would be there.

And so would he.

In order to avoid anyone who might be watching for him at the airport, he had flown to Málaga; he would drive the two hours up to Seville later in the week. But when he approached the Hertz kiosk, he did find someone waiting for him. A man he knew well. A fellow operator from his former unit.

Angel "Fig" Figueroa stood off to the side of the Hertz desk, twirling a keyring on his finger. "Long time, no see."

They shook hands the way warriors do. It had been more than six months since he had last seen Fig. In that time, Rainey—Mouse and Tonka, too—had left Delta and permanently signed on to work in the CIA's Directorate X, formerly known as Directorate 12. Filling the spots they had left behind in the Joint Services Group were men like Fig, Babe and Jazz. JSG—pronounced "jay sig" by insiders—was a secret unit within the DX where some of America's most elite special operators went via temporary duty assignment to assist the CIA in carrying out some of its more difficult and assuredly dangerous clandestine and covert affairs. They came from places like the Army's ACE (aka Delta Force) and Special Forces, the Navy's DEVGRU, the Marine Raider Regiment, and elsewhere.

"So you're my Spanish tour guide?" asked Rainey in French-accented English.

"Si, señor," said Fig smiling like a used car salesman. When they were away from the crowds of tourists, Fig murmured, "The others are already up in Seville doing recce."

"Good."

"You do know that once you're inside, you'll be a sitting duck."

"Yes."

"You don't seem too concerned about the fact that this could be a setup?"

"I'm not, actually. In my mind, there are far easier ways to put me on the X," said Rainey casting his eyes toward the afternoon revelry. "If Moses was intent on killing me, I don't believe he would have come up with this elaborate story about my father. Add to that what we've already uncovered…"

Fig pulled the rented SsangYong Rodius into the street. "I get what you're saying, Bronc, but maybe that's part of the strategy. Maybe logic is part of the deception, if you know what I mean."

"I'm tracking. But… Just call it a gut feeling."

"Could be gas," said Fig with eyebrows raised.

Rainey didn't even crack a smile. "Anything's possible."

There was something nagging at him though. Before leaving the safe house in Grimsby, Rainey had asked Job what the other thing was that he wished to discuss prior to his consideration of a meeting with Moses. In true Job Jackson fashion, he deflected the question and told him it could wait.

"I don't know how you listen to this stuff, bro." Fig had switched on the car stereo on and found it tuned to a local classical music station.

"What?"

"This classical music crap."

"It's not for everyone, I'll grant you that. But give it a chance. You just might be surprised at how quickly it grows on you."

Fig frowned.

"I'm serious."

"I know you are. That's the problem."

♦ ♦ ♦

From the safety of their hotel room, they spent the next few days communicating back and forth over a secure link with the team in Seville. In between briefings, rather than suffer the boredom of being cooped up in the hotel room—nice as it was at the seaside Hotel Vincci Málaga—Rainey explored the city and quickly fell in love with its rich history and transcendent charm.

On one of his first expeditions away from the hotel, he discovered the Alcazaba fortress and the Castillo de Gibralfaro. He imagined what it must have been like in ancient times, looking out over the sea at sunrise from atop the castle walls. The Burger King he'd passed on his way there—a different type of castle for a different type of people—should have seemed strangely at odds with the looming medieval ramparts that rose up over the highway. Yet somehow it worked. Málaga seemed to be a place where old and new coexisted in perfect harmony.

On the second day, his penchant for craftsmanship—the idea of making, forging, fixing with his bare hands—caused him to seek out Pedregalejo a little further up the coast, in the old fishing district. He had seen a brochure in the hotel lobby that advertised the boat building there. He was soon pointed to a man named Pepe who was teaching a group of men and women out on the beach how to build *jábegas* in the way the Phoenicians once did. Rainey stripped off his shoes and socks, rolled his khakis up to his calves and joined them. Fifteen minutes in, his shirt became damp with sweat, so he peeled it off and let the sunshine rain down on his lean, muscled torso. Even after the others had tired and gone, he continued to work.

It was freedom, a man set loose to his labor.

For hours, he lathed and sanded oak timbers on the shore of paradise with Pepe offering occasional good counsel to his handiwork. After he had finished, he and Pepe shared a few spits of grilled sardines, which had been salted and cooked over an open flame in a sand-filled wooden boat. The aromatic mixture of fire, grilled fish and sea air made him never want to leave. When that time finally did come and the sky was nearly indigo, Pepe smiled proudly and labeled him a natural shipbuilder. Rainey was welcome back any time he chose to return. The sea and the timber would be waiting, Pepe said.

Mimicking the patterns and pursuits of a tourist, Rainey drifted through the designer shops along Calle Marqués de Larios and the surrounding pedestrian thoroughfares. From the shadowed tile walkways that wove between the multi-storied buildings, he marveled at the exquisite architecture, the detailed workmanship. The years it must have taken to design and build such intricate structures. Obvious were the historic influences, which dated all the way back to 770 BC, when the

Phoenicians founded the city. During each one of his little daytime escapades, he discovered something new, some hidden gem—the watchmaker's shop, the quaint little bookstore that smelled of old paper, leather and fresh-brewed coffee. He toured the Picasso museum in the former Palacio de Buenavista, the Museo Interactivo de la Música on Calle Beatras and even indulged in a bit of *helado* as he strolled past the Roman amphitheater.

In the evenings, Rainey split time between La Tetería and the Café del Viajero, where he found he could tuck in and relax, sip some coffee and really let his mind go to work. Through all of it, even when ordering from the baristas, he remained in character, speaking only in French-accented English. For he was now Lucien Joubert—venture capitalist by day, itinerant playboy by night, adrenaline junkie at all points in between. The passport in his pocket may have labeled him a Canadian, but Monsieur Joubert—the happy traveler he was—considered himself to be a citizen of the world.

It was strange though and perhaps the reason he was feeling a little guilty. Of all the thoughts about his father and the current operation, one thing continued to tug at the fabric of his soul. He realized it now as he milled through the Old City, seeing couples mingling about, hand in hand and arm in arm: he desperately wanted someone to hold and to love. He hated to admit it, especially after the little dust up with Maddie outside their childhood home, but... He missed Kayla.

She told me to tell you she said hi.

A breeze swept in from the coast, bringing with it the sweet smell of the sea. Rainey lingered a few minutes more then turned and headed back to the hotel.

He stepped into the elevator and hit the button for the top floor. Just as the doors were beginning to close, two boys, each about eight years old and soaking wet from having just come from the swimming pool, scampered in.

Rainey's expression softened and he managed a friendly grin. "Bringing some of the pool back to your room, eh?"

They looked at him quizzically then ignored him altogether. The boy closest to him shook his shaggy wet mop of hair, lashing streaks of water over Rainey's face and shirt. At the same time, as if suddenly spurred on by a demon, the other began pushing all the buttons on the panel in front of them. They fell into loud laughter then started pushing each other, each time harder than the last. The one closest to Rainey stepped on his shoe and made no attempt to apologize or to move away from him. The young hooligan stepped on his shoe again when the other boy shoved him.

When the doors opened and the torment was over, the boys sprinted from the lift and disappeared down the hall, their feet thumping loudly against the thin carpeted floor.

Rainey stepped off and looked at the trail of wet footprints the boys had left behind. He stood there for a second and spat, *"Petits morveux."* Little brats.

30

THE drive up to Seville took more time than expected due to a three-car crash just outside La Puebla de Cazalla. It was just past 7:00 P.M. when they rolled into the eastern edge of the city. The concert wasn't until tomorrow night so there was still plenty of time to walk the streets around the Teatro de la Maestranza to get a better sense of distances and sight lines. Rainey had studied the street maps, surveillance images and video so thoroughly during the past several days it felt like he had been here before.

The safe house, a spacious two-bedroom affair, was nearly equidistant from the theater to the northwest and the Catedral de Seville to the northeast. The men who greeted him and Fig were in good spirits considering they had been confined to a small grid of the city for the past several days and had been extremely busy.

"Looks like you got a little sun down in Málaga."

"Hey, Babe. Yeah, I got a little."

"How nice for you," said Jazz from the kitchen. "While you've been checking out the girls on the beach, we've been sweating our nuts off up here."

"Ignore him. He's a little cranky today," said Babe. Jazz responded by spewing an obscenity which Babe ignored with a chuckle. "But seriously, we all understand what's at stake here."

Babe and Jazz were both Delta operators like Fig. The three of them were now attached to the DX's Joint Services Group along with another teammate named Booster, who was still back home recovering from injuries he had sustained last year. Fig, Babe and Jazz would be Rainey's security force. Shooters, if need be. Deltas were among the best in the world. But hopefully no guns would be needed here in Seville.

"Any updates on Moses?" said Babe.

"None that I'm aware of. Job's been quiet. He's dealing with what happened in London. I think we've had all the updates we're gonna get," explained Rainey.

"What happened in London?" said Jazz.

"The Brits and Job tracked down the guy who they believe was behind the attacks in Hull. They were about to raid the guy's flat when the whole place blew. They're still investigating, but word from Job is that the guy worked for Scotland Yard, and he was dead before the explosion. Preliminarily they suspect the blast was triggered when the raid team tossed in the stun grenade. Killer must have rigged it that way. A man was seen running from the back of the apartment building just before the explosion."

"Crazy, bro."

"No doubt," said Rainey. "Where's Shepherd?"

"It was his turn to run for grub. He should be back soon," said Babe.

Rainey nodded. "Good deal."

Shepherd, that is, Mark Alcott, had been Rainey's detachment commander back when they had served together in 3rd Special Forces Group. He had later moved on to the Defense Intelligence Agency as a senior intel ops officer before finally landing in Job Jackson's shop at the CIA. He was put to work in various capacities within the DX to include running surveillance operations in some of the most hostile environments on the planet. Rainey was thrilled that Alcott was involved in this operation; the guy was one of his biggest role models. He was a gifted leader of men. And leading men in combat was no easy task. What's more, Mark Alcott was a faithful man of God.

When the food finally came, Rainey and the team reviewed the operational details once again. Rainey noted where the men would be inside and outside of the theater, where the exits were in relation to his seat. Alcott had already been to two shows earlier in the week and with the aid of the others had meticulously noted the security procedures inside, the number of staff present, traffic patterns outside and where local police were likely to be posted to facilitate the ingress and egress of attendees. There was only a cursory inspection of handbags, no pat-downs. That was good and bad. Rainey would be able to wear a gun. So would any hostiles.

Jazz would stay at the safe house and monitor the radio net and a computer screen on which would be displayed everyone's physical location by way of the GPS beacons they would be wearing. Jazz and Alcott had initially had a minor dispute over this point, because Jazz thought Alcott should run the op from the safe house, be the eyes and ears of it all. But Alcott overruled him. He would be inside the theater. Mark Alcott was a man who liked to lead from the front.

Rainey examined the tuxedo he would be wearing. *A tux. Ugh.* Rainey was vehemently opposed to formal wear. Unless, of course, it was part of the operation. He slipped his arms into the jacket and spied himself in the bedroom mirror.

"Fits great," said Alcott.

"It's a little snug in the arms." Several times, Rainey practiced drawing a pistol that he would be wearing at the small of his back. He twisted to his left, twisted to his right, bent forward. "It'll work."

"Good, because that was the last one I could find in your size. You good?"

"I'm good."

"All right. Let's go for a walk."

◆ ◆ ◆

Rainey wore a short-sleeved, blue linen shirt, which he'd left completely unbuttoned over a plain white T-shirt and tan cargo shorts. He pulled on a Sevilla FC ball cap then stuffed a pillow from the sofa under his T-shirt, which made him look thirty pounds heavier, and secured it in place with KT tape. To complete his ensemble, he strapped on a pair of black Teva sandals.

As he was adjusting the pillow and the tape beneath his shirt in the bathroom mirror, Fig leaned in and handed him a Glock 19. Rainey eased back the slide, made sure it was hot then pushed it into an HTC holster he wore inside his waistband.

"Be careful, will ya?" said Fig.

"Will do."

Alcott soon joined him in the living room, wearing a Real Madrid knockoff jersey and a wig of long black hair held in place by a thin, black leather headband.

"Aw man, Shep. You look like the *Barbara* of Seville," said Rainey.

"Hilarious."

"Or maybe Cher," jabbed Babe.

"C'mon, Babe. He's a lot prettier than Cher."

Alcott shook his head. "Everyone's a comedian. Let's just go, okay."

From the safe house, Rainey and Alcott looped around to Calle Almirante Lobo where they turned westbound. They crossed over Paseo Cristoból Colón and stopped when they reached the corniche, pretending to look at the lights out on the Canal Sevilla-Bonanza. A dinner cruise drifted by at a snail's pace. A young girl standing in a cone of light waived at them from the aft deck. Rainey, the stereotypical Seville tourist, waived back with a happy smile.

"Babe will be anchored down the canal a few hundred meters to the north. He's last resort, but also your fastest way outta here."

"Gotcha."

They headed north along the waterfront and, during their nonchalance, inspected the façade of the Teatro de la Maestrana.

"I'm sure you noticed from the intel that the sightlines aren't great out here due to the traffic and the trees. Rest assured it will be worse tomorrow night with all the people milling around out here. You can also expect a decent police presence. The two groups I saw earlier this week were not nearly as well-known as Pollini. Trust me. It's going to be crowded."

They worked their way back across Cristoból Colón and continued east on the north side of Calle Dos de Mayo.

"So how're you doing?"

"Whaddya mean?" said Rainey.

"I mean, how are you holding up? This can't be easy."

Rainey shrugged.

"You believe he's really alive?"

Rainey squinted down the narrow roadway, past pedestrians and people riding bikes. "I want to believe. I want him to be alive more than anything."

Alcott patted him on the shoulder. "We're all rooting for you, brother. If he's alive, we'll find him. That's a promise. We're all behind you on this."

"Thanks. It means a lot."

Rainey stopped several times pretending to check his phone, an oblivious tourist out for an evening stroll. Each time he did, the wind blew the hair from Alcott's wig against his face. Rainey glanced over at him as he swatted the strands away. With his head tilted down into the glow of his phone, he chuckled.

"What?" said Alcott.

"Dude, you look like a washed-up, Spanish soccer star."

"Looks who's talking, chubs." Alcott drummed Rainey's pillow belly with the back of his fist.

Rainey scratched his doughy belly in a way that caused both of them to snicker.

"All right. Let's head back. I'm as prepared as I'm ever gonna be under the circumstances."

31

THE following night, Rainey straightened his bow tie in the reflection of his car window a few blocks away then adjusted the cuffs of his shirt as he headed toward the theater. "All right, people. Showtime."

"*Good to go,*" came Alcott's voice in his earpiece. *"It's starting to fill up in here, Bronco. I'd get moving."*

"Roger, that."

Rainey walked the sidewalk and joined a string of others moving toward the entranceway. As they turned to go inside, his eyes moved upward to the large letters affixed to the façade of the Teatro de la Maestranza. Thoughts snapped in his mind like the flash bulbs of paparazzi cameras. Is this a trap? Who the devil is Moses? Will he show? How does he know Dad?

I'm trusting you, Lord. You're my shield.

A sleepy-looking man in a black coat and starched white shirt greeted him at the door then waved him along. A modern lobby dominated by wood opened up on either side of him. A sea of people, some in black tie others in no tie at all meandered about. He detected several languages right off the bat. English was still the dominant tongue, but he also heard Spanish, German, French, Chinese and of course Italian.

It's a regular U.N. in here.

♦ ♦ ♦

A man dressed in a lightweight gray jacket, khakis and leather brogues that were worn at the toes, stood along the corniche in front of the theater. He had been chain-smoking cigarettes by the water's edge as he watched for his target. Just a moment ago, he had seen him enter through the main entrance.

The man's weathered face glowed in the flame of his lighter as he fired up a fresh cigarette. He flipped the Zippo closed then dropped it into his pants pocket. He pinched the cigarette with two of his sausage-like fingers and sucked in deeply, his eyes shrinking into mere slits. Letting the cloud of blue smoke escape his lungs, he spoke into the radio mic in his shirtsleeve.

"He's here."

♦ ♦ ♦

Zarek Tarło sat upright in the electrician's van further down the promenade. He echoed the words to his team members scattered inside and around the building. The two men in uniform standing by their police motorbikes on the street corner to the south. The mustached man walking the sidewalk selling carnations from a cardboard box. The handsome couple strolling hand in hand by the waterfront, young lovers and dangerous killers each. The striking raven-haired woman inside, milling about the crowd in a tight black dress, a friendly expression on her face and an Astra A-70 strapped to the inside of her left thigh.

"All right people. Do not lose sight of him. And be careful. Reagan Rainey is very smart and extremely dangerous."

Tarło slipped out his phone and dialed a number.

"Yes?" said Stedman Carter.

"He's here, just like we figured."

"Good. Let me know when it's over."

"Will do." Tarło pocketed the phone and gazed down the street through the windscreen of the van.

The driver beside him restlessly played with the strap of the Vityaz-SN in his lap. "Why don't we just kill Rainey and be done with it?"

"Because Rainey is not the only threat now. This Moses person is a big wild card. Could be an even bigger problem than Rainey. We play it smart, though, and Rainey will lead us right to him. Then we kill them both."

◆ ◆ ◆

Rainey sliced his way through the glitterati with grace and poise. He held his head in the confident manner of a man who was accustomed to such pomp and circumstance yet had no desire for it. Once again, he was Lucien Joubert, a man blessed with considerable means and the rugged good looks that could steal hearts. Break them, too. Monsieur Joubert was a friendly but shy aristocrat. Whether he was aware of it or not, Rainey—er, Monsieur Joubert—had managed to strafe the senses of an ample-breasted woman in a silvery blue evening gown moving about the throngs like a shark circling its prey in shallow water. The woman came close once then retreated just as quickly. She seemed to be sizing him up, getting a feel for his movements, his countermeasures.

"There's a blonde on your three," Alcott warned. *"She's checking you out pretty good. Don't let it go to your head."*

Rainey smirked, but it came out as a polite smile to anyone who might have noticed.

"Remember, Bronc. Moses could be a woman."

His head tilted slightly to the right as he feigned an inquisitive perusal of the venue's interior design. He first noticed her bound-up golden locks, then the rest of her, which was shamelessly spilling from the top of her gown. Out of the corner of his eye, he could tell she was looking right at him.

He continued exploring the lobby with his discerning craftsman's eye. As if by accident, he allowed his gaze to land on her again. She was staring at him now in an obvious manner, her forehead lowered, her breasts rising and falling as she breathed. Rainey's inner, early warning detection system was pinging loudly inside his head. The woman had acquired her target and was now locked on.

To him.

Rainey kept his eyes moving as any normal person would do while standing in one place for any length of time. At one point, he checked his watch and then for the third or fourth time read through the evening's program.

Again, Alcott's voice in his ear: *"I'm taking my seat. I'll watch for you."*

Rainey had a tiny mic in his bow tie, but made no attempt to reply to Alcott's radio traffic.

Alcott would be in the second balcony in an aisle seat, able to quickly move if the need arose. Because Moses mentioned in his blog post that he was hoping to meet after the show, the team figured that was when he planned to make his move. But they would be prepared for anything, at any time.

Rainey followed behind a rotund man that smelled of onions and aftershave. The man moved like a penguin a few inches at a time toward a set of grand double doors that had just been propped open. An attendant in a burgundy vest and pressed black slacks stood on either side ready to instruct people on how to find their seats.

When the big man in front of him shimmied forward again, Rainey was able to spy the upper recesses of the auditorium. The house lights were turned up. It had been quite some time since he had been to the symphony. Last time, in fact, had been with his mother after returning home from his fourth overseas deployment. He loved everything about the symphony. The intimacy, the sense of order and logic, but most of all, he loved the tranquility. It was the complete opposite of how it was in combat.

As if he had been chosen to lead a battlefield charge, the crowd in the lobby suddenly began huddling around him. He imagined himself a cracker that someone had just tossed into a fish pond.

Pangs of claustrophobia tickled at his senses as more and more people poured into the lobby. The hordes squeezed together to become one mass. He became instantly aware of every touch, every poke, every nudge. He focused for a moment on the pistol in his waistband. Could he reach it? He would have to clear bodies, but yes he could get to it if need be.

Rainey turned to his right and greeted an old man roughly his height with a scrawny, gray beard and a liver-spotted head of thinning white hair. Behind wire-rimmed spectacles, were a set of black eyes that, perhaps once vibrant, were now clouded and dull. Their shoulders touched as a riptide of concert-goers pushed closer. The old man's eyes brightened as he offered an awkward smile, a wordless acknowledgment of their mutual suffering.

In the next instant, the throng shifted and the old man was sent into him with a whispered grunt. With a fluid grace, Rainey stepped to his left to counter the assault. As he did so, his left elbow connected with someone on the other side of him. He turned to offer a quick apology and found the woman in the silvery blue dress, the Shark as it were, staring up at him, a shock of desire in her eyes.

"*Excuse-moi, madame.*"

"*Ah, un Français,*" she said, continuing in muddled French. "I was guessing either Italian or…*Israeli,*" she murmured. "But no. You are a Frenchman. How *marvelous.*" She jiggled as she giggled.

"Close," said Rainey with a grin that seemed to urge her on. "Canadian. *French* Canadian."

The woman made a pouting face. "Canadian? You are a long way from home, my dear. You are new to Seville then, yes?"

"First time, yes." Rainey's eyes continued about the room, searching for threats, for anyone who might be focused on him.

"I'm Pilar. My friends call me Pía." She held out her dainty right hand, which was adorned with a gleaming ruby in an intricate, gold setting.

Rainey took it in his rough hand and smiled. "Lucien."

"You have very strong hands, Lucien." She said the name as if she were savoring the sound of it on her lips. "*Lucien.* I knew a Lucien once. At university. A real scoundrel, he was. Are you a scoundrel, *Lucien?*"

"Only on weekends."

The Shark erupted in laughter, which her dress could hardly contain. A few people in the immediately vicinity took notice. While some of the men stole a glance or two, their female counterparts in one way or another signaled that they had been affronted, but in a civilized kind of way. A subtle roll of the eyes. A carefully, upturned nose. Though, as Rainey would later recall, there was one woman who dared to rebuff the mores of the symphony and whispered a rather loud unflattering Italian version of the word "tramp."

"Well, Lucien," she said, raising an eyebrow. "Perhaps we'll bump into each other after the show."

"Perhaps."

A man behind him tapped him on the shoulder and pointed him forward with the patience of a drill sergeant. Rainey turned and offered a polite apology. When he turned back, the Shark was gone.

"You think she's Moses?"

"I don't know," he said, discreetly covering his mouth. "Could be. Right now the odds-on favorite."

He walked into the auditorium. It was considerably cooler than the lobby. The air was fresher, too, with a hint of molasses. There was also something else. Something more pungent. He canted his head backward as he breathed it in. It was glue, the type used to affix industrial carpet to a cement floor.

Rainey walked to his row and sidestepped across to his seat. He folded the bleached wood chair out and relaxed into the pale olive cushion. He sighed with an amused grin, crossed his legs and made a dispassionate attempt at finding the Shark.

Alcott: *"She's on your four. Midway up the second terrace. Five seats in. Don't look back or she'll notice. I'll be your eyes. You just enjoy the show."*

32

Southern Venezuela

THEY had tracked the men ahead of them without much trouble. Having to do little bushwhacking themselves made their trek both easier and faster. They came to an abrupt halt when they suddenly heard voices carrying through the vegetation in front of them. Crouched down now, in the flora with weapons at the ready, they each remained frozen and silent.

Maddie could feel her heart pumping in her chest. Her eyes were wide with anticipation as they swept back and forth looking for movement through the tree trunks, leaves and vines.

"Here."

"Wait. Let me get my footing."

Mouse looked at Maddie. The two voices were thick with a strange accent. "Russian?"

She shook her head as she strained her ears.

"She's right," said Evelina. "It's definitely not Russian."

"Okay. Give it to me."

"Careful."

"Almost sounds Italian," said Maddie.

Evelina squinted. "Maybe." Evelina looked at her GPS unit. "Okay, the plane is about three hundred meters ahead. There's the ravine." She held up the small screen so they could each see.

According to the information Humphreys had provided, the plane had crashed into a tangled mess on the side of a deep ravine, which wasn't wide enough for a helicopter to access. And the river below was too steep and fast-moving for any attempt to reach it by boat. The rescue team, Humphreys had said, had to stage a short distance away and then rappel down over the rocky cliff to get to the wreckage. The bodies had to be extricated and hauled back up on long rope lines. It was an incredibly dangerous enterprise especially during the rainy season, much like it was now.

Evelina had everyone perform a quick comms check then pointed to Maddie and Mouse. "Okay. You guys, see if you can work your way around to the eastern side of the ravine. Try to get eyes on the plane. The jungle is thick, so you're not going to be able to get great overwatch, but do the best you can. Tonka and I will stay here until we hear from you."

"Roger that," said Maddie.

"Keep your head down, rook," said Tonka.

"You, too, big man," said Maddie, patting him on the shoulder as she and Mouse set off through the jungle.

◆　◆　◆

Maddie and Mouse found a small stream about three yards wide cutting through the flora. They had to watch their footing on the wet rocks, but it was a hundred percent better than having to whack their way through the native jungle with a machete. They moved quickly down the slope keeping one hand free to brace against slips and falls, the other one firmly on their weapons. Maddie's HK MP7A1 was the size of a large pistol and was easy to maneuver even with the suppressor screwed on. Mouse's Citizen Arms SBR was slightly less so.

The stream widened as it neared the edge of the ravine. Maddie stepped carefully out of the water and steadied herself against a rubber tree. As she waited for Mouse to follow suit, she gazed out over the ravine. The other side was twenty yards away. She followed the chalky limestone cliff facing her down to the white froth of a river that was raging from left to right.

"Whaddya think?" said Mouse gazing over the edge beside her.

"I'd say it's probably a forty- or fifty-meter drop." She inched closer to the ledge and craned her neck to the left. "I don't see any plane."

"Must be up around that bend there."

She nodded. "If we can cross somehow, we'll have the high ground. We'll be able to see what they're up to."

"Hard part is getting over there without breaking our necks."

"You're not scared are you?" she said.

Mouse frowned as he looked down again. Water was plowing through the jungle with a steady roar.

She smiled. "C'mon. I think I have an idea."

"I'm not gonna like this, am I?"

She shed her rucksack and pulled out a climbing rope and three locking carabiners. "Still remember how to do a Tyrolean traverse?"

"Yep, I was right. I don't like it."

Mouse unslung his rifle and propped it against a tree stump. While Maddie rigged up her harness, he found a long, flat rock and tied one end of her rope around it several times until he had a rudimentary grappling hook. He then walked to the edge of the ravine, checked for anyone who might be watching then looked for a target. He stepped a little closer to the edge and made sure of his footing and that the loose loops in his left hand were good to go. He looked back over his shoulder and made sure Maddie was clear then wound the rock in the air five or six times and threw it over to the other side. The rock landed in the middle of a strangler tree. Slowly, he drew up the slack and pulled the rope backward. It caught. He tugged on it again this time with far more force. Suddenly, it let loose and he fell backward. Maddie quickly reached out and braced him.

They exchanged glances.

Mouse checked his grappling hook and, satisfied it was still in good shape, repeated the process of throwing it over the ravine. This time the rock held. He tied off the rope on their side of the ravine then tested it with his full weight.

"She good?" said Maddie.

"As good as she's gonna get."

"Okay. Cover me."

"Yeah, yeah. Just don't fool around out there."

"Don't worry," said Maddie. "I don't plan to. Wait till I'm set then I'll cover you as you cross."

"Roger that."

Maddie clipped herself onto the rope and spun the carabiner lock then clipped her rucksack on as well. As she pulled herself across the rope, the pack would drag behind.

She sat down in the harness, her life at the mercy of the rope line and Mouse's makeshift grappling hook. She set out across the ravine. A third of the way across, she looked down then up river. She scrutinized the edge of the jungle then continued pulling herself over in a steady hand-over-hand technique.

Once she had her feet on terra firma, she unclipped herself and her ruck from the rope. She quickly dug out her MP7 and tucked into a spot from which she could cover Mouse. When she was set, she gave him a thumbs-up.

He acknowledged her signal then knelt down. Maddie then focused her attention up and down the tree line. In her peripheral vision, she saw Mouse fold up his rifle, remove the suppressor and push both items into his rucksack then clip onto the rope. He was halfway over when all at once the heavens unleashed and began to pour buckets. She squinted as the rain pelted her face.

Great.

33

OUSE wiped his eyes. He was dangling from the rope and facing the sky as the torrents pounded him. Bobbing up and down ever so slightly he turned his head and sucked in some oxygen. He put both hands back on the rope and was about to start moving again when the line began to vibrate. At first he thought it was the heavy downpour, but then the rope lurched like someone had given it a good tug. His eyes shot wide as he whipped his head toward his grappling hook.

It was still holding.

He turned back the other way, focused on the tree to which he had anchored the rope.

What the…

Someone was standing by the line. A man in military uniform with an AK slung over his shoulder. He had the rope gripped in one hand and a long blade in the other. He was sawing the knife back and forth.

◆ ◆ ◆

The rain stung her face. She was soaked all the way through yet she remained focused on the other side of the ravine. Somewhere within the jungle, there were five armed men.

Maddie's eyes swept back and forth. The rain had turned the tan limestone on either side of the divide to a dull brown. It had also brought with it a fog that was getting thicker by the second. She held the gun like they'd taught her in the Academy. She was a natural, her instructors had said.

Maddie flexed her hands one by one as she gripped the gun. The traverse had caused a slight cramping in her fingers.

Water dripped from her eyelashes, her nose. Her head moved slowly back and forth. Her honey-colored eyes mere slits. She noticed Mouse in her periphery but did not look at him. Not until his body movements began to convey alarm.

Maddie squinted into the rain and fog.

Oh my gosh!

A man on the other side had appeared: an apparition in the miasma. Dark gray against the jungle background. He was…

Cutting through the rope.

◆ ◆ ◆

Mouse steadied himself with his left hand clinging to the rope. He reached for the FNS-9 on his right hip, wrapped his hand around the grip and pulled it from the holster as he bobbed up and down in his harness. The rope lurched and he dropped an inch or two. His heart was pounding in his chest.

He brought the gun up along his leg. He had to be careful he didn't hit the rope. He was about to squeeze the trigger when he noticed a black smudge suddenly appear just above the man's left eyebrow.

The knife fell first. It slid out of the man's hand, deflected off an exposed tree root and like a cliff diver gracefully arced into the air before finally disappearing into the river below. The man went next but was far less graceful. His head fell back and his knees folded over. He lifelessly clambered against a tree then sloughed forward. He went down on an angle until he hit the first jagged rock jutting from the side of the ravine. This sent him into a slow spin. And that's how he entered the strong foamy current.

The gun dangling in his hand, Mouse watched as the water quickly whisked his would-be killer away for all eternity. He holstered the gun and cast his eyes toward Maddie's position. He got another thumbs up. He returned the hand signal and quickly finished his traverse.

◆ ◆ ◆

Maddie stayed in position until Mouse had his rifle out and was ready to go.

"Thanks."

"Just doing my job," said Maddie.

"Yeah, but that was one heck of a shot."

Maddie shrugged. "C'mon. I want to see what these guys are up to."

They crept uphill through the jungle, stepping around walls of thick, lush and very wet vegetation. The rain was letting up a bit, but still came down in a stiff shower. Soon they had worked their way past the bend in the ravine. They moved toward the edge slowly, careful not to lose their footing and stumble.

In order to stay hidden, they remained about six feet back from the edge. They tucked behind some logs that formed a slanted T and gazed down across the ravine.

There, perched on the other side of the ravine, about twenty-five yards down, was a small white plane—a Cessna 206—turned various shades of brown from the years of mud running over it. One of the wings was snapped in half.

"Can you read the tail number?" asked Maddie tugging out a pair of Steiners.

Mouse pressed his cheek against the stock of his rifle and peered through his scope. "Yes."

Maddie popped the lens caps off. Her lips mirrored Mouse's as he read them off. This was the place where her father had died.

Dad. *Daddy.*

She swallowed hard, lowered the binoculars and took a deep breath. She let it out. Then looked again.

The aft section of the cabin and fuselage were still intact, but the cockpit had been decimated. It was as if the plane had opened its mouth and vomited its contents. Seats, instrument panels, wires, and other indeterminate chunks of manmade items lay scattered about at the front of the plane.

Maddie keyed her radio. "Bucket One, do you copy?".

"Roger, Four. I copy." Evelina's voice was scratchy with static.

Maddie keyed her radio again as Mouse kept watch through his scope. "We're in position. They are now minus one."

"Come again?"

"There is one less man in their party."

"I copy. You think he alerted any of the others?"

"Not sure, but he forced my hand."

"Roger that. We're about forty meters southwest of the plane. We have eyes on two of them. Looks like they're spreading out to set up watch. Another one is going down over the edge."

Maddie cast the binoculars upward, following the rocks, rutted mud and tiny waterfalls to the top of the ravine. A man in a harness was rappelling down over the edge. He was dressed the same as the man who had tried to kill Mouse. Venezuelan military uniform. "Roger that. I've got one guy on a rope headed toward the plane."

"You guys see anyone else from your pos?"

"Negative. Just the guy on the rope."

"Roger that, Four. We need to— Stand by. Ah crap!" Evelina's voice was cut off by a crackle of automatic gunfire.

34

W*E are in contact! I repeat we are in contact!"* Piercing cracks of gunfire thundered across the jungle.

Maddie looked at Mouse with pleading eyes.

He nodded. "Go."

She heard Mouse trying to raise Evelina and Tonka on the radio as she tore off through the jungle. Neither of them responded. The gunfire grew louder and more intense. A small war had erupted.

Maddie scrambled through the foliage toward a large tree that lay across the ravine. She had considered going back to the rope line where they had traversed earlier, but that was too far away. Plus, the guy with the blade may have compromised the rope's integrity. Thing could snap when she was halfway across. It was still a big gamble to climb across the tree, but she decided to go for it. Her friends were in trouble. They needed help.

Now.

Maddie shot up a steep grade, mounted a knoll before sliding her way toward the downed tree. She was careful not to go too fast here. If she slipped, she would be a goner. The tree was about the diameter of a telephone pole, more than adequate to hold her weight. She rubbed it with her gloved hand. The rain on the smooth tree might as well have been ice.

More gunfire

It's now or never.

Maddie checked up and down the ravine for enemy soldiers then swung her MP7 around to her back. She hefted herself onto the log and began to inch away from the bank. A loud burst of gunfire startled her just as she was gaining her balance. Her left foot slipped. She felt herself falling. She reached out and bear-hugged the log with all her might. The wood was rough and greasy against her face. She stilled her dangling legs and tried to take control of her senses. Her right hand began to lose purchase on the tree. It became a claw. Scraping for any bit of friction or crack it could find. But it was no use. She was slipping.

No! Please, God! No!

She dug deep, lunged and adjusted her grip. She locked onto the tree, her heart hammering away inside her chest like a riotous mob pounding on a police car. Maddie concentrated on her breathing and her vice grip on the log.

Get control. You're good, Maddie. You're good.

She stopped writhing and just hung. She took several giant breaths and then swung her right leg out. The tip of her boot brushed a rock. She tried again. The rain began to pick up. It was as if someone were dousing her with a fireman's hose.

Focus! Get a grip! You can do this. You have *to do this.*

Her arm, shoulder and chest muscles were on fire. Maddie kicked out again. This time, the sole of her boot stuck. She started inching herself up. Suddenly the ground gave way. She felt her stomach drop. Her eyes shot wide. She hugged the tree even tighter, trying to take in gulps of air to replenish her muscles which were desperate for oxygen.

This is it, Maddie. One more time. Do this or it's over.

A rifle belched from somewhere nearby on the other side of the ravine. She ignored it. She kicked out once again. Her boot landed on a rock. She held it there and swallowed more gulps of air. Then with everything she had in her, she pulled herself back up onto the fallen tree. When she had finally regained her balance, she just lay there, arms and legs hanging on either side of the tree. She closed her eyes and let her lungs work.

Wow. That was close. Thank you, Lord. Thank you. Thank you. Thank you.

She focused on distributing her weight evenly as she slowly set off again. As she moved across the wet log, the plane soon came into view on her left. She looked toward the other end of the log, then up and down the edge of the ravine. She was fully exposed. If anyone saw her now she'd be the easiest target ever.

Her eyes darted back to the plane. Through the wreckage, she saw the man on the rope. He had reached the plane and tied himself off. He had also shed his backpack. It hung from a piece of metal jutting out from the mangled cockpit. Her view was blocked for a second as she continued to slide across the log. When she saw him next, he was manipulating something in his hands. A clamor of gunfire ripped her head back to the jungle ahead of her.

It was close. Too close.

Maddie reached up and swept a lock of wet hair from her face.

Keep moving. You're almost there.

She was a few yards from the other side when she caught sight of a man in uniform shuffling through the trees. He was armed with an AK-47 and was working his way toward the fight which was somewhere in the jungle on her eleven o'clock. So far, the man hadn't noticed her. But if he turned his head a few degrees to the left, she was toast.

She stopped crawling, hoping he would continue past her. The river below was a raging ocean tide. The rain beat against her head and back—a trillion little hands trying to push her to her death.

It was only a matter of time till he saw her.

Maddie slowly sat up and straddled the log. Bracing herself with her left hand, she reached back for her sub-gun. Her fingertips brushed against it.

Come on, come on!

The man's head turned toward her. He did a double take.

Their eyes locked.

Maddie's hand found the grip of the gun. She whipped it up just as the man was bringing his own rifle to bear. She squeezed the trigger twice, snapping off two short bursts that ripped into the center of the man's torso. He grimaced and leaned forward. His lifeless body rolled over the edge and was quickly devoured by the raging monster below.

She didn't bother to look for the guy on the rope again. She just wanted to get off the X. She continued across the slick log until she found enough footing to dismount. A few paces into the foliage, she crouched and thanked her Maker once more.

"Bucket Three, I'm on the other side."

Mouse: *"Copy that. I see you. Listen, I've seen a couple of muzzle flashes not far from your pos."*

"I copy. Thanks. I'm going dark."

"Going dark. Roger, that."

"Moving now."

"Copy that. Be careful."

35

MADDIE clawed up the slope over mud and rocks and roots and leaves. She kept low as she moved into the darkened jungle. She turned to the sound of gunfire, people shouting in the distance and began to chart a course through the vegetation. With the natural white noise from the water in the ravine and the rain pummeling her from above, she couldn't make out what the voices were saying. But they were definitely male.

When the guns were humming, she sprinted, using the noise to camouflage her rapid movement through the jungle. When they fell silent, she crept like a tiger over, under, around and through the legion of obstacles, nary making a sound. She kept her MP7 in a low-ready position and prepared herself for a sudden, intense gunfight. The people at the Academy had trained her well, but this was real: her first foray into combat. Truth be told, she wanted—needed—to know what she was really made of. There was no greater test of a person's constitution than combat.

She would have her wish.

Maddie rounded a rocky outcropping. The terrain here was greasy and slippery. She placed her left hand on the rock to steady herself. It was slick with algae or something that at least resembled algae. She stepped carefully, paying special attention to each footfall. The jungle was quiet now.

As she circled the rock, she noticed the outline of man. His head jerked toward her. Maddie raised her gun and squeezed the trigger with clinical precision. Her rounds thudded into his chest and neck. As he fell backward he fired a burst from his AK into the air. Her gun was suppressed. His was not.

Men were suddenly crashing through the jungle toward her from somewhere on her right. No sooner did she turn her head to seek them out than rounds slammed into the rock beside her. She fired a few rounds in the direction of their muzzle flashes then dove. Hot lead chiseled an arc into the rock where she had just been standing and followed her to the ground.

Maddie speed-crawled a few yards through the greenery then stopped. Silently, she looked over her shoulder. The rock was marred with chalk-white dotted lines that were perfectly parallel to one another, as if some primitive tribe had carved them by hand eons ago. She inched forward and hid beneath a shiny green plant with leaves the size of pizzas. She drew herself under it and waited. She cast her eyes to the dirt. A plump, lime-green snake hissed at her and quickly slithered away.

That's right. Get lost!

Two silhouettes appeared against a backdrop of dark jungle canopy. Her hunters stood ten yards apart. They were big and sinewy. The closer man was eight yards away. He had a bushy mustache that the rain had turned into a greasy, black grub. His brow was thick, his face leathery with jagged scars from years of bad acne or war or both. The other was taller and younger. The sleeves of his fatigues were rolled up to his biceps, which were pulpy and tattooed. He'd made an attempt at a full beard but it was patchy and ill-groomed. She noticed his mag pouches were nearly empty. He had one left not counting the one in his AK.

Maddie pushed her suppressor through the plant, moving the leaves aside carefully. Her first round hit the closer man in the temple.

He disappeared from view as if he had unexpectedly stepped into a grass-covered pit. The second man spun, dropped into a crouch and froze. His eyes were wide, his head snapped back and forth. She heard him calling out for his buddy in whispered shouts. But there was no reply. The man shuffled a few steps forward, sweeping the muzzle of his AK-47 back and forth. He would shoot at the slightest provocation.

Maddie squinted through the rain and steadied her aim. Her MP7 coughed again. Several wide holes appeared on the man's neck and head. He listed and fell, leaving a mist of blood in the air that the rain quickly scrubbed away.

◆ ◆ ◆

Mouse watched the man laboring on the rope. The guy's feet kept slipping from the rock, which was slick with fast-moving little waterfalls. After several moments of apparent frustration, the man looked up and sighed then started climbing again. Mouse fired two rounds into the limestone above the man's head, causing him to flinch and let go of the rope in his right hand. He dropped several feet before he was able to reclaim the rope and brake.

"Sorry, pal. You stay put," he whispered.

The man dangled for a spell then righted himself against the cliff. Once he had his legs planted, he turned and seemed to be searching for whoever was shooting at him.

Mouse smiled behind his scope though he knew the man had no chance of seeing him. "*Hola.*"

◆ ◆ ◆

Maddie lay there motionless till she was sure it was safe to move, then reloaded and reclaimed her feet. The jungle was silent now except of course for the constant thrum of rain. She slalomed through the underbrush, ignoring the cold rainwater that soaked every part of her body. With each step, the water inside her boots squished between her toes.

She had made it fifty yards before seeing another human being, dead or alive. Where were Evie and Tonka? It was like they had just vanished. She was about to key her radio, when a man appeared. His uniform was smeared with mud. He had the build of an elite soldier and he moved like one, too—intrepid, athletic and smooth. His face was resolute and chiseled, his hair cropped close to his scalp. And he looked seriously pissed off. Maddie crouched, canting her head back and forth, so she could follow him through the tangle of vegetation. He was not hunting. He held his carbine low and was pacing through the jungle with purpose. Then she saw why. Behind him were two figures. The first one was female.

Evie.

The second was Tonka. He appeared to have been shot in the upper left arm or shoulder. Both of them were bound with their hands behind their backs. Aside from the occasional wince at the corners of his eyes, Tonka was stoic. He was a rock.

"Move!" A uniformed man cross-checked him in the back with an AK causing his head to snap back and his legs to stumble. "Let's go! Let's go!"

Tonka straightened. He stopped dead in his tracks, turned and faced the man. He stared at him like a dog protecting a bone. The man shouldered his rifle, held the muzzle within an inch of Tonka's face. Tonka didn't flinch, didn't move a muscle. He just stood there looking at his captor squarely, fearlessly.

"Move! Or die!"

Tonka held the man's gaze for a few seconds then slowly turned and resumed his pace behind Evelina.

A third hostile outfitted like all the others—Venezuelan military uniform and AK-47—brought up the rear. The three of them were leading Evelina and Tonka back toward the ravine. Maddie waited till they were past her then made sure there were no stragglers. Satisfied there were none, she stepped out into the wet trampled vegetation and began following them. She was careful to stay far enough behind so that the last man wouldn't hear her. She synched her footsteps with his when she could. *Hang tough, you guys. I'm coming.*

The dark, constricted jungle soon gave way to an area that had been cleared by machetes. The closer they got to the ravine, the lighter it became. There was a rope anchored to a Brazil nut tree. The rope led to the ravine and disappeared over the edge. *The man on the rope.* The plane must be directly below.

Maddie stepped off the freshly blazed trail and sunk into a spot from which she could observe and think. No sooner had she crouched down than another man stepped into view. He regarded the two prisoners with a scowl. "So, *these* are the ones who have caused me so much trouble. Put them over there." He pointed to the ground in front of a large log.

"Sit!" barked one of the men in uniform.

Evelina and Tonka didn't budge. Their faces brimmed with defiance.

One of the men slugged Tonka in the face. "*Now!*"

Evelina lowered her head and bull-rushed the guy who had hit Tonka. But the man beside her grabbed her by the hair before she got going, yanked her back and belted her hard across the face. Evelina yelped and crashed to the ground.

The men laughed.

Maddie's body shot alive with rage. It took every last ounce of self-control to not break into a sprint and start shooting. But she was too far away. She would be seen or heard before she'd ever be close enough to kill them all. Plus, Evie and Tonka might get caught in the crossfire. She had to get closer. She gritted her teeth, stepped back out onto the trail and crept forward at a snail's pace.

The man that seemed to be in charge walked to the edge of the ravine then returned to a spot in front of Evelina and Tonka. He drew a pearl-handled pistol from the holster on his hip. It was a full-size Kimber .45. "Feisty little thing, aren't you?" He pointed it at Evelina. "Now. Just who are you and why are you here?"

36

MADDIE had an idea. She ducked into the foliage and picked up a large rock. She chucked it to her right. It was big enough that it made quite a racket even with the rain droning on.

The boss man flipped his hand up and ordered one of the soldiers to go check it out. Maddie slipped between the leaves, which fell closed behind her like a curtain. She quickly positioned herself beside the path that she knew the man would take. She waited till he was just past her then leapt out behind him, all at once throwing her right arm around his neck. The crook of her elbow sunk deep under his chin. She locked her hands together and squeezed. With her right shoulder pressed against the back of his head, she kicked the back of his knee and hopped backward, allowing herself to fall on her stomach, the bad guy on his back. It happened so fast, the man had no time to counter. As they both hit the ground, the man's neck snapped with an audible crack. Maddie released her grip, rolled away and disappeared back into the jungle.

She quietly returned to the spot from which she could see Evie and Tonka. Her odds were better now, but still not great. She checked her magazine. Even though there were a few rounds left, she reloaded with a fresh one.

The three remaining men stood around her teammates forming a perfect isosceles triangle. The man with the Kimber leaned forward. He lifted his pistol to Evelina's forehead and cocked the hammer. "You no talk?" He shrugged his shoulders. "Very well. Bye-bye, pretty girl."

Maddie was running at full speed before she even realized what she was doing. She fired at the man with the Kimber first, hitting him in the pelvis, chest and right arm. The gun flipped out of his hand as he fell over dead. His bookends whipped their heads around. Simultaneously, they swung their guns toward her. Maddie drilled the guy on the left in the neck and face. She then snapped her muzzle to the right. As she fired again, her foot slipped on a wet root and she cartwheeled into the bushes. The last man stood there, legs apart, rifle shouldered. His gun jack-hammered for what seemed forever. Maddie tucked herself into a ball. Bullets snapped all around her, chewing up the earth and trees. Mud jumped up and splattered her face while bits of leaves floated like moths in the air.

When the gunfire stopped, Maddie took a quick drag of air and popped up to shoot, but her target had moved. The man was now a freight train charging right for her. She saw his rifle disappearing into a single point as if it were happening in slow motion. She heard her instructor's voice resounding inside her head as she canted her shoulders forward and twisted her abs ever so slightly to the right. *"Center mass! Slow is fast. Fast is slow."* Both eyes open, she engaged the trigger of the sub-gun in three smooth pulls. Four, five, six splotches became one bloody mess on the man's sternum. He tumbled into the foliage and didn't get up. Maddie trod over to him and kicked him hard in the nuts to make sure he was dead.

She squinted against the rain and turned a full 360 degrees. Satisfied the coast was clear, she ran over to her teammates. "You two okay?" Evelina and Tonka were seated on the ground, their backs pressed against the fallen tree. Maddie yanked a Zero Tolerance folding knife from her pants pocket and quickly cut them loose. Evelina had a big welt under her left eye and Tonka's left shoulder was bleeding. Both of them were covered in mud as if they had been dragged through the jungle at one point.

"Splendid," said Evelina. "Thanks to you."

"What about you, big man? Looks like you took one to the shoulder."

"What, this?" said Tonka, examining the wound. "Clipped me is all. I'll live."

Evelina picked up an AK from one of the dead men. "Be right back. Gonna go get our gear."

Maddie nodded as she stood. "Bucket Four to Bucket Three."

"Go ahead, Four."

"Troops are safe. How's the dope on the rope?"

"Looks a little testy."

"Good. Cover me."

"Roger that."

Maddie stepped through the trees to the ravine. She looked across to where she knew Mouse was secreted, gave him a thumbs-up then peered down over the edge. She saw the top of the man's head and shoulders. She curled her tongue and whistled loudly, causing him to look up. "How's it hangin'?"

The man glared at her.

"Hands! Let me see your hands! Now!"

The man lowered his head.

"Careful, Four. I can't see his hands," said Mouse.

"Hey, numbnuts! Get your hands up! Now!"

This time when the man looked up his empty hands came up, too.

"Good. Now put them on the rope and climb. Try anything funny and you're a dead man!"

"Okay. Okay. I comeeng."

Maddie held her sub-gun on him as he ascended. She glanced back as Evelina came chugging back through the jungle with her and Tonka's gear.

"I've got zip ties in my ruck," said Evelina. "As soon as he is up here, put him on the ground."

"Roger that." Maddie watched the man. As he reached the edge, he paused. "All the way, dude. Let's go!"

His head tilted back toward the rapids. He was panting. "Tired. Need break."

"You can have a nice long break after you get your butt up here."

The man frowned as he set about hoisting himself up to the top of the ravine. Maddie led him at gunpoint a safe distance from the edge then ordered him to the ground. The man complied without protest. Evelina was on him in a flash zipping his hands behind his back. Maddie covered her as she patted the man down for weapons and stood him up.

Maddie looked up toward Mouse and gave him the high sign while Evelina walked the man over to Tonka and shoved him to the ground.

"There. Have a seat." Evelina stood in front of him, crossed her arms and looked him in the eyes. "Your friends are dead. You're all alone. It's over. Cooperate and try not to piss me off and maybe we'll let you live."

The man's face twisted into a grisly smile.

Maddie was still standing at the edge of the ravine. She could see deep inside the cabin of the plane now. A seat was folded forward. One was folded back. Another was shoved against a window on its side. Wires and insulation and pieces of something that looked like vinyl or plastic hung from the ceiling. The rain had turned to a mist so faint that particles of water just hung in the air. Meanwhile, the sun, though it was heading quickly toward the horizon, was beginning to show itself. Several streaks of gleaming sunlight were probing the jungle canopy. Maddie stared deeper into the plane.

It couldn't be.

There on the floor toward the back of the plane, caught in a sparkling ray of sunshine that had shot through one of the only unbroken windows, was a book. Not just any book. The Bible. It was not only intact, but seemed to be in perfect condition, untouched by the crash and years of impossible elements.

A somber feeling washed over her. Her throat knotted. At that very moment, she felt God's presence. Her eyes began to well up with tears.

Daddy, what happened to you?

The sound of Evelina's voice ripped her from her reverie. "What are you so—?" A pause. "Maddie, look out!!!"

The explosion was enormous. It sent her backward through the air and into the bushes. A red-orange fireball shot into the air. A plume of thick, black smoke that was visible for miles slowly mushroomed up over the jungle.

Maddie tried to move, tried to breathe.

Then everything went black.

37

Seville, Spain

FOR his third encore, Pollini performed Chopin's Nocturne in D-flat major, Op. 27, No. 2. As the last note faded into silence, the crowd stood and went wild, Rainey right along with it.

Alcott: *"Look alive, all. Concert is ending. Bronco, your female friend is looking in your direction."*

"Outstanding! Just exquisite." His words were meant for Alcott, but blended in perfectly to the other offerings of adulation coming from the audience.

The house lights came up and the crowd continued to buzz. There was a cackle of laughter off to his left. Down in front of him two women were still shouting praises toward the stage in Italian.

He followed the throng toward the lobby. As he stepped through the auditorium doors, an arm grabbed him. He tensed, but refrained from pulling away.

"Oh, Lucien, what a performance! What an absolutely *marvelous* concert! What did you think? Please tell me you loved it." The Shark squeezed his left arm and pressed herself into him nearly spilling out of her dress in the process. Reagan Rainey might have been embarrassed at such a display, but for the worldly Monsieur Joubert this type of thing was routine.

"It was fabulous. Pollini at his best. I especially enjoyed the Schumann pieces." The remark was intended to be provocative.

"Yes, they were very good. But my favorite was when he played Stravinsky. I just adore Stravinsky." She clung to him, as if he were a life raft in a stormy sea. "Soooo. Are you up for a drink, my Lucien? Where are you staying?"

You're not Moses.

"I'd love to, but I really can't tonight. I hope you understand."

"Oh, *pooh.* Are you sure? I make very good company, Lucien." Her eyes flashed with desire. "Very good."

Rainey pushed the fingers of his right hand halfway into the pocket of his tuxedo jacket the way wealthy, confident men sometimes do. Something familiar brushed against his fingertips. He pulled out a small sheet of paper and read it with the casualness of a man checking his billfold then slid it back into his pocket. "Sadly, yes, I'm quite sure."

"Very well. But if you should change your mind, I'm staying at the Gran Melia Colón, Room 306. I will be up late should you decide to call."

He smiled as he slipped from the Shark's clutches and bid her a fond goodnight. Rainey walked outside and turned left. He moved down the sidewalk till he reached the black BMW sedan Alcott had rented for him. He ducked in, started the engine and drove off.

"Shepherd, you up?"

"I'm up Bronco. Go."

"Moses made contact. Clean up the safe house and get the team to Ronda. Find a hotel. Then book a room for me at a separate hotel. Someplace that has a lot of entry/exit points. I'm gonna take the scenic route."

"Something wrong? Are you good?"

"Everything's fine. But if I'm being followed, I don't want you guys getting burned. We have to consider the possibility that Moses now has me under surveillance."

"Understood."

"Let me know when you're all set and we'll go from there."

"Roger that."

38

Ronda, Spain

FOUR hours later, Rainey was approaching the Plaza Concepción Garcia Redondo from the north on Calle Comandante Salvador Carrasco. At the traffic circle, he turned right onto the narrow, one-way Calle San José and gunned the engine. If he was being followed, he wanted Moses, or whoever it was, to think he was just performing routine surveillance detection maneuvers.

Seeing nothing in his rearview mirror, he continued down the tight alley till he came to a stop sign. He hit the unlock button on his door several times as he waited for traffic to pass. He proceeded through the intersection and turned left onto Calle Molina, then made a quick right onto Calle Pozo. Once he was all the way around the corner, he brought the car to a quick stop. In the same instant, his right rear passenger door clicked opened and someone with a suitcase climbed in. Rainey quickly got back up to speed. To anyone watching, it would seem as though he had never stopped.

"What's up, Fig?"

Fig was lying across the back seat, having already shoved the suitcase to the floor behind Rainey. "You tell me."

Headlights swept across his face as Rainey put his indicator on and turned left onto Calle Jerez. "Moses made contact."

"Yeah, I know that. But what's going on? Why are we in Ronda?"

"He wants to meet here tomorrow. I hope."

"You *hope*?"

"I'll explain later."

Fig slipped an envelope between the seats. "Here's your reservation info. Room is registered under the name Eric Bishop. We're over at the Berlanga. Shepherd's waiting for a debrief, so whenever you get settled..."

"Good deal." Rainey drifted to the next block and turned left onto Calle Padre Mariana Soubiron.

"Your kit's in the suitcase."

"Thanks, bro."

"Don't mention it."

Rainey continued for a few more blocks then made a quick right onto Calle Naranja and braked hard without skidding. As the car lurched to a stop, Fig rolled out, closed the door behind him and disappeared down the sidewalk in the opposite direction, hands in his pockets and a ball cap pulled low on his brow.

Rainey squared the block then parked on the street near his hotel. When he got to his room, he put a wad of chewing gum over the peephole and double-locked the door. He hefted his suitcase onto the bed then closed all the blinds and drapes. He walked back to the suitcase and dug out a rugged laptop. As he waited for it to power on, he devoured a couple of chocolates he had scooped up from the front desk.

When the computer was up and ready, he clicked on an icon for a proprietary DX VPN and waited for the connection to establish. Soon he was staring at Alcott and the others in a large window on the screen and himself in another smaller window in the upper, right-hand corner.

"Fig back yet?" said Rainey.

Alcott turned around in his chair. "He just walked in."

Rainey explained in more detail what had happened back in Seville and why they were now in Ronda.

"You want to see the video?"

"Absolutely."

"Okay. I'm gonna have Jazz take over now." Alcott disappeared from the frame and Jazz slid into view.

Rainey leaned forward in his chair.

"All right, Bronc, you should see it in a second or two." Jazz smoothed his trimmed beard with one hand and tapped the touchpad with the other.

Another window popped up on the screen, which Rainey quickly enlarged. He waited a few seconds then the video clip began to play. One of Rainey's tuxedo shirt studs had actually been a pinhole camera and had given Jazz a live video feed of events as they unfolded at the concert hall. This was the footage from that video recording.

"We never get a great shot of his whole face. Just his lower jaw and chin. And it's always from the side."

Rainey studied the figure on the screen: the old man who had bumped into him and somehow slipped the note into his jacket pocket.

Moses.

When the clip ended, Rainey played it again. Then again. He stopped it several times and stared at the man.

"Well, we know one thing for certain," said Alcott in the background. "He knows what *you* look like."

Rainey nodded as he crossed his arms.

"What about the voice?"

"I've already uploaded the file to the XOC. There's no match. But they said the guy was speaking with a fake Italian accent. His native tongue could be Russian or one of the Northeast Caucasian languages."

"Well, that jibes. Moses said in his letter that he was Russian. Anything else?"

"Nope. That's it."

Fig chimed up in the background. "I don't get it. Why is he jerking you around? Why make you come here?"

Rainey glanced at the scrap of paper on the table next to his laptop. "He's just being careful. Number one, he wanted to see if I'd show. Number two, he wanted to assess whether or not I'd come alone."

"So you think we convinced him you were there by yourself?"

"That remains to be seen. My guess is that he's still a tad suspicious. I would be if I were in his shoes."

"Can I see the note?" said Alcott, appearing over Jazz's shoulder.

Rainey picked up the note and held it in front of the tiny camera at the top of the screen.

Alcott read it out loud. "Up for a little rondo in Ronda? Be at the center of the Puente Nuevo tomorrow at noon. Moses."

"We don't have to worry about prints or other bios. There was nothing on the letter or the envelope that surfaced in Lisbon." said Rainey. "Won't be any on this either."

"What's a *rondo*?" said Fig.

"It's a form of music that has a recurring theme or element," said Babe from somewhere off camera. "A kind of refrain. Don't you know anything?" He shrugged when they all looked at him. "What? I may be a snake eater, but I'm a cultured snake eater."

"He's right," said Rainey. The expression on his face was as serious as his muse. "The Triumph folks used musical code names for their targets. Don't ask me why. The two that concerned my dad were Echo and Keynote."

"You think rondo could be another code name?" said Alcott.

"It's possible. Could also just be a clever little play on words. In any case, we need to get some rest. Let's link up again tomorrow at oh eight hundred."

"Sounds good. That'll give us time to do some recce."

"All right. Goodnight ladies."

39

WHAT *are you up to, Reagan Rainey? Yes. Moses must have gotten a message to you somehow at the concert.*

From a small parking lot at the northwestern tip of the city, Zarek Tarło stared out into the pitch black Andalusian wilderness. A pinprick of light appeared far in the distance, a vehicle traveling on some dusty mountain lane. He squinted and followed it with his eyes until it was gone.

Being up here, perched like a bird of prey, he understood why this city had been so difficult to conquer over the centuries. You could see for miles and miles. No wonder Ronda was known as *The Eagles' Nest.*

A stiff breeze swept up from the expansive valley below and buffeted him, pulling his shirt taut against his frame. The outline of a pistol appeared at his waist. He yawned and his ears popped.

The two men behind him were sucking on cigarettes and talking in hushed voices. For ten solid minutes, they had discussed exercise routines and protein shakes. Now the topic was women. They were going back and forth about the physical traits of a popular American singer when his phone buzzed inside his pocket.

Tarło swiped the screen and held the phone to his ear, all the while picturing the man on the other end. He was probably leaning against a street lamp sucking down cigarettes like they were going out of style. Tarło never complained about the way he went about his business though. The guy was one of his best watchers. The man and his skilled surveillance team had followed Rainey all the way from Seville to Ronda. Meanwhile, Tarło and the shooters had stayed a few miles behind, ready to strike at a moment's notice.

"Yeah?"

"He's at the Hotel el Tajo."

"Did he meet with anyone?" said Tarło.

"No. And he's still by himself."

"Okay. The other surveillance team is standing by. In another hour, we'll rotate you and your team out. I'm not taking any chances. I don't want anyone falling asleep on this one or getting burned. Rainey's gonna lead us right to Moses. I can feel it. Neither one of them is leaving Ronda alive."

"Are you sure we have enough people to carry out an urban assault? Ronda is full of tourists and the streets are narrow and congested during the day."

"Don't worry. I've taken that into consideration. There are more hitters on the way. They should be here by morning. With a little added surprise."

40

RAINEY wiped beads of sweat from his forehead as he moved through the crowded Carreterra Espinel. He paused for a spell in the shade of a busy bazaar and discreetly checked to see if there was anyone following him. The bustling pedestrian activity made it difficult. Sure as he could be that he was clean, he continued down the narrow walkway alive with slow-moving tourists and fast-talking merchants peddling their wares with practiced predation. He skirted past a series of magenta-colored chairs and tables wrapped in white cloth. Hunched over one of them, a young couple sat eating sandwiches. The girl's purse hung from her chair back. If he were a thief, he could have easily snatched it and disappeared long before she knew it was gone.

He ambled down the tiled stone thoroughfare and wove through several seniors with maps and brochures discussing what they should see next; harried men and women with strollers and diaper bags; a man with a sunburned bald spot and a chubby-legged toddler strapped to his back. Rainey emerged onto Calle Virgen de la Paz and back into the hot sun. A local policeman with a fluorescent yellow shirt and black pants stood officiously on the other side of the street, a rock amidst a steady current of people sweeping past him in either direction. Like any good cop, he had found a small sliver of shade from which to carry out his duties. The officer removed his hat with a grimace and wiped the wetness from the top of his head with the palm of his other hand. He looked at Rainey as he set his hat back in place and let a long, pronounced sigh seep through his lips. With his cheeks puffed out such as they were, he took on the expression of someone blowing out birthday candles. Rainey avoided eye contact, knowing it might cause the policeman to take a particular interest in him.

Turning left and crossing to the shady side of the street Rainey caught a glimpse of the hulking, black bull monument on the far side of the Plaza de Toros. He drifted by shops stuffed with bullfighting trinkets, hand-painted ceramic plates and stand after stand of post cards.

The aroma of meat over a fire wafted from the Hotel Restaurant Don Javier. His stomach growled as his eyes flicked to the left. He checked himself in the reflection of a large plate glass window across the street, making sure his little arsenal was still concealed.

Rainey wore a plain, white T-shirt under a loose-fitting, gray button-down shirt with his sleeves rolled up and the top two buttons left undone. His shoes were Merrells—as comfortable as they were tough. Under his shirt, he wore a Glock 19, two extra mags for it, two thirty-round mags for his SBR and a blowout kit. All of it fit neatly on a High Threat Concealment (HTC) Low Profile System. One of the things he liked most about the covert belt system was that it held all of his hardware snugly to his frame with little to no printing. On his back, hidden inside what looked like an innocent, touristy green and gray backpack, he carried his short-barreled rifle—an HK416C with a pullout stock and a Trijicon MRO red dot optic. He had six more magazines in the ruck, not counting the one in the gun. Each of them was topped off with 5.56mm NATO rounds. The magazines were grouped in two sets of three, and were seated nicely behind two rip-down Velcro flaps, one on either side of the main pocket. Alcott had insisted he arm himself in such a way due to how vulnerable he would be out on the bridge. And Rainey didn't object. In fact, he loved this configuration.

At the Plaza de España, the road became a setted traffic circle. The bust of Antonio de los Río Rosas, the famous Rodeño politician, rose up from within a flower garden at the circle's center against a backdrop of whitewashed buildings.

Rainey stayed along the right side of the plaza where the sidewalk was wider and the shadows were longer. He stopped just beyond a small pharmacy and stepped under the first of several sepulchral archways along the elegant, stone façade of the Parador de Ronda. From here, he studied the flow of people and vehicles. He tried to pick out anyone who might be watching him, a tough feat even for someone with his level of training and experience. The best surveillance people were ghosts.

Finally, he turned his attention to the bridge. The Puente Nuevo, or "new bridge," spans the modest Río Guadalevín and a rocky chasm known as El Tajo Canyon, which is every bit of 393 feet deep. Built in the 1700s to connect two sections of the city, the bridge is markedly similar to aqueducts the Romans constructed in ancient times.

He looked at his watch.

11:56.

Just as they had planned earlier this morning, Alcott, Fig, Jazz, and Babe were all strategically positioned around the bridge. Alcott was seated at a table back in the plaza behind a pair of trendy European sunglasses and a Brad Thor paperback. At his feet was a businessman's leather satchel inside which was his own HK416C. He hadn't even looked up when Rainey strolled past a minute ago.

Fig was perched on the landing outside La Pilastra del Torero on the other side of the bridge. He was playing the part of an amateur photographer. However, the khaki camera bag slung over his left shoulder didn't contain lenses and spare battery packs but rather an HK MP7A1 and six magazines.

Then there was Jazz. The short, wiry tough guy with the sharply trimmed beard and even sharper tongue was rocking a stroller back and forth in front of a shop that sold handmade leather goods on the far side of the bridge. He was the stranded dad left outside to tend the sleeping baby as wife and mother-in-law went shop to shop spending his money. What was made to look like a baby all wrapped up and shrouded from the hot sun, was really his LWRC M6A4, otherwise known as an Infantry Automatic Rifle—the modern version of a SAW.

Babe, who was crossed-trained as a sniper, had set up shop on the rooftop of an apartment building on Calle Ermita, on the east side of the gorge. Lying behind a suppressed Citizen Arms .308 Win. carbine that was outfitted with a powerful scope, he would be the angel watching over them.

Rainey looked at his watch again.

11:58.

Ignoring the din of the plaza, he slowly scanned back and forth, left to right. His eyes reached the far side of the bridge and then came back to its center.

11:59.

The Lord is on my side; I will not fear. What can man do to me?

He cupped his hand over his mouth. "Here we go. Moving to the X."

41

AOB Vichada
Eastern Colombia

THE first thing she recognized was the thumping of chopper blades. Then a man's voice. He was shouting. "…okay, Maddie!"

She tried to sit up, but found herself restrained to a backboard. Mouse was seated next to her. Beyond him through the open cabin door was the jungle. They were flying low, maybe a hundred feet above the treetops. The helicopter banked a little then leveled off again.

She felt a hand resting on her shoulder. Canting her head to the left, she saw Evelina and Tonka. Evie gave her a pat and said, "Chicks rule!"

Tonka's left arm was in a makeshift sling, the upper portion of his shirt had been cut away and a white dressing taped in place. A spot of blood the size of a dime had soaked through. He smiled and with his good hand gave her a thumbs-up.

Evie leaned down next to her, the gusts through the open cabin whipping her ponytail and stray locks about her face with hurricane force. "Be there soon. Rest easy, girl."

There? Where was there?

Her head hurt as she tried to make sense of what had happened. Why was she now strapped to a backboard in the back of a Black Hawk.

Mentally, she began to take stock of her body, starting at her feet. She wiggled her toes inside her boots then moved her ankles. Her calves were good. Knees... *Ouch!* Her left knee throbbed. She tried working the joint, but her legs were strapped down. It was stiff. If she could only bend it, the pain would go away, she assured herself. She pushed the thought from her mind. Okay, what else hurts?

Hips, stomach, chest felt fine. Her lower back was tight and sore, like she had been punched in the kidneys more than once. Shoulders, neck? Ugh. Neck is stiff, too. She had a splitting headache, but nothing she hadn't experienced before in her many years of martial arts.

She clenched her fists and went about rolling her wrists and tensing her biceps and triceps. All good. Now back to that knee. She concentrated. It felt swollen. She forced it to move this time under the wide nylon strap, but grunted when pain shot through her body.

"Relax, Maddie. One more minute." Mouse grabbed her hand. "Sit tight. I know it sucks."

She closed her eyes, took a deep breath and swallowed. *God, I'm in Your hands. Help me face whatever the outcome with courage.* She didn't know how badly she was hurt, but one thing was racing through her mind now. What was Wes going to think? He had wholeheartedly supported her decision to go work for the CIA, but would that support endure? Her first overseas assignment and she's coming back on a stretcher. She would never admit it, but part of her—the selfish part—didn't care. She clenched her teeth and tried bending her knee once more. It moved a little more than before, but the pain was excruciating. What if she was going to lose her leg? Then what?

In a fleeting second, she wanted to cry, but then she gritted her teeth and snarled. No. I will not cry. I am never out of the fight. I will never quit.

Never!

Adapt and overcome.

Mouse looked down at her. He squeezed her hand. "You're one tough chick, Maddie. You hang on."

As the Black Hawk set down, she realized there were two other choppers that had been flying with them. A platoon of heavily armed commandos emptied out of them. Two of them were frog-marching a man in a muddy uniform across the way. He was blindfolded and his hands were zip-tied behind his back. Things were starting to come back now. *The log.* She had climbed across a ravine on a log. A man in a uniform—the same type uniform the guy being led across the field was wearing—tried to kill her. She had shot him in the chest. She had killed others, too. Evie and Tonka. She'd found them. Tonka had been shot. In the shoulder, yes.

Events were flashing in her mind now.

The man with the Kimber. The other soldiers with AKs. She saw a rope. There was man on a rope. She remembered now. He was beside the plane. She had made him climb up the rope. Evie's voice echoed in her memory. *"Maddie, look out!"*

That was the last thing she could remember.

Mouse grabbed his rucksack in a fist, hopped out then turned and snatched another pack, too. It was hers. She recognized it. She'd been wearing it in the jungle. He said something to the door gunner that she couldn't quite make out just before three athletic-looking men in camouflage fatigues appeared and began pulling her out. One of them reached across her and gripped the edge of the backboard. She read his shoulder tabs from top to bottom.

Special Forces.

Ranger.

Airborne.

They carried her across a patch of dirt and scrub grass into a modest one-story structure. They turned into the first door on the right and entered a large general purpose room. On one side were a briefing table and chairs, a white board and a large monitor. On the other was a small table stacked with radio equipment and computer hardware. They carried her to a separate area within the room. It was stocked with bins of medical supplies and several olive-drab, foldable cots. A fourth soldier quickly unfolded one of them then helped the others slide her onto it.

Now free of the straps, Maddie quickly tried sitting up—a bird let out of a cage.

"Easy, now. Easy. Just relax." A black man with a full beard appeared in front of her, coaxed her back down. "Lay back now. Let me take a look at you. Okay? It's all right."

Tonka entered the room and dropped his gear just inside the doorway. He walked over to the cot and looked at Maddie. "Listen to him, Maddie. Sgt. Bradley is the medical sergeant here. And he's one of the best in Special Forces. We did the Goat Lab together. You're in good hands. Besides, I'll be right here."

"I'm good. I'm okay," said Maddie. She tried to sit up again, ignoring the jackhammering inside her head.

"Maddie, seriously. Sit back!" barked Tonka. "What is it with you Raineys?"

Sgt. Bradley leaned forward and grinned. "Call me Xavier, okay?" He began evaluating her, getting her vitals. "Can one of you tell me what happened?"

"There was an explosion," said Tonka. "She was blown backward, landed pretty hard on her back. She's got a goony on the back of her head the size of a golf ball. She never lost consciousness, but she was dazed pretty good. Didn't really seem to know what was going on till a few minutes ago."

Sgt. Bradley nodded. "I see. What hurts, Maddie?"

She grimaced.

"I can't help you unless you tell me what hurts."

"My head and my left knee. My lower back is a little sore, too."

"Anything else?"

"No."

Sgt. Bradley began looking at her eyes, studying her pupils with a small penlight. He asked her a series of questions to test her memory. Afterward, he examined the knot on the back of her head then rolled her pant leg up to her thigh. There was already a large bruise on the back of her knee. He palpated her entire leg for broken bones then focused on the knee. He tested it for ligament damage by performing a series of pushes, pulls and twists. "Have you ever had knee problems before? Sprains, tears, that type of thing?"

"Nothing serious."

"Can you bend it?"

"A little."

"Show me."

Maddie slid her heel toward her butt. Her knee rose from the cot several inches. She wanted to scream, but instead she just gritted her teeth. Her forehead started to glisten. For a moment, she paused and grunted a quick breath then winced as she continued.

"Okay, okay. Don't hurt yourself," chuckled Sgt. Bradley.

"Now what?" said Maddie as Sgt. Bradley gently helped her lower her leg to the cot.

"Well, you definitely have a concussion. Without further testing, I'd say it's a grade two. You should get some rest and take it easy for the next week or two."

Maddie frowned. She hated the idea of being sidelined. Especially on her first assignment.

"As far as that knee is concerned, at a minimum, you should get an x-ray, but I also recommend an MRI just to be safe. Afraid I can offer neither out here. I don't *think* you have any torn ligaments, but I can't be a hundred percent sure without an MRI. For now, ice and elevation are your friends. I'm gonna wrap your knee. It'll give you a little extra support and will help with the swelling till you get to where you're going. Tell me if it's too tight."

"All right. Thank you."

42

"WHERE are we anyway?" said Maddie examining Sgt. Bradley's handiwork. He had already packed up his things and left them alone to talk.

Tonka adjusted the fit of his new sling. "Advanced Operations Base Vichada. Eastern Colombia. Evie called in the cavalry after you took that gainer. There was no way we could hike out with a prisoner *and* you in that condition."

"Where is he anyway? Is he talking?"

"Mouse and Evie are watching him No, not yet. He's playing Mr. Tough Guy. But don't worry. He'll talk."

Maddie slid off the cot. "So what happened to you and Evie?"

"We had eyes on two of them and were moving in closer, when all hell broke loose. Guys started coming out of the woodwork from all over. We held them off as best we could. They closed on us pretty fast after I got plinked. Stripped us of our guns and commo gear and slogged us back to their leader. That's when you came along. Mouse said you pulled some circus crap on a log or something to get to us. Crazy stuff. We said this before, but it's so true. You and your brother are so much alike, it's starting to get a little freaky now."

"How nice." Maddie made a sarcastic smile.

"I'm serious."

"You said there was an explosion."

"Yeah. They blew the plane. You were standing right above it when it went. The explosion knocked you back about five meters. I give you high marks for form, Maddie. Ever do any cliff-diving?"

"Funny." Maddie squeezed her wrapped knee, turned it from side to side as she mused. "Someone didn't want us to find out what brought down that plane."

"No doubt about that. But it's all good. Evie's already got someone from Lynn Street running down the photos Humphreys took after the crash." Lynn Street was a term they sometimes used amongst themselves for Directorate X headquarters in Arlington, Virginia. Incidentally, it was just a few blocks away from Carter Tower.

Evelina slipped into the room. "So what's the good word? How you feeling, Maddie?"

"Sore, but… Gonna take a lot more than that to keep me out of the fight."

Evelina smiled. "Somehow I knew you'd say that. What about you, big guy?"

Tonka showed off his new sling. "Patched up and ready to rock."

"Okay, good," said Evelina.

Maddie shuffled across the room, testing her knee. "So what's the game plan?"

"Chopper to Tolemaida. There, we'll hop a jet. And our new friend is going with us."

"*Swan!*" boomed Tonka.

They both looked at him like he had two heads.

Tonka beamed proudly. "That's your new name. Swan. As in *swan* dive. It's perfect."

"Beautiful," said Maddie shaking her head. "Just beautiful."

Once their gear and prisoner were loaded into the refueled Black Hawk, they bid AOB Vichada, the Rangers and 7th Group ODA team assigned here goodbye and flew west to Tolemaida Air Base. It was dark when they arrived. A DX jet was waiting for them on the tarmac. Their blindfolded prisoner was quickly led onto the plane and strapped into a special transport seat in a small, square room aft of the main passenger compartment. A stern-faced crew member dutifully appeared with a syringe and injected a strong sedative into his arm. She stood over him until he was out then wordlessly took a seat and strapped into her lap belt.

Maddie hopped up the stairs on one foot and eased into a seat on the starboard side of the plane where she could elevate her leg. She reclined her seat a few notches and rubbed her eyes. She was tired, exhausted really. The adrenaline dump had long worn off and now she could barely keep her eyes open. Yet somewhere deep within her soul, was the residue of exhilaration. An exhilaration like none she had ever before experienced. She took no joy in the killing of other human beings, but knew that it was sometimes a requirement of the job. She did, however, take satisfaction in knowing she had earned the respect of her peers.

Mouse dropped into a seat facing her and grinned. "Hey, Swan."

"I see you've been talking to Tonka."

"Whaddya mean?"

"Shut up."

"Just glad you're okay. Here." He handed her a Styrofoam container.

"What's this?"

"Dinner. You earned it. Saved each of our butts. You're solid, Swan. You can definitely handle your biznass."

"Thanks, Mouse." She thumbed open the lid and greedily eyed the colorful bounty before her. Thin cutlets of grilled chicken lay over white rice and a mix of diced peppers, chopped onions and sliced tomatoes. Sides included chunks of papaya and a halved strawberry guava. She held it up to her nose. It smelled positively wonderful. She turned to him, a sparkle of delight in her eyes.

He winked. "Stick with me kid and you'll never go hungry."

Tonka squeezed into a chair across from them. "He's right. I don't know how he does it, but no matter where we are, Mouse is always good for scrounging up a decent meal."

Mouse held up a plastic fork full of succulent white chicken meat which he quickly made disappear. He smiled as he chewed. "It's a gift."

Evelina strode up to the others and plopped down in the sofa. She had a phone pressed to her ear. "Okay, I understand. See ya when I see ya."

"What's up, Evie?" said Mouse pointing with his empty fork to the food container he'd acquired for her. "Dig in before it gets cold."

"Thanks, Mouse. I will in a sec. I have one more call to make."

They were airborne again in less than fifteen minutes.

43

THEY shot north over the Caribbean. In the inky black sea far below, Maddie could make out the lights of several cruise ships headed for Aruba. Oh, how nice it must be to be perfectly oblivious to everything going on in the world. Most people were. She massaged her knee, lost in her logic. It's weird, she thought. That's really what they were fighting for, those in the intelligence and special operations communities and the military at large. They were fighting so Americans and all people frankly could be left alone in safety, so they could continue being oblivious.

Her thoughts turned to Ray. Where was he? What was he doing? Was he safe? Would he find out what had happened to Dad? If he really was alive, Ray would find him. He would do anything, go anywhere. When Ray was committed to doing something, he would not stop until he succeeded. He was the most driven person she had ever known. She was so proud of him. He was such a good man, a stellar role model.

Be safe, big brother, wherever you are.

The pounding in her head had subsided somewhat, but her knee was still thick and stiff with swelling. She lifted the icepack from the bandaged joint and smirked at the cold splotches of pink-red skin along the edges of the dressing. She looked over at Evelina who was poised behind a laptop. Mouse and Tonka were both snoozing.

"Do we know who he is?"

Evelina shrugged. "He didn't admit to anything back at Vichada and that includes his identity, but based on the prints I rolled, his name is Mihai Cioabă. Forty-two years old, Romanian by birth, but also has Dutch citizenship. Served in the Dutch military from the mid-nineties through two thousand three. KCT."

"KCT? What's that?"

"*Korps Commandotroepen*. Dutch special forces. Did tours in Bosnia and Macedonia. Hard to tell what he's been doing since. One thing's for sure, he gets around. Netherlands, Bulgaria, Greece, Czech Republic, the UK, Brazil. Been in the U.S. a dozen or so times prior to oh seven.

"Oh, wow. Here's where things really get interesting. He's got a couple of red notices lodged against him. Seems he's wanted by the French. Something to do with a bombing that occurred in a Paris suburb in oh eight. Left six people dead including a French government official and a senior member of the DGSE. Israelis and Dutch want him, too. Killed an IDF officer in Ashdod in oh nine. In two thousand twelve, he was involved in the theft of classified information from a Dutch naval officer."

"Busy guy."

"Yeah." Evelina tapped a few keys. "Guy's a blank slate after two thousand twelve. No address, no employment record, no anything. At least under his real name, that is."

"You think he'll tell us anything?"

Evelina canted her head toward Maddie, looked her dead in the eyes. "He'll talk."

"You seem pretty confident."

"Let's just say I've seen this type of thing before. With guys a lot nastier than him."

Maddie held the icepack against her knee, wrapped a towel around it. "I guess I'm just confused. Where are we going?"

Evelina grinned. "Get some rest."

Maddie looked out the window again. The darkness below was absolute. Her eyes quickly grew heavy. She'd always thought you weren't supposed to sleep with a concussion, but she could no longer keep her eyes open. Besides, Evelina seemed okay with it and she had far more training and experience than her. Maddie shifted her slender frame to a more relaxed position, took a deep breath and let it out through her nose. And then she was out.

When she next opened her eyes, she found Evelina gently rousing her by the arm. She squinted and blinked then thought to check her watch. She'd been asleep for two hours. Maddie wiped her eyes and mouth and looked out the window. It was still pitch black outside. Suddenly, something triggered in her mind as she began to make out the faint outlines of land in the distance. Sparse pinpricks of light dotted the terrain. She craned her neck trying to see further ahead. In a few minutes, the jet banked to the left and she was better able to see what lay beneath them.

"Evie, is that what I think it is?" said Maddie, straightening in her seat.

"Buckle up, Swan. Things are about to get interesting. Seriously, buckle up. We're about to land."

44

Ronda, Spain

RAINEY stepped forward into the crowd. He moved like a tourist, casual and weary-footed. But inside he was ready for anything. Adrenaline was already coursing through his veins. A fickle breeze tugged at his shirt as he moved out onto the narrow two-lane bridge, called Puente Nuevo. He followed the sidewalk on the western side of the setted roadway. Instantly, he felt naked, exposed. Every instinct in him screamed to get off the bridge, that this was a trap. And yet he remained outwardly calm and lazy-eyed.

When he reached the midpoint of the bridge, he stopped and turned toward the old stone parapet; it was all that separated him from the deep gorge below. Behind a section of wrought-iron fence that was set into the wall, he gazed long and hard out over the canyon. The view was glorious. It stretched for miles and miles over forests, fields and orchards. Far in the distance were the rugged Cádiz Mountains in the Parque Natural de Sierra de Grazalema. The peaks and ridges cut a jagged line into the pristine, azure sky. God's fingerprints were everywhere.

Rainey pushed his sunglasses up on his forehead. *Here I am. Now where are you?* His eyes followed the contours of the craggy canyon down to the thin thread of river below him. The slope swept up on his left to a wall of white-washed buildings with tiled roofs. Several colorful towels hung from a quiet third-floor balcony. They fluttered in the wind like flags and pennants on a Navy ship. Two floors below and one building over, a lithe woman relaxed back into a brown wicker chair. Her hair was long and flowing, the color of fine gold. She held a magazine—pages folded back—in her left hand. She used her right hand to sip at something in a glass that might be red wine. The woman set down the glass, turned to the next page, then propped her bare feet on the railing and playfully bobbed them back and forth as if in rhythm to a tune only she could hear.

To his right there were congregations of people perched along the railings next to the Parador de Ronda. It was a popular spot for tourists to take in the spectacular view of the canyon and the iconic Puente Nuevo.

Moses could be anywhere.

A pair of young couples passed behind him. The women were gabbing in German about the refugee crisis in Europe while their men followed closely behind discussing the opening week results of the Bundesliga. A blue panel van with a dented front quarter panel nudged toward the bridge. Likewise, a silver Kia compact with squeaky brakes approached from the other direction. Rainey scrutinized each face as it passed by.

Suddenly, the buzz of a motorbike drew near. He nonchalantly turned toward it. A teenaged boy with floppy black hair and aviator sunglasses slalomed through a string of pedestrians and more oncoming traffic like it was second nature. The boy wore black athletic shorts and a pink polo shirt with the collar up. He was Moroccan or Algerian, or maybe even Libyan. One thing was certain: the boy was staring at him. Rainey was already rehearsing his movements, how he would draw, shoot and move to cover. He considered his shot angles, his target background and the innocents still flowing around him.

The boy was within spitting distance now. Rainey bent his knees slightly, staggered his right foot behind his left. His body was alive with energy, his right hand poised like a quick-draw artist in the Wild West. But the boy continued past without further provocation, mounted the hill to the south and disappeared with a turn in front of the Hotel Poeta de Ronda.

Something tugged his pant leg. Rainey twisted around and saw a young girl, maybe ten years old standing in front of him, dwarfed by his strong American frame. Her delicate hand shot out, a piece of paper in its grasp. No, it wasn't a piece of paper. It was a brochure for the Parador de Ronda. The confused look on Rainey's face prompted the girl to say, "For Rainey. You take."

His eyes rose, moved to the left and to the right. They searched for anyone observing him. However, the bustling of tourists and cars continued, making the task nearly impossible. If someone were watching, they could be anywhere. In the window of that building over there, sitting on a bench behind sunglasses like Alcott in the plaza or even milling among the legion of tourists. Moses could walk right past him and he would be none the wiser.

The girl implored again, this time a bit louder, "For Rainey. You take!" She pushed the brochure closer.

Rainey accepted it with his left hand. As soon as he'd claimed it, the girl spun on her heels and ran off. She was gone in a matter of seconds. Obviously a local.

"Whatcha got there, boss?" came Fig's voice in his earpiece.

Rainey leaned against the balustrade and slowly opened the brochure. In one of the middle sections, a photograph had been circled. There were no other markings in the brochure, no notes scribbled in the margins. Nothing. Rainey dropped the brochure to the sidewalk. When he bent down to pick it up, he said into his lapel mic, "Moving to the terrace of the Parador hotel restaurant."

He heard each man say "copy" as he folded up the brochure and slid it into his back pants pocket. Alcott quickly chimed up again. *"Shepherd to Bronco. I'm working my way toward the promenade now. Let me get ahead of you. The rest of you guys, stay put for now."*

Rainey discreetly replied, "Roger that." The others responded likewise.

The terrace was a good place to meet. It was situated on the back-side of the hotel and overlooked the deep Tajo Canyon and wide expanse of mountain valley into which it emptied. The location was public and at the same time out of view of any potential surveillance personnel posted around the bridge.

Moses was smart.

45

RAINEY set off back across the bridge toward the Parador. Alcott was already moving through the wrought-iron gate that issued onto the promenade—a long gradual slope of tiled slate. Tan and gray stone masonry walls and black iron fencing ran along either side of the walkway, keeping the wide-eyed tourists from falling to their deaths.

Rainey moved at a steady pace, but didn't rush. He wanted to give Alcott time to do his thing: blend in and get first eyes on the terrace, which was situated at the back of the Parador. A handful of people were stopped along his route, holding cell phones in the air and liberally snapping photos of the area, each other and every inconsequential thing in between. A trio of giggling high school-age girls with a selfie stick was really going to town. He shuffled past them and continued on his route.

Alcott was fifty meters ahead with his own phone out. He was stopped now. Rainey slowed his gait as Alcott snapped a few photographs then held the phone up in the air as if recording a homemade documentary for posterity. He was good. It was hard to act oblivious in a crowd while also being alert to everything going on around you. But Alcott did it masterfully.

Rainey swatted at a fly and walked on. A bead of sweat ran between his shoulder blades and down his spine as Alcott turned the corner to the right and disappeared from sight. Rainey stopped at the corner and gripped the railing with both hands as if he himself were mesmerized by the stunning view. He studied the enormity of the valley, the beauty, each ridge and wrinkle in the earth. In his periphery he saw Alcott just short of the terrace, turned toward the railing with his cell phone pressed to his ear. He was speaking loud enough to be heard by passersby.

"C'mon, Sheila! It's safe. I'm telling you, you have to see this. It's gorgeous." A pause. "You're not gonna *fall*. Oh my gosh!"

Inwardly, Rainey grinned, but on the outside he was a blank slate. His eyes followed the downward slope of the valley then flicked up to the right. The terrace was long and straight and a continuation of the promenade on which he stood. It was tucked beneath three floors of hotel rooms, each with its own, private balcony. Rainey counted fifteen separate rooms.

Only a handful of tables on the terrace were occupied. An old man sat alone at the far end. He was hunched over a cup of coffee and a pastry that hadn't been touched. A partially folded newspaper lay in front of him next to a porcelain vase of fresh, colorful flowers.

There you are.

Rainey strolled past Alcott without the slightest acknowledgment and approached the old man's table. He stopped beside the empty chair and waited for the old man to look up from his newspaper.

There was a modicum of hesitation in the man's voice as he said, "Good afternoon, Mr. Rainey. Please, have a seat."

Rainey pulled out the chair and sat down. "Moses."

The creases in the man's face stretched into a wry smile. "How did you like the concert? It's getting some great reviews." He tapped the paper with his middle finger. His hands were large and powerful and liver-spotted.

"Fine. But I'm not here to discuss Pollini."

"No, of course not."

A waiter appeared beside them. Rainey asked for coffee and the man quickly scampered off.

"You said you have information about my father."

Moses nodded. "I do. I ha—." He fell silent as a man brushed by and sat down in the corner, two tables over.

Rainey sat with perfect posture, his hands resting on his thighs, his feet shoulder-width apart. He was ready to spring; he was ready for anything.

The man across the table swept a forelock of thinning gray hair from his brow. His eyes were cloudy gray marbles and moved in a way that bespoke a familiarity with the art of deception. Though he did well to mask it, he was keenly alert to everything going on around him. His mannerisms were graceful and uncontrived, charming in fact. In a crowd of people, Moses would be the last person anyone would label a spy. Yet Rainey noted some subtle contradictions in the man. He had a face that was aged, yet his frame was athletic and well-proportioned even for someone with half as many years. Rainey stared into his eyes again. They could be contact lenses. Hard to tell. He didn't know why, but the hair on the back of his neck was standing on end.

"I want to show you something," said Moses. He flipped the newspaper open revealing a thin computer tablet. He pushed it across the table. "Hit play."

Rainey swiped his index finger across the screen and the tablet came alive. A video file had been opened but remained frozen in dormancy. A large sideways triangle in the center of the screen beckoned. Rainey tapped it. At first the screen went blank then a dimly lit room appeared. The footage was shaky and at times unfocused. Slowly it became clear. It was a prison, at least what looked like a prison. An old prison, World War Two-era perhaps. The relative height and movement of the camera's lens led him to believe that the footage had been captured surreptitiously, as if the camera were secreted on someone's person or inside a briefcase.

The lighting increased and a long, dark corridor with cinder-block walls painted burgundy and an arched, white ceiling appeared. There were rooms on the left and rooms on the right. Each of them had a sturdy door with thick black iron bars. At the second door on the left, the camera stopped, turned. As the camera moved closer to the door, he could see through the bars and into the tiny room beyond. It was dark and bleak inside. The only visible items were a metal bucket, a dog dish and a thin mat that was soiled and worn. The camera jerked to the left and a figure materialized in the shadows. It was a man. He lay motionless in the corner, his back to the camera.

Rainey swallowed.

There was a rustling from the tablet's speaker as a man's muscled hand appeared from behind the camera lens and gripped one of the bars in the cell door. The hand rattled the cage. Metal clanged. When nothing happened, the hand shook the door again. The clanging this time was much louder. For a moment there was still nothing. No noise, no movement. But then slowly the prisoner began to move. It was obvious the man was in quite a bit of pain and discomfort. His movements were stiff and awkward as if he'd not changed position in days or maybe weeks. He was grotesquely thin. His threadbare shirt hung on his bony frame in a way that caused images of emaciated Jews in concentration camps to flash through Rainey's mind.

The man's right arm swung up. He was laboring to turn. The forearm had been broken, maybe more than once, and had not been properly set before it healed. The prisoner steadily worked himself up into a seated position, drew his legs back in an attempt to stand. His head bobbed backward. He took a breath and pressed on. Rainey's heart was already pounding against his sternum when the man finally turned toward the camera. He couldn't believe his eyes. The man had aged. His face was haggard and sunken, marred with deep-set wrinkles and a gray beard that had not been trimmed in ages. But there was no mistaking it.

The man was his father.

46

THE screen went black as the video clip ended. The knot in Rainey's throat was painfully thick. It felt like he'd swallowed a softball. When he blinked, a tear streaked his cheek. He quickly smeared it away and looked across the table with renewed vigor, rage bubbling beneath the surface. He could sense the adrenaline releasing into his system.

Moses had a legitimate look of concern about him. "I'm sorry you had to see that."

"Where is he?" growled Rainey.

"He's—" Moses went silent.

"What? What is it?"

Moses leaned toward him and in a voice just above a whisper said, "The man that just walked by, the one now seated behind me at the corner table, is he with you?"

"No," said Rainey hedging ever so slightly to his right, till his eyes landed on the man seated at the corner table. When the guy had first sat down, Rainey felt something trigger in his mind, but didn't know why. Now he did.

"You recognize him?"

"Yeah." Rainey's jaw flexed. "He was outside the concert hall last night selling carnations."

Moses nodded.

Suddenly, the radio came alive in his ear. It was Fig. *"Bronco, three cars just pulled up in front of the hotel. I count six men. And they're moving toward your pos in a hurry."*

"You didn't come alone did you?" said Moses.

Rainey ignored the question, lowered his forehead. "Are you armed?"

"No. Why?"

"Because things are about to get very ugly, very quickly. Watch the blog. Day minus one. Hour plus six. Understand?"

"I understand."

"When I move, you move. Got it?"

"Got it."

Rainey jumped up and rushed the man at the corner table. The sudden approach caused the man's eyes to jolt with surprise. He tried to stand and at the same time draw a pistol from his hip. His table rocked forward and nearly upended, causing his coffee to spill and his utensils to clang together.

Rainey struck him hard in the throat with the blade of his palm before he could free his weapon. The man clutched his neck with both hands as he crumpled to the ground unable to breathe. Now whether he radioed his buddies or not, all they would hear was him gasping for air. Rainey spun back around. Moses and the tablet were gone.

Fig: *"I've got company. Two guys in blue jeans are… Crap! I've just been made. They're armed with SMGs. All of them."*

A woman taking pictures with her cell phone on the corner of the promenade shrieked. At the same time, someone further up the footpath—a man—yelled, "Gun!"

A crackle of gunfire echoed down the canyon.

Fig: *"Contact! I'm in contact! Two guys on the bridge!"*

Jazz: *"I got your back, bro. Hold that spot."* A loud blast of automatic fire followed. Jazz's IAR. Had to be. *"Come toward me, Fig! Move!"*

Babe: *"Bronco, the plaza's teeming with tangos. You and Shep are gonna have to shoot your way out."*

"Roger that!" Rainey knelt down and ripped off his rucksack, pulled out his SBR and threw the Ferro Concepts Slingster over his torso. He extended the stock, flipped the selector switch and signaled Alcott.

Babe: *"I got four guys with SMGs running into the hotel. Two more going down around back on the footpath."*

"Roger that."

Alcott sprinted over with his own SBR out. "Bronco! Where's Moses?"

"He split. We gotta move!"

"No kidding!"

Gunfire suddenly raked the stone wall beside them. They both dove to the ground and crawled through an open door, which issued into the large hotel dining room. Bullets stitched up the outer brick wall of the hotel. The glass in the large windows shattered and fell like stage curtains. People screamed and scattered.

It was pandemonium.

Alcott slid forward, poked his head outside the doorway and a burst of rounds sent him back inside. "I got two men posted up on the corner of the footpath with long guns. One's kneeling, the other's standing. They're blocking off the terrace. Looks like they want us to go through the hotel!"

Rainey scanned the dining room. Most people had made it out alive. Most, but not all. A young boy lay dead, blood still oozing around his small lifeless form. A woman, presumably the boy's mother, screamed and wept loudly over his lifeless body. She shook him as if trying to wake him from a deep sleep.

Rage consumed him. The muscles in Rainey's face visibly shook. *How dare they?*

He looked left. He could see into the kitchen. Someone was huddled down behind a stainless steel table, frozen with fear. Rainey made a fist to stop his hand from shaking. It was one of the body's natural reactions to an adrenaline spike. He keyed his mic. "Can anyone get a bead on the two guys on the footpath?"

Babe: *"I can see one of them. Head and shoulders."*

"Take him out. You see the other one, hit him, too."

"Roger that."

Rainey picked up a butter knife, wiped it clean with his shirt and tilted it around the threshold of the doorway through which he'd just dove. As he remained scrunched on the floor, he squinted at the reflection of the two men sealing off their exit. He swallowed as he adjusted his grip on the butter knife and held it steady. It all unfolded on the blade of the knife. The head of the man standing suddenly exploded and he fell over. It sounded like a wet sponge being thrown against the floor. The kneeling man whipped his head around, a look of confusion mixed with alarm on his face. The lone gunman flattened himself to the ground, grabbed his shirt collar and barked something into his lapel, still pointing his weapon in the direction of Rainey and Alcott's position.

"Good hit. One down," said Rainey.

Babe: *"Copy."*

The gunfire up in the plaza continued. Every so often Fig and Jazz would chime up as they held their positions on the south side of the bridge. Police sirens began to wail.

Alcott looked at Rainey. "Brah, we either fight our way through the hotel or we take our chances with the dude on the footpath and hope there aren't any more shooters where we can't see."

"No brainer," said Rainey. "Wait! What's that?" There was a thumping noise in the distance. It was coming from further down in the valley. The clamor quickly grew louder.

Crap!

Jazz: *"Bronco and Shep, there's a chopper coming up the valley."*

"Roger that. We hear it."

No sooner had Rainey finished his transmission than a black and gray Bell 427 swooped up from the valley below. It drew level with the terrace and hovered there, a mere thirty yards away. The cabin door was open and a man wearing a ball cap turned backward sat with his feet on the step bar. He was pointing a KAC Stoner LMG with a box magazine in their direction.

"Shepherd!" Rainey grabbed Alcott by the shirt and yanked him back. Both of them scrambled along the floor as the Stoner announced its presence in thunderous fashion. Bullets shredded the room. Tables and chairs flipped and splintered, lights burst and glass shattered. Dust consumed the entire room. A small fire broke out along the one wall. Smoke alarms shrieked and the sprinkler system came alive. Cones of water shot down from the ceiling.

"Listen, the guys in the hotel are waiting for us. We can't go that way."

Rainey snapped his head back and forth. "Agreed."

The gunner in the helicopter ripped off another burst. They both pressed their faces to the shiny tile floor.

"But the terrace is just as bad now!"

Rainey looked up. "Wait here. I have an idea." He crawled across the floor like a house centipede. He slid into the kitchen and took refuge behind a tall metal cabinet. He sat up and searched the room. After a few seconds, he punched the cabinet. None of the ingredients for his initial idea were readily available. He moved further into the kitchen, poked his head up to see what else he had to work with.

Hmm. All right. That might work.

"What are you doing?!" called Alcott just as the guy in the chopper unleashed another barrage.

When the jack-hammering stopped, Rainey yelled, "Almost done!" He finished his little concoction and swam back across the floor to Alcott.

"What's that?"

"How 'bout Rainey's Rum Punch? I don't know." Rainey looked down at his creation: a bottle of rum and a Sterno Culinary Torch, which he'd coupled together with plastic wrap.

"Brah, I hope that works."

"Only one way to find out. See that brick wall over there?"

"Yeah."

"It's pretty thick. Should be good cover. On three, head for that wall. It'll divert their attention long enough for me to serve them up with this."

"You sure?"

Rainey grinned. "No, but the longer we hang around, the more likely that gunner and his buddies are going to put us down for the count."

Alcott looked toward the helicopter through the opening. The chopper hung there like a giant angry wasp waiting to destroy them. "Let's do it."

Rainey popped on the torch and turned the flame up as hot as it would go. "Ready?"

"Ready."

Alcott shot up and sprinted across the room. As he ran, the gunner tracked him with his muzzle. Bullets nipped at his heels, ricocheting deep into the hotel restaurant. Alcott dove behind the wall just as 5.56mm rounds punched into the brick and mortar. At the same time, Rainey stood up and ran to the door that led out onto the terrace. He hesitated only long enough to take a target glance at the helicopter then stepped forward and threw his IED for the center of the main rotor. He didn't wait to see if his aim was true. As soon as it left his hand, he spun and did a Pete Rose slide back to safety.

Both the chopper pilot and the gunner saw what was happening but could do nothing about it. The IED dropped into the blades and disappeared in a fireball which doused the cabin in flames. The small explosion must have damaged the motor or perhaps one of the rotor blades because the chopper began to whine loudly in protest. Almost immediately, it began to spin out of control. Despite any measures the pilot was taking, the helicopter spiraled into the canyon leaving a corkscrew of black smoke in its wake. It slammed into the grassy bottom with a flash of fire and continued to scream and lurch.

Then it exploded.

Holy cow. It worked.

Alcott raced back over to him, threw out his hand to help him up. "Nice work, Bronc. Let's move."

Fig came on the radio again. Rainey could hear the staccato of gunfire over his message. *"Two more cars just pulled up from the north. Add four more tangos to the mix."*

It sounded like a warzone up there. Guns hummed, people screamed, tires screeched, sirens blared. What on earth was going on? Where did Moses get to? Was he still alive? Rainey and Alcott prepared to move on the lone gunman on the footpath before any more men joined the fight.

"Babe! Shepherd and I are coming up the footpath. Hold your fire!"

"Roger that."

Gunfire boomed again from the plaza. Something exploded.

Rainey broke out into a sprint. Alcott was right on his heels. As he drew near to the corner, he slowed. Where was the guy on the corner? Had he fled his position? Or had he just withdrawn around the bend?

Rainey sliced the pie. Suddenly, a rifle muzzle jabbed at his face. Rainey parried it away with the business end of his SBR. The man's momentum propelled them both toward the wall. The man latched onto him. Rainey's feet came off the ground and for a split second he thought they were both going into the canyon. Rainey released the grip on his carbine and clutched at the man, countering the force with urgency.

Alcott stepped forward, held his rifle a few inches from the side of the attacker's head and fired. The man instantly went limp and Rainey shoved him to the ground.

47

RAINEY and Alcott ran up the footpath toward the war going on in the plaza. Several cars had been abandoned on the bridge. One of them was on fire. Only minutes ago, the place was a tourist's paradise. Now it was a warzone. The air was hazy with gun smoke, which the noontime sunshine colored a shade of slate blue.

He and Alcott ducked behind the wall and tried to get a sense of the size and location of the enemy force. They had the entire plaza blocked off, including the bridge. Their sedans were parked at odd angles. Rainey easily counted eight men. Some were armed with long guns, some with submachine guns. Each of them was posted up at a position of good cover. If he and Alcott ran out into the plaza now, they wouldn't stand a chance. Unless…

"Jazz! You up?"

"I'm up. Go ahead."

"We're at the top of the footpath. See my hand?" Rainey stuck his hand above the wall, waved it back and forth.

"Yeah. I see it."

"What about you, Fig? You see me?"

"Roger that. I see you."

"Okay. I need you guys to lay down suppressive fire while Shep and I cross the bridge." Rainey looked at Alcott with eyes that said we can do it. "Keep your fire on the eastern half of the bridge and we'll run the western. Copy?"

"Jazz copies."

"Fig copies. Say when, boss."

"Okay. On my three-count." Rainey and Alcott gripped their weapons and gulped a big breath of air. "Here we go. In three, two, ONE!"

Rainey and Alcott leapt up and bounded through the gate leading into the plaza. They cut to the right and made for the bridge. As they zigzagged through the empty cars, a guy behind one of them stood up with an SMG. His eyes went wide as he shouldered his weapon. Rainey yelled for Alcott to keep running as he veered toward the guy with the gun. Rainey launched into him like a missile, planting his shoulder into the center of the man's chest. The man made an *oomph* sound and they both went to the ground. Rainey got to his feet first, but the guy was quick and shot up with an uppercut. Rainey absorbed the blow with a grunt. He reached out and grabbed the man's shirt with both hands. He pulled the man toward him and at the same time rolled onto his back, pushing his right foot into the man's abdomen. The man disappeared over the balustrade and into the canyon, letting loose a primal scream as he fell.

Rainey jumped up and sprinted as fast as he could along the western side of the bridge. Fig and Jazz each continued to fire. Rainey was halfway across the bridge when he saw a terrified little girl balled-up and screaming. She was tucked into a small alcove set into the wall from which tourists could look down into the canyon. Rainey swerved over and scooped her up in one arm. With his free hand, he held his rifle from swinging wildly and ran for his life and the girl's.

When Rainey reached the other side, he blew past Fig, Jazz and Alcott. With the girl still tucked under his arm, Rainey darted beneath an archway at the front of a long row of shops, which he hoped was out of the line of fire from the shooters in the plaza. From the doorway of one of them, a frantic woman screamed. She ran to him, her arms wide and eyes wrecked with tears. He bent over and gently placed the girl in her arms and directed her to get inside and to stay down.

Rainey turned back toward the fight, posted up behind a concrete support beam and yelled. "I'm up! Let's go!" As his teammates raced toward him, he fired across the bridge at anyone who posed a threat. When the trio was past him, he turned and sprinted after them. They rounded the corner onto Calle Tenorio and kept running.

◆ ◆ ◆

Zarek Tarło fired again. The muzzle of his Beretta ARX 160 was red hot. He and his men had been trading rounds back and forth across the bridge with two shooters that were apparently here in support of either Reagan Rainey or Moses. How his surveillance teams had missed them he couldn't fathom, but he would deal them later. Whoever these two men were, they were skilled practitioners of urban warfare. Their tactics and calm under fire were top-notch.

He ducked down and reloaded, scanning the plaza as he did so. From his position, he easily counted eight men, *his* men, who were down for the count and two more with gunshot wounds that didn't look good. They would probably be dead, too, in a matter of minutes.

He radioed his men. Only four responded. *Four* out of eighteen.

Impossible.

Tarło popped up to fire when he caught movement in his periphery. His finger poised on the trigger, he rotated his head to the right. *There he is! Reagan Rainey.* There was another man with him. They were both armed with short-barreled rifles. The second man wasn't Moses. That much was certain. His watcher on the terrace had already radioed the teams with Moses' description the moment he'd laid eyes on him. No, the second guy must be with Rainey. Probably CIA, too.

He watched Rainey and the other man crouch down by the gate, which led to the footpath. He could no longer see them. Tarło craned his neck. What were they doing? He had his answer a few seconds later.

Both men leapt up, burst through the gate and turned to cross the bridge, now a gauntlet of abandoned cars and motorbikes that were parked at all manner of angles and riddled with bullets. A maroon Toyota Camry was aflame in the middle of the bridge. The ravenous fire spewed thick, black smoke into the perfect blue sky. It could have been Dublin during the Troubles or Sarajevo in the 90s. Ronda had become a warzone.

Tarło leveled his carbine at Rainey's back. *You're mine.* Suddenly, rounds punched into the truck that he was using for cover. He jerked back his head just as several of them chewed into the metal grille and headlamp assembly in front of him. A mist of glass and plastic wafted around the corner of the truck and into his mouth and nose. The taste was gritty and had the tang of chemicals. He scraped the tiny particulates from his tongue using his front teeth and spat them to the ground, coughed and spat again.

He popped his head up and ducked immediately. Another fusillade ripped long ovals across the truck's hood, sparked off the bumper and chiseled white scuff marks into the stone setts of the road. When he was finally able to manage a solid peek, he saw Rainey's three gun-toting helpers sprinting away on the other side of the bridge. And no Rainey.

Tarło leaned into the truck wheel and rallied his troops. "Everyone, get to the bridge! Now! They're heading south!" Moses had already vanished. He wasn't going to let Rainey get away, too. Come hell or high water, Reagan Rainey was going to die in Ronda. "Move it!"

He slammed a fresh magazine into his gun and jumped out to lead the charge. He saw the muzzle flash first on the far side of the bridge. Then came the chattering report of an SBR, the snap and sizzle of rounds whizzing past him. The two men sprinting beside him dropped to the roadway as if someone had just flipped a switch and shut off their life force.

Still, he ran. He ran like a madman as adrenaline surged through him. He had made it several paces onto the bridge when something that felt like a hammer hit him in the right bicep. He slowed and shook his hand, trying to force the feeling back into his fingers. He quickly spied his arm. His shirtsleeve was already soaked through with blood.

A feeling of light-headedness washed over him and he dropped to his knees. He scrambled behind a car and rolled to a seated position. Tarło pulled out a combat tourniquet and applied it to his arm with the speed and efficiency of a man who had practiced for just such a scenario. When the tourniquet was secure and his arm throbbed from a lack of circulation, he gripped his carbine and forced himself to slow his breathing. He tilted his head upward and took in the entirety of the plaza turned battlefield. People—not all his—lie dead and dying, vehicles and buildings were littered with bullet holes, puddles of shattered glass gleamed in the sun like diamonds. Police sirens and car alarms wailed.

The grime of war smeared across his face, he tucked his rifle into his left shoulder and ground his teeth. He spouted off a string of vulgarities, stood up and spun toward his foes, prepared to fight to the death.

But instead of gunfire, he was greeted only with silence.

48

RAINEY and his three teammates ran a block until they were off the main thoroughfare. As they slowed to a walk, Rainey noticed Jazz was bleeding from his right thigh.

"Is it bad?"

"Nah, man. I'm good."

"You sure?"

Jazz glanced down at his leg. "Yeah. Just got me in the meat. Hurts like a mother, though."

"Here we go," barked Fig, still leaning into the open window of a little Renault Kangoo that was parked in front of the Restaurante Duquesa de Parcent. The driver had been kind enough to leave the keys in the ignition. They promptly crawled inside and pulled away. Tiny as the van was, it barely fit through the cramped streets. Fig eventually nosed out onto Calle Armiñán and eased down on the accelerator so as not to be conspicuous. The road leading out of the city was sloped and curved forcing Fig to apply constant pressure to the brakes.

The men inside the van were quiet, especially Rainey. He sat in the back on a stack of folded bedsheets, his SBR in his lap and angled toward the floor. His eyes were as intense as ever, and though it may have seemed like they were scanning the streets for threats, his focus was now elsewhere. The video clip of his father played in his mind over and over again, interrupted only by a voice beside him—it was Alcott's—radioing Babe, giving him updates on their progress and a location for them to meet in the south end of the city.

In a matter of minutes, they piled into Babe's sedan, leaving the borrowed van parked on a vacant side street. They continued south on the A-397 toward Marbella. It wasn't until they were coming down out of the hills of southern Spain and the hazy Mediterranean appeared in the distance that Rainey snapped from his reverie. He had already described his short meeting with Moses and the video clip to his teammates. They were both stunned and motivated.

Rainey dialed up Job from the back seat. He told him about what had happened in Ronda, the encounter with Moses, and the video clip of his dad. Job listened to all of it without interruption then offered him careful instructions which included where they should ditch their gear and how each of them would leave the country. Spain and the United States were close allies, especially in the War on Terror, but Spanish authorities would be livid if they knew Americans were operating on their soil, let alone involved in such a highly visible incident without their knowledge or permission. The truth would eventually shake itself out, but for now Rainey and his team needed to get out of the country with the least amount of fanfare possible.

When they reached the coast, Babe turned the car north toward Málaga. Despite a short detour to patch up Jazz's leg and dump their gear—a DX support staff member would later collect it and make it disappear for good—they made decent time to the airport without having to drive at excessive speeds. They left the car in the lot with the windows down and the keys in the ignition after wiping it clean of fingerprints and cutting out a part of the back seat where Jazz's leg had bled.

Rainey and Alcott boarded a flight to Milan, Fig and Babe one to Munich, while Jazz would hang loose for a couple of hours then fly to Geneva on Swissair. The plan was for all of them to link back up in Zurich in two days at an address Job had provided and to keep a low profile in the meantime.

49

Guantánamo Bay, Cuba

MADDIE walked back inside from the oppressive heat. It was only a little past 7:00 A.M., but the humidity was already suffocating. Her leg was still stiff and swollen, but it felt markedly better than it had a few days ago.

The door, marked simply "Camp Zero," fell shut with a whoosh. The chill from the building's air conditioning was immediate and it was glorious. She rubbed the goose bumps on her forearms as she followed Evelina down the empty corridor. It was nothing to look at, this prison. The cinder block walls were painted a bland cream color. The tile floor was dull and worn down the middle. But it was clean. And secure. Very.

Camp Zero was designated a restricted access site even among those stationed at Gitmo. The staff assigned here was a mix of current and former CIA employees. Those who no longer worked for the Agency were contract employees. It was smaller than the other prison camps here. In fact, it really wasn't a prison camp per se. It was more a temporary detention facility for very special prisoners to roost in between interrogation sessions, which were conducted in a separate section of the multi-building complex.

The nearly three days of waiting had driven Maddie and her fellow warrior spies crazy, but such was the business of intelligence. She was learning that waiting was perhaps the biggest part of the job. But now the waiting was over. They had just been given the good news: the man, named Mihai Cioabă, was talking.

She sat down beside Evelina in a conference room. Tonka and Mouse both waltzed in a minute later and plopped down across from them. Each of the men had a sandwich and a bottle of water.

"Always eating," said Maddie with a grin.

"C'mon, Swan. Gotta feed the pythons." Mouse jokingly flexed his biceps. "They don't like to go hungry."

Maddie was still shaking her head at Mouse's goofy antics when the conference room door swung open again. In walked Job Jackson with a stack of files tucked under his arm. He closed the door behind him then took a seat at the head of the table.

"All right. Here's the deal. Mr. Cioabă is talking. So far, he's had some interesting things to say about what he and his associates were doing in Venezuela and about the person for whom they work. They were sent there to destroy the plane."

"Mission accomplished," said Maddie.

"Yes, well…"

"Who sent them?" said Evelina.

Job opened the top file, extracted several sheets of paper held together with a paper clip. "His name is Zarek Tarło." He passed the dossier to Evelina.

"Zarek Tarło?!" said Mouse, sitting up. "I once knew a Zarek Tarło. We did some joint training ops with him and some of the GROM teams about three, four years ago. What's he got to do with this?"

"Who's Zarek Tarło," said Evelina.

Mouse propped his elbows on the table. "He's a deputy commander of GROM, Poland's counterterror unit."

"*Former* deputy commander," clarified Job. "He now runs an outfit called RWS, LLC. Per its articles of organization, RWS is a security consulting firm based in College Park, Maryland. But according to our friend down the hall, they do much more than consulting. Much more."

"Mercs," offered Tonka.

"Exactly, but RWS is not some backwater, soldiers-of-fortune operation—big men with big tattoos and big guns for hire. Huh-uh. No, RWS is high-speed. It hires only the best. Most of the staff are Special Forces types or have that kind of training. They're skilled operators with real-world experience, i.e. combat experience. The company employs former and *active-duty* security and intelligence officers all over the world, too. As a result, they have access to blank passports and other identity documents, which help them slip in and out of countries as needed. Each employee generally has four, five aliases depending on how active he or she is. Since two thousand twelve, Cioabă has been living under one of his aliases. That's why he's been off the grid. Last, but certainly not least, RWS maintains a very selective clientele. Very powerful, too.

"Now, Cioabă doesn't know who the company's clients are—only Tarło does—but he does know Tarło. And he's agreed to help us find him. Cioabă says he last knew Tarło was en route to London to deal with an RWS agent that botched an operation. Guy worked for Scotland Yard. Name's Rory Alvin."

"Worked?" said Evelina.

"Yes. He's dead. But I'll get to that. Seems that RWS had some kind of logistical snafu and therefore had used him to hire some local talent to kill…," Job stopped, looked at Maddie. "To deal with Ray and Pappy as well as a former Agency employee by the name of Ernie Wells, who has been living in England. Don't worry, Maddie. They failed. Ray is fine. So are Pappy and Wells.

"The investigation into who tried to kill them led us to Alvin's flat in London. Tarło must have beaten us to him by minutes. He rigged the flat so that when the raid team tossed in their stun grenade, the whole place blew. Alvin was later found in the rubble. He'd been strangled.

"Bottom line: whoever hired Tarło and his company does not want whatever it was your father was working on to come to light." Job quickly filled them in on what was known about Ben Rainey's part in Operation Triumph. "We believe the same person might be behind the assassination of the DNI."

"Assassination?" said Evelina. "I thought he died of a heart attack."

"We're confident it was made to look that way. Bureau's already been notified. They are proceeding with utmost discretion." Job explained his meeting with McManus's wife and the files that she discovered missing from her husband's safe. "The files were in an envelope labeled, *Artifacts of Triumph*."

"Artifacts of Triumph?" said Mouse. "More like artifacts of conspiracy."

"Somehow Zarek Tarło and his mystery client connect to all of it. To Moses and his letter. To Ben Rainey. And to Operation Triumph. Ray's already working on the Moses angle. I need you guys to find Tarło. He doesn't work from some cushy office. He works in the shadows. Same as us."

There was a quick knock on the door and a staff member entered. She went directly to Job, leaned over his shoulder and whispered into his ear. Maddie watched with anticipation. They all did. Something had happened. Job's face turned grim at the news, whatever it was.

When the lady was gone, Job stood. "I'm sorry, but I need to take a phone call. Hang loose for few minutes. I'll be right back."

A few minutes turned into an hour. When Job returned his eyes were red. He sat down and pursed his lips as if he were fighting back tears.

"What is it?" said Maddie.

"I just spoke to Ray. He had a meeting with Moses in Spain." Job shook his head. "I don't believe it—."

"Believe what? What is it?"

"Maddie, it looks like your father really may be alive."

It hit her like a ton of bricks.

"Moses showed Ray a video clip of your father. He's in some kind of prison or at least what looked like a prison. He didn't appear to be in good health."

She shot up, pressed her palms on the table. "Where?"

"We don't know yet. We don't even know when the footage was captured. It could have been years ago. It could have been days ago. Their meeting was cut short. Someone launched an attack on them. By the grace of God, Ray and his team managed to escape without serious injury. Moses' status is unknown, but Ray's hoping he can make contact again. That's if he got out alive."

"It's Tarło. It's gotta be," said Evelina.

"I'm thinking you're right."

Maddie shoved her chair over and walked to the far corner of the room. She wanted to cry, wanted to fight, wanted to do something, anything other than just sitting here and talking. But she had to contain her emotions. Emotions wouldn't get her dad back. She unclenched her fists. "What now, Job? What do you want us to do?"

"Find Tarło. That's your mission now. Find him and then we find out who hired him."

50

FOUR hours later they were headed out of Reagan National in a Directorate X Chevy Suburban. It had taken them that long to hatch their plan.

"Are you sure you want to do this?" said Evelina.

Maddie gripped the door handle. "Absolutely. Besides, it's my idea. It's only fair that I be the one in the crosshairs should anything go wrong. Just cover my backside."

"Don't worry. We will."

They dropped her off outside her building in D.C. She wanted to clean up and give Wes a call before she went shopping. She needed to hear his voice and let him know she was okay. Her working for Directorate X and the CIA was going to be a challenge for both of them. It would certainly test their relationship. But if anyone could do it, they could.

She checked her messages then took a hot shower after which she threw on jeans and an old American University T-shirt. The cabinets in the kitchen were mostly bare. There was nothing in the fridge either except a gallon of milk that was a few days past its sell-by date. She settled on a bowl of Lucky Charms as she mused about her father. The revelation of him being held somewhere and treated like an animal infuriated her.

Maddie was like her brother in many ways, neither of them needed additional incentives when they had set their mind to something. Both were incredibly self-motivated and stubbornly resolute in their pursuits. It was a Rainey thing. And they were darn proud of it.

The thought of finding Tarło consumed her. He had information that could potentially lead them to her dad. Maddie bowed her head over her cereal and prayed.

Father God, thank you for giving us Your Son to die on the cross to save us from our sins. Thank you for your grace and mercy and endless love. I'm deserving of none of it. Thank you for keeping us safe in Venezuela, for watching over me and my friends. You are great, God. You are faithful and true. Please, oh God, please, please, please, if my father is truly alive, comfort him. Let him know somehow that you are there working in mysterious ways for Your glory. Please, grant me and Ray and the others strength, courage and clarity in order to find him alive and bring him home for good. I ask all these things in Jesus' name. Amen.

Maddie finished her cereal. She dropped her empty bowl in the sink, rinsed it out and picked up the phone. It was Sunday and she knew Wes would likely be at his mom and dad's house outside Lovettsville, Virginia. He had a large, tight-knit family and they almost always congregated there after church for a huge Sunday lunch. It would soon be football season, too, when half the family watched football while the other half played board games or talked about their families and the kids played in the woods outside or engaged in otherwise harmless mischief. She loved every minute of it. She wished she were there now.

The phone rang a few times until Wes finally answered with a hearty hello. She could hear loud jovialities in the background. Laughing and story-telling.

"Maddie, how are you, *where* are you?"

"I'm fine, honey. I just stopped in town to pick up a few things before I head back out."

"For how long? Can I see you before you go? I'll leave right now."

"No, no. Don't do that. Stay and have fun. I just wanted to tell you that I love you."

"Maddie, is everything okay?"

"Just pray for my mom, pray for my whole family right now. That's all I can say for the time being."

There were a few seconds of silence then, "Okay. I will. I love you, Maddie."

"I love you, too. Say hi to your family for me."

"Will do. They miss you. And so do I. Terribly."

Maddie smiled into the phone. "I miss you guys, too."

"Promise me you'll be careful."

"I promise. All right, I gotta go. I'll see ya when I get back."

"Bye, my love."

51

THE oversized wooden door swung open as the doorbell chimes were still echoing inside the cavernous foyer. A silver-haired man in a black tuxedo jacket with tails and neatly pressed gray slacks greeted her. Vera Lysniak flashed a faux smile and stepped inside, waited for the butler to close the door. It latched behind her with a quiet, sturdy thud. With the submissive eyes and perfect posture of a dutiful servant, the butler held out one of his white-gloved hands. "This way, if you please, madam."

He led her through the house without question or comment. Her arrival had been expected. Vera had never been here during daylight hours, always after dark. Some would say she did her best work in the dark. Or in the shadows, to be precise. The mansion was magnificent, everything about it. In fact, this was not a mansion. A mansion was like a tool shed in comparison. This was a palace.

Her heels clopped along the polished floor. The Old World design was divine. The woven tapestries and dark, wood-paneled walls, the three-story, stained-glass window straight ahead put a twinkle in her eye. They soon passed beneath a gigantic, wrought-iron chandelier that must have taken a small army of men or a crane to hang. Two long staircases swept upward on opposite sides of the room. The tops of them disappeared somewhere behind her at a height that in a normal house would be equivalent to the fourth floor.

They turned left through an archway and set off down a long hall. She counted six slender tables along the sides of the corridor, all of them hand-carved teak, atop which were colorful vases. One of them was probably worth more than the whole of her estate. They each had a dedicated lamp housed in a rectangle of brass that set them in a subdued light. It could have been a museum. There were rooms on the right and the left, some doors open, some doors closed. She'd been in a few of them before. The study with the Aubusson rug and the leather-topped, walnut desk. The library with endless tomes, most of them first editions—books for which some people would give anything just to glimpse once in a lifetime.

Midway down the hall, they came to a gilded rosewood grandfather clock that chimed thrice. Here they turned to the right, which brought them to yet another hall every bit as long as the first. Vera switched her handbag to the other arm and tried to keep pace with the butler who could walk a line like the sentinel at the Tomb of the Unknown Soldier.

Finally, they came to a spacious parlor and continued across to a set of French doors that put them outside onto the smallest of the main house's three verandas. Stedman Carter was sitting at a glass and wrought-iron table beneath a mammoth pergola canopy. A wall-mounted, 60-inch plasma TV was switched on and tuned to a number of business and news channels, though the volume was muted. Carter set a china cup into a saucer and stood as she negotiated the half dozen steps onto the terrace.

"Vera, good afternoon. Glad you could come."

"Hello, Stedman."

Carter asked his servant to bring out another tray of tea. The man bent forward a few degrees at the waist and said, "Very well, sir," then receded back into the house.

"So where's your wife?"

"Still in Paris, spending my money."

She smiled. "Oh, how nice."

"Please, have a seat. Would you like something to eat?"

"No, thank you. The tea will be just fine."

Carter held the back of the chair until Vera was seated then pushed her in. He smoothed his tie as he circled back around to his own chair.

Vera followed him with eyes of predation. "So how are you?" she said.

Carter let out a hefty sigh. "Not good. They got away."

"They what?"

"Rainey and Moses, they both got away. Zarek's people blew it. I don't know how, but they did. And now I don't know what to do. Can you believe that, Vera? For the first time in my life, I don't know what to do."

She placed her handbag on the table. Oh, how she relished this moment, when a man as powerful and charming and gorgeous as Stedman Carter was as vulnerable as a baby rabbit. She looked at the back of her hands, her red-polished nails. She would stroke his ego, build him up and ensnare him with her deviousness and womanly wiles. Plying not only her gainful wisdom but her body as well, Vera would own Stedman Carter in one fell swoop. It had been this way with the president of the United States. Even to this day, she owned Grantley Winslow. And the poor fool didn't even know it. Yes, they were the closest of friends, but truth be told she controlled, manipulated, used him for her own devices. Though she would admit it to no one. Not ever. And so it would be with *billionaire* Stedman Carter

"Come now, Stedman. All is not lost."

"Vera, were you not listening? They got away. If this Moses guy really does have information about Ben Rainey, worse yet, if Ben Rainey is still alive and the CIA finds him, we will be ruined! Have you forgotten what that means for the president's campaign? Ben Rainey shows up alive and tells America what he knows, there will *be* no more campaign."

"Relax, my dear. Calm down. Now, I've been thinking. The incident in Ronda has been all over the news. No one knows what happened or why. I can tell you one thing, the president is pissed at the Agency. They never informed him about the meeting in Spain. He hates them to begin with and would positively love to embarrass them in spectacular fashion. The question is: how can we embarrass the CIA in such a way that doesn't harm the administration? Better yet, that also hands us the election in November."

"You have an idea, don't you?"

She smiled. "Maybe."

He sat quietly and listened to her musings. When she was finished, he was giddy with excitement. "Vera, you are incredible."

"And I'm just getting started, Stedman."

"Say, how about a dip in the pool before you go?"

"But I don't have a suit."

"Who said you need one?"

"Oh, Stedman, you *are* a naughty boy."

52

College Park, Maryland

THE following day, a shiny, black Mercedes Benz AMG GLS63 with dark-tinted windows pulled into the parking lot of a modest office park that consisted of four one-story, brown brick buildings. There were no signs, no evidence whatsoever to indicate the names of the businesses within. The only way to differentiate between offices was by examining the suite numbers—white vinyl decals at the upper right corner of each door.

"Please be careful. Remember, anything doesn't feel right, get the heck out. Not sure I like the fact that there are two Raineys to worry about now. One is bad enough."

"Relax, Pappy. I appreciate the concern, but I'll be fine. I can take care of myself."

Saul Baker's eyes were in the rearview mirror. "I know you can, but… Just be careful, will ya? I'll be praying everything goes smoothly."

Maddie grinned. "I will. And thanks."

She alighted from the back seat of the SUV and stepped onto the sidewalk, doing due diligence not to break an ankle in her black Gianvito Rossi pumps. Her knee was still sore, but at least the swelling had subsided. She adjusted her pencil skirt at her hips, pulled the sides of her business suit forward, and slid her Fendi handbag to her elbow. She wore her lustrous brown hair in a bun and a pair of tortoise-shell eye-glasses that seemed to draw attention to her intelligent, amber eyes.

A mustached man with a cream-colored T-shirt and green work trousers came around the corner of the building. In one of his cal-loused hands, he carried a pair of red-handled shears, the other a thick cigar. He lumbered across the lawn toward a trailer that was parked in the corner of the lot. Jammed inside, were riding mowers, gas-powered trimmers and other tools. As Maddie drew near, his eyes clumsily fell to the hint of cleavage at the neckline of her blouse. His face screwed up into a goofy smile and he nearly walked into the handicapped parking sign jutting up from the sidewalk.

Completely in role, Maddie paid him no mind. Instead, she shuffled around a clump of fresh-cut grass that lay in her way as if by merely touching it, even with the sole of her shoe, she might contract some exotic disease for which there was no known cure. Finally, she turned left onto the straight cement footpath that led to the door of Suite C-8.

◆ ◆ ◆

Mouse, Tonka and Evelina sat along the street in a champagne-colored Dodge Caravan with blacked-out windows. They were far enough away to be invisible, but close enough to keep eyes on Maddie.

"There she goes," said Evelina.

Mouse leaned into the side of the van, his eyes following Maddie intently. When he turned back, he saw Evelina staring at him with eye-brows raised. "What?" he said.

"Dude, she's Bronco's *sister*," said Tonka.

"I know that. I can't help that she's hot. Oh… Well, uh… Evie you're hot, too. Don't—"

"You're kidding me, right?" said Evelina, both hands on the binoc-ulars in her lap.

Tonka dropped his forehead into his hands and slowly shook his head back and forth.

"What? What'd I say?" said Mouse, his cheeks reddening. He looked at Tonka for an escape.

Evelina rolled her eyes. "You're pathetic. You know that, right?"

Mouse turned his palms up and shrugged as if he had been accused of a crime that he did not commit.

Evelina—the compassionate judge—shook her head and administered his parole. "Relax, tough guy. I grew up with five older brothers. Just try to stay focused, okay?"

◆ ◆ ◆

The reception area was small and plain and smelled of recently vacuumed carpet and computer paper. Upon her entry, a middle-aged woman with short blonde hair and narrow eyeglasses looked up from a widescreen computer monitor on a glass and metal desk. The quick appraisal of Maddie's form and figure snapped her visage from cold, calculating centurion to eager-to-please concierge.

"May I help you, miss?"

"I certainly hope so. Is this the office of RWS."

"Yes. It is."

"Very good. My name is Frannie Green. I'm looking for a Mr. Zarek Tarło."

"Is he expecting you?"

"No."

"Well then, I would encourage you to schedule an appointment for another time. Mr. Tarło is very busy."

Maddie wrinkled her nose. "No, that won't work. I need to see him now. I assure you, it will be worth Mr. Tarło's time to meet with me."

The woman's face hardened. The centurion had returned. "I'm sorry, miss, but Mr. Tarło cannot meet with you right this minute. Now, if you would care to schedule an appointment..."

Maddie narrowed her eyes, jutted out her left hip, the quintessential Washington D.C. power player who was more than prepared for a battle of wits and wills. With a not-so-subtle edge in her tone, she said, "How soon will he be available?"

"He won't be back in the office until Wednesday at eleven."

"Are you sure he can't meet with me anytime sooner, today preferably? I work for a very powerful man, a man whose influence is hard to fathom. Perhaps even for someone like you. He was told that RWS provides *special* services to a select clientele and that Mr. Tarło would be able to help him with his…um…private matter."

"On whose behalf are you here?"

Maddie parried with a condescending explanation as if the woman were too naïve to know better. "I'm sorry, but my boss has a penchant for absolute discretion. He insisted that I deal directly with Mr. Tarło and that even his name be spared until such time."

"I see. Well, RWS prides itself on complete confidentiality."

"Excellent."

"But I'm afraid Mr. Tarło really is unavailable at the current time. Perhaps you would care to meet with one of our other associates."

Maddie shook her head impatiently. "No, no. I've been given strict instructions to only deal with Mr. Tarło. My boss isn't going to like this. He had his heart set on RWS for…well, for reasons best left unsaid. Just between you and me," she leaned closer, "he's willing to pay a *lot of money* for Mr. Tarło's close, personal attention to this delicate matter. But, hey, if you're not available, you're not available. Am I right?"

"If you want to schedule something for Wednesday, I can squeeze you in at eleven-thirty."

"No, that'll be too late. The senator, I mean…." Maddie blushed. "Do me a favor, forget you heard that."

The woman smiled as if she'd been the first to draw blood.

"As I was saying, my *boss* needs the job done within the next few days. I guess he'll just have to find someone else."

"Who did you say you were again?" said the receptionist.

"Frannie Green."

"Do you have a card, Miss Green? Or is there a number at which we can reach you in case there would be a change in Mr. Tarło's schedule?"

"Certainly," said Maddie, sensing a nibble.

The woman accepted the business card, examined its contents. She was still picking at the embossed letters with her thumbnail when she said, "And you were referred to RWS?"

"Yes, that's right."

"May I ask who made the referral?"

"No. You may not. What I mean, is that he asked that his name be kept in strict confidence. I am, however, permitted to mention that the job will not involve travel to Spain, which should come as a relief to Mr. Tarło."

"Spain?"

"Yes. I'm told the Andalucían area especially is rather hot right now."

"I'm not sure I understand."

"No?" Maddie held her gaze.

"I'm sorry, no. Nevertheless, Miss Green, I will pass your message along."

Maddie slid on her expensive sunglasses, exited the RWS office and pressed down the sidewalk at a pace that suggested she had other important business ahead of her. As she approached the vehicle, Saul hopped out and scurried around to open her door.

She said nothing as she climbed in. Instead, she frowned into her smartphone, which had never left her hand even inside the RWS office, and made a show of appearing unsatisfied with the brief encounter.

Saul held the door with both hands as he waited for Maddie to pull her legs inside the SUV. "She's watching from the window. Play it all the way through, my dear." He closed the door, tugged on the bill of his chauffeur's cap and reclaimed his place behind the wheel. The vehicle nosed into traffic and Saul's eyes appeared in the rearview mirror. "How'd it go?"

Maddie kicked off her heels and sunk back into the seat. "Good. They bought it."

53

Rockville, Maryland

THEY congregated in the back room of Founders Coffee Shoppe, which was normally reserved for holiday parties, banquets and other large gatherings but was now empty and quiet. The only sounds came from the other side of a set of sliding double doors: the muted din of diners; the occasional outburst of laughter; the shrill wail of a baby's cry. The proprietor had ushered them inside a back door before whisking off to retrieve place settings. He promptly returned with utensils wrapped in navy blue napkins and arrayed them around the table for his guests while a waitress took drink orders. He gave Saul a big hug and then shook hands with each member of the team. Due to the sensitivity of their office, no names, real or otherwise, were divulged.

Maddie slid into a chair, crossed her legs and picked up a menu as the owner withdrew into the kitchen. "You come here often, Pappy?"

"Whenever I'm up this way, yeah. The owner is retired Bureau. Worked CI. You know…a spy hunter. We crossed paths quite a bit over the years—on the Pitts and Hanssen cases and Ames, too. He's as solid as they come. Guy will do anything for you, too. I brought your brother here a couple years ago. He absolutely loved it. It's one of his favorite places to steal away to, but don't tell him I told you."

"Is that right?" said Mouse conspiratorially.

"Yep. Locals love it, too. Especially the cops. That's the best indicator of whether a restaurant is good or not, ya know. If the cops eat there, it's gotta be good. And clean."

Maddie pointed to the wall. "Well, I can see why Ray loves it." The restaurant was adorned with prints of famous paintings, small plaques with stenciled quotations from men like Washington, Franklin, Madison and Jefferson, along with framed replicas of historical documents and letters. Affixed to the wall beside her was a print of Arnold Friberg's famous painting, *The Prayer at Valley Forge.*

"That's Ray's favorite. Mine, too. Amazing isn't it? Ray's got a rather good reproduction hanging in his study. I find the image to be incredibly moving. Consider it: George Washington, a man so pivotal in our nation's history, there on his knees, bowing his head in submission to Almighty God. If only we had leaders like that today, men and women of courage, who dare to honor God and do what's right in His eyes, regardless of whether or not it's right for their party or their own self-interest. I think that's the first step to solving our country's ils, you know. We, all of us on a daily basis, need to humble ourselves before God and seek His will. And do what's right."

"I thought Washington was a deist, Pappy. Why would he be praying?" said Evelina.

Saul frowned. "Washington was *not* a deist. No, sir! He was a faithful man of God. You don't have to take my word for it. The evidence exists; it's out there. In fact, it's shocking just how much God was involved in the nation's founding. But sadly, the predatory revisionists, the progressives and their elite media co-conspirators have corrupted American history. They want to color over our godly heritage, our *real* history. But such is the nature of deception. As we well know. Deception, successfully employed, fosters further deception. It can harden hearts and confound the most erudite of mankind. It can even breed contempt for the truth."

Tonka nodded. "Heck, Pappy. They've taken God out of everything else in this country. Shouldn't surprise anyone that they would try to remove Him from our heritage."

Mouse agreed with a hearty nod. "I can see why you and Bronco get along so well. He says a lot of the same stuff. It doesn't take much to get him going."

A smiling waitress brought them coffee and water then took their orders. Maddie dropped two cubes of sugar into her cup and poured in a few drips of cream, gave it a careful stir with her spoon.

Leaning away from them, Evelina pressed Maddie's phone to her left ear. She was listening again to Maddie's little dust-up with the receptionist. Maddie had recorded the whole thing with her phone in plain sight. Sometimes the best way to camouflage a deception was operating right out there in the open. When the audio clip was over, Evelina looked up. "Wow, Swan really nailed the Miss Snooty Pants routine. You're a natural, Maddie. She probably called him the minute you left the office."

Mouse sipped his coffee. "Any bets on how soon Tarło calls?"

"A few hours tops," said Evelina. "If that veiled comment about Ronda isn't enough to get them going, the images of Maddie in that dress will be. RWS has to have at least one camera inside the office whether it was visible to you, Maddie, or not. Yeah. Smart money says he'll call inside three hours or so. I figure that will be long enough to run the phone number on the card and the tag on the Benz."

"Seriously?" said Mouse. "You think it'll be that soon?"

Evelina smiled. "Based on the way these two reacted, um yeah."

"Whaddya mean?" said Maddie.

"Nothing," snapped Mouse, his face turning bright red just as the waitress appeared with their food.

"Let's just eat, okay?" suggested Tonka. "But just for the record, I'm with Evie."

54

THE flight from Spain had been long and taxing. To avoid scrutiny, he had driven to Barcelona where he boarded one of Stedman Carter's private jets and flew to Baltimore. An RWS employee had picked him up there and had driven him home. Now, nearly 24 hours after the disaster in Ronda, his arm was sore and stiff and he had a splitting headache. All he wanted to do was rest and forget Reagan Rainey and Moses, whoever he was.

Zarek Tarło stepped across the threshold of his luxury townhouse on R Street NW and into the welcoming comfort of home. He dropped his duffel bag and maneuvered into the living room where he fell into a recliner, careful not to bump his slung arm. He closed his eyes and laid his head back. He was just starting to nod off when one of his cell phones buzzed inside his pocket—not the phone he used to communicate with Stedman Carter, but his RWS work phone.

Leave me alone.

He almost didn't answer, but decided it was probably important. In fact, it had to be, because he had already given the office staff strict orders not to bother him unless it was for something that just couldn't wait. His plan was to relax the rest of the day then check in with Carter in the morning. He had already briefed him on what had happened in Ronda, already endured the initial barrage of rage from a man who was accustomed to getting what he wanted. Always. But what could they have done differently? Someone with a lot of talent and a lot of firepower had helped Rainey or Moses or both. It was perplexing how his people had missed them. Indeed, the mission was a miserable failure. Stedman Carter would be on the warpath for good now. That would be both bad for business and for him personally. But right now he was too tired and sore to think about it anymore. He needed sleep.

The phone continued to buzz. He held it in his left hand, cracked his eyelids and confirmed that it was the office calling.

"Yes," he said, his eyes falling shut again.

"Mr. Tarło, sir, it's Gladys."

"Yes, Gladys. What is it?"

"Someone dropped by the office a few minutes ago."

"Who?"

"She called her herself *Frannie Green*. Said she was referred to RWS, but wouldn't say by whom."

"C'mon, Gladys, speed it up. I'm tired. Just tell me why you called."

"She mentioned Spain, sir."

There was a pause.

"Sir? Are you still there?"

"I'll be right in."

55

College Park, Maryland

WHADDYA got?" said Tarło, staring at the computer monitor on his desk.

The receptionist sat down across from him, a yellow legal pad in her hands and her half-moon reading glasses on the tip of her nose. "The number is untraceable. And nothing's come back on the tag yet either, but I'll keep trying it."

"Okay." Tarło played the video footage again. He scrutinized every inch of the woman who had presented as Miss Frannie Green in the RWS front office two hours earlier. She had a sleek, athletic build. Heck, she was drop-dead gorgeous. Dressed like a million bucks, she appeared to have access to money, too. And based on the allusion to Ronda, Frannie Green was very well connected. But how could anyone know that he was in Ronda? It's just not possible. Unless someone was talking.

He stroked his forehead. "Has the team in Venezuela checked in yet?"

"No, sir."

Tarło tilted his wrist, drew back his shirtsleeve and noted the time.

"They're due back tomorrow," said the receptionist. "Maybe they had trouble with their comms. You know, couldn't get a signal out. It *is* the rainforest, sir."

"Thank you, Gladys. But something's not right. We have to assume the team has been compromised. In any case, someone is talking."

"What are your wishes, sir?"

"Dust off the burn bags. I want everything gone within the next twelve hours. *Everything*. Laptops, servers, phones, files, you name it."

"Consider it done."

"But first, alert whoever we have in town and put them on standby. I have a feeling I'm gonna need them."

"Yessir," said the receptionist before scurrying out of the office.

Tarło picked up a clean cell phone and punched in the number on the business card. It rang twice before a strong, confident and very female voice came on the line.

"Uh, yes. Miss Green, please."

"Speaking. And you are?"

"Zarek Tarło. You wanted to see me?"

"Yes, that's right. Well, I did, but we are no longer in need of your services. It seems word about what happened in Ronda has reached my boss's ears. Pursuant to my advice, he has now decided to stay clear of you *and* RWS. You understand."

"Wait, wait. I don't know what on earth you're talking about."

"Come now, Mr. Tarło. Let's not play games."

"Miss Green, if that is in fact your real name, I assure you that I do *not* play games."

"Yes, well…"

"It seems your employer has been given some bad information. Please, allow me to take you to lunch and maybe we can resolve this. For both our sakes."

"I don't know. My boss was pretty upset to hear about Ronda."

"I don't know who you work for, but trust me, RWS had nothing to do with Ronda or any other place in Spain. Frankly, miss, it's very disturbing to hear that RWS' reputation has been compromised. In my business reputation is everything."

The woman hesitated. "Well, you *were* highly recommended."

"Please, fifteen minutes. That's all I ask."

"All right. I'll give you fifteen minutes. No more. My time is precious. Do you know where the Torpedo Factory Art Center is?"

"Yes, I think so. In Alexandria."

"That's right. Be there in three hours. On the riverfront I'll be wearing a red American U T-shirt and blue jeans."

"Thank you, Miss Green, thank you. I trust we—."

Click.

"Miss Green?" He looked at his phone.

The line was dead.

Tarło stood as one of his subordinates rounded the corner into his office. "Where is she?"

"She's in D.C. Outside the Library of Congress."

He pulled a pistol out of his top drawer and pushed it into his waistband. "Get everyone to the Torpedo Factory Art Center. This one's not getting away."

56

Zurich, Switzerland

REAGAN Rainey hopped over a log and continued running along the narrow, dirt path. For a little over an hour now, he had been winding through the dark, pine forest as thoughts wound through his mind. He pressed the pace faster ignoring the fact that his lungs and legs were already burning. He climbed a hillock and gritted his teeth. He ran harder, faster still.

When he broke through the trees he was nearly sprinting. The trail dipped then rose sharply over another knoll before finally emptying into a long meadow of lush green grass. The rich azure of the *Zürichsee* stretched out beneath him. Rooftops dotted the hillside beyond the water, poking through the summer haze like lighthouses in a dense fog. In the far recesses of the horizon, the snow-capped Alps danced and shimmered in a catch of sunlight. Ray turned his eyes upward to the dozen or more lazy clouds suspended in a sky that glowed silver and blue and white and purple. He had never seen a more vibrant, grander proclamation of the glory of God's creation.

He slowed to a walk and took it all in. There were times in his life when he knew God was trying to get his attention. He came to a wooden fence and stopped, put his hands on the rough timber and leaned forward.

He breathed. His body was alive with endorphins brought about by the tremendous amount of exertion he had just inflicted upon himself.

Sweat dripped from his nose and chin. He peeled off his T-shirt, dabbed his face with it then slung it over his shoulder. He gripped the fence with both hands. The texture of the wood reminded him of his father. Whenever he was home on leave, he would take Rainey out to the workshop and teach him a trick or two. How to select the right wood for a job, how to carve it just right. How to sand it so it felt as smooth as silk. It was from his father that he'd acquired his passion for working with his hands. Whether it was pounding on a slab of iron or lathing a plank of cedar, he relished the idea of creating something useful, something beautiful from nothing more than a few raw materials. He wondered if on a subconscious level, it was his way of maintaining the connection with his father.

Rainey recalled the promise his dad had made to him when he was a kid: *someday these tools will be yours, Ray*. He'd forgotten it over the years but it had just now come back to him. Suddenly, he saw his father again in the video clip, beaten and broken. For a fleeting second, he thought he might break down. Not because the man in the clip was his father, though that was a huge factor that weighed on him, but because he was an American who had been abandoned, left behind, given over to the enemy.

Betrayed.

How must he feel? What were the thoughts that had surely run through his mind over the years? Did he ever once think that he had been forgotten? By his country, by his family even? It was one of the most reassuring things for anyone being sent into harm's way to know, an axiom by which he and his teammates lived, from Special Forces to Delta to today in the CIA's Directorate X.

No one gets left behind.

Yet there he was—his *father*—stuck in a dank prison cell in some unknown hellhole.

Rainey fell to his knees, bowed his head. He prayed for his father. He prayed for the American who'd been left behind. *"God, You are the*

One True God. The God of all creation. Your power is great, oh God. Please, I pray that You will lead us to him. Allow us to bring him home, Lord. Whether he's alive or… Please, God, I pray that You will lead us to him."

He stood and brushed the dirt and grass from his knees, wiped the sweat from his forehead, chest and arms. Somehow he felt at ease. As if God had taken the weight of the operation off his shoulders. He stared into the distance as his breathing returned to normal.

He turned around at the sound of a car door being closed. At the top of the meadow, set against the edge of the tree line was a mammoth chalet that could easily be confused for an alpine resort. Jazz stood at the edge of the largest deck—one of five—put his hand to his mouth and whistled. Rainey threw his hand in the air in acknowledgment then watched as Jazz waved him in.

Rainey jogged up to the main house, still wondering who owned the place. He took a set of wooden steps that led to the first deck two at a time and went inside. He wiped himself off once more then tossed his T-shirt in a laundry chute in the hall.

Fig was the first one to greet him. "Job's here."

"Good."

"Dude, I hope you plan on taking a shower."

Rainey would normally joke back, but he was too focused now to think about anything other than the information Job had for them. Like schoolkids assembling for homeroom, they all appeared in the main living room, which was as spacious and grand as the lobby of a five-star hotel.

Babe, Alcott, Fig and Jazz plopped onto a massive tan sectional, which faced a stone fireplace that went all the way to the polished wood rafters in the ceiling. The peak was easily fifty feet above them. Rainey grabbed a bottle of water from the kitchen and returned. The wall to his left was nothing but windows. He had been in some pretty neat places over the years, but never had he attended a briefing with a backdrop such as this. The view of the *Zürichsee* was spectacular. And the way the sunlight illuminated the natural beauty of Switzerland was downright awe-inspiring.

He took a swig of water as he glanced outside then turned to face Job who was over by the fireplace. Rainey's eyes flitted up to the wood and iron chandelier that hung over them. It was the size of a baby grand piano.

They had each made it here without incident. Rainey and Alcott had come from Milan by train the previous day and had been the first to arrive. A caretaker let them in when they had knocked, handed over a set of keys and a number to call when they were finished with the place then disappeared. The house had everything: plenty of living space, upwards of twenty-five bedrooms, a fully stocked, restaurant-style kitchen, gym, game room, movie theater, indoor swimming pool, sauna. It truly could have been a resort.

"Who owns this joint, Job?" said Fig.

Job took a seat in a wing chair and crossed his legs. "An oil tycoon in Texas. He's a friend of the program. Guy loves America. Let's just leave it at that." He opened a briefcase on the coffee table and pulled out a small stack of papers. "So let's talk about Ronda. I take it that you guys haven't heard… The media is reporting that the Agency is to blame for Ronda *and* for Hull. It's a complete PR fiasco."

"How do they come up with this stuff?" said Alcott.

"They've cited *inside sources*."

"That's ridiculous!" barked Jazz. "It was an ambush for crying out loud!"

"The administration is piling on, too. They're putting all of it on the director. POTUS and his cronies have wanted Thompson's head for years. They have long wanted to install their own yes-man. But up to this point, they could never find a viable reason to get rid of him without coming off as petulant partisans. Thompson has been a devoted public servant his whole life, holds an impressive record of achievement and is respected by his subordinates and the public at large. What's more, our allies like him and our enemies don't.

"But POTUS has called him on the carpet. He's going to make an example out of him, do some grandstanding, if you know better. The election is doubtless playing large in this. What better way to stir up his base than to spank the CIA and blame it on prior administrations? Lap dogs in the media really eat that stuff up.

"There's a press conference scheduled in a few days. Word is that POTUS is going to lambast the director and the Agency publicly. Show him the door in a shameless performance unless we can come up with something that would prevent that."

Fig shook his head. "That's crazy. Guy's freakin' off his rocker."

"Someone was waiting for us," said Rainey darkly. "Whoever it was, I think they leveraged the blog. Tried to take Moses and me out at the same time. It's the only thing that makes sense."

"I think you're right." Job passed some papers around. "This is who we think is responsible. But not just for Ronda... He's also behind what happened in Hull, the DNI's assassination, Venezuela, too. Name's Tarło. Zarek Tarło. I understand some of you may be familiar with him. He's a former deputy commander of GROM." Job quickly filled them in on the operation in Venezuela and events that transpired since, including the information that was gained from the RWS operative, Mihai Cioabă.

"Dude! So let's go find Tarło," pressed Jazz. "Put his nuts in the grinder!"

Job shook his head. "I've got people working on that. I want you guys to stay on Moses. If he made it out of Ronda, and it looks like he did—Spanish authorities haven't found any bodies that look like him—then we need to track him down and find out what he knows. The fact that he was willing to meet with you, Ray, and did so, says a lot."

"Just hope he's not too scared to surface now," added Alcott.

Rainey stepped forward and examined the papers being passed around. "He isn't."

"What do you mean?" said Job.

"I mean that I looked him in the eyes. There was a calm about him, certainly a readiness for action. I didn't see fear."

"There's also the possibility that Moses was in on the attack. You know... Set us up."

"Doesn't add up, Jazz. He was in just as much danger as me. He actually pointed out the guy from Seville, the one from outside the concert hall. Moses had nothing to do with the ambush. But if Tarlo was following the Schumann blog, he could have had people deployed to Seville, waited till they saw either Moses or me then followed one of us. Likely me. It was a good plan. Take us both out at the same time. They certainly came with plenty of firepower."

"You're right," said Alcott.

Rainey paced around the room, stopped in front of the massive wall of windows. He finished off his bottle of water then sat down on a rustic, wooden chair beside an end of the sectional. He leaned backward, crossed his arms and began scratching his unshaven face.

"What is it, Ray? I know that look," said Job.

"How did Tarlo know about the blog to begin with?"

Job nodded. "I've been thinking the same thing."

"Yeah, who knew about it?" said Alcott.

"Well, outside of the people in this room, very few others. The director, of course, the case officer through whom the letter surfaced and the deputy chief of Lisbon Station."

"Who else?"

"Let's see now. Thompson had a meeting with POTUS. I'm sure he briefed him on the full contents of the letter."

Rainey leaned forward, put his elbows on his knees. "Which included the way in which Moses wanted to communicate. Who all was present at that meeting?"

Job's face turned grim. "I don't like where this is headed, Ray."

"I don't either."

57

RAINEY hefted Job's briefcase onto the dining room table. He popped it open and pulled out a laptop computer and a special thumb drive that would keep the computer's activity both secure and invisible. He opened the laptop, powered it on and cracked his knuckles as he waited for it to boot up. He pushed the thumb drive into the USB slot. In a few seconds an icon flashed at the bottom of the screen. Good to go.

Fig and Jazz had gone into town for dinner, while Babe and Alcott were using the time to get in a good workout down in the exercise room, which left Rainey and Job alone upstairs in the main living space.

"You seriously think someone in the president's circle is working against us?"

"Tell me I'm crazy," said Rainey.

Job rubbed his forehead. "I can't. Because I think you're right." He sighed. "First chance I get, I'm going to have a long talk with the director. I want to know who was there in that meeting when the letter was first discussed."

"What if the president *is* somehow mixed up in this?"

Job frowned and the question went unanswered. The possibility that the president of the United States could be involved was a lot to process, which was likely the reason he changed the subject.

"Listen, I need to talk to you about Maddie."

"What about her?"

"Ray, she's…"

"Yeah?"

"Maddie was brought on by the Agency. In fact, she is working for me in the DX."

Rainey stopped typing, looked up from the screen.

"She came on back in January. Started the Academy the same time you did. We kept you guys on different rotations at the various training programs around the country in order to prevent you from crossing paths. Her idea. Not mine."

Rainey stood up and walked across the room. He was hot, red hot. He put his hands on his hips and stared long and hard out the window. The recollection of Maddie and Wes on the dock tiptoed into his thoughts. *That's why they seemed so desperate for each other's company. They hadn't seen each other in six months.* "Why didn't you tell me?"

"I'm telling you now."

"Yes, but why not sooner?" implored Rainey.

"She thought you might pitch a fit, try to go over her head and kill her chance of joining."

"She would have been right, because I would have, Job. Can you blame me for wanting to protect my sister?"

Job remained quiet for a minute then said, "I know you'll always think of her as your little sister, Ray, but Maddie is more than capable of doing this job. She's not six years old anymore. She's a grown woman. She's intelligent, athletic and tough, and, next to you, the most stubborn person I know. There is not an ounce of quit in her. Does that remind you of anyone? Does it?"

Rainey's eyes narrowed as he crossed his arms.

"I know what you're thinking, Ray. Believe me, I do. But the simple truth remains: we need women like her. They bring a lot to the table. They can do things and go places that men like you and me cannot."

Rainey sighed, closed his eyes. "I get that, Job. I just don't like it. In fact, I *hate* it." He swiveled at the hips. "Is she aware of the things she'll be asked to do, be *ordered* to do?"

"She is. We had a long, candid discussion before I greenlighted her for the Academy. She's the perfect recruit, Ray—one in a million. The DX is better off for having her."

Rainey walked back over to the laptop, sat down behind it.

"Listen, I know what is going through that big brain of yours. You're scared for her. You're worried. I experienced those exact same thoughts and emotions when she first came to me. Part of me is still scared and worried, but a bigger part is proud of her. I recall going through the same thing back when you enlisted, when you were select-ed into SF and then moved on to Delta. It's no secret that I have al-ways thought of you and Maddie as my own children. But something I've learned, especially over the past year or so, is that God is sover-eign. He's in control. Try as you might, you can't control the ones you love, even if you think what you're doing is for their own good. You have to let them live free to make their own choices. You just have to pray they make wise ones. In the end, you have to put your trust in the Almighty, have faith that He will watch over them."

Rainey's fingers were poised over the keyboard. He stared at the backs of his hands.

"You want to know how she did at the Academy?"

"I can only guess that she excelled."

"Excel, she did. Her scores were off the charts." Job cleared his throat. "Higher than yours, I might add."

Rainey typed a string of characters into the Web browser and hit ENTER. He decided to push his emotions deep down inside. "How is Wes handling it?"

"Very well, actually. Better than I would be if it were my fiancée who had gone off to play warrior spy."

"Says a lot about his character. He's good for her."

Job leaned against the table. "I've heard good things so far."

"She's already in the field?"

"Maddie is the main reason we have the information on Tarlo. But I'll let Mouse and Tonka tell you about that the next time you see them."

Somehow he felt relieved. Maddie was teamed with Mouse and Tonka. Good. They were two of the best operators he knew. Normally, they'd be working with him. Now, he understood why Job had temporarily assigned them elsewhere. It was a wise move. Job had teamed Maddie with people he trusted, people who would look out for her with extreme prejudice as she got her feet wet.

"Evie, too. She's had nothing but praise for her. I think she likes having another warrior chick in the mix. The two of them have become fast friends. They seem to work well together."

"*Evie?* Who's Evie?"

"Oh, that's right," Job chuckled. "You know her by a different name. Well, you're DX now, so… Evie is short for Evelina Krantz."

"That who I think it is?"

"The one and only," said Job.

"Warrior chicks, huh?"

"Hey, they can both kick *my* butt, I know that."

"Well, that's not really saying much." Rainey smirked as he clicked inside the dialogue box on the Schumann blog then began to type.

Job hunched over his shoulder. "I was wondering when that Rainey sense of humor was going to show up. Better late than never."

"It's the time difference."

"Riiiiight," said Job as he leaned closer to the screen. "*Cernaral?* You spelled it wrong."

"No I didn't."

"I don't get it then."

"It's kind of an inside joke. One that I'm sure Moses and other fans of Schumann *will* get. This *is* a Schumann blog."

Job seemed bewildered.

"It means Vienna, Job. If Moses is Russian, and I don't doubt that he is, Vienna is a place he'll likely feel comfortable."

Job shook his head with a grin. "Clever. And I agree. Do it."

Rainey posted the message then pressed his back into the chair with a sigh. His unfocused eyes were still glued to the screen.

Job placed his hand on Rainey's shoulder. "We'll find him, Ray."

Rainey shut down the computer, closed the lid. "I hope you're right."

"You'd better get going. I'll brief the others. Be careful, will ya?"

"You know I will."

He showered quickly then packed a small overnight bag before heading out. He was climbing into the driver's seat of a black Ford F-150, one of four vehicles belonging to the estate and left for the Agency operatives' use, when Fig and Jazz pulled into the driveway. The two men crawled out of a BMW sedan and strolled over.

Fig stood next to his open window. "Hey, Bronc. Where you off to?"

Rainey smiled. "To see a man about a clarinet. Job will fill you in."

Then he backed out and drove away, leaving a dust cloud in his wake.

58

Chemnitz, Germany

H E had just walked through the door of his flat. It was the first time he had been here in weeks. It didn't look like much. The walls were bare, the quarters were cramped and the fridge perpetually empty, but it was a safe haven—one of a dozen or so he kept around the world for times such as these.

Demyan Rostov paced to the sliding glass door, which fronted the Museum für Naturkunde—the Museum of Natural History. He peeked through the vertical blinds. The door was still locked and the balcony beyond just as he had left it. A small table that the birds had obviously been using as a perch was pushed to one side. A dented metal folding chair lay on its side and was propped against the wall. To his right was a potted plant that had long since died. Several pathetic, brown ribbons of what used to be green stalks stretched from the soil, over the edge of the pot and through the balcony's iron railing as if they had tried to escape their isolated torment but failed—men shot dead on a prison wall and left to rot.

He placed his carry-out on the bar in the kitchen and pulled up a stool. Suddenly, the neighbor next door started playing his music again, some dreadful techno crap. The incessant thumping was making the walls shake and severely souring his mood. Rostov closed his eyes, wishing it all away. It only seemed to get louder. He rubbed the bridge of his nose and spat a vulgar swear word.

It had been so long since he'd been here, he had nearly forgotten about the neighbor on the other side of the wall. Until the first pulse-pounding beat. The man was a slug. He never left the apartment, always had the same music playing and kept it cranked up until the wee hours of the morning.

Enough is enough.

Rostov stepped into the hall. It was empty. He walked to the neighbor's door and knocked. The door swung open and the filthy pig appeared. His hair was greasy and long, his chalk-white belly strewn with scraps of wiry black hair hung over the waistband of his boxer shorts because his "YOLO" T-shirt was two sizes too small. He hadn't shaved in days and his eyes were bloodshot from popping pills, which the vile man-child was wont to do.

"Könnten Sie bitte die Musik ausschlagen?" Could you please turn the music down?

The man looked at him with a vacant stare then barked out a pejorative and slammed the door in his face.

Rostov took a deep breath, looked up and down the hallway then knocked again. This time when the door opened, he shot into the apartment, punched the man in the throat and shoved him to the floor. He turned and closed the door then advanced again toward his prey. The man was rolling around on the beer-stained carpet like a beetle on its back. Rostov stepped closer with pure hatred in his eyes. He kicked the man in the stomach. Then kicked him again.

He kicked him in the chest and stomach, kicked him in the groin then stomped on his head again and again until the man went limp, gurgling in his own filth.

Rostov stared down on him with disdain then walked over to the stereo, which was still booming. He reached out and turned the knob slowly until the volume was at a more respectful level. Then he went to the kitchen, tore off a few paper towels from a roll on the counter and wiped the blood from his shoes. He placed the bloody towels in a plastic shopping bag he picked off the floor then rolled it up into a ball.

The hall was still empty when he left the man's apartment flat. He returned to his own, dropped the plastic bag in the waste bin then washed his hands in the sink. Rostov climbed onto the stool and sat stock still for several seconds. He squinted, trying his best to hear the music. Finally, he smiled.

Perfect.

He scooped a forkful of smoked salmon into his mouth and fired up his laptop. He first searched the news sites for updates on Ronda. By all accounts, it was still unclear what or who was involved in the gun battle. Some speculated that it was the work of Islamic terrorists, others that it was a war between factions of organized crime. The biggest lead Spanish authorities had, it seemed, was the helicopter that had been recovered from the bottom of the canyon. How Rainey managed to knock it out of the sky was still lost on him. He was just thankful to have made it out alive and unscathed. He credited Rainey and his people for that. If it hadn't been for them, he would be dead.

He took a bite of one of the potato cakes on his plate then clicked on a bookmarked link, which took him to the Schumann blog. He scrolled down through a dozen or so posts. One person compared Schumann to a modern American composer he'd been studying at university.

"Please," said Rostov aloud. "No doubt a com-*poseur*." He grinned at his wordplay.

But the grin quickly faded when he saw the next post. It was from Rainey. It had to be.

"Heard some Schumann the other day played by a group of barbarians who wouldn't know the difference between a strophic and a rondo. I don't care what the program said, it wasn't exactly Carnaval. *Lol. Perhaps it was just a cruel prank. Now that I think about it, I bet the man who sold me the ticket had a good laugh at my expense. No matter, I have a ton of books here to read. Surely one of them will take my mind off such a dreadful experience. But first, I have to get some work done. I've got a paper due Friday at 8:00 a.m. that I haven't even started. Yikes! Time to get to the library."*

Rainey was being cryptic. Obviously, he thought someone was monitoring the blog. Of course! That's how whoever launched the attack in Ronda knew they would both be in Spain. Probably followed one of them from Seville to Ronda. Now he just needed to figure out what Rainey was saying.

Rostov read the post again, and then a third time much slower than previously. He keyed on the references to '*Carnaval*' and 'a prank.'

'*It wasn't exactly like* Carnaval.'

Carnaval was one of Schumann's most famous works for piano. He had used a type of cryptogram in the musical composition. Rainey was telling him in a sense that there was a code within the blog post.

A thought occurred to him.

Schumann had also composed a piece called, *Faschingsschwank aus Wie—Carnival Prank from Vienna.* "Carnival" was not exactly *Carnaval.*

It soon became clear. Rainey was telling him Vienna.

Okay. What else?

He smiled. '*Friday at 8:00 a.m.*' He remembered what Rainey had said to him on the terrace before all hell broke loose.

"*Day minus one. Hour plus six.*"

Rostov did the calculation in his head. Friday minus a day was Thursday. And 8:00 A.M. plus six hours was 2:00 P.M.

But where in Vienna?

He studied the post again. '*Time to get to the library.*' Of course! The library. But which library? Surely Rainey knows there is more than one library in Vienna.

Think, Demyan. Think!

Rostov read the blog once more. It seemed to have been written from the perspective of a student.

A school.

A *school* library.

Yes! That's it! The Vienna University Library was the largest library in all of Austria.

So… Rainey wants to meet in two days at the university library at 2:00 P.M.

Rostov looked at the clock on the microwave.

6:37 P.M.

If he left now, he could be in Vienna at a little after one in the morning. That was more than enough time to do some reconnaissance and planning. He quickly finished his meal, tossed the empty food container in the waste bin and grabbed his car keys from the kitchen counter.

Reagan Rainey, here I come.

59

**Alexandria, Virginia
1:00 P.M.**

A patchwork of white clouds meandered past the marina and out over the Potomac. Maddie sat on a bench with her feet stretched out. A wide ray of sunshine shot across the planks of the boardwalk. She could feel its heat tickling at the tops of her feet and bare ankles.

She had on a red American University T-shirt, skinny jeans with the bottoms rolled up and brown leather Hush Puppies loafers. Her shimmering espresso-colored hair she wore tied back in a perfect ponytail. The big sunglasses on her face had two purposes: number one, they screamed, "I'm rich, gorgeous and way out of your league, approach me if you dare;" and number two, they hid her eyes while she scanned the people swirling around her.

"Stand by, Swan. You have company. A white male, green Celtics T-shirt and cargo shorts is moving toward you now. He's on your nine." It was Evelina in her earpiece.

Maddie crossed her legs and began to bounce her foot. She checked her watch as if she had more important things to do, then crossed her arms, too.

The man stepped up next to her, a brochure in his hands. "You, uh, want some company?"

Maddie lowered here sunglasses an inch, looked at him. "Excuse me?"

"Well, you look like you're here alone. Just saying, maybe you'd like to hang out together. Name's Pete." He held his hand out and smiled.

"Buzz off, creep."

"Look I didn't mean to—"

Maddie glowered at him. The man's smile sunk, his spirit dimmed. It went against her nature to be mean to people, especially when they were being so nice. But she didn't want this guy ruining the meeting with Tarło or getting himself hurt. Or both.

Sorry, pal.

"I, um... Look, I'm suh, suh, sorry to have bothered you." The man offered up his hands in defeat, nodded and trudged off.

Evelina: *"What was that?"*

Maddie acted like she was checking the screen of her smartphone. She managed a whisper without moving her lips. "False alarm."

It was kind of a strange feeling being out here exposed like this, but not one she hadn't experienced before. She had felt the same way when she was sliding over the ravine on the log in southern Venezuela. Though in this case, there were people watching her back. To be precise, there were *fifteen* people watching her back. The bulk of them were FBI agents. After the meeting with Tarło had been set up, Job notified Chris Miller—a supervisory special agent with the FBI's Washington Field Office and the man in charge of the investigation into the DNI's assassination. It was quickly determined that Evelina, Mouse, Tonka and, of course, Maddie would assist the FBI with their investigation but on strict terms that included operating under aliases. It was critical to the overall mission of the CIA's Directorate X that their status as covert operatives be stringently protected and therefore no one could know their true identities. That included the FBI.

Maddie tightened her ponytail and avoided looking for the FBI agents that she knew were out there—at the table by the window inside the Blackwall Hitch, or on the patio of the Chart House; the man and woman holding hands on the bench over there, lovers out on a date; the guy standing by the ticket booth for the Potomac Riverboat water taxi, or, maybe the young man kneeling by the railing, tinkering with his bike tire.

On the other hand, she did know where her teammates were posted. Mouse had pulled the short straw and was serving up sundaes and waffle cones at the ice cream trolley back along the Art Center building. Meanwhile, Tonka and Evie were hovered over a table with an umbrella, enjoying Bread and Chocolate pastries at the opposite end of the esplanade. Even Saul was in on this one. He and an FBI agent were sitting in a Defender B-class boat with a Coast Guard team from Station Washington. They were tucked in along the coast just up the river near Tide Lock Park.

Evelina: *"Look alive, Swan. Got another one heading your way. White male. Mid to late forties, wearing a gray button-down shirt and black jeans. Arm in a sling. Ten meters away on your four."*

A man sat down next to her. Maddie turned her head. He had close-cropped hair that was once black as night, but was now on the verge of being overrun with gray. His arms were tan and muscular. Like Evie had said, his right arm was in a sling. There was a small tattoo on his left forearm of an eagle holding a lightning bolt. His hands were meaty and rough.

"Miss Green?" he said, his eyes still focused on the water.

"Mr. Tarło, I presume."

"I wasn't sure you'd show."

"Why's that?"

He grinned.

"Mr. Tarło, I agreed to meet with you because I am hoping to come to some kind of understanding. You see, my employer is hopeful that the information he received regarding your exploits is somehow erroneous. I will tell you that he is desperate for someone of your caliber to handle a major problem for him. And it is my job to find that someone."

"Yes. And just exactly what information did he receive?"

"Well, truth be told, it was me who received the information." She winked. "I have some incredibly well-placed sources, mind you. Suffice it to say that I have it on good authority that you—that is, you and your company—are responsible for the unfortunate mess in Ronda. As well as..."

"Yes?"

Maddie made a show of checking for interlopers with feigned subtly then leaned toward him. "The death of the DNI."

She might as well have kicked him in the groin. His reaction would have doubtless been the same. "Miss Green. I don't know where you're getting your information, but I assure you that it's nothing but fiction. RWS is a reputable business with a flawless track record."

"Come now, Mr. Tarło. Don't insult my intelligence. You and I both know the truth."

His eyes narrowed. She had his full attention. *Good.*

Maddie crossed her legs. "We are quite similar, you and me. We both work for people with ungodly amounts of money and power, and we are both paid quite handsomely to keep them that way no matter what it takes. Am I right?"

He didn't respond.

"Now, like you, I am pragmatic. I know that my boss wants you bad. He is convinced that you are the best man for the job, and he's *desperate*. And therefore so am I. Now, I've used some of your competitors on prior occasions and frankly there is no comparison with your company. You are the best I've come across thus far. So... Whatever trouble you have gotten yourself into, I am sure it's nothing I haven't dealt with before. I have friends in high places, Mr. Tarło, and I can be *very* persuasive when I want to be. But in order for me to help you, I have to know everything, every detail, no matter how insignificant you may think it is. In return, I can guarantee you monetary compensation that is double your normal fee. Half up front, half when the job is complete. If you accept and are successful, you also stand to gain a powerful and trusted ally with unfettered access to the highest levels of government."

"You make an interesting pitch, Miss Green. Hypothetically, if I did know what you are talking about, I would most certainly demand triple my usual fee."

Maddie smiled. "I think I can make that work."

"And yet I still don't know for whom I would be working or anything about the job. As long as we're still speaking hypothetically, that is."

"First things first. How much damage are we talking? Meaning the DNI and Ronda. Is there anything else I should be concerned with? I need to know exactly how much work I've got cut out for me."

Tarło looked around. "Lady, I don't mean to be rude, but…"

"By all means, you won't offend me. We're talking business here."

"How do I know you're not a cop or are working for the FBI or something?"

Maddie chuckled. "Mr. Tarło, I can assure you that I am *not* a cop and I most certainly do not work for the F-B-I."

I'm working with *the FBI, but not* for *the FBI.* Maddie made the distinction in her mind. Funny how important a little preposition could be.

"I'll tell you what. I don't want you to do anything you're not comfortable with. Take a couple hours and think it over. If you decide against my offer, no harm done and we can both forget all about this. But if you *do* decide to take me up on my offer, I will need to know by three o'clock tomorrow afternoon. No later. There are things at play here that have me on a very tight timetable. I'm sorry that I can't be more forthcoming, but that's just my situation. I hope you understand.

"You have my card. Call me by three P.M. tomorrow at the latest. If I don't hear from you by then, I'll assume you've decided to decline my offer."

"That sounds reasonable."

"Very good. Now, you'll have to excuse me. I must be getting back."

They shook hands after which Maddie walked back through the Art Center, crossed N. Union Street and entered the parking garage. When she reached her DX-provided Cadillac CTS, she started the engine, shifted into gear and made her way out to the street.

Maddie eased up to the stop sign at Cameron Street and glanced in the rearview mirror. A blue Buick pulled from the curb and fell into traffic three cars back.

She smiled.

Hi there.

60

ZAREK Tarło walked to the railing and stared down at a few cigarette butts surrounded by an armada of grass clippings floating on the water. He looked up, gazed across the river and sighed as he pulled out his secure phone and dialed Stedman Carter.

"Yes?"

"We need to talk in person. ASAP."

"Where are you?"

"Alexandria. Old Town."

"That's no good. I'm in New York. Can it wait until tomorrow?"

"No."

"All right. Well, I have meetings through the rest of the day and a dinner with the mayor later tonight that I can't get out of. Then tomorrow morning I'm flying to Chicago. Why don't you come here? We can meet at my condo. Say five-thirty?"

"I'll be there."

Tarło pocketed his phone. *What are you up to, Frannie Green?*

He had the distinct feeling that things were starting to unravel. His team from Venezuela hadn't been heard from yet. That alone was enough to cause serious concern. And now this chick, calling herself

Frannie Green, had suddenly materialized out of thin air and was driving hard to the hoop to get him to do a "job." He had no clue how she might know about Ronda and the DNI's murder. But he would. By God, he would.

He took a circuitous route back to his Range Rover on N. Royal Street. There was a chance that this broad, Green, was up to something and that for starters it just might include having him followed. But a large part of him was hoping she was legit. Not only was she confident, articulate and intelligent, but she was beautiful. If Frannie Green was for real, then she might well be worth courting for recruitment. She could be a valuable asset for him and RWS. And if he'd learned anything from Stedman Carter over the years it was to always keep your eyes open for good people with special talents. They were hard to come by in this business.

He pulled into Reagan National, bought a plane ticket to New York City then dropped into a seat to wait for his boarding call. Fifteen minutes later, an old man in a "Virginia is for Lovers" T-shirt, carrying a tan canvas duffel bag, plopped down across from him. He was out of breath and appeared to be irritated.

Poor guy. Probably pissed at himself for buying that shirt.

♦ ♦ ♦

Saul Baker set his duffel bag down on the floor and glared at the airline counter. "Fools! Every last one of them. I swear!"

His face was still screwed up with displeasure when he caught the man across the way looking at him. "They delay your flight, too? The jerks!"

"Uh, no," said Tarło.

"Well good for you. I had my lady friend race me down here, so I could go running through the stinkin' terminal. I get here without so much as a minute to spare and do you know what they tell me?"

Tarło shrugged.

Saul made a satirical face. "'Sorry, sir, but your flight has been delayed.' Do you want to know why my flight is delayed?" Saul didn't wait for an answer. "Because they're all dopes. That's why!"

Tarło withdrew into his chair.

"Where ya headed?"

"New York."

"Yeah? New York, huh. The Big Apple. Ha. I'm off to Portland, myself. Oregon, that is. There're two Portlands, you know. One is in Oregon, that's the one I'm flying to, if these idiots can ever get their act together, that is. Then there is Portland, Maine. Ever been?"

Tarło sighed and checked his watch.

"Beautiful country up there. Little tip for ya… If ya ever get the chance to go to Maine, ya gotta stop by my friend, Cal McHenry's place. It's called McHenry's Oceanside Grille. It's right by the Portland Yacht Club. Place serves the best lobster on the entire East Coast."

"I don't like lobster."

"Ya don't like lobster? What the…? What kind of person doesn't like lobster? I've been all over this here country and ya know what? You're the first person to ever tell me they don't like lobster. Tarnation!"

"Listen. I'm not in the mood to talk, okay?"

"Not in the mood? Well *sorry*! Guy who doesn't like lobster isn't in the mood to talk. Ha! Ya know, forget I told you about Cal's place. He doesn't want your kind there anyway. Tell you what… I'm gonna go sit over there. You okay with that? Ya *jerk*!"

Tarło rolled his eyes. "Perfect."

"*Perfect*. Oh, okay. Well you—whoever you are… You can just cram it!" Saul stood up and bent down to pick up his duffel bag. As he reached for the handle, he dropped his book—a Vince Flynn paperback he'd been holding in his left hand—and inadvertently kicked it under Tarło's chair, or so it would seem to any onlookers. He crouched down next to Tarło, screwed up his face and began searching for it, purposely crowding the man. Saul nudged Tarło's leg out of the way.

"Wait! Just wait, will you? I'll get it. If it'll get you outta my face any quicker." Tarło leaned forward and stretched his arm beneath the seat.

After several seconds of this, he knelt in front of the seat and located it. When he sat back down, he held out the book. "Here! Now go bother someone else."

Saul snatched the book from his hand and glowered at him. "There is no decency in this country anymore."

"Ah, shove off, old man!"

Saul walked away with a sour face. He rounded a corner and looked back over his shoulder. Verifying he was no longer in Tarło's field of view, his frown turned upside down.

Gotcha. Ya jerk.

Saul crossed the terminal, turned down a short corridor and approached a door that was marked "Private." He knocked twice and the door swung open.

A gravel-voiced FBI agent named Zepp waved him inside the security office then closed the door. He patted him on the shoulder. "Well done, Mr. Baker. You sly old dog."

"Cake." Saul handed the duffel bag to another agent who was seated at a metal table behind a laptop and some other gadgetry. Next to him, a security officer kept watch over a wall of video monitors which played live feeds from the surveillance cameras throughout the airport.

The agent unzipped the bag, performed a cursory check of the equipment within, then placed the bag on the table but out of the way and resumed his focus on his computer screen. Inside the duffel bag was a sophisticated electronic device that looked like it could be a wireless modem for a home computer network, but was really used to capture cell phone data from unsuspecting targets. The technology wasn't new, but it was the first time Saul had ever used it. While Tarło had been distracted with Saul's angry, old man routine out in the terminal, the device in his duffel bag had sniffed out and collected the data from Tarło's cell phones.

The agent at the laptop ran his fingers over the keyboard then turned toward Saul and the senior agent. "He's got two phones. Both utilize high-level encryption."

Saul grimaced. "No good?"

The agent smiled. "I didn't say that."

"Oh and by the way, he's flying on American Flight Two Twenty-nine to JFK." The ruse with the book had allowed Saul to sneak a glimpse of Tarło's boarding pass, which had been sitting on the seat next to him under a pair of sunglasses.

"Yes, I know. I have two agents at the American desk now. Zepp pointed to another agent in the room. "Notify the New York Office. I want a surveillance team mobilized and ready to go before he lands at JFK. I'll alert Miller."

"On it, boss."

Saul leaned over the shoulder of the agent at the computer, a cell phone now pressed against his cheek. Saul was on the line with someone at the Directorate X Operations Center in Arlington. "Are you getting this?" He chewed his bottom lip as he waited for a response. After it came in the affirmative, Saul said, "Good. Update the chief."

61

Washington, D.C.

IT wasn't until the following day at 2:16 P.M. that her phone vibrated. She looked at the screen. It was Tarło.

Maddie accepted the call as she turned toward the window inside the Dansbury Club. She pealed back one of the thick drapes in the dimly lit lounge and stole a peak at Tarło's watchers. They were out there on the street, in three cars with two men per. Evelina, Mouse and Tonka, each now assigned to one of three FBI surveillance teams respectively, had given her regular updates on their status.

Yesterday, after leaving the Torpedo Factory, Maddie had driven to a tall office building in Arlington, in which the DX had long rented three floors of office space for a variety of cover companies that came and went in much the same way clandestine operations did. *Frannie Green's* office was on the sixteenth floor and boasted a commanding view of the Potomac and the nation's capital beyond. If any of Tarło's men had followed her up, they would have discovered her office suite locked and dormant with a glass and stainless steel placard on the wall that indicated, "Green Executive Services, LLC., President Francesca Green, Meeting by Appointment Only." Maddie found it somewhat comical that there were no phone numbers anywhere in sight, but decided that it was rather smart in her case, because it added an element of exclusivity to Miss Frannie Green's mystique.

There in the office, Maddie had changed into a sandstone-colored business suit and awaited Saul, the dutiful driver, to arrive in the Mercedes. Together they had traveled to Philadelphia where Tarło's watchers should have seen Miss Frannie Green conducting discreet meetings with a busy executive and a woman who was meant to appear as some kind of aide-de-camp for a city politician—really just two DX operatives who, like her, were playing a role. After that, Maddie and Saul shared a nice dinner at R2L then decided to rough it in a suite at the Rittenhouse for the night.

Early this morning, Saul had driven them back to D.C. where Maddie and a number of other seasoned DX operatives reconnoitered at various locations in order to bolster the validity of Frannie Green's enterprise. They had been to the Capitol Building, a financial investment firm, the Hart Senate Office Building, the Cannon and Rayburn Buildings, the Library of Congress twice, a corporate law office known to represent high-profile clients and finally the Dansbury Club, a private social club for D.C.'s aristocracy. Turns out Saul knew a board member there who had eagerly agreed to sponsor them for the day.

Maddie had enjoyed running Tarło's people all over town. She and Saul had used their knowledge of how difficult it was to follow someone, especially in large urban areas, to their advantage. But they purposely never lost them, because that wasn't part of the plan. Rather it was to frustrate them, tire them out, get them hungry and grumpy. And that's just what they did. Meanwhile, Evelina, Mouse and Tonka had rotated in and out with their FBI teams in order to stay fresh and alert.

"Hello?"

"Miss Green. Zarek Tarło."

"Yes, Mr. Tarło. I've been waiting for your call. Have you made a decision with respect to my offer?"

"I have. I'm going to decline."

"Oh? I'm sorry to hear that. It's really quite unfortunate."

"Is it?"

"Yes, well, I suppose if I were in your shoes, I might consider my offer a risk too big to take, too. Well, from my perspective, it was worth the shot. I know my employer will be disappointed. But, I'll keep you in mind for future projects if you'd like. Good luck with your situation. I hope everything works out."

"What do you mean, my *situation*?" hissed Tarło.

"Honestly, Mr. Tarło, I should like to think you know better. These matters are best not discussed over the phone, but since you asked… I meant your situation with the DNI's murder investigation, and what's happened in Hull and Ronda."

"Hull now, too? Listen lady—"

"Come now, Mr. Tarło. There you go playing games again. And who was it that said they don't play games?" Maddie snorted. "The attack at the Institute outside Hull. The men involved, they worked for you. Well… They didn't work *for* you but were hired by you." She made the statement as if it were common knowledge. "I really wish you would reconsider my offer, because I could be a great help to you. You're sure you won't change your mind?"

"Yes, I'm sure," he growled.

"Well then, I'm just wasting my time, aren't I? Thanks for calling, Mr. Tarło. Now, if you'll excuse me, I really must get back to work. Good luck to you." She disconnected the call before Tarło could speak again. Maddie smiled into the screen of the phone.

Burn, baby, burn.

62

Baltimore, Maryland

TARŁO walked through the empty warehouse, his footfalls echoing throughout the hollow chamber in a rhythmic *clip-clop* pattern. It wasn't always this way. Often the warehouse was chock-full of crates that contained anything from small arms and high explosives to sophisticated radar detection systems, surface-to-air missiles and other cutting-edge American technology. All of it was illegally produced—some using stolen military designs—in various secret factories around North America that were owned by Stedman Carter.

Yesterday three shipments went out that were bound for ports in Qatar, Liberia and Pakistan with their final destinations being Syria, Mali and Iran, respectively. The laborers, the people who worked here day-in and day-out, would likely be shocked if they ever found out about the role they played in such an enterprise. Stedman Carter's illegal arms empire spanned the globe and had done so for decades. And Charm City Logistics was a key cog in its successful operation *and* its secrecy.

To the staff here, he was known as Hal Truett, a no-nonsense, heavy-handed regional operations manager. Hatchet Hal, as he was sometimes called behind his back, would appear from time to time to ensure quality control was top-notch, but more often than not, ended up putting the fear of God in the employees in one way or another. Rewards were aplenty for those who exceeded standards. Similarly, punishment for a poor attitude or a poor performance evaluation was doled out in equal measure, and was—in the most severe cases—more than a swift kick in the pants and a severance check.

After the meeting with Carter in his 432 Park Avenue condo, Tarło had come here to lay low and think. There was a residence hall in a separate and secure area of the warehouse. It was austere to be sure, no frills or luxury accoutrements here, but it was safe and quiet and gave him and his people a place to hang out or crash if they were headed out to safeguard a particularly sensitive shipment or likewise had just returned from a clandestine operation abroad.

The residence hall had its own private entry and exit points and consisted of twelve bunkrooms, a kitchen, lounge area, a briefing room and a small locker room with showers and a bathroom. In an adjoining warehouse, which RWS leased from one of Stedman Carter's real estate companies, Tarło kept a fleet of vehicles ranging from sub-compacts to ubiquitous work vans along with a rather impressive armory. It was from here that he had called Frannie Green.

Tarło stopped in the middle of the empty CCL warehouse, looked around then shouted at the top of his lungs. Had there been any employees on the premises, they would have doubtless come scrambling from every nook and cranny to see what madman had gained entry to their workplace.

His primal scream faded into the roar of traffic, the blare of a honking semi up on O'Donnell Street. Tarło drifted back into the residence hall and sat down in the briefing room. He stared at the wall, seething with rage. His chest rose and fell with heavy breathing. He rubbed his chin then pounded the table with a fist.

He dialed one of his men. "What's her status?"

"She's at the Dansbury Club, boss. I'm really beginning to hate this broad."

"What do you mean?" replied Tarło.

"Freakin' woman has run us all over. I haven't eaten since yesterday before the Torpedo Factory. Can't we just smoke this chick?"

"Shut up and stop complaining. Just stay on her. Her time is coming." Tarło ended the call and dropped the phone onto the table. He pulled a knife from a sheath in the small of his back, stared at the blade for several seconds. A glint of light caught in the shiny steel as he turned it over in his hands. Finally, he brought it down hard onto the tabletop, twisted the tip of the blade so that it left a deep gouge in the Formica. His eyes were alive with rage.

Your time is coming, Miss Green. Believe me, it is.

63

THE night had been a blur. For the better part of the past five hours, Maddie and her "date" had been rubbing elbows with the cream of Washington society at Congressional Country Club in Bethesda, Maryland. Though the Agency had clamored for either Mouse or Tonka to be her personal protective detail for the evening, the FBI balked, citing laws and territorial issues. Eventually, a compromise had been reached when Mouse suggested an FBI HRT man with whom he had trained on occasion. Gerald Easter was handsome and affable, but more importantly, when the situation called for it, was a warrior's warrior. Former 82nd Airborne and Army Ranger, Easter was a man who knew how to fight.

It was sometime after midnight when they turned onto her street. The house was at the end of the block on Juniper Street NW and was situated in a quite wooded area on the threshold of Rock Creek Trail. To their credit, CIA and FBI teams had worked tirelessly for the past two days to turn it into the home of one Frannie Green, busy Washington power-player, restless and secret political operative and royal pain in the butt. They had placed photos and other mementos around the house, on walls and credenzas, just enough to give it the spice of believability. They had also taken care to rig every room for audio and video recording. The finishing touches consisted of releasing doctored files associated with Frannie Green's Cadillac and driver's license into the Washington DMV system when they were all done. Since the meeting with Zarek Tarło yesterday at the Torpedo Factory and her brief stop at the office in Arlington to change, this would be the first time Maddie was alone and therefore the time when the CIA and FBI stakeholders believed Tarło was most likely to strike. She had clearly stirred up a hornet's nest.

The FBI man, Easter, pulled the BMW into the driveway and escorted her to the door.

"Kiss me," she said quietly.

"What?"

"On the cheek, make it look gentlemanly."

Easter—playing the part of Edward Hargrave, the wealthy son of some D.C. political so and so—gave her a polite peck on the cheek. Then in a voice meant for public consumption, he said, "Thank you for a wonderful evening, Miss Green. If you're free this weekend, I'd love to see you again. There is a perfect little place in the Caribbean that I'm sure you'd enjoy. It belongs to my family. I hope you're not one to get seasick."

"Oh, Edward, you really are a rascal. We'll see." Maddie smiled and batted her eyes coyly. "I had a marvelous time tonight. I'd ask you to come inside, but I have an early start tomorrow."

"Understood. Give my best to the senator."

"I will. Goodnight."

"Night then."

Easter waited until she was inside and the door was closed then backed out of the driveway and drove away.

◆ ◆ ◆

A man, who was hidden in the woods across the street from the house, activated his radio. "Guy just left."

Tarło looked into his rearview mirror. "Copy that." He had a nagging feeling in the pit of his stomach that he was being followed. If anyone were tailing him, though, they were doing a stellar job of staying out of sight. But Zarek Tarło was a man who always trusted his gut and for that very reason, he began a series of maneuvers that would ensure his solitude.

At this time of night the University of Maryland wasn't exactly bustling with activity, but there was usually enough going on by which to get lost. He hooked a counterfeit faculty-parking permit on his mirror and drifted down Fieldhouse Drive. He turned into the parking garage on Union Lane, descended to the second level and pulled in next to a minivan with an OBX decal on the back bumper. He quickly kicked off his boots and put on running shoes. He changed out of his black T-shirt and threw on a light gray polo that was a size too big then tugged on a Terps ball cap before finally strapping on a Jansport backpack.

◆ ◆ ◆

Steve Zepp, the FBI man in charge of the surveillance detail assigned to monitor Zarek Tarło's movements, twisted in the front-passenger seat. He watched as Tarło's sedan turned and headed away from the main road. "Okay, people look alive. Target just turned onto Stadium Drive. Air One, do you copy?"

"Air One copies. I got him."

"Unit Three, take Baltimore Avenue and hold a position somewhere near Lakeland," said Zepp.

"Ten-four. Heading there now."

"Air One to all units. Target has turned into the parking garage on Union Lane. He's disappeared from view. Air One has lost visual. I repeat, I've lost visual."

◆ ◆ ◆

Tarło snuck down a set of stairs and entered the Cole Student Activities Building. When he came out the other side, he passed the tennis courts and headed for the large parking lot that was almost always filled with student vehicles. He searched for an older model Honda. They were plentiful on college campuses across the country and easy to steal especially with the shaved key he had in his pocket. In a matter of minutes, he found a mid-90s Civic. He stepped to the driver's door, inserted the key and after a few jiggles was inside.

Thirty minutes later, he was crossing Rock Creek on West Beach Drive NW. He pulled off the road just north of Parkside Drive and killed the engine. It was a relatively deserted area this late at night. But what made it the perfect spot to leave the car was the fact that from here it was only a short walk through the woods via a trail that dumped out onto Frannie Green's street. He could practically walk to her front door without being seen.

As he set off down the trail, he keyed his radio. "What's the situation?"

"It's quiet, boss. All clear."

"Copy that. Be there in a few."

64

TARŁO settled in beside the man in the woods. His name was Ludwik. He had been one of Tarło's best operators in GROM. It's why he strongly recruited him when he'd founded RWS. He and Ludwik had done special reconnaissance work together for years but never quite like this. There was something just not right about Frannie Green, something he couldn't put his finger on. Spending as much time as he did with Stedman Carter and those with whom he rubbed elbows, Tarło had certainly seen his fair share of pushy elites, which is why he had strong reservations about Frannie Green. Something didn't ring true with her. For one, she never cursed. In his experience, all of the calculating, vengeful women he had ever come across swore like sailors. Take Vera Lysniak, for example. She could use a particular cuss word six, seven different ways in a sentence. A noun, verb, adjective. Heck, even a preposition.

Hopefully after tonight he would know for sure if Frannie Green was on the up and up, even if that meant she was who she said she was and knew what she said she knew.

"Everything set?"

"Roger that. Just like you wanted."

Tarło grinned. "Good. Can I have a peek?"

"Sure. Here." Ludwik reached over the stock of his sniper rifle and handed him a pair of night-vision binoculars. "Shall I make the call?"

"Go ahead."

Ludwik picked up a phone, the type that some in their business referred to as a burner phone. It was a prepaid cell phone, one that anyone could buy at Walmart or similar stores for which there was no contract and thus no name associated thereto.

Tarło was close enough that he could hear the whole conversation.

"9-1-1. What's your emergency?"

"Yeah. There is a man—"

"Sir, why are you whispering? I can hardly hear you."

"I don't want him to see me."

"You don't want who to see you?"

"The man with the knife. I… I saw a man with a knife come outside my neighbor's house. He was covered in blood. I think he may have killed someone. I know a woman lives there with her two kids. Her boyfriend… I think it's her boyfriend. Oh my gosh! Oh my gosh!"

"Sir. Sir! Calm down. What's the address you're calling from?"

"Uh. Seventeen forty-one Juniper Street, Northwest. Please, God!"

"And the address where the man with the knife is?"

"Seventeen forty-five. Huh! He just came outside again. He's… He's coming… He's…" Ludwik disconnected the call then powered off the phone and removed the battery.

Tarło patted him on the arm. "Nicely done, brother. That should do the trick."

Not long after, they could hear sirens and engines screaming. They grew louder. Flashing LEDs lit up the entire neighborhood.

"Get the survey teams out of there. Do it now."

Ludwik clicked the channel knob on his radio and relayed Tarło's order to the men who had been keeping tabs on Frannie Green for the past two days. Three vehicles that were parked in various, strategic locations within the neighborhood slowly pulled away and disappeared.

Patrol cars soon raced onto the block. Police officers, some with guns drawn flooded the street. A team of uniforms approached the door of Frannie Green's house as FBI agents in tactical gear emerged from the house next door and a moving van parked up the street.

It was mass confusion.

Amidst the chaos, Tarło studied the front door of Frannie Green's house as cops and FBI agents argued and pointed fingers on the front lawn. After twenty minutes, Frannie Green appeared on the porch, wearing a nightgown. Two men and a woman followed closely behind. They were clearly dressed for action. Tarło recognized the two men but couldn't recall their names. He sunk deeper into the brush, focusing on the figures inside his ATN NVB3X-3 night-vision binoculars.

"See the two guys on the porch?" said Tarło.

"The ones in plain clothes? Yeah."

"You remember them?"

Ludwik peered through his scope. "One on the right looks familiar. Who are they?"

"They're Delta. Like Rainey. Or at least were." Tarło and his Polish GROM teams had trained with Delta and other JSOC special mission units in sensitive counterterrorism operations in years past. "Crap," he whispered.

"What is it?"

"I just remembered," said Tarło. "Those two guys there. They were on Rainey's team."

"Seriously?"

"Uh huh."

"So, now what?"

Tarło grinned. "Now, Ludwik? Now, the real game begins."

65

Dickerson, Maryland

AFTER the FBI, police and everyone else had cleared from Juniper Street, Tarło and Ludwik followed the woman known to them as Frannie Green. It wasn't easy, because it was just the two of them, but they had managed. They were professionals after all and were used to adapting to the ever-changing situations that arose in their business.

Two men, presumably FBI agents, had driven Frannie Green here to a farmhouse in the middle of nowhere, which as it turned out—according to the GPS unit they were using—had an address of Dickerson, Maryland. Instead of trailing them onto the narrow, private lane that shot off Comus Road, however, Tarło and Ludwik had decided to park their cars in a grove of trees due south of the farmhouse, on a gravel cut along Old Hundred Road that farmers used to access their fields with combines and other implements of husbandry.

They crouched behind an old rusted tractor that looked like it had died and been left to rot twenty years ago. Tarło consulted the night-vision binoculars. The place was dark and quiet. The outbuildings that were situated around the house were devoid of livestock. There was a large barn over to their right. The door was wide open. Other than a 70sera Ford stake body that had two flat tires and a few piles of farm-related junk, it appeared to be empty.

"Gotta be an FBI safe house," said Ludwik.

"Yeah. It's perfect. For them and us."

They surveilled the house for nearly an hour while they waited for more of Tarło's RWS people to arrive. In the meantime, he and Ludwik checked the full circumference of the house for a security presence.

There was none.

The sky along the eastern horizon was still jet black when the two FBI agents surprisingly emerged from the house and climbed back into their Ford Explorer. It was the only vehicle parked by the house. Tarło checked his watch.

4:19.

The agents swung around the crushed gravel lot and sped off toward the road. Tarło ducked as the SUV's headlights swept past his position.

"No girl in the vehicle," he whispered into his radio.

Ludwik: *"Roger that. She's still inside. I can see her silhouette in the second-floor window on the back of the house."*

"Copy that. She's ours. But let's wait till the others arrive."

"Roger."

Soon six more of his men arrived and skulked to his position. They were dressed in tactical gear and were all wearing NODs. Tarło looked at them and whispered, "You three, fan out and keep watch. Kill anything that moves. Go." When they had disappeared into the darkness, he turned to the remaining trio. "You guys, Ludwik is waiting by the back door. Let me know when you have her."

◆ ◆ ◆

Maddie paced across the tongue-and-groove wooden floor of the bedroom. Events from Juniper Street were still swirling in her mind. She was tired and the FBI agents who had left her here weren't exactly friendly considering how everything had gone down.

Her thoughts turned to Wes. She missed him dearly, wished she could hold him and that he could hold her. She longed for his embrace. Oh, if he could see her now.

Maddie silently offered a quick prayer then eased down onto the bed. Her knee was swollen and stiff from all the time on her feet, but she had endured worse—like that time when she won a judo tournament with a severely sprained knee.

She clicked off the antique lamp and sighed into the blackness of the room.

◆ ◆ ◆

Ludwik now joined by three of his mates crept up to the back door. He gave a hand signal and they stopped. He examined what they were up against and chuckled quietly. Nothing more than a brass hook closure on the screen door and an old skeleton-key lock on the entry door. He pulled out his multi-tool, dealt with both doors and was inside in less than forty-five seconds.

The four men moved through the kitchen, weapons poised and ready to fire. If not for the NODs, they would have seen a colorful blend of ivory, jade green and vermillion. There were some papers strewn about on the table—blank statement forms with FBI letterhead, an empty cereal bowl and three coffee cups in the high-backed, cast iron sink. The scent of chamomile played at his nose as Ludwik ducked into and out of a pantry and signaled it was clear. They prowled into a dining room and passed a ten-person wood table that stretched across the room like an airport runway.

The stairs leading to the second floor were off to the left. Ludwik signaled for two men to stay put while he and another man checked the next room, a large living room. It was decorated as though it were still the 1930s as was much of the house. In the middle of the room was a large, floor-model radio, the kind that families used to huddle around after a long day's work on the farm and listen to their favorite programs. An upright piano stood along the wall and appeared as if it hadn't been played in years. On the opposite side of the room was a mammoth red-brick Colonial fireplace, cased in wood which was coated with an ivory enamel finish.

Ludwik motioned to the men and they stacked up behind him again. He edged around a wall, pointing his MP5 to the top of the stairs. They were wooden, probably oak or walnut with a well-worn carpet runner that shot down the middle. He placed his foot on the first step then steadily eased forward until his full weight was on the board. It creaked softly causing him to grimace.

The next few steps were squeakers, too, but the rest were silent and solid under the stress of their boots. There were four doors along the second-floor hallway, not counting the bathroom directly in front of him. Its door stood open and Ludwik could easily see that it was empty and contained no threats. As they made their way to the top of the stairs, they intuitively split into two two-man teams. Ludwik's went to the right while the other team headed to the left.

The first door he came to was cracked and held the majority of his focus. Not just because it was slightly ajar, but because it was the bedroom in which he had seen the silhouette of Frannie Green.

Ludwik swallowed and wiped the sweat from his brow with the back of his gloved left hand before he pressed forward. He tilted his head back to the man behind him without taking his eyes off the door. He felt the man squeeze his shoulder.

Ludwik gripped the handle of his MP5, stretched out his left arm and gently placed his hand against the door. He nudged it open.

66

MADDIE froze. Her eyes were wide in the darkness. She thought she had heard something. A squeaking noise. But couldn't be sure. There was an intermittent breeze outside that had the branches of a large maple tree scratching the side of the house like a bony-fingered beast clawing at her senses.

Her breath caught in her chest as she heard another sound. This time she was positive it was coming from inside the house. She craned her head toward the bedroom door.

It was moving.

◆ ◆ ◆

Ludwik followed the door as it swung into the room. Surprisingly, it made no noise. His eyes and muzzle swept the room until they landed on the figure on the bed. She was lying on her side with her back to him.

Perfect.

He took another step.

Click.

The lights instantly came alive in the room. He was blinded in his NODs. There was a whoosh and a tinkling sound as his teammate beside him fell to the floor. He batted off his NODs and jerked his head around the room, squinting at the window. There was a small dime-size hole in the glass.

Sniper!

It's a trap!

Gunfire erupted from down the hall. Then just as quickly there was silence.

Before he could move to cover or key his radio, a figure materialized in front of him, grabbed the suppressor of his MP5 and yanked him off balance. At the same time, the figure kicked him in the knee, the stomach, the knee again. His adversary latched onto his weapon with both hands and twisted it from his grasp, cracked him in the face with a powerful butt strike that shattered his nose.

His eyes were still adjusting to the sudden light but he was far from out of the fight.

Ludwik lunged toward the figure, but the figure countered with another lightning-quick strike to the face this time with the snout of the suppressor. Immediately blood began leaking from his forehead.

He stepped back to gain his senses. He looked at the person in front of him. It was Frannie Green. She was pointing the weapon—his weapon!—at him.

"Want to try again?" she said with a snarl.

"I thought you were in bed."

Maddie fired a three-round burst into the pillows and blankets that had been bunched up to look like a person lying on their side. "You know what they say when you assume something in this business, right?"

Ludwik smiled, put his hands up.

Then rushed her.

Maddie stepped to the side and fired a burst into his head then stood over his lifeless form.

"You're dead."

♦ ♦ ♦

Alarmed by the sudden bursts of gunfire, Zarek Tarło tried in earnest to raise his men on the radio. When no response came, he stood up, drew a pistol from a holster on his waist.

"They're all dead." The voice was familiar, but he couldn't put a face to it.

Tarło turned his head to the left and saw an old man with a 12-gauge pump-action shotgun.

"It's over, Tarło. Drop the gun."

He looked toward the house then back to the old man. "I know you. You're the man from the airport."

Saul Baker stood there stone-faced. "Virginia is for lovers, but here in Maryland they believe in strong deeds and gentle words." He lowered his voice. "Now, drop the weapon. I'm not gonna say it again."

Tarło grinned. "You set me up, didn't you?"

Saul shrugged. "I knew it was you who pulled that stunt on Juniper Street. Had to be. Figured I'd let you think you had the upper hand. Espionage one oh one, ya know?"

"Well played, old man. Well play—"

With that Tarło spun to shoot. But Saul was expecting it. He blasted him in the chest at close range with one round of double-aught buck, which caused Tarło's entire body to jolt before collapsing to the ground.

Saul gazed around. The silence was deafening. He leaned over, rifled through Tarło's pockets until he found what he was looking for.

A cell phone.

He consulted the incoming and outgoing calls and texts. It was the one Tarło used to communicate with Stedman Carter. He smiled as an idea formed in his mind.

He opened the text conversation again and tapped out a message. A response came within seconds. His face illuminated in the soft glow of the phone's screen, Saul whispered into the cool night air.

"Gotcha."

Then, with his own phone, he dialed the FBI.

◆ ◆ ◆

Carter's phone chirped, signaling it had just received a new text message. He read the notification on the home screen with tired eyes. It was Tarło. He fingered the screen and the full message opened.

"We got the girl."

Carter punched out a reply. "Good! Take her 2 warehouse in Bmore. Wait 4 me there."

"On our way."

Finally, he would find out who Frannie Green really was and where she was getting her information.

67

Baltimore, Maryland

THE Charm City Logistics warehouse on Dillon Street was quiet and dark and traffic outside was minimal. But that would all change in a matter of thirty minutes or so when the predawn sunlight bled into the eastern sky and the city of Baltimore came alive with the prospect of a new day.

Carter's driver/bodyguard pulled into the lot and parked beside Tarło's Chevy Tahoe. Carter got out and strode to the door with the bodyguard trying to keep up. He entered a dimly lit hallway, his hard-soled shoes proclaiming his arrival like drums of war. He pushed open the door to the residence hall and paced through to the briefing room.

It was empty.

Hands on his hips, he looked around. His forehead creased with wrinkles. "Zarek! Zarek, where are you?!"

"In here, boss." A voice dampened by the cement-block walls hearkened from down the hall.

Carter spun on his heel and marched toward the lounge, just one room down. He stormed into the room and froze. There sitting on the sofa in the middle of the room was an old man with a satisfied grin on his face.

"Who the heck are *you*?!"

"Me? I'm nobody. But these guys…," he nodded toward the corner of the room. "These guys are somebody."

At that moment a bevy of federal agents rushed him, jamming guns in his face. "FBI! Don't move!" A variety of curse words peppered their careful instructions.

Someone cranked his arm behind his back and shoved him against the wall, causing a small bulletin board to fall to the floor. As he was being cuffed, he realized the grunts from out in the hall were coming from his bodyguard. A scrum of agents had pinned him to the floor. A female agent issued commands as she dug her knee into the small of his back and a big, burly guy with a mustache and red cheeks pressed his face against the concrete.

When the excitement was over, an FBI agent stepped into the room. He wore a lightweight navy jacket over his bright white dress shirt and powdered blue tie. A gold badge dangled from a chain around his neck. He looked as fresh and lively as Carter looked exhausted. The agent assessed everything with a slow, confident turn of the head Finally, a grin stretched across his face. "Well done, guys." He approached Carter, leaned over his right shoulder and spoke in a calm, clear voice, which demonstrated the authority of his office. "Stedman Carter, my name is FBI Supervisory Special Agent Christopher Miller. And you are under arrest."

"Arrest?! For what?!"

"For being stupid, slick." Saul sipped a can of Pepsi to which he'd helped himself from the kitchen. He rose to his feet, sized up the billionaire then held the soda can in the air as if toasting the agents for a job well done.

"Hooked a big one this time!"

Miller nodded. "Yes we did. Now get these turds outta here. We've got a whole warehouse to inventory."

The place was jam-packed with crates the agents would soon discover held all manner of illegal arms destined for nation states that were by no means friendly to the United States.

Saul smiled and patted Miller on the arm as he drifted toward the exit. "Better you than me."

68

IT was two days ago, while on his way to the airport in Zurich that Rainey had telephoned the man at his shop in Vienna. The man was polite enough, but maintained he had just finished for the day and was on his way out the door. Rainey, likewise, was cordial and quick to the point. He presented the man with an offer, which he knew was just too good for anyone in his position to pass up. The man had asked only a few questions then agreed to Rainey's bullish commission, promising to get to work straight away. When Rainey stopped by later that night, the man was already well underway. They had quickly struck up a conversation about music that before long turned to the man's daughter, who was in a back room practicing her violin. She was as gifted a musician as her father was a craftsman.

Rainey now sat in the quaint café across the street. He had been sipping coffee and pretending to read a newspaper for the last twenty minutes as he waited for the man to arrive and open his shop. The storefront was a perfectly authentic rendition of Viennese style and culture. Its baroque façade was formal and well-maintained, elegant and beautiful though not overdone. Somehow it blended in seamlessly with the more modern businesses that lined Josefstädter Strasse.

There was a small sign above the wood and glass door that said, *"Friztl Klarinetten,"* with the Ls both taking a respectable shape of a clarinet. It was consistent with the rest of the storefront, clever but not gimmicky. But then again a man with the reputation of Claus Fritzl had no need for flashy signs or colorful banners. His work product spoke for itself and was all the advertisement anyone in his field needed.

Fritzl was particularly famous in this part of the world for his craftsmanship. If you were fortunate to play a Fritzl-stamped clarinet, you were likely an exceptionally gifted musician or someone who had a considerable amount of money to throw at a hobby. In Rainey's—er, Herr Johann Deistler's case, it was the latter.

The idea had come to him after recalling a story Saul once told him about how he had used a violin shop to pass messages back and forth with an agent in East Germany. A similar approach might work here, plus it would allow him and the team to observe Moses and anyone on the street that might be following him. Rainey was determined to make this meeting work and not become another Ronda.

At three minutes to eight, the lights inside the shop came on. Claus Fritzl appeared in the window. He straightened several articles of paper set atop a glass case then regarded his wristwatch. It was precisely 8:00 A.M. when he paced to the door and flipped over a sign that indicated his shop was now open. If the businesses in Vienna were anything, it was punctual. Rainey squinted over the newspaper. Fritzl unlocked the door then turned and walked toward the back of the store until he disappeared from view.

Rainey dropped a five-euro note on the table and waded across the street. He entered the shop to the sound of a single brass bell. The front room seemed larger now compared to when he had been here the other night. Probably just the lighting. Several aisles of shelving stretched off to the left on which was everything from clarinet accessories to sheet music to books and DVDs on how to master the clarinet.

"Herr Deistler! Guten Morgen," said Fritzl from behind the counter.

"*Jawohl. Guten Morgen.*" Rainey stepped toward the man and they shook hands.

Fritzl beamed with pride. "I've been busy on your clarinet. Would you like to see it?"

"I would love to."

Fritzl donned an apron then waved him behind the counter. They walked through an open door and into the man's workshop, which was easily double the size of the storeroom out front.

"I envy you, Herr Fritzl. Your shop is something else." Rainey picked up a block of grenadilla wood, felt the smooth texture. He considered what it must be like to earn a living doing this type of work. No gunfights. No bombs bursting. Just the sweet tranquility of working with one's own hands to create something beautiful, something useful from nothing more than a few raw materials. He pined for the chance to be in his own shop back home. There were so many things he wanted to do, projects he wanted to complete, but he never seemed to have the time.

Someday...

"It is my sanctuary, Herr Deistler."

"Yes. I understand completely."

Fritzl pulled back a work cloth, picked up the clarinet and handed it to Rainey. "Here. What do you think so far?"

Rainey turned it over in his hands, examining every last intricate detail. "Magnificent. You are a true artisan, my friend."

"Thank you. Obviously, I still have some more work to do."

"As long as it's ready by two."

Fritzl smiled. "I will be finished by noon."

"Excellent." Rainey pulled out a wad of money, handed it to Fritzl.

"But Herr Deistler, it's not finished yet."

"No matter. You are an honest man, Herr Fritzl. Your handiwork bears witness to this." Rainey looked him in the eyes. "And I've thrown in a little extra for your trouble."

Fritzl quickly counted it. "*Five thousand euros* extra? Herr Deistler you are too kind."

"You earned it." He shook the man's hand again. "Oh, I almost forgot. A case. Do you have a suitable case that I may purchase for my clarinet?"

Fritzl walked to a cabinet, pulled out a black leather case and set it down on a clean cotton cloth atop his workbench.

Rainey opened it, stroked the plush burgundy velour of the interior then smoothed the lines his fingers had left in the soft fabric. He lifted a small leather tab and inspected an inner storage space for extra reeds, a cleaning kit and other accessories.

"On the house."

"No, no. I can't—"

"I insist, Herr Deistler."

Rainey grinned. "Very well. Thank you."

"I will see you at two then?"

"Actually, no, I'm afraid not. I have an appointment that I must keep. But a friend of mine will be in to pick it up. He will probably be here around two twenty-five or so. I hope that isn't a problem."

"No problem whatsoever. I will be here and so will your clarinet."

"Very good. It was a pleasure meeting you, Herr Fritzl."

"Likewise, Herr Deistler. And thank you for your business."

Rainey exited the shop and turned left. He hooked another left onto Albertgasse then cut through Hamerlingpark. He strode up Kupkagasse then swung around the corner and hopped into his rental—a silver Peugeot 308—and headed north through the city.

At the first red light, he picked up his phone and punched in a number. When the call connected, he said, "I'm clear. It's a go."

"Roger that. We're all set," said Alcott.

"Good. All right. Catch you boys later."

69

DEMYAN Rostov had been studying the area around the university library all morning and a good chunk of yesterday. He had been trying to get inside Rainey's head while also getting a feel for the rhythms of the city. Clearly, the man was taking no chances now. Rainey was making sure the meeting was wholly on his terms. That meant that there was a high probability that he was being watched, which didn't bother him as long as it was only Rainey's people keeping tabs on him and not whoever was responsible for Ronda.

His watch said 2:05 and yet there was still no sign of Rainey. He looked around the library again. It was crowded with people of all ages, as it was open to the general public not just to university students and faculty. An uneasy feeling settled in his stomach. Was he at the right place? It occurred to him that Rainey might be waiting for him in a specific section of the library and not by the main entrance.

Rostov stood up and walked to a help desk. He asked specifically where the books on Romantic-era composers were located. The lady gave him a questioning stare over the top of her half-moon-shaped reading glasses before directing him to the Departmental Library on

Musicology, which was just around the corner from the main university library.

Rostov hustled over there. As he walked, another thought shot through his head. What if Rainey wasn't planning to meet him here at all, but had left some kind of message for him. If he were in his shoes, that's what he might do.

Yes. That's what he's doing.

When he found the right section, he slowed his search. There were so many books. Where to start?

No place better than at the beginning…

He slid out the first book on Schumann and opened it. Inside the front cover was a piece of computer paper that had been folded in half. Rostov hesitated. He looked left and right, making sure no one was watching. Then he unfolded it. It was a note. And it was written in Russian. Clearly this was meant for him.

"Go to the clarinet shop on Josefstädter Strasse. Ask for Claus."

Rostov tucked the paper into his pocket and gently placed the book back on the shelf. Again he took stock of his surroundings. Convinced he was clean, he made his way out of the library and flagged a taxi. The driver nodded without enthusiasm when he mentioned the clarinet shop. Seven minutes later he was standing in front of the storefront on which was a sign that read, *"Fritzl Klarinetten."*

He felt the heat of eyes on him though there was no way he could possibly know who here on the street or maybe in a nearby window was focused on him. This was foreign to him. He was ill-accustomed to not being in control. It gave him a sense of unease, but he was not afraid. A man like Demyan Rostov didn't know the meaning of fear.

He pushed into the store and glanced around. His eyes floated up to a mosaic of photographs of a brown-haired girl in various stages of childhood. In each picture, she held a violin. Dozens of ribbons and citations hung in a glass cabinet to the right. And there were countless newspaper clippings pinned to a corkboard on the wall behind the counter. Doubtless the girl was the proprietor's daughter.

"Ja. Guten Tag. Was kann ich für Sie tun?"

"I'm supposed to ask for Claus?"

"*Jawohl.* I am Claus. Herr Claus Fritzl. Oh, yes, of course! You must be here to pick up the clarinet."

Rostov grinned. "Uh, yes."

"It's all ready for you." Fritzl bent down behind the counter. When he stood, he had a black leather case in his hands and a giant smile on his face. He passed it across the counter as if it were packed with explosives and any false move might cause them to go off.

Rostov clutched the handle in like fashion. "Do I owe you anything, or…?"

"By all means, no. Herr Deistler has taken care of everything. Please tell him that I am very grateful for his patronage. And I miscounted when he was here. He didn't give me an extra five thousand euros. He gave me an extra *fifteen*. His kindness has allowed me to pay for my daughter's lessons again. You don't know how happy this has made her. And me!"

"I will."

"*Guten Tag!*"

"Same to you."

Rostov retreated across the street into the café. He asked for a cup of tea while he gathered his thoughts. He parked himself in a booth at the back and placed the case on the seat beside him. When his tea came, he took a sip then popped open the case and set his eyes on the clarinet within. It was beautiful. The waitress even said so on her way back through.

He didn't understand. There was no note, no message, no nothing. Just a clarinet. He frowned as he plucked each piece of the instrument out of the burgundy fabric, lined them up on the table. Some wisecracking Brit a few tables away called out, "Aye! Play us tune, why don't ya."

Rostov ignored him and continued his examination. He opened the small storage pocket, rifled through the extra reeds, cork grease and cleaning cloth. He sighed. Then he caught a glimpse of the edge of a piece of paper sticking out of the lower joint as it rested on the table.

He tilted his head and peered through the cylinder. Rostov coaxed out the scrap of curled paper with his fingertip and opened it. This time the note was written in English.

"Novaragasse 35. Apartment #4. And bring the clarinet."

He packed the pieces of the instrument back into the case and finished his tea. As he stood he pulled his shirttail down so no one would see the pistol in his waistband. Rostov drifted outside and hailed a cab. He spouted off the address and then relaxed back into the seat. They were out there. He was convinced Rainey and his people were watching him. He was still searching for them when he realized the driver was speaking to him. Rostov caught the man's questioning gaze in the rearview mirror.

"A clarinet," he said. But based on the driver's queer expression, he hadn't been asked about what was in the case. "I'm sorry. What?"

"Nevermind," barked the driver with a few slurs under his breath. "Novaragasse dead ahead."

Rostov paid the man and climbed out. Novaragasse was a one-way street in Leopoldstadt, the second municipal district of the city. It was a rather affluent area of Vienna with stores, museums, cinemas, upscale homes and apartment complexes. The buildings on either side were five stories high and seemed to press in on him and the street below. He had the sense that he was in a shooting gallery.

Number 35 was on the opposite side of the street. He walked toward the door again assessing the likely positions of a surveillance team. He saw threats everywhere. Behind the twisted window blinds five floors up. The scruffy-faced man in the side-view mirror, two cars down the street. The woman with dark sunglasses and an athletic build in running gear now coming right toward him. He tensed, ready to act. When she had trotted past, he relaxed and stepped up the two steps to the door of the apartment building. There was a brass panel on the wall beside him with sixteen black buttons and corresponding white labels. One of the labels was unreadable, another one was missing. The label for Apartment Four had been scribbled out with what looked like black magic marker. Above it, someone had written a name, but not just any name, the very name that he had used to communicate with Rainey since the beginning. A name that now, when he read it aloud, sent chills down his spine.

"Moses."

70

EMYAN Rostov pressed the button, which made a high-pitched buzzing noise that echoed into the street.

"Ja?" A man's voice hearkened from a small speaker set within the brass plate.

"Ich habe Ihre Klarinette." I have your clarinet.

Click.

The magnetic lock released and he stepped inside. The lobby was quiet and elegant if not aged. Dust particles danced in a bright band of sunlight that sliced through the window in the door behind him. He squinted as he looked back toward the door then shuffled forward.

A door on his left stood open. As he drew near, he heard a man whistling a tune that was a local favorite. Rostov stopped in the foyer and studied him. The man was hunched over a floor sink filling a metal bucket in what turned out to be a supply closet. He was dressed far more for his utilitarian duties than for vanity's sake. His olive-colored khaki shirt and pants were a little tight and his work boots were well-worn. The man grunted as he bent forward to his limits exposing the top half of his backside in the process. Rostov politely looked away while the man continued with his affairs.

When the man's rear was no longer showing, Rostov cleared his throat in order to draw his attention. The man rotated his head halfway to the right as if trying to decide whether or not he had heard something.

"Excuse me, sir. Apartment Four. Which floor, please?"

The man rose to his feet with a wince then waddled around. "Eh?"

"Apartment Four. On which floor is it?"

"Can't you read?" The man pointed to a sign with a spray can he was holding. "Apartments start on the second floor, go all the way up to the top. Number Four is on two. But elevator is out of order. Have to take the stairs."

Rostov turned to locate the door to the stairs.

"Watch the floors now. I just got done cleaning them."

Rostov glanced back and realized the man had the spray can aimed at his face. A small puff of compressed gas was the last thing he saw before he lost consciousness.

♦ ♦ ♦

Jazz caught the man under the arms as he fell forward. He was joined almost immediately by Babe and Fig who had been staging in the disabled elevator. Together the trio picked up Moses and ushered him out a door at the end of the foyer and into the courtyard to a waiting Mercedes-Benz Sprinter van. The back door swung open and Alcott leaned out, pulled the unconscious man inside as the others climbed in after him.

"Good to go," said Alcott in the direction of the driver.

Rainey eased off the brake and exited the courtyard through a narrow opening that dumped them out onto Aloisgasse. "What about the clarinet?"

"It's right here," said Babe. "I got it right here."

"Sweet," said Rainey.

In the back of the van, Jazz nudged Alcott with his elbow and whispered, "What's the deal with the clarinet?"

Alcott shrugged. "How on earth should I know?"

◆ ◆ ◆

It wasn't until they crossed the Danube and were well on their way to Brno that Moses began to stir. Rainey had since traded places with Babe. Alcott and Fig had already relieved the man of his pistol and performed a thorough inspection of his clothing, shoes and belt for weapons, phones and tracking devices. As expected, he carried no form of identification other than a Spanish passport, which, as they would later learn, was a rather high quality counterfeit.

Rainey took a swig from a bottle of water as he waited for Moses to fully regain his senses. He screwed the cap back on and dropped the bottle in a cup holder in the woodgrain console beside him. The man's face was puckered, his skin leathery and aged. Wisps of thinning white hair were combed neatly in place on his liver-spotted scalp. His bushy, gray eyebrows rose and fell, twitched and turned along the tops of his wire-rimmed glasses in such a way that made Rainey imagine they were squirrel tails. Rainey thought the man was going to sneeze when his nose wiggled at one point. It was bulbous and a distinct shade of purple and seemed to draw attention from the other far less interesting features of his face.

Moses opened his eyes and blinked. They drooped at first but gradually came alive. He squinted. "Reagan Rainey."

"The one and only."

Moses tried to shift in his seat but stopped when he discovered he was restrained with thick zip ties. "Are these necessary?"

"You tell me?" said Rainey.

"If I wanted to harm you I could have shot you in the concert hall in Seville or on the terrace in Ronda."

Rainey stared at him for a minute then nodded to Fig who flipped out a blade and cut him free.

Moses rubbed his wrists. "Thank you."

"Forgive me if I seem a bit more direct than I was in Spain, but who the heck are you?"

"Yes. Well... I will show you. Just remember this: if I wanted to kill you, you would already be dead."

Rainey's forehead scrunched up as he studied him. "What do you mean *show* me?"

Moses smirked. "I mean *show* you." He brought his hands up and began clawing away at his face and head.

Rainey's heart quickened. He prepared himself to act, to fight. They all did. Alcott pulled a Glock from his waistband.

When Moses was finished peeling off the disguise, he lowered his hands to the armrests and looked up in silence.

Rainey already had his own pistol in his hand and now pointed it at the center of the man's chest. "Rostov."

"Who?!" blurted Jazz.

"*Demyan Rostov.* He's a Russian assassin." Rainey swallowed and gripped his pistol, the muscles in his forearms and biceps showing. "He tried to kill me last year. How many times was it?"

The others in the van were switched on and staring daggers at him.

"Easy fellas. Easy now. Remember, Rainey... I could have killed you in Seville and again in Ronda." Rostov held up his hands in surrender. "I mean you no harm. You or your friends. Seriously."

"I don't believe you."

"It's true. I'm a changed man."

Rainey's eyes were aflame with intensity.

"I want to help you."

"Why?"

"Partly to atone for my sins."

"And?"

"The other reason is my own and shall stay that way. You'll have to forgive me, but that's the only way I'll lead you to your father."

"And what if I just shoot you right here?"

"Then you'll never know what really happened to him or where to find him. I'm your only hope. I'm willing to lead you to the Promised Land. Please. At least hear me out."

"You make one false move and I'll shoot you right between the eyes."

"Fair enough."

After several seconds, Rainey lowered the gun but kept the muzzle trained on Rostov. "Talk."

"You remember the video clip I showed you?"

Rainey nodded.

"It was recorded a week before I delivered the letter to the case officer in Lisbon. Sorry about that, by the way. But that was the best way I could think of to reach you."

"How did you know he was CIA?" asked Rainey.

"Sentinel. He gave us all kinds of information."

"Who's Sentinel?" chimed Jazz.

Fig smacked him on the back of the head. "Would you shut up?"

"What?" said Jazz.

Rainey ignored Jazz's interruption and didn't bother to explain that Sentinel was the code name the Russians had given their deep-cover operative, a man the DX eventually identified as a high-level CIA employee. The extent of the exposure as a result of his betrayal was still being parsed by various agencies within the American intelligence community. So far what Rostov had said made sense. "Us. You mean SVR?" *Sluzhba Vneshney Razvedki* was Russia's foreign intelligence agency.

Rostov nodded. "Your father is alive, Rainey. And I know exactly where he is being held and what it's going to take to get him out of there."

"Why are you doing this? What's in it for you?"

Rostov's eyes turned toward the darkened van window. "I'm afraid that's my business."

"Cut the bull, Rostov! You know what? Hunting down and killing bad guys, that's my business. I could put a bullet in you right now and it would make a lot of people very happy."

"Yes. But like I said, you'd never find your father then. He is *alive*, Mr. Rainey. And I am willing to lead you to him. Do you want to save him or not?"

"Suddenly I'm *Mister* Rainey." He shook his head. "How can I trust you after what you did last year? You killed Americans. Some of them were friends of mine."

Rostov lowered his head. "I feel bad about that. I do. I don't deny what I did. I guess you could say that now I'm trying to make up for it. It won't bring those people back, nothing will, but… I owe this to you."

The van hit a bump and everyone gently rocked. Rainey drew a deep breath while he mused. For the life of him, he couldn't figure out what would possess this trained Russian assassin to help him.

"There *is* one thing," said Rostov.

"Uh-huh. Let's hear it."

"You have to promise that your government will stop hunting me."

Rainey looked him dead in the eyes. "It's not my place to speak for my government. You know that, Rostov."

"Speak for yourself then. One warrior spy to another. Promise me that when this is all over *you*, Reagan Rainey, will no longer hunt me."

71

Prague, Czech Republic

THEY reached the city limits after dark. Along the way, Rainey had put a call into DX headquarters for Job and requested he fly to Prague for an in-person meeting. What Rainey needed to talk about was too sensitive to discuss otherwise.

Babe turned off Koblenova just before the Pepsi plant and followed the pavement to a gate in a chain-link fence. A small vinyl placard hung on the fence next to an adjacent guard shack that plainly read, "P&D Press, s.r.o. A Division of MHP Global." After a brief conversation with Babe through the driver's window, the guard gave them a set of specific instructions and waved them through.

Though it would never appear in an official account of the operation, the fact remained that MHP Global was an international publishing house and a strong partner of the Greenbriar Foundation, the front organization for the CIA's Directorate X. The P&D Press facility in Prague was the company's European headquarters.

The team pulled into a garage bay in a separate, secure area of the property anecdotally referred to as the Greenbriar Room, or GR, among DX operatives. This was an area that was set aside for clandestine operations although the size and capability of a GR varied greatly across the spectrum of Greenbriar Foundation affiliates. In this case, there were lodging accommodations and a place to keep up to three vehicles securely under roof.

For the next several hours, Rostov presented him with files stored in a cloud-based account and information regarding his father while the others stood by and provided a vigilant, armed presence. What Rainey learned in the process was nothing short of shocking.

In the morning, Rainey left the team and Rostov at the P&D Press building and traveled by tram westward into the heart of the city. He alighted at the Náměstí Republiky stop, circled the block and performed a series of surveillance detection maneuvers before continuing down Celetná Lane toward Old Town Square.

The city was already teeming with tourist activity and the typical morning throngs, which allowed him to blend in with little effort. He understood why people came here. Prague had old world charm. The architecture was simply stunning, the setted streets were clean and lined with shops right out of a storybook. The toy store on his left reminded him of a simpler time in world affairs, back when people made things with their bare hands, carried on conversations in person not over the phone or on social media and actually knew what was going on in the world, which didn't include celebrity gossip.

He passed a jeweler and a currency exchange kiosk, a souvenir shop that specialized in crystal in the artful traditions of Bohemia. Two lovely ladies in summer dresses were walking toward him. Their happy chatter became a whisper as they drew near. The one on the left, a brunette that bore a striking resemblance to Kayla, his college sweetheart, flashed a smile and made eyes at him as they passed. He offered a polite grin and immediately heard giggling as he continued on his way. His thoughts soon became overrun with memories of Kayla, their college romance and what Maddie had said before he had set off on the operation. *"She looks good...didn't see any wedding ring on her finger either...got the sense that she's still carrying a torch for you."*

She still loves me.

He shook his head.

Stop it, Ray. Stay focused.

The Belgian chocolate shop on his left reminded him of the fact that he hadn't eaten anything yet. The information Rostov had disclosed last night was that jarring that it had chased away any vestige of an appetite. Even this morning, he hadn't been hungry enough to eat. But the intoxicating allure of chocolate now had his stomach growling like a mean dog.

Rainey entered the Old Town Square and veered toward the Jan Hus Memorial. For several minutes he stood there, gazing up at the sculpture of a man who dared to challenge the status quo, dared to risk life and limb for truth and the foundational church doctrine of justification by grace through faith. For his efforts, Hus was burned at the stake. But because of his courageous stand, he helped spark a movement now known as the Reformation. In the way Wycliffe had influenced him, Hus inspired countless others, most notably a German man named Martin Luther.

Like George Washington and others, Rainey believed in the principle of deeds, not words. Faith put into action. But was faith enough to endure years of anguish, imprisonment and betrayal? Though the situation wasn't exactly the same, he wondered if faith had been able to sustain his father all these years as it did men like Jan Hus in his time.

Rainey was still ruminating when the anachronistic sound of horse hooves against the cobblestone broke him from his reverie. He looked at his watch then set off again.

He looped around and approached the apartment on Žatecká from the north. The front door was unlocked and the reception desk empty. Rainey trotted up the stairs to the fourth floor and knocked. Job's bodyguard opened the door and at the sight of him pivoted and allowed him to enter. The man then stepped into the hall and disappeared as Job had doubtless instructed.

"I'm up here."

Rainey cast his eyes upward to the sound of the man's voice then wound up a wood and wrought iron spiral staircase to a posh living room. Job was standing by a window that faced Prague Castle.

"How bad is it?"

Rainey wordlessly walked to the sofa and sat down.

"I see."

"He's alive, Job. My father's alive."

Job stared at him, the rising and falling of his chest visibly quickening. His eyes began to well up as he paced over to the chair across from Rainey and eased into it. The spymaster gripped the arms of the chair as if it were a rollercoaster car. His mouth opened but no words came out. Finally, he took a deep breath and composed himself. "I can't believe it. Ben… Alive." He wiped tears from his face with his fingertips. "Okay. Lay it on me."

"It's Rostov."

"*Demyan* Rostov? As in the Russian assassin? The man who tried to kill you last year? And me for that matter."

Rainey nodded.

"Ray, I—"

"Relax. I know what you're gonna say. That it could be a trap. That he still wants me dead. Trust me, Job, I've considered that."

"But you don't believe that to be the case."

"I didn't say that either. There is clearly something going on here, something for which we have no calculus. Yet. He's up to something. I know that, but…

"But what?"

"Look, he easily could have killed me in Spain, but he didn't. Regardless, I believe what he's saying about my father. I looked into his eyes, Job. He's telling the truth." A pause. "You're thinking how can I be so sure, right?"

"Ray, deception is—."

"It's because I've seen the files that prove it."

"What files?"

Rainey opened the satchel that was still slung over his shoulder, removed a stack of files he had printed out in the Greenbriar Room in the P&D Press facility and pushed them across the coffee table that separated them. "These files. My father's alive, Job. He's *alive*. I know what happened to him and exactly where he is. And I'm willing to risk everything to go get him."

72

HE sat quietly by as Job poured through document after document. The files that Rostov had turned over detailed a whole host of things. First and foremost, the files supported what they already knew from their conversations with Ernie Wells about Operation Triumph and DNI Hank McManus. In addition, they confirmed that Ben Rainey did have an extensive network of spies inside Russia and several of the now-former Soviet states. Almost all of them had been pointing fingers at a KGB veteran by the name of Levka Borovsky—who from 1995 through 1999 was head of a special counterintelligence unit within the FSB—as one of the biggest sellers of leftover Soviet military hardware to include large caches of rockets, missiles, even nuclear warheads. The list went on and on.

"So our old friend Borovsky is Keynote." The sarcastic reference had to do with the fact that Levka Borovsky was determined to have been the brains behind the plot Rainey foiled last year. In the aftermath, Borovsky had been expelled as SVR director by the Russian government and, for reasons that were still not very clear, had since gone into hiding.

Rainey nodded. "In most cases, he worked through a broker, who per Operation Triumph had the code name, Echo."

"It says here that that man is Stedman Carter."

"Indeed, it does."

Job shook his head. "Remind me to fill you in on a few things when I'm done." He patted the stack. "This explains so much. But where did all of this information come from?"

"Interrogations, recovered dead drops, wiretaps."

"No, I mean where did Rostov get these files?"

Rainey grinned. "He stole them from Borovsky."

"Unreal. I mean, I just can't— My gosh!"

"Both Borovsky's and Carter's empires were built on criminal activity. Not just that, they betrayed their countries as they got rich. Word is they were really tight back in the late eighties and nineties, but eventually, as Rostov explained it to me, Carter became too big for his britches. Outgrew his role as broker and became one of Borovsky's biggest competitors. The men had a bitter falling out about ten years ago. Rostov said they hate each other now."

"I still don't understand why McManus had Wells destroy the Triumph files."

"Read on," said Rainey. "Third paperclip."

Job flipped to the spot and scanned the text, his index finger leading the way. His hand was midway down the page when he abruptly looked up. "Holy cow!"

"That's right. *POTUS*. He had just become senator by then. Thanks to the fabulous mainstream media of our time there are still stretches of the president's past that are a complete mystery. Only a few brave souls have ever dared to allege publicly that he's a Muslim and a radical one at that. Though he's never admitted it. And never will. Not until he's out of office. And even then…"

"I see your point."

"Clearly, his policies over the past four years have demonstrated that he has no love for Israel. I don't recall him ever once condemning the anti-Israel bile that's regularly spewed by Islamic fundamentalists. Do you?"

"Sadly, no."

What Rostov's files highlighted—and what Ben Rainey's agents with respect to Operation Triumph had uncovered—was a meeting that took place in May of 1996 on a yacht off the coast of Cyprus between Levka Borovsky, Stedman Carter and a young American man said to be representing an Islamic aid foundation later identified by U.S. intelligence agencies as a terrorist organization. There was a long discussion about acquiring a nuclear weapon or at the very least enough enriched uranium to build a bomb that would send Israel into oblivion. The young American was none other than Grantley Winslow, as in sitting United States President Grantley Winslow. And there were photographs, audio and video recordings to supplement every report.

"Now we know why McManus was killed," added Rainey.

"Yeah. He was probably blackmailing Carter or POTUS."

"Or both." Rainey sunk back into the sofa. "If you read on, you'll see how the Russians came to find out about my dad. Seems they received an anonymous letter much the same way Rostov left his note for us. The author identified my dad as an American CIA officer and detailed what he was working on. Even suggested that if the Russians wanted him they were welcome to make him disappear without repercussion. The author had referred to his betrayal of my father as a *gift*. Mentioned that any *artifacts of Triumph* would be taken care of, too."

"McManus."

"That's my guess. Carter probably put him up to it."

"Why Carter?"

"For one, no one knew back then that Winslow would one day be president. So it stands to reason that McManus was doing Carter's bidding. And two, what better way to make the problem go away than to have my dad die in an innocent little *plane crash*," said Rainey with air quotes. "Carter had the resources to make that happen."

Job's face fell back down to the printed-out documents as Rainey mused aloud. "For Borovsky, it couldn't have been any sweeter. He got to eliminate a key impediment to his black market dealings and at the same time was able to round up a whole network of spies for the FSB. Heck, he probably got promoted."

"Things are all making sense." Job told him about the operation to net Zarek Tarło. "FBI followed him to a meeting he had with Carter in New York. Surreptitiously recorded him ordering Tarło to capture, interrogate and kill… Uh… Maddie. Except they didn't know it was Maddie."

"What?!"

"Relax, Ray. We've already taken Tarło down. Actually, he's dead." Job related how things unfolded back home with Maddie and the others. "Last I heard, feebies had just scooped Carter at a warehouse in Baltimore. For now, everything is being kept quiet.

"Well, this should be the final nail in the coffin. For him and the administration," said Job.

"Whaddya mean?"

"I spoke to Thompson about who was at the meeting in the Oval Office after the letter from Moses first came to light."

"Yeah, and?"

"Based on everything I now know, I have no doubt that Vera Lysniak is the one who leaked the info contained in the letter."

"I don't follow."

"The NSA."

"National Security Agency?"

"No, the other NSA—the president's national security advisor."

"Valetta Ivory? What's she have to do with any of this?"

"She reached out to Thompson yesterday morning. They've been close friends for years. She passes on tidbits of info here and there for the betterment of our national security position. The administration might be a virulent political machine, but Ivory is the exception. She is someone who puts country above all else, including self-interest. She's a true patriot, Ray.

"Anyway, Ivory attended a big shindig at Stedman Carter's mansion the night prior to McManus' death. She didn't think anything of it at the time. Only remembered later, you know, after the DNI's death was classified a homicide."

"She saw something?"

"You could say that. She saw McManus stealing away with Vera Lysniak during the party. Said McManus looked worried about something but after their brief encounter, his demeanor had changed for the better. Also according to Ivory, it seems that Vera and Stedman Carter have grown especially close over the past few weeks. The fact that Carter is in this thing up to his eyeballs has me convinced that Vera is our leak."

Rainey dragged his fingers through his short, brown hair as he aired his thoughts. "So, Vera tells Carter about the letter and the blog. Carter has Tarło and his people try to kill us in England and then Spain. Yeah, makes sense."

"Also explains why Carter sent guys down to the site of the plane crash in Venezuela. He wanted to destroy any possible evidence that would show how the plane was actually taken down." Job related how the DX was able to track down the missionary's son, who procured some old photographs that clearly substantiated the fact that the plane had been brought down by some type of bomb. "If Ben was supposed to be dead, they needed a plausible story and a body. So McManus likely fabricated reports about Ben meeting with one of his agents in Venezuela, or something along those lines, then they killed those missionaries. Bomb explodes over the jungle, plane falls into no-man's land. No witnesses to worry about. Gosh… McManus, Carter and Lysniak… What a bunch of freakin' scumbags.

"Until Rostov and his letter, everything was copacetic. But the notion that your dad could be alive was just too dangerous a proposition for everyone involved. McManus, Carter, POTUS. Ben knows way too much. Even after all these years, he is still a massive threat to everything they have built on lies, greed and betrayal.

"Ray, you know, you just may have saved Thompson's career and his reputation."

"No, Job. *We* did. All of us, together. As a team. But our work has only just begun."

"You're absolutely right." Job straightened the files and sighed as if he'd just run a 5K. "You eat yet?"

"No."

Job hurried out of the room. When he returned, he had a tray of pastries and two cups of piping hot coffee. "All right. Let's get down to business and bring your dad home where he belongs. Now, where is he? Where's Ben?"

73

RAINEY sipped his coffee while his chocolate eyes burned with intense concentration. The hot liquid washed down his throat and trickled into his empty stomach. "He's in a place the Russians call, Secret Facility Number One Eleven, the reference being to Stalin's SF, Number One Ten. It's a gulag, Job, as in the traditional sense. Prisoners are subjected to hard labor, beatings and all kinds of humiliations. There is no due process, no nothing. Most of the people taken there are in some form or fashion political prisoners: journalists and other outspoken critics of the government. But there are a few foreign nationals, like my dad—intelligence officers operating without official cover and the like who are deemed too valuable for traditional arrest and detention.

"The fact that my dad remains alive can only mean that he still knows something…or Borovsky thinks he does. See, the prison operates under Borovsky's authority. He has complete autonomy to run it as he sees fit. It's been that way for years. The men who work there are all hand-picked for their loyalty and brutality."

"What happened? How did it go down?"

"He was snatched off the street in Tallinn. Quietly ushered across the border and taken to SF One Eleven. From what I can tell, he's been there ever since."

Job was motionless as he soaked it all in. "Where is this *SF One Eleven?*"

Rainey took a bite of *trdelník* then chased it down with another sip of coffee. "It's situated due northwest of Moscow, near the small town of Kholm. It had at one time been a small, secret base used by the Red Army back in the thirties and forties. Officially, the base has long been abandoned, locked up and fenced off from the public. However, since the fall of the Soviet Union, it's been used as a secret prison—a black site—for particularly troublesome actors deemed detrimental to the Kremlin.

"Rostov said that there are currently about thirty inmates." Rainey pulled a manila folder from his satchel, opened it and removed the first paper inside. He unfolded it and smoothed it against the coffee table. "This is a map of the facility. The prisoner quarters are on the first and second floors below ground." He pointed with his finger. "My father is being held in this cell right here. On the second sub-level."

"What is this?" Job pointed at a large rectangular section on a third sub-level.

The muscles in Rainey's jaw flexed. "That is the cellar. It's where the most vile humiliations, torture and executions are carried out.

Job slid to the edge of the chair and cradled his face as he mulled over the map. "What do you have in mind?"

Rainey extracted a yellow legal pad. It was full of handwritten notes. At the top of the first page was a heading that was underlined twice: **Concept of Operation**.

Job carefully read each page. When he had reached the end, he rubbed his eyes. "I can't believe Ben is alive. After all these years, I…" He trailed off, clearly lost in his emotions. "And the Russian president is aware of all of this?"

"No question, he's aware. *And* complicit."

Job stood and paced around the room, gazed out the window. "So what is Rostov's motivation for helping you find your dad? Not just that.

Those files have the potential to cause irreparable harm to the Russian Federation as a whole. Why would he do such a thing?"

"I'm still working on that," said Rainey.

"Could it really be that he's a changed man?"

"It's possible, but like I said before, I think he's up to something."

"But what? That is the question," said Job.

"Don't know. What I *do* know is that my dad is alive."

"You're right. Well, there's no way POTUS is going to authorize this. I mean, what you're proposing is a covert operation on foreign soil. *Russian soil.* And a black site to boot. Not to mention, saving Ben's life is tantamount to suicide for him." Job milled around the room. "But I am not about to put Thompson on the spot, either. Make him stick his neck out any further than it already is. If he has no knowledge of this then better for him if this ends in disaster. Tell you what. If I order you to do this then I'll be the one to take the heat if it goes bad. I owe it to Ben. He's my best friend."

"I appreciate that, Job, but no. I don't want anyone subjected to an order like that."

"Then what, Ray?"

"This has to be completely black and completely voluntary. I will explain it to my guys. But for my plan to work with all of its contingencies, we're going to need more people. It's all there in my notes."

"Say no more. I'll get on it right away."

"But they each have to understand that they have the option to decline. I'm not going to force this on anyone. Promise me you'll give them the option to say no."

"You have my word."

"Good. Oh, there is one more thing that I should mention. In return for Rostov's help, I promised him that I would no longer target him…you know…when this is all over."

"You did what?" said Job.

"Trust me. Everything is gonna be fine."

"You seem awfully optimistic."

"Because this fight is righteous, Job. God has led us this far. I trust that He will take us the rest of the way. Not saying it'll be easy, but all I can do is trust Him. That and fight like the dickens to bring my dad home. God as my witness, I'm *gonna* bring him home or I'll die trying."

Another tear streaked Job's face. "Your faith is a lot stronger than mine, Ray. But I'll do whatever it takes to get Ben back. I know he would be so proud of you. I know I am."

"Thanks."

Job flipped to a fresh page on the legal pad and jotted down some notes. "Okay. Let's touch base this evening. Hopefully by then I will have a handle on everything and everyone we'll need to proceed. We'll smooth out any rough edges then. Deal?"

"Deal."

74

WHEN Rainey had returned to the P&D Press facility, he spoke to each of his teammates alone and in private at which point he explained what he and Job had discussed including the part about their chance to opt out of the operation. None of them equivocated for a second.

They were all in.

Pleased with their decision, Rainey then took Rostov aside and presented him with his plan for the operation. Rostov initially suggested a way for Rainey and his teammates to get into the country, but Rainey, fearing a snafu or even some kind of trap at the border, advised him that they would enter the country on their own terms, which would remain secret, even from Rostov.

Rainey's rescue plan involved a prisoner drop-off. It seemed to give them the best chance for success. He didn't bother to mention all that he had in mind for the operation, only the part about how he and his teammates would be dressed as FSB Alpha Group troops and would be staging the drop-off of a high-value prisoner. Alcott had volunteered to be the prisoner. Rainey, the only one who spoke fluent Russian among them, would be the driver and thus would deal with the guards on the gate. Once they were inside, the meat and potatoes of the operation would begin. The only thing Rostov had to do was get them into the facility where Ben was being held, nothing more, nothing less.

It was after nine o'clock at night when Rainey's phone hummed against the table. He picked it up without delay. "Yes?"

"Everything is a go: gear, people, the works. It's all been set into motion. Just how you wanted," said Job.

"Awesome. I'm gonna cut our friend here loose."

"All right. Hey, I want you to know that I will be praying for you. We're all behind you."

"Thank you, sir."

"Godspeed."

Rainey ended the call then asked Fig, Babe and Jazz to drive Rostov to the airport. Before they slipped the blindfold back on, Rainey gave the Russian one last glimpse and a thinly veiled warning. "I gave you my word. And I intend to stand by it. Just don't double-cross me."

"I appreciate that. Thank you. I'll see you in three days," said Rostov.

Rainey shook his hand. "Three days."

♦ ♦ ♦

Aboard an Aeroflot plane to Moscow, Demyan Rostov kicked off his shoes and reclined in his seat. He reached out, pulled the phone from the seatback in front of him and dialed a number. He rolled his sleeves up while he waited for the call to connect. When a gruff baritone came on the line, he spouted off a code phrase and waited until it was checked for its veracity. Finally, the call was put through to the intended recipient.

"Da?" The voice was familiar but one he hadn't heard face-to-face in quite some time.

"It's me, Sasha." Sasha—one of Rostov's many aliases.

"Ah, Sasha. So, you have good news?"

"Da. I did it."

"You didn't!" The man on the other end howled with laughter, which soon became a wet cough. "My star pupil has done it! I cannot believe it. You were always my favorite."

"Believe it, sir. In three days you will have your revenge."

"And you, Sasha, will have your freedom."

"I will send you the details by the usual method." Rostov drummed his fingers against his thigh.

"And I will be ready to devour them," said Levka Borovsky.

75

**Novgorod Oblast, Russia
Three Days Later**

REAGAN Rainey slipped out of his sleeping bag and into his Merrell hikers. It was still dark as he crept out into the chill morning air. He stalked a few paces into the woods and took a leak then stoked what remained of the small campfire outside their ramshackle abode with a stick. A few shy embers came to life, offering a soft red glow against the blackness of the Russian forest. He gently pushed a loose bundle of dead grass and pine needles into the hot coals, dropped a few twigs on top and blew softly into his creation until a flame caught. He laid another handful of kindling on the fire as it grew. When it really started to take off, he eased a pair of small logs he had collected onto the pile.

Normally, he would have erred on the side of caution and done without the fire—no need to draw unnecessary attention to their presence, but in this case, they were deep in the forest, far from any road and had scouted out the terrain thoroughly before setting up camp. They were actually in what looked like a summer youth retreat, not unlike those in the States where fathers and sons bonded over campfires and hunting and fishing. Except this one was long deserted and had since been reclaimed by the forest. It was probably fifty or sixty years old. Not much was left to show for it in the way of structures. The only one that hadn't caved in or collapsed entirely from decades of heavy snowfall was a small bunkhouse with a short rise of roughly hewn steps, on which a lightning-struck tree had fallen and destroyed. But once they had chased out the lone occupant from the premises, a rather pesky raccoon, the place was perfectly suited for their purposes. They would soon be gone anyway.

They had flown from Prague to Minsk where a DX support staff officer greeted them. The man didn't ask any questions, he simply drove them to a dirt track that cut through the woods and across the Russian border. It was a route sometimes used by smugglers, he'd said. His last words to them had been wishes of good fortune at whatever it was they were up to. Clearly, he had done this type of thing before.

Once inside the Bear, they had linked up with another support staff officer who drove them to a lakeside dacha outside Nevel. There, she provided a detailed map and directions to where they were going and the safest route to get there. She also gave them the keys to the vehicles they would use which contained the weapons and other gear needed to effect the operation.

Rainey had no idea how the support staff did the things they did at times, he just knew that they did them. Often in this business there were more questions than answers. In any case, the support staff folks were the unsung heroes of the intelligence world. They never got the glory, never had movies made about them, but what they did behind the scenes and in the shadows, day-in and day-out, was absolutely critical for mission success and he loved them immensely because of it.

Now, hunkered down over a fire in the wilderness, miles northwest of the small Russian hamlet of Pogost, memories of Afghanistan drifted into his mind. The smell of woodsmoke, dirt, trees, and a hint of animal dung took him back to a particular night in Kunar Province before he and his A-team from 3rd Group set out on a perilous operation that left two of them dead. He thought of them often, thought of their faces and the jokes they liked to tell. He realized that this mission was about more than bringing back his dad. It was about bringing back an American who was thought to be dead. He wished he could in some way bring back all who had died serving the red, white and blue.

Rainey knelt and offered up a silent prayer. He thanked God for providing him and the whole of mankind with a way of eternal salvation. He thanked Him for allowing him and his teammates to get this far and asked for the continued safety of all who were involved in the operation. Lastly, he asked that the mission would be a success and that he would be able to honor the promise he had made to his mother to bring his dad home.

"You're up early."

"Big day ahead," said Rainey, stirring the fire.

Jazz walked over, pulled his hands from his pockets and warmed them in the heat of the fire.

"How's the leg?"

"Sore, but not bad considering."

"Good," said Rainey.

"Say, you really believe in all that God stuff don't you?"

"Yes, I do."

"I don't know," said Jazz. "Always seemed a little hokey to me."

"Why's that?"

"Just seems like a crutch, is all. No offense."

"None taken," said Rainey. "But I have to say, living without knowing for sure what is going to happen to you when you die… I mean let's face it, bro, we're all going to die at some point and in this business it could happen anytime. Must be a pretty empty feeling not knowing."

Jazz kicked a stone into the fire.

"Listen, brother, you have kids. What if I told you that you have a Father in heaven who loves you so much that he sent His Son, His *only* Son to die on the cross to take away the sin of the world, *your* sin and *my* sin."

"I just don't get that. Why would God do that? I mean what's the point?"

"Because the penalty for sin is death. It's not me saying that; it's what the Bible says. Someone had to die because man chose to sin. If Christ hadn't died on the cross, we would all be doomed to spend eternity in hell when we die. But the good news is that Christ rose from the dead not only to fulfill what was written in Scripture, but to demonstrate to the world once and fall all, that the God of the Bible is the One True God. He is able to defeat death itself.

"But unless we accept it, unless we make the personal decision to believe in our hearts, we can never know true salvation and will never spend eternity with God in heaven when we die."

"Bro... You shoulda been a preacher."

"Yeah, well... Every Christian is a preacher, or should be. Some just have a church building and a congregation."

"But why does God allow believers to suffer? Why would God do this to your dad? He's what you call 'saved,' right? Why would God let these Russian turds haul him off to a gulag and torture the heck out of him?"

Rainey's eyes fell back to the fire. "I don't know. I..." It took him a moment to compose himself. "I don't have all the answers, Jazz. God never promised that bad things wouldn't happen to good people. Think of it in terms of *our* world, doing what we do... No one ever told us we'd never face adversity in carrying out our objectives, but it's all about how we deal with it and overcome it. All I can tell you is that I rely on my faith to get me through the tough times. To be perfectly honest, I'd be a wreck without God in my life."

"I'll think about it."

"I can't make the decision to accept Christ for you, bro. I sincerely hope you do, but it's ultimately up to you. If you ever want to talk more, I'm here for you, brother. I got your back."

"Thanks, Bronc. You're a good man and a good friend. And by the way, we're gonna find your dad. I have no doubt."

"Thanks, brother. I appreciate that. I really do."

76

BY midday, they had received final word from Job via sat phone that the op was still a go. Everything and everyone was in place. They had kept the conversation short and vague for the sake of the NSA and any other agencies, foreign or domestic that might be listening. The idea was to keep the operation black and for that to happen there could be no record of it, even back home on American soil.

Rainey and his team were an hour from launch. They were now suiting up and making last checks of their weapons and radios. All of them save for Alcott, who would play the prisoner, wore black FSB Alpha Group BDUs complete with patches on the shoulders. On the left, was the Russian flag, on the right, a green and black tactical version of the Alpha Group emblem. They were each armed with a tricked-out AK-12 and an Arsenal Strike One pistol, which they carried in a thigh rig. The only thing on each man that wasn't Russian-issue was the radio due to the need to maintain operational security with their comms. Even their watches and boots were Russian-made.

"You ready, Bronco?" asked Fig.

"I'm ready. Before we launch, I just want to thank you guys for all you've done and for signing on for this—for me and my family. I don't know what's going to happen when we get on target, but I love each of you like you *are* my family. You're each my brother." He went around the cramped room and shook each man's hand.

"Let's do this," said Babe.

"For Ben," said Alcott.

"For Ben," the rest echoed in unison.

Rainey pulled on his balaclava and switched into game-time mode. *For you, Dad.*

He climbed into the driver's seat of the navy blue Volkswagen Transporter as Babe guided Alcott into the backseat after applying zip ties to his wrists and ankles and pulling a hood over his face. Fig and Jazz would follow closely behind in a black Mercedes Benz G Class with tinted windows.

They performed one last comms check and then set off, leaving their staging area just how they had found it.

It was exactly 53 minutes later that they pulled into Kholm, a small town that was humble in appearance. An old woman with no teeth and sloped shoulders, wearing a dull-colored shawl and mismatched socks rocked back and forth on a bench as they rolled by. She was alone yet she was speaking in an animated way, mouth chomping up and down, gnarled hands shooting out this way and that. Lady sure was riled up about something.

Rainey rolled to a stop in front of some kind of administrative building and waited. Seconds ticked by. Where was he? Rostov was supposed to meet them here. Rainey consulted the directions in his head again. Yeah... They were in the right place.

The door of the building suddenly opened and Rostov strode out. Rainey studied him, looking for any clues that would indicate he had changed his mind and was setting them up for a situation from which they just might have to shoot their way out.

Rostov climbed into the front-passenger seat of the VW.

"You're late," said Babe.

Rostov twisted and gave the men in back a quick glance. "Relax. I had to use the bathroom. My, my. You guys look very convincing. If you don't mind, how did you—?"

"I do mind," snapped Rainey.

Rostov smirked.

"What's so funny?"

"I guess I just thought there would be more of you."

"This is all we need," said Rainey.

"I hope you're right, because once I get you in, you're on your own."

"I wouldn't have it any other way," said Rainey.

At Rostov's direction, they turned off the main road onto a gravel lane that snaked through a dark forest of pine and birch. There was a small red and white sign fastened to a tree that when translated to English read, "RESTRICTED AREA. NO TRESPASSING. LETHAL FORCE AUTHORIZED."

"Makes you feel all warm and fuzzy inside," quipped Babe.

Again Rostov grinned. "*Da.*"

A gate appeared around the bend. Rainey pulled up in front of it. A man dressed in camouflage fatigues, holding an AK-400 stepped from a small guard shack. Another man stood back and covered him as he approached Rainey's door.

Rainey lowered his window and greeted him in Russian. "Hello, Comrade Private."

"Please state your reason for being here."

Rostov leaned over and held out his credentials. "Private, we are FSB and are transporting an important prisoner! Let us in, you idiot."

The guard studied the ID for a few more seconds then nodded to the other man who, in turn, walked to a wooden post, his rifle hanging close to his thick frame from a single-point. The man lifted his arm and pressed a big square button on the post then turned and watched them with the cold, dead eyes of a killer. Immediately, a motor whirred and the gate squeaked open.

Rainey dropped the van into gear and eased down on the accelerator. He checked the rearview, verifying Fig and Jazz had made it through the checkpoint as well. They drove for another mile before coming to a chain-link gate that was twenty-feet high, topped with razor wire. Another guard approached. Just like before, Rostov barked at the man and held out his wallet badge. This time, however, there were four additional guards and a giant Caucasian Shepherd that one of the men kept on a short leather leash. The dog barked twice then fell silent as its handler issued a loud, terse command.

They were finally permitted to enter after a guard with a circular, lighted mirror on a stick had walked the circumference of each vehicle and verified there were no explosives secreted in their undercarriages.

"Park over there," said Rostov. He pointed to a spot near the edge of the old parade grounds. "Good. Now, wait here. I have to report in. It will just be a minute. When I return, we'll head over to prisoner intake."

Rainey was silent as the Russian assassin alighted from the van and scurried across the grass. Rostov yanked open a thick metal door without looking back. Several guards patrolling the grounds eyeballed them suspiciously. Prisoner intake was a good 200 yards further into the complex. The building had at one time housed a swimming pool, weight gym, basketball court and training rooms where troops learned hand-to-hand combat techniques. The plan called for Rostov to follow the facility protocols, which meant he would check them in at the main office building, obtain any specific orders from the watch commander, then return to the van and escort them the rest of the way to prisoner intake. Standard operating procedure for new prisoners at intake, as explained by Rostov, dictated that new captives be stripped of their clothing, hosed down, permitted a few minutes to dry off then dealt a brutal beating that would almost always require several weeks of healing. It was all part of the welcome-to-hell treatment, which had only gotten worse since Levka Borovsky had been given full operational authority over the facility by the Russian president.

"I don't like this, Bronco," said Fig in his earpiece.

"Neither do I, bro, but trust the plan."

"Oh, I do. I just don't like it. Feels like we're sheep being led to the slaughter."

"I feel ya, brother. Just be ready to move." Rainey checked his watch. "Shouldn't be long now."

77

ROSTOV marched swiftly down the hall to an office. When he entered, two muscular men with submachine guns greeted him.

"Is he here?" said Rostov. He already knew the answer to his question. Borovsky's bodyguards wouldn't be here otherwise.

The one on the left jerked his head toward the inner office door and Rostov pressed further inside.

Levka Borovsky stood up as he entered. "Demyan." The old Russian spymaster beamed with excitement. "Is it true? Reagan Rainey is really here?"

"I told you I would get him to come, didn't I?"

Borovsky clasped his hands together. "Yes! You did. But I can't believe it! Your plan actually worked. He came willingly."

"See for yourself."

Borovsky walked to the window and gazed out across the square piece of grass where Soviet troops had once stood in formation, drilled and prepared to fight the Germans. "And he thinks he is going to rescue his father?"

Rostov answered with a wry grin and Borovsky erupted in boisterous laughter. "There is one more thing."

"Yes? And what is that?"

"This." Rostov leveled a pistol at him.

Borovsky turned around. If he were surprised, his face didn't show it. "Demyan. I don't understand. What are you doing? You would betray me?"

"No, Levka Mironovich. It's you who has betrayed me." Rostov paced toward him till he was only a few feet away. "I've done your bidding without question for years. Last year was the first time I have ever failed you. And just like that you wanted me dead. I knew you would send your assassins, but none of them are even remotely as good as me. I am the best."

"You are, Demyan. You are the best."

"Please. Apparently, that meant nothing to you when you put the contract out on me. Well, Levka Mironovich, in doing so, you left me no choice. I approached your fiercest enemy from the Thieves' World and made him an offer he couldn't refuse."

"How much is he paying you?"

"That's not important. This is about more than money. This is about respect and true freedom—freedom from your heavy-handedness, freedom from your loathsome commands; freedom from your death warrant.

"I knew you wanted Reagan Rainey dead bad enough that the mere chance to kill him would be enough to lure you out of hiding. I could think of no other way to find you, but to let your hate accomplish it for me. It's why I orchestrated all of this."

"Demyan. I raised you and…"

"And you taught me well. 'Trust no one,' you always said. Surely, you understand this."

Borovsky raised his chin in defiance. "Go ahead, Demyan. If you are going to shoot me, do it face to face. No back of the head stuff."

"As you wish, but first I have a message to pass on from your old friend."

"Yes? And what is that?"

"Your family is next. Every last one of them." He smiled as Borovsky's eyes grew wide then raised the integrally suppressed Ruger .22 cal. pistol without the slightest bit of emotion. The first, whisper-silent bullet hit Borovsky right between the eyes. He sent three more rounds into his head and face after he was down, for the sake of the reports that would later follow. After all, he wanted to make a good impression with the new Russian mafia boss who was paying him.

The bodyguards knocked then entered. Surely, they had heard the commotion of Borovsky falling to the floor if not the metallic action of his pistol. "Is everything all right?" said the first man.

"No." Rostov pointed behind the desk. As both men looked to where their boss lay, he raised the gun again and fired two rounds into each man's head. Neither of the bodyguards got off a single shot before falling to the floor dead. Rostov picked up a handheld radio from the desk and issued a few terse commands. He paused to give Borovsky's corpse one last look then rushed out of the room.

Freedom at last.

78

RAINEY consulted his watch again. He spoke into his lapel mic. "Something's not right. He's taking way too long. You guys ready? Looks like we're gonna have to go to plan B."

Fig: *"Jazz and I are ready."*

"Okay on my count," said Rainey. "In three, two—."

Suddenly, a man came running around the corner of the building and stopped. He was shouldering an RPG7 and had it aimed right at Rainey's vehicle.

"Ah crap," whispered Babe.

"What is it?" said Alcott tilting his hooded head toward Babe.

"One of the guards has an RPG with a thermobaric round pointed in our direction."

"Great."

Demyan Rostov emerged from the office building, sauntered across the parade grounds with a broad smile on his face as several armed men maneuvered into position around the two vehicles with rifles raised and ready to shoot. At his side was the SF 111 watch commander, evident by his uniform and regal gait.

"Make one false move and you will be blown to bits," hearkened Rostov.

Rainey checked his watch again.

Come on.

Rainey spoke into his lapel mic again. "Wrecking Ball, this is Priority, I need you to step it up. We have a situation here."

A voice in his earpiece: *"Roger that, Priority. Wrecking Ball copies. We're two mikes out. I repeat. We're two mikes out."*

"Good copy. Two mikes." Rainey's hands lay across his AK-12. He flexed his fingers. "Sit tight boys. Just a little longer. Babe, I think you can free our prisoner, now. But do it carefully."

Babe slid a knife to Alcott, who discreetly clipped out of his bindings then reached under the seat and pulled out an AK-400, unfolded the stock and held it between his knees with the muzzle pointed toward the floor.

Rostov shouted from the grass, "Now, listen very carefully! Each of you slowly put your hands up against the ceiling and keep them there. If you make any sudden movements, my friends here will fire. Do it now!"

"Do it guys," said Rainey.

They all raised their hands and pressed them against the ceiling of their respective vehicles.

"Whole thing was a trap, huh Rostov?" yelled Rainey through his open window.

"Yes and no."

"And my dad? It's all fiction… Isn't it?"

"Oh your father is alive, actually. That part was true. Remarkably, he's one of the few who have endured all these years. But alas, he won't be alive after today. You see, you are going to watch him die. Then I am going to kill you—once and for all. And your friends… We have prepared special accommodations for each of them. I don't have a beef with them, so I'm going to let them live for the time being. If they manage to survive twenty years or so of interrogation and torment, maybe another brave team of operators will come and try to save them." Rostov howled with laughter.

Rainey tilted his wrist. "Twenty-five seconds, guys. Hold fast. Wizard, if you're out there, hit the RPG man first."

The former Delta Force sniper, now a permanent fixture within Directorate X's Joint Services Group, clicked an affirmative response with his radio.

Rainey's forehead was moist inside his balaclava. Things were about to get very loud and very chaotic, but he kept his mind on the goal, which was finding and rescuing his father from these evil monsters. So far, things hadn't gone exactly according to the way he had planned them, but that was usually the case. Try as you might, there were always unknown variables in this business. The key was adjusting quickly while remaining focused on the mission.

And, of course, staying alive.

One of the armed men outside jerked his head toward the sky.

Here we go.

The first AH-6 Little Bird helicopter zoomed overhead, barely high enough to clear the treetops. The armed men on the ground all followed it across the sky with their eyes. It was just human nature to do so. As they did, the man with the RPG took a bullet to the base of his skull and fell. Then so did two, three, four of his buddies. The M134 Minigun on the second incoming AH-6 hummed, chewing up the rest of the armed men in the parade grounds. Then as quickly as it had appeared, it circled out of sight.

Rainey punched the accelerator. Fig did the same in the SUV. Together they raced across the compound toward the building where Ben Rainey was being held captive.

Babe alerted the elements in the air. "Priority to Wrecking Ball, we are moving to the target now."

"Ball One copies."

"Ball Two. Good copy."

The two attack helicopters buzzed back and forth over the facility, hitting the guard towers with extreme prejudice then took turns covering Rainey and his team from the air.

Rainey drove the van as fast as it would go. As they neared the door they would enter, he said into his radio, "Ball Three. You're up."

"Ball Three. Roger that." The third Little Bird, this one an MH-6 with an operator strapped into a bench on each side, swooped down. It was on the ground only long enough for the two men to step off and move to a position of cover.

Rainey slammed the brakes and skidded to a halt, sending up a shower of gravel and dust. Fig was right behind him. Everyone dismounted in perfectly choreographed movements. Alcott who had already shed his hood, posted up outside the door with the other two operators. The trio would hold security as Rainey and the others forged into the prisoner block.

The door was locked, but the team was prepared to blow it from the start. Fig slapped a shape charge against it and the men all turned away as it blew. They pressed inside, weapons up and ready. The hall was damp and dimly lit. They hustled to the stairway twenty yards down on the left. As they were just about there, a guard came around the corner at the end of the hall. Rainey and Babe fired simultaneously and the man dropped in a heap.

They took the steps to the second sub-level smoothly. As they descended, a horrific odor of rotten flesh smacked at their senses. They ignored it and continued on. There was a sturdy metal door at the bottom of the stairs secured with a magnetic lock. Rainey said one word and Fig again stepped forward. He affixed another small shape charge to the door and the others prepared for action. The blast buckled the door and filled the corridor with dust and gray smoke, which they shot through and left in their wake.

Ben Rainey's cell was five doors up on the right. Everything was the same as he had seen it on the video clip in Ronda except in reverse, since now they were coming in from the opposite direction.

Each cell door was made of thick black iron bars. Rainey kept his muzzle pointed downrange, and tried not to focus on the door of his father's cell, but it was no use. As much as he had prepared himself mentally for this very moment, its gravity was crushing. What would his father look like, what would he say? Would he even recognize his own son? And in what kind of shape would his mind be? Prolonged torture and imprisonment were enough to drive some men to madness. A jumble of emotions assaulted him, threatened his focus. But the two men with AKs that just whipped around the corner in front of him snapped him back to the task at hand. Rainey squeezed the trigger of his AK-12 in chorus with Babe. Their muzzles flashed brilliantly in the dark bowels of the gulag. Their aggressors slumped to the hard, damp floor.

Rainey continued past his father's cell and dropped to a knee. Jazz did the same to protect their rear. Both of them would hold security in the corridor while Babe and Fig worked the cage. Fig reached inside the breach pack that Babe wore on his back, extracted a tool commonly referred to as a "hoolie." He jammed the one end of it into the joint between the wall and iron door then leaned into it. He grimaced and pried with all his might. "Ugh. Won't budge."

"Give it to me," said Babe, one of the most naturally powerful men in the entire American special operations community.

Fig quickly passed him the hoolie.

Babe gripped it like a baseball bat. First, he beat on the block right beside the iron. If the hoolie were an axe, he could be Paul Bunyan chopping down a tree. After several whacks, the block cracked and pieces spilled to the floor. Babe then dug the flat end of the tool into the void and worked it back and forth with abandon. Once he had a really good bite, he took hold of the hoolie and leaned backward, tugging on the tool with both hands. The muscles in his whole body bulged with his efforts. Finally, the whole thing, frame and all, dislodged from the wall and clanged to the floor.

He handed the hoolie back to Fig and turned while Fig secured it back in his pack.

"Okay," said Fig.

Babe let out a breath of exhilaration and gripped his rifle. He patted Rainey on the shoulder and said, "I got this, bro. Go get your dad."

Rainey traded places with Babe and entered the cell. Fig was already inside. There, sitting upright on a thin mat spread out on the floor was a scrawny, gray-haired man.

His father.

79

BEN Rainey had a look of contrition about him. A man who had suffered unspeakable acts for years, he had no more fight left in him. He grimaced with his hands up in surrender. "Please. No more. I can't…"

Rainey tugged off his balaclava. The eyes of father and son met for the first time in twenty years.

Immediately, Ben's eyes sparked to life. A smile creased his face as he burst into tears. "My son!"

"Dad!" Rainey went to him, reached out his hands. They embraced, both of them weeping with joy. "I missed you, Dad! I missed you so much!"

"Oh, how I've missed *you*."

Fig snapped some photos of their reunion and the inside of the cell with his phone then tapped Rainey on the shoulder. "Bronc, we gotta go."

"Dad, we've come to take you home."

He held Rainey's face in his broken hands. "*Home*. There is no sweeter word."

"You said it. Now, we need to strap you in to this. It'll be easier on you this way and we'll be able to move quicker."

"Whatever you say. As long as you don't say I'm dreaming."

Fig had already prepared the roll-out stretcher from the Sked Tactical Rescue System he had worn on his back. He and Rainey helped Ben into it then secured the straps.

"Ready, Dad?"

"I've never been readier."

Rainey took the strap by Ben's head in his left hand and nodded at Fig. They lifted simultaneously then gripped their rifles with their free hands.

"Comin' out," said Rainey.

"Roger that. We got ya," said Babe. "Jazz, you got the lead."

"Roger that. Good to go," replied Jazz.

They left the same way they had entered. When they reached the door that led outside, they paused. Rainey radioed Alcott. "Shepherd, how do we look?"

"Still solid, Bronco."

"Roger that. Ball Four, we're standing by and ready to exfil."

The pilot in the fourth Little Bird, another MH-6, responded in his Southern drawl. *"Bawl Four. Thassa good copy. Comin' eento the LZ now."*

Jazz watched for the helicopter to land. When it did, he called out to the others, "Ball Four's on the deck. Let's jet."

The men stormed outside. They sprinted past Alcott just as gunfire popped from somewhere on their left and sparked against the side of the chopper. Alcott and the JSG operators directed their muzzles toward the seven or eight men maneuvering toward them, armed with AK-9s, AK-47s and RPGs. They knocked down several of them and kept shooting toward the ones that had managed to duck behind cover. A door to one of the buildings shot open and more armed men appeared like ants spilling out of a disturbed anthill. That is until Ball One buzzed back into view and obliterated every last one of them with his minigun.

Alcott screamed into the radio. *"Ball One! Look right! Man with a SAM!"*

A man in camouflage with a Russian Verba MANPAD was peeking around the corner of an outbuilding.

PSHOO! PSHOO!

All at once the man and his shoulder-fired missile disappeared in a spectacular cloud of fire and dust. Ball Two had swung around and struck with two of its Hydra 70 rockets.

"Thanks, Ball Two."

"What are friends for?"

Reaching Ball Four, Rainey and Fig slid Ben into the open cabin and strapped him down. Fig climbed in after him and buckled himself in, too. Then it was Rainey's turn. Jazz ran around to the far side. He and Babe would ride on the bench seats above the skids. When everyone was secured, they signaled the pilot and the Little Bird lifted off and headed for the same route it had taken to get here, which was but the tiniest of openings in an otherwise impenetrable area of Russian air space.

Rainey glanced back. Ball Three was dropping onto the landing zone. Alcott and the two JSG operators hustled to it. A man in a ghillie suit—Wizard—emerged from the woods, lumbered across the open space to the chopper and fell inside. He strapped in then aimed his suppressed Citizen Arms purpose-built .308 Win. toward the ground, in case any remaining threats popped out.

When Ball Three was off the ground, Rainey pulled a remote from his vest. He leaned to the side and eyed the two vehicles they had used to penetrate the facility, making sure Ball Three was clear of them. Then, he powered on the remote and in quick succession pressed the only two buttons. Both vehicles blew apart, the explosions flashing brilliantly against the dark, wooded landscape.

"Here ya go, sir!" Fig wrapped a thick wool blanket around Ben to shield him from the chill air shooting through the open cabin.

Ben smiled. "Thank you. Thank you, all!"

Rainey held his father's hand the entire forty-five minute ride out of Russia. He just couldn't let go. The operation was a rousing success. He was elated and felt a tremendous sense of accomplishment. From the looks on the other men's faces, they all did.

By the time they landed, the choppers were running on fumes. They set down in a field just across the Latvian border. It was the same place from which the helicopters had come. Two semis were waiting for them along with a team of people to disassemble each aircraft.

The Little Birds would be quickly packed inside and the trucks driven back to the airport in Riga to await a flight back to the States aboard a cargo plane owned by a popular commercial freight company, with whom the Greenbriar Foundation just happened to be strategic partners.

Meanwhile, Rainey and the others were all hustled away in groups of three, each group in a different vehicle with a different destination.

80

Landstuhl, Germany

RAINEY sat by his father's side in a secure room at Landstuhl Regional Medical Center. Doctors had said that Ben would need to stay here for at least a few weeks until his condition improved. Twenty years of prolonged captivity and torture had taken their toll on his body, but he was in good spirits considering.

There was a knock on the door and Job peeked in. "Ray, they're here."

"Okay." He looked back at his dad, patted his arm. "Dad, there are some people here to see you. I'm gonna step out. Okay?"

Ben nodded with expectant jubilation.

Rainey closed the door quietly behind him as he made his way into the hall. When he saw his mom and sister sitting with their backs to him in a small waiting area, he nearly lost it, but he kept himself together long enough to greet them. They turned at the sound of his voice. "Hi, guys."

They both leapt to their feet and rushed toward him. Wes and Iris were there, too, but they held back, respectfully giving the Rainey family some space.

"Ray! How is he? Can we see him?" blurted Maddie.

"Yes. Just be gentle."

Sarah and Maddie hugged and kissed him then headed for the room. Maddie waved to Wes. "C'mon, sweetie."

"I don't want to intrude on a personal family moment."

"Nonsense, Wes. You *are* family," said Sarah. "Iris, you, too. Come on, the both of you. It's fine."

Rainey nodded. "She's right. Please. Join us."

◆ ◆ ◆

Maddie pushed the door open slowly. She let her mother enter first then followed her into the room. The moment she laid eyes on her father, her legs became weak. She nearly fell to her knees.

"Daddy!," she cried. "Daddy! Oh, thank you, God! Thank you! Thank you! Thank you!"

She scurried to the bed, reached out and fell into her father's embrace. Not for a second did she ever think this moment was possible. But here he was. *Alive.* After all these years, he was alive and in her life again.

"Daddy, I love you! I love you so much!"

"I love you, too, kiddo."

◆ ◆ ◆

Sarah, always the graceful one, swept toward him, her eyes racked with concern for his condition. Was it really true? Was her Ben really alive and here? Their eyes met as she came to him and only then did she believe it. She bent down, latched onto him and wept with her whole body. They both did. All the years of sorrow and grief and loss let loose at once. The floodgates were open and she didn't care one bit.

◆ ◆ ◆

Rainey walked to the other side of the bed and joined his family in their moment of reunification. He was never one to let others see him cry, but now he couldn't help himself. He stretched out his arms and hugged them all at the same time.

Wes, Iris and Job stood inside the door, rivers of tears racing down each of their faces. It was a moment few could ever imagine let alone witness.

They clung to each other for hours. They laughed. They cried. They regaled the Rainey family patriarch with details of their lives, brought him up to speed on world events, but really just enjoyed their joyous time together.

Finally, a nurse encroached into the room and advised them that Ben needed rest but that they could visit him again in the morning. Sarah objected and was permitted to stay. Anticipating this, Job had already rented a comfortable house a few blocks from the medical facility for everyone else to crash.

No one was going home without Ben.

81

THE summer air was cool, the night quiet and serene. Rainey sat by himself on the deck of the rented house, his feet resting on the railing and a cup of hot coffee couched in his hands. The glow of the moonlight illuminated his face, giving it a bluish tint.

He was still trying to process the events of the past few weeks. He marveled at the Hand of Providence. God's grace and mercy were indeed limitless. His father's faith in God was truly remarkable, an inspiration. He had seen firsthand the evidence of it scrawled into the wall of his father's cell. There had been no time to dwell on it during the operation, but now the words chimed in his thoughts like the bell in a clock tower at high noon.

"Jesus loves me. This I know."

Another memory came with the suddenness of an IED. He and his sister would sometimes sing that very song in the car or around the house when they were little tikes. He remembered something his father often said after they had sung it. Each time. Every time.

"Hope of the world, guys. Hope of the world."

"I hope I'm not interrupting anything."

Rainey glanced up. "No, Job. Just reflecting is all."

"I'm still trying to get my head around it, too." The older man pulled a chair closer and sat down. "So, I've been in contact with some of our people in Moscow and elsewhere regarding the fallout from the operation."

"Thing I don't understand is why would Rostov go through all the trouble with the letter, the meeting in Spain, the feigned assistance to help me save my dad if he was just planning to kill me in the end? There has to be more to it."

"Reports are still coming in, but I may have the answer to your question. Word is that the Russians found Levka Borovsky and his bodyguards inside the prison. They'd been shot. By a pro."

"Rostov." Rainey rested his head backward on the chair. "But why?"

"Borovsky had been lying low since last year. No one had been able to find him. Perhaps the fact that a number of Russian organized crime bosses, competitors all, wanted him dead had something to do with it. We're hearing now that Demyan Rostov approached one of them, offered to kill Borovsky for a cool five mill. To do so, he first would have had to figure out a way to lure Borovsky out of his hole."

"Me. I was the bait."

"Looks that way."

"According to our Russian sources, Borovsky had a contract out on Rostov. This was apparently after last year because of his failure to kill you. I'm guessing Rostov made some kind of deal with Borovsky that would void the contract. Like if he were able to capture you and bring you to SF One Eleven."

"But it wasn't a deal at all. It was Rostov's plan to get to Borovsky," reasoned Rainey.

Job nodded. "Precisely. I think you were just unfinished business. Icing on the cake. Rostov couldn't resist. There is something else you should know."

Rainey stopped sipping his coffee, canted his head toward Job.

"They haven't found his body... Rostov's I mean. He's still out there."

Rainey closed his eyes, shook his head. "Are you telling me that he got away?"

"Unfortunately, yes. For the time being."

Rainey's eyes narrowed as he mused. "You know where he is?"

"Not yet. But we're working on it. I'm optimistic we'll have something soon. The prints we pulled off that clarinet should certainly help."

The door behind them creaked open. A feminine figure shifted through the shadows of the moist night air, fell into a chair next to them.

"I just wanted to thank you both," said Maddie. "I still can't believe it's true. Dad… Alive."

"Me, either, sis. But there's no need to thank us. You had as much to do with his rescue as anyone."

"He's right," said Job.

Maddie smiled. "Thanks."

"You're welcome, Swan."

Maddie did a double take. "Who told you?"

"Let's just say it wasn't a little birdie."

"*Mouse.* I'm gonna kill that guy."

"Relax. I like it." Rainey sat up in his chair. "Listen, I talked to him and Tonka. I heard about the job you did. They had nothing but good things to say about you and those are guys I trust to tell me the truth. If you weren't pulling your weight they would have told me."

"What are you saying? That you approve of me working for the Agency?"

"I'm saying I'm proud of you, sis. And that I love you. The DX, especially, is better off with you in it. To be honest, I didn't like the idea of it at first, but… You're all grown up now. You're smart and you can take care of yourself. You're solid, Maddie. America needs people like us. We are the tip of the spear and I wouldn't have it any other way. But there will be days when you want nothing to do with this job. It will break your heart, crush your sense of justice at times, ruin relationships, steal friends and colleagues from you. It can be a beast. Trust me. But don't ever let it take your spirit or your grit. Not ever. Above all, resolve yourself now to hang on to your faith. Tuck it deep down inside, wrap it around your heart like the flag, because there will be times when it's all you have.

"I say all this not to scare you or make you second guess signing on, but because I love you and care about you. I know you can do this job. Hearing guys like Mouse and Tonka talk about you the way they did… It makes me proud to be your brother."

"Aw shucks." She made a goofy face then got up and hugged him. "I love you, too, big brother."

Rainey cleared his throat. It was a gesture he'd perfected when he wanted to eschew any show of emotion. "So, Job. What's the latest on the director?"

"I'm not sure exactly. I know he has a meeting with the president in the morning. Have to wait and see. He doesn't tell me everything, you know."

82

Washington, D.C.

CIA Director Ken Thompson walked the West Wing hall like he had done countless times before. The hard soles of his polished brogues yielded not a sound against the carpeted floor. His approach was silent but for a few loose coins in his pants pocket. The jangling made the Secret Service agent posted outside the door to the Oval Office look his way, but his arrival was not a surprise. The people inside were expecting him.

He greeted the agent with a grandfatherly nod then paused outside the door, taking just enough time to straighten his tie and offer a silent prayer. When he entered, all heads turned toward him. The wolves eyed their prey greedily. They licked their lips, salivating for the feast they were about to devour.

Thompson, his chin up and face a blank page, paced toward them without hesitation. He had no retinue, no dutiful aides scurrying along in his wake. The truth was his only companion today and the only one he would need.

"Morning, Ken. Have a seat."

"Good morning, sir. Thank you."

Vera Lysniak sat in her usual post, at the end of the sofa nearest the president. Her legs were crossed and she was bobbing the toe of her shoe—a sublimation of the anxiety of an impending battle.

Thompson regarded her as the adversary she was. He sat on the sofa opposite so he could face her head-on and did so entirely on purpose.

"Do you have your resignation letter?"

"No, Mr. President, sir."

Vera couldn't help herself. "No?! Why in God's name not?"

The tiniest of smirks leaked from the corner of Thompson's face. "Because I'm not resigning."

"Good! It's your funeral then. You're fired!" she said.

"No. I think not."

"What's going on Ken? Those were your only options. I hate to be crass. But she's right."

"No, Mr. President. I'm not going anywhere. You see it's you who will be standing in the unemployment line. That is unless you go to prison with Vera, here."

Vera leapt to her feet. "What?! How dare you come in here and—"

"Vera, please. Sit down." President Winslow waited until she did so, then looked back at Thompson. "Ken, I'm not sure I understand. What's going on?"

Thompson pulled a digital voice recorder from his jacket pocket and placed it on the coffee table. He looked directly at Vera as he pressed PLAY.

There was a rustling noise at first with a squelch of static then the audio became clear. The color drained from Vera's face when Stedman Carter's voice boomed on the recording.

"I don't care who she is, Zarek. I want you to grab her and make her talk. Do you understand, me? How in the world could she know about Ronda?! Someone is giving her information. I want you to find out what she knows then kill her. Just make sure no one ever finds her body."

"I understand."

Carter barked out a string of curse words, then: *"It's bad enough McManus is coming back to bite us. I told Vera we should pay him more money, but noooooo she wanted him dead for the president's sake. The election... The precious, bleeding election. You know what? Screw the election! Screw Vera! Look what I have to deal with because of them. No more!*

"*This Frannie Green is messing with the wrong man. Whomever she's getting her information from is dead, too. No more answering to conniving Ms. Lysniak. She started all of this with that stinkin' Moses letter. We still don't know who he is! Ugh!*

"*I'm going to finish it. This is going to end!*"

"*How do you think Green knows about McManus and Ronda? You think she has a source in the FBI, maybe the CIA? Maybe she's Moses.*"

"*I don't know, Zarek, that's what I'm saying! I want you to find that out. I don't care what you have to do to her. Cut her fingers off, strip her down and douse her with acid. Be creative, for heaven's sake. Just make her talk!*

"*Vera's grand plan... I should have put my foot down from the beginning. How could I have ever gotten involved with that witch?*"

Thompson clicked off the recorder. The silence in the Oval Office was deafening.

"That was just *part* of a conversation between Stedman Carter and a man who worked for him by the name of Zarek Tarło. It was captured by the FBI in New York as part of their investigation into the DNI's assassination. You will be interested to know that Carter was picked up late last night in Baltimore. Tarło's dead.

"Oh and by the way, if you care, Ben Rainey *is* alive. He'll be back in the country by week's end. I hear he's got one heck of a story. One that complements perfectly the records we have from Levka Borovsky. Something about a young Grantley Winslow soliciting the purchase of a nuclear weapon for his Islamic fundamentalist buddies in May of ninety-six. Seems there are photos and other rather compelling evidence as well. Stuff that even your media friends can't cover up."

The president was nearly catatonic. "Vera, what have you done? How could you do this to me?"

"What have *I* done? Don't you dare talk to me like that! You knew about everything from day one. I made you what you are today. You would be nothing without me."

Thompson dropped the recorder back into his pocket. "Listen, you guys can argue all you want after I'm gone. In any case, this is how things are going to go. You, Mr. President, are going to step down. Say it's due to health reasons, say it's that you want to spend more time with your family, I really don't care what you say, just so long as it's done gracefully and with respect for the Office. America doesn't need another White House scandal. Especially one of this magnitude. Your running mate can step in and finish out your term. If he wants, he can assume the race for the presidency as well…or whomever your party decides on to do so. You have until the end of business today.

"If you should choose to stay in office and continue your campaign for reelection, that's fine, but then the recording will go public. I know people—honest people—in the media, too, who would love to scoop a story like this. You should know that the FBI, the Attorney General and the leadership of both parties in the Senate and the House already have copies."

"That's blackmail."

"No, sir. It's justice with all due discretion for the American people. They don't deserve a president who does what you've done. They deserve a president who holds honor in high esteem. Men of humility, integrity and moral courage built this country. You sir, couldn't hold the Founders' water.

"Now, I'm giving you a choice. You can either step down with grace or be impeached and indicted along with Vera and her guy pal, Stedman Carter. Ultimately, it's up to you.

"Vera, my dear, you have a choice as well. You can either go with the FBI agents standing in the hall on your own or you can be perp-walked out across the White House lawn. Either way you are leaving here with federal agents."

There was a knock on the door that punctuated his statement.

Vera's hate-filled eyes narrowed. "You will not get away with this."

"It's not about getting away with anything. It's about making things right. And it's about bringing home an American hero, a man who has spent the past twenty years of his life in a secret Russian prison, where he was forced to endure unimaginable acts of depravity. But I don't expect you to get that. Not with the way you've behaved."

The knock came again and this time the door opened afterward. Two FBI agents stepped across the threshold and waited.

"I'm serious. The choice is yours, Vera."

"You haven't won. You have no idea what kind of fight you're in for."

"Tell that to Stedman. His attorneys are already angling for a deal."

Thompson stood up and walked out. Even in triumph, he was too much of a gentleman to laugh in the faces of his adversaries.

83

IN a conference room not far from the Memorial Wall inside CIA headquarters, a small gathering of people sat idle as its members awaited the ceremony that was about to begin. Rainey detected a hint of carpet cleaner in the air as he stared at the American flag standing at the front of the room. The joy he shared with his mom and sister, and of course his father, was tempered by the guilt and sadness he suffered for the families of the other men and women of the CIA, whose fortunes were still unchanged. Job didn't have to explain it for him to know that this was the first time in the Agency's legendary existence that an operative without artifice had turned up alive after being officially declared dead. The star chiseled into the Wall—the one that represented Ben Rainey—had been premature as it were. The entire Agency was buzzing with excitement because of it. The rumor mill was working overtime, too, as staffers not apprised of the highly compartmentalized details went about theorizing how the operation had been pulled off and who could have possibly been involved.

After a week in Germany, they had been flown home to American soil. It was still hard for him to fathom. Dad… Alive and home for good.

Ben had been looked after at Walter Reed for a little more than a month before doctors finally permitted him to go home. A nurse was assigned to monitor his care for the foreseeable future and would stop in to check on him once or twice a week at the family's Annapolis home.

No one made any mention of the ceremony that had taken place by the Wall in May of 1997—the one the Agency held to memorialize and honor their fallen, specifically Ben Rainey. It was as if to talk about it would darken the history that they were now living. However, though the ceremonies were indeed polar opposites by their very nature, the parameters were the same. Only immediate family and other Agency-invited guests were permitted to attend. Photography of any kind was severely restricted. And there was to be no discussion, let alone public disclosure, of any of the proceedings or identities of those present. Any failure to comply with these rules and others could compromise sources and methods, they were told. Of course Rainey knew that much of this was for the benefit of the Agency staffers in attendance, some of whom could be real sticklers for protocol even if those protocols were outdated and unnecessary.

The room stirred as Director of the Central Intelligence Agency Ken Thompson entered, a few aides trickling in behind him. He had the bearing of a powerful CEO and dressed like one, too. There were no wasted movements in his gait, no fraudulent facial expressions. Thompson strode to the lectern and offered a genuine smile. He placed both hands on the dark, polished wood and gazed out over the small group, which consisted of the Rainey family including Wesley Kuehle, Job and Iris Jackson, Saul Baker and some others that played lesser but equally important roles in the career of Benjamin Rainey. Though he and Maddie were present, they were not there in any official capacity. To be sure, the fact that they were employed by the agency within the Agency—to wit, Directorate X—was a tightly held secret, and for that matter, highly classified information. And so it was that today they were here simply as the loving children of a covert operative who was suddenly and miraculously back among the living.

"Good afternoon, Rainey family and honored guests. It is with great honor and felicity that I stand before you today as we celebrate this truly momentous occasion." He turned and faced Ben Rainey. "Though it may be difficult for me to render in mere words just how much joy and encouragement your safe return has brought to the members within these hallowed halls, I will try.

"On a personal level, I can tell you that I have been moved in a way that is both humbling and inspiring. Ben, yours is a remarkable story, one that demonstrates a rare faith not just in Almighty God, the Sustainer of all things, but in your country and countrymen as well. Your actions in the most difficult and horrific of situations are a true testament to your strong character, patriotism and predisposition to serving your fellow man. Benjamin Paul Rainey—Ben—on behalf of this Agency and a grateful nation, I want to officially welcome you home and say thank you."

Everyone burst into applause. Ben's eyes sparkled with tears. His bottom lip quivered as he grinned with the modesty for which he was well regarded. With his left hand, he reached up and dabbed his nose with a tissue then adjusted himself in his wheelchair. He turned toward Sarah who cradled his right hand in her lap. She was stroking the back of it gently with her fingertips.

"In addition…" Thompson turned toward an aide. The man handed him a small wooden case then retreated to a position along the wall. "I feel it only fitting to do this here, now, with your family and closest friends present." Thompson flipped a sheet of paper on the lectern. "I've had the privilege of serving in the capacity of director of CIA now for three administrations. Never before have I known a man quite like Benjamin Rainey. I can tell you there is no one more patriotic, more dedicated to the proposition of America. His commitment to service, and his relentless drive to complete the mission are legendary. He is the embodiment of everything it means to be an American. His indomitable spirit, resolve and quiet confidence are contagious to boot. And don't expect him to ever tell you about his exploits, even if he were permitted to do so. Because, you see, Ben Rainey is one of the most humble men I've had the pleasure of knowing. He's a model for everyone within the Agency and the Community overall.

"Thus, it is with great joy, that I present to Benjamin Paul Rainey, for exemplary conduct, bravery and fortitude in furtherance of the interests of national security, the Distinguished Intelligence Cross. Congratulations, Ben."

Again the room erupted. Saul Baker hinged forward in his seat behind Ben Rainey and patted him on the shoulder. There wasn't a dry eye among them as Ben wheeled to the front of the room. He didn't look quite as infirm as the day he was pulled from Special Facility No. 111, but the signs of his internment were still evident.

"Thank you, Mr. Director. Thank you, all. I'm not one for speeches, so I'll keep it brief." Ben regarded the medal in the open case then set it in his lap. It was the CIA's highest decoration and was usually conferred upon its recipients posthumously. "For those wondering, 'How did you do it, Ben? Where did you get the strength to endure the torture, to go on living in those horrendous conditions?'" He paused. "Do you know what it was? It basically came down to two simple truths. The first one is this: *Jesus loves me. This I know, for the Bible tells me so.* And the second can be found in the book of Psalm, in chapter one eighteen, verse six, which reads: *The Lord is on my side; I will not fear. What can man do to me?* I can only attribute my survival to the will of God. His grace and mercy are indeed everlasting. Even in my darkest hours, His love was there. I felt it. Love from my Heavenly Father, as well as the love of my blessed wife, Sarah, my son, Ray, and daughter, Maddie. Love was, and is, the source of my comfort." Ben looked at his family, paused as his emotions threatened to overpower him. He pursed his lips then finally said, "I love you guys."

Sarah and Maddie both smiled through their tears.

Then there was Ray. Outwardly, he was his usual stoic self. But on the inside, he was a little boy staring in admiration at his first and still-biggest hero. When no one was looking, Rainey smeared the moisture that had swelled in his eyelids and wiped his nose with the back of his hand.

"I also want to express my gratitude for the love and faithfulness of my dear friends. You know who you are. Without them, I would be nothing. Thank you all, once again. God bless each of you and may God bless America."

84

Washington, D.C.
Two Weeks Later

THE streets were lined with colorful mounds of the casualties of fall. The leaf trucks would likely be along in the morning to vacuum them up. As he turned onto Wisconsin Avenue NW, his headlights illuminated a man wearing a Philadelphia Eagles ball cap turned backward and a flannel shirt with the sleeves rolled up to his elbows. Long shadows danced around him as he labored away in the evening darkness, working his rake like an oar in the mighty rapids of a raging river.

Rainey drove past the café and turned at the next street. It didn't look half bad. Plenty of escape routes if he needed to bail. He drifted the Bronco into the meager parking lot to the rear of the café and shut off the engine. A stiff breeze kicked up. The large vehicle rocked back and forth. He took a deep breath as a battalion of leaves scurried across the blacktop, scratching and rattling as they went. A warm sensation rose up out of his shirt. The anxiety had been building since the last time he had seen her—a hurricane a few miles off shore. He had always chosen to ignore the weather warnings. *It'll go away*, he'd told himself. But this time he couldn't ignore it. The hurricane had made landfall.

He leaned over and checked himself in the mirror then took a deep breath and stepped out. En route to the front entrance, he had to side-step three groups of clueless, college-age kids with their heads down in their phones in order to avoid a collision. What did the kids used to do without their all-consuming phones?

The café was just outside the campus of American University. It had a quaint, old Colonial America feel to it that was authentic and not touristy. The walls were paneled in rich wood, the tables round and intimately set. *Great*, he thought. He had specifically told Maddie that he didn't want to go anywhere that would convey to Kayla that this was anything more than two old friends catching up. Friends that just so happened to be in love at one time.

No, Ray. Don't go there. She's probably moved on even if you haven't.

Yesterday, he'd called the number Maddie had collected from her and left a message that went something like this: *"Hi, Kayla. It's Reagan. Maddie said she ran in to you a while back and well, I guess I've finally drummed up the courage to call. Sorry I missed you. I know it's been quite some time, but if you're interested in getting together over coffee, I'd love to say hi back, in person. I'll be at the Mt. Vernon Café—it's near AU—tomorrow night at seven. If you decide not to show, I'll understand. But I hope you do. Take care, dear— I mean… Take care, Kay."*

Rainey had no idea whether or not Kayla would show, let alone if she had even received his message in the first place. The voice-mail greeting had been a generic one in a computerized voice. A reverse phone number lookup had revealed that the number was registered to an office line within the athletics department of George Washington University. A subsequent Google search of the name Kayla Chapman had cleared up whatever mystery remained. Kayla was the head coach of the GW women's soccer team.

He tucked into a table deep in the café with his back against the wall and pulled out a Robert Ludlum paperback. If Kayla didn't show, at least he would get in some good quality reading.

◆ ◆ ◆

At 7:05, he heard the bell above the door jingle and some leaves scrape across the threshold as a college kid and his girlfriend entered. They were holding hands and had the goofy look of love splayed across their young faces. He sipped his coffee and realized a sense of jealously had taken up residence in his mind. He shook it free and refocused on the pages of his novel.

It was nearly 7:30 when he placed the business card he often used as a bookmark back into the book and resolved himself to the idea that she wasn't coming. Rainey turned toward the young couple, enthusiastic in their love and wished himself back in school with Kayla on his arm.

He sighed and pushed back from the table. The sound of his chair legs on the hardwood floor nearly drowned out the jingling bell at the front of the café. He canted his head so he could see past the occupants of another table and was immediately mesmerized. There, standing just inside the door, was Kayla Chapman and she was absolutely radiant.

Rainey stood to get her attention. When her eyes fell on him, he swallowed. It was as if they were seeing each other again for the very first time. She certainly did not look like the girl he'd known in school and yet there was something warmly familiar about her. Gone were the functional ponytail and women's royal blue Casio G-Shock, the tight, faded blue jeans, Duke Soccer sweatshirt and Nike running shoes. Kayla now wore a navy, roll-neck sweater beneath a charcoal anorak and gray slacks that accentuated her athletic, feminine lines. He followed her legs all the way down to a sexy pair of ankles that disappeared into a pair of black leather booties. Her brunette locks were longer now, too; they swished about as she set off toward him. His heartrate immediately quickened. His palms began to sweat. The heads of four young college-age men huddled over a table in her path snapped up and followed her movements as she swept past them. She grinned as she drew closer. Even in the dim light of the cafe, her electric blue eyes shone bright. She'd always been a natural beauty, but now... Now, she was stunning.

He blinked and forced himself to breathe. No one had ever been able to do this to him: turn his insides to jelly.

No one but Kayla.

◆ ◆ ◆

A few leaves shot past as the door fell closed behind her. Kayla drew the strap of her handbag further up on her shoulder and searched the café from right to left. She was late, but knew he would still be here. Reagan was persistent like that. It was one of his most endearing qualities. It had definitely played a huge role in his success on the soccer field back in school. He could have been a great one, even gone pro if he had stayed in school and not dropped out to join the Army. One particular memory flashed in her mind.

It was the semifinal game against Virginia in the 2003 NCAA Men's Division I tournament. Reagan, the freshman forward phenom, had scored both of Duke's early goals despite a stingy Cavaliers' back line. Late in the second half, he received the ball again near the center of the field and was tackled to the ground violently—a clear foul the referee should have called but didn't. Reagan, in typical fashion, leapt to his feet and with unbridled rage, charged after the Virginia player who was dribbling away with the ball. But Reagan was never one to lose his temper. He was never out of control. He was the type of person who used his rage to fuel his drive to succeed, to accomplish his goals. And that's just what happened.

Reagan raced after the ball with reckless abandon. He applied relentless back pressure as the ball was passed once, twice, three times. Other players might have given up after the second pass, but Reagan was different. He was driven like no other she had ever known. Reagan lunged and managed to block the fourth pass. The ball ricocheted into space near the corner of the goal box. He sprinted for it, fighting off a speedy sweeper all the way. When Reagan finally won the ball, he pulled off a move that is still talked about by historians of the NCAA men's soccer tournament. The defender twisted backward and fell as if he'd been shot with a sniper's bullet. Reagan left him behind with a few powerful strides and headed for goal. Another defender suddenly came running in hard, but Reagan—the magician he was—stopped on a dime, pulled the ball back with his toe and let him go sliding by. Then, he rolled the ball forward with the sole of his boot and stepped into a shot that might have been a missile. The ball was still on the way up as it rocketed past the keeper's outstretched hands and found the side netting in the top right corner of the goal.

Kayla grinned as she recalled Reagan's trademark primal scream after scoring the winning goal. She could still see him there on the field when the final whistle sounded. He was just as gracious in triumph as he was in defeat. He, in his blue and white striped jersey and black, satiny shorts, walked to a Virginia player who had dropped to his knees. Reagan leaned over, placed a hand on his shoulder and consoled him. She could still see him trotting toward her after she and some of her women's team girlfriends had made their way onto the field to congratulate him. She and her friends had talked about him for some time afterward. Not just because of the way he played the game, but because of his rugged good looks. They were particularly smitten by his well-defined leg muscles that rippled beneath his grass-stained shorts when he ran, the way his shaggy brown hair fell across his forehead and those eyes. Oh, gosh, those eyes. They were rich, milk-chocolate brown and he knew just how to use them. One look and they could make her melt, especially when combined with that utterly intoxicating smile of his.

She remembered the scent of the cologne he always wore and how she used to purposefully search it out on his neck when he pulled her close in the chilly autumn dusk during walks across campus. It was a pleasing scent that reminded her of woodsmoke or Christmas or trips to her family's winter house in Vale.

Kayla scooched around a table of rowdy guys. Based on their ID holders and keychain lanyards, it was obvious they were AU students. They stopped talking and stared at her, mouths agape, as she waded past. She ignored their gawking and pressed toward the man she had come to see.

She stopped when she reached his table. It was as if they were the only people in the café. Everything else became white noise. She stood in front of him and took all of him in. He still possessed those sumptuous chocolate eyes, but somehow they were different. They seemed to bear a quality her mind just could not put to words. They had most certainly seen terrible things. Seen death. Seen war. Was that why they were different?

Physically, he appeared to be in far better shape than he had been in during his college days. He was even more muscular, more powerful. He'd grown an inch or so, too. The way his left hand was pushed into his pants pocket made the muscles in his arm flex within the sleeve of his sweater. Her heart skipped a beat.

When he finally grinned, she saw a glimmer of the old Reagan, her Reagan, but instead of easy optimism, the happy-go-lucky vibe for which he was well liked back in school, his face exuded something else. *What is it?* she thought, as she studied his rugged features. Seconds felt like minutes. Then it occurred to her. It was a hyper alertness, an intensity that lay below the surface, something that he was doubtless well accustomed to keeping hidden. But Kayla could see it plainly. It made him seem dangerous. And she liked it. Truth be told, she was attracted to him now more than ever before.

"Hi."

"Hi, Reagan." It felt so good to utter his name again.

He pulled out her chair and stepped back. But she didn't move. They both stood there looking into each other's eyes with unknown expectation.

Rainey smiled. A word began to form on his mouth, but it was quickly cut off by her terrific bear hug. Kayla wrapped both arms around him and squeezed. Tears began to swell in her eyes.

"Welcome home, Reagan. Welcome home." She didn't know why she had said it. But the words just felt right. It was one of those times in life when speech came before thought. All emotion—her soul completely naked and exposed.

◆ ◆ ◆

It seemed like minutes had passed till he realized he was hugging her just as tightly. The day he'd left for boot camp was the last time he'd held her.

Rainey didn't want this moment to end. As his own tears began to streak his face, he suddenly sensed the eyes from the other patrons in the café. But he didn't care. He never wanted to let go of her again.

Her voice drifted up from his chest. "Let's get outta here."

He pressed his cheek against the top of her head, breathed in the aroma of her hair. It smelled of flowers in springtime. "Okay."

They slipped out the back door and set off down Macomb Street. Soon they found themselves on a bench on a leafy street due east of the National Cathedral. They sat and talked for more than an hour, trading stories and catching up on each other's lives. It felt like old times. Kayla couldn't believe his dad was alive and she said as much several times over. When a natural lull in the conversation finally came, Kayla looked up into the heavens as he continued studying her. Surely, the November night sky was a sight to behold. But so was Kayla Chapman. The moonlight caught in her eyes causing tiny flecks of cobalt and turquoise to undulate around her pupils like islands in the bluest ocean. Her lips appeared as soft and supple as a satin pillow. He wondered what it might be like to kiss them again. He was watching the nickel clouds of her breath in the air when she turned back. They regarded each other wordlessly for several moments until a car horn bleated from the next street over. When Rainey looked back at her, she was fidgeting with the zipper of her jacket pocket.

"Sorry for being late by the way. I was down in Durham watching the Duke girls beat Northwestern earlier today. Flight back was delayed for some reason. Then I hit traffic outside of Dulles."

"No need to apologize. I'm the one who should be apologizing. I'm sorry, Kay. I—"

"No, Reagan. No." She reached up and cradled his face in her hands. They were chilly against his skin. "No more apologies. You've done enough of that over the years. I surely didn't make it easy on you by ignoring your letters and emails. I'm not going to say your leaving didn't hurt, because it did. But I respect you for why you left. Fighting for your country doesn't come without sacrifice for those who go off to war and for those who are left behind. But…" She sighed deeply, causing a gunmetal-gray cloud of breath to fill the chill air. "I think it's time we both got on with our lives. We certainly can't change the past. It's time we stop dwelling on it."

Rainey took her hands in his, warmed them against his chest as his eyes fell to the street. "I understand."

"No, I don't think you do. What I'm saying is that I want you in my life. I love you, Reagan. I've always loved you. And I'll never stop loving you."

Rainey looked up. She was so beautiful. He felt a sensation come over him as he stared deep into her bright sapphire eyes. He looped his arm around her and pulled her closer. "I love you, too, Kay. I love you, too." Kayla tilted her head back, closed her eyes and offered up her lips. A spark of static electricity snapped as they kissed.

Rainey's head began to swirl and he lost all sense of time.

85

Kota Belud, Sabah
East Malaysia

DOWN came the rain again. It pelted him like tiny stones. Demyan Rostov hunched over on his paddleboard as the sea churned and sputtered all around him. He worked his way toward the shore, squinting into the torrents that were screaming down from the heavens. It had been much more enjoyable here early in the year. Yes, it would rain, but the sunshine was always quick to follow. But now, with the rainy season in full swing, it was starting to cramp his style. He was contemplating moving elsewhere at least until the resorts opened back up in March. Maybe there was someplace nice on the Peninsula he could stay. He had heard it was still pleasant there, especially on the west coast.

A gust of wind blew the rain sideways and nearly whipped the paddleboard from his grasp. He gripped it tightly until he was on the sandy footpath within the protection of the thick tropical flora. After twenty yards, he tossed the board and paddle in a spot where the wind couldn't reach them and continued up the slope. Halfway up the hill, the soft, sandy track gave way to a mixture of sand, dirt and stone. His feet weren't yet toughened to the point that they could endure the gravel's bite. He kept to the side of the path and used the fallen fronds of the palm trees like stepping-stones.

The house was contemporary by local standards with a stucco exterior that had been bleached white by the sun and decks that offered stunning views far into the South China Sea. He particularly liked spending time beneath the thatch-roofed gazebo. Most of his female conquests, did, too. There had surely been many.

The previous owner—a Saudi prince—had never once visited the place, or so the real estate agent who had sold it to him had said. Perhaps it was this dreadful rainy season that had kept him away.

Rostov climbed the stairs and pushed in the French doors. He stopped to brush the wet sand from the bottoms of his feet then pressed further into the house. He crossed through a roomy drawing room and ascended a flight of stairs to the second floor. When he reached the landing, he turned toward the kitchen and froze.

There on the island countertop something stood like a centurion. It cast a long, knife-like shadow across the tiled surface. Rostov slowly twisted to his right as a figure emerged from the darkness. "But he promised…"

"You're right, he did. But I didn't." Maddie raised her arm. At the end of it was a Glock 19 with a suppressor. She fired three rounds into him then walked back over to the counter and retrieved the clarinet.

She collected her shell casings then slipped out the front door, locking it behind her. When she was on the gravel lane that led back to the Jalan Baru-Baru, she reached down into her woven handbag and clicked her radio back on. She brought it to her mouth. "It's done."

Mouse: *"Copy that. ETA two mikes."*

"Copy."

Maddie hung back in a grove of jackfruit trees as the clamor of the rain grew. She was grim-faced, but suffered no regrets over killing Rostov. Her conscience was clear, especially after seeing the photographs of the pre-adolescent girls in his credenza. Demyan Rostov was a vile human being. The world was a safer place now that he was dead.

When she heard Mouse approaching on the motorbike, she swept the rain-slicked hair from her forehead and stepped onto the shoulder of the road. He stopped long enough for her to climb onto the seat behind him then continued on at a normal pace.

They exchanged no words, no high-fives or other forms of congratulation. They were professionals. Killing wasn't something to celebrate; it was just a necessary part of the job.

Maddie marveled at how fast Job had found him. The first real break had come fairly quickly, when the prints recovered from the clarinet were crosschecked against Interpol's fingerprint database. It turned out that Malaysian authorities had been investigating a series of unsolved murders, rapes and child abductions that began early in the year. Most of them were limited to the cities and towns of Malaysian Borneo, but there were a few scattered along the west coast of the Peninsula as well. The prints recovered from several of the cases were positively matched to the prints Demyan Rostov had so kindly deposited on the clarinet when he had handled it in Vienna.

Job focused the search on Southeast Asia, a place in which he himself had extensive history. He alerted the stations in Kuala Lumpur, Brunei, Singapore, Jakarta and Manila. Each of them was forwarded pictures of Demyan Rostov taken from the surveillance footage at the D&P Press facility in Prague.

When the station chief in Brunei called about a foreigner—a Caucasian man—who was rumored to have just returned from abroad and again taken up residence in the expensive plot of land near Kotah Belud, Job sent a DX team to investigate. Indeed, the house was well beyond the means of the average Malaysian citizen. After a quiet examination of the real estate agent's records, the noose tightened further. It was learned that the house had been acquired through a purchasing agent who was suspected of having ties to Russian organized crime.

A surveillance team was dispatched to watch the house, which wasn't easy as it was in a remote, tropical location along the coast. Nevertheless, within a few days he was spotted. That first night, they followed him down to Kota Kinabalu where he seemed to be trolling for young women to seduce or abduct. They documented everything including the layout of the house. One night, when Rostov had gone out in search of pleasure, several DX operatives stayed behind and burgled the home. They mapped out each floor, carefully searched through his things, noting the placement of each weapon, and even located the trophies he had collected from the victims of each of his crimes.

His routine consisted of morning swims or excursions along the coast on his paddle board, midday jogs along the Jalan Baru-Baru and nightly forays into the resort-rich areas where he preyed on young women with lots of money and an appetite for tales of derring-do.

In the end, Maddie was glad to have been selected for the assignment. It gave her and her family closure and put an end to an out-of-control crime wave in Southeast Asia.

She looked at her watch, smeared the rain from its face. *Good, I'll be home in time for Thanksgiving.* It would certainly be a special one this year in the Rainey household.

There was no doubt about that.

ACKNOWLEDGMENTS

I would like to start off by thanking the **Author my life—the Lord of lords and King of kings**. He reigns supreme. Always has and always will.

To my beautiful and hardworking wife, **Jill**, I could not have written this book—or the first one—without you. Your love is amazing. I am eternally grateful for all you do for me and our children as I pursue a dream. Thank you for your sacrifice and support and for sharing your life with me. I am a better man because of you. I love you!

Claire and **Jackson**, I love you guys more that you will ever know. Thanks for putting up with me during the ups and downs of writing. You are each a gift from God and bring me so much joy. God has big plans for you both. I can't wait to see what they are as you grow and mature. I know that I am blessed to be your dad.

Thank you to **Donald** and **Diane Harbaugh**. You set the standard. Your faithfulness to God and His ways—and also each other—is something I seek to model in my own life, with my own family. Thanks also for the sacrifice, encouragement and support over the years. I love you

Much appreciation goes to **Charles Douglass**. Since I was little, you've always been such a faithful servant of God. It hasn't gone unnoticed. Thank you for walking the walk. To the rest of **my family**, I am grateful for each one of you and for the support you've given me over the years, not just with my writing. You've helped me become the man I am today.

Without a good foundation, the biggest buildings would crumble. I've been blessed to build my dreams on a good educational foundation. The **teachers** I had at **Christian School of York** from kindergarten all the way through 12th grade, were dedicated, loving and top-notch educators. But most of all, they demonstrated to me what it means to be a mature follower of Christ. Thank you for your dedication to biblical instruction and for your sacrifice.

Thank you to **Beth Soles** for your keen editing skills and critical eye for content. The manuscript was far better because of you.

Many thanks to a fellow author and brother in blue, **Joshua Hood**. Anything you ever need, you know where to find me. And I know where to find you: hidden in the woods outside my living room window. Lol.

Jeff Wilson, your kindness is Tier One! Thanks, my friend.

Author and CSY alumnus, **Mike Dellosso**, thank you for your godly example, support and wisdom.

To **Steven Wilson**, American vet, author and Christ follower, thanks for your friendship, kindness and support. And for the multimedia help along the way.

Without the wise counsel and gracious assistance from **Jan Thompson** and **Luana Ehrlich**, I would likely still be rubbing sticks together in my writing cave and looking for that first spark. The *Warrior Spy Thriller* series is off and running because of you guys. Thank you!

Janey Mack, I appreciate your time, friendly insight and guidance.

Last year, I had the good fortune of meeting **Chris Miller** and **Eric Bishop**. In addition to being good, patriotic dudes, they are insatiable readers and dedicated fans of the thriller genre in particular. I'm blessed to call each of them friend. Thanks for your support and friendship and for the timely texts and tweets that do nicely to keep me laughing.

Marshall Vosburg, *vielen Dank für die Hilfe bei Deutsch.*

Many thanks to the **Real Book Spy, Ryan Steck**, for the incredible job you do day in and day out for the entire thriller genre. I don't know when you sleep, bro. I'm thankful for your support, enthusiasm and everything you bring to the world of books. You are a force!

As this book was nearing publication, another hero went home. **Terry O'Hara**, aka Scott Harvath, supplied me with daily shots of inspiration through his social media posts. Terry was a former NYPD detective who developed esophageal cancer as a result of his response to Ground Zero on 9/11. He was a *real* American hero who lives on in our hearts. His legacy is that he loved life, fought the good fight with all he had in him and always did so with a smile on his face. Rest easy, brother. We'll take it from here. Forever #TerryStrong!

There are a number of people out there who contributed valuable information to me as I wrote this book but who wish to remain nameless. You know who you are. I am grateful for your time, assistance and your service to the cause of freedom.

Thank you to all **my brothers and sisters in blue** at home and around the world, and all those who, in the name of service, duty and honor, run *toward* danger. I salute you. Stay safe out there.

To all the **great authors** out there, past, present and future, you push me to strive for excellence. Thanks for your commitment to the craft.

And finally to the **readers**. Without you, none of this would have meaning. I love you, all! Please continue sharing the thrill with family, friends and co-workers. Word of mouth is an author's best friend. Also, please consider posting a review on Amazon, Goodreads, and elsewhere if you enjoyed the book. Reviews are critical for authors these days and each one is very much appreciated.

Whether you are a reader, an agent or publisher, feel free to drop me a line. I love hearing from fellow book addicts. You can always find me through the website: **DonyJayBooks.com**.

God bless!
DJ

ABOUT THE AUTHOR

DONY JAY is a graduate of York College of PA, with a B.S. degree in criminal justice. He serves as a detective for a suburban police department in Pennsylvania. When he's not reading or writing, Dony loves spending time with his family, staying fit and cheering on the Philadelphia Eagles. Above all, he's a follower of Jesus Christ. According to Dony, the tenets of a rich & rewarding life include faith, family and freedom. In that order. He resides in south-central Pennsylvania.